A PLACE CALLED HOME

JO GOODMAN

ZEBRA BOOKS
KENSINGTON PUBLISHING CORP.
http://www.kensingtonbooks.com

ZEBRA BOOKS are published by

Kensington Publishing Corp.
119 West 40th Street
New York, NY 10018

All Kensington titles, imprints, and distributed lines are available at special quantity discounts for bulk purchases for sales promotion, premiums, fund-raising, educational, or institutional use.

Special book excerpts or customized printings can also be created to fit specific needs. For details, write or phone the office of the Kensington Special Sales Manager: Attn.: Special Sales Department. Kensington Publishing Corp., 119 West 40th Street, New York, NY 10018. Phone: 1-800-221-2647.

Zebra and the Z logo Reg. U.S. Pat. & TM Off.

ISBN-13: 978-0-8217-7418-2
ISBN-10: 0-8217-7418-2

First Printing: December 2011

10 9 8 7 6 5 4 3 2 1

Printed in the United States of America

Chapter 1

Kids made women look twice at a man. Usually in a good way. That was the lesson of these last twenty-seven days. Mitchell Baker had never really thought about it before—had had no reason to—and now he was considering that with what he'd learned, maybe in the future he would rent a kid from time to time, take him to the park, ride a bike, play touch football or catch (depending on the season), and wait for the women to gravitate toward him. They seemed to be fascinated, well, at least interested, in a man on his own enjoying himself with his kid. In this case, three kids.

It helped they were pretty cute tagalongs. He couldn't take any credit for that, though, and he didn't point it out to the inquiring women until pressed with comments like "She has your eyes" and "I can see where they get their athletic talent." What his eyes had in common with eleven-year-old Emilie's was the color green. As for athletic talent, Mitch had never noticed he was particularly gifted in that area while the twins, just turned five, were almost preternaturally coordinated.

When he pointed out that the trio didn't exactly belong to him, the women weren't noticeably less affected. In some cases, their curiosity was piqued and they hung around to offer helpful parenting hints, stain removal advice, and occasionally, a phone number. Life was good.

Mitch slouched in the burgundy leather chair in his lawyer's office. Under the high gloss cherrywood table his hands were folded loosely in his lap. His thumbs tapped out a rhythm because it was not easy for him to be a body at rest. He was dressed casually: jeans, Cole Haans, white Oxford shirt (lightly starched). The cuffs of the shirt were rolled crisply to three-quarter length, revealing forearms that were dusted with golden brown hair and leanly muscled. On his right wrist he wore a watch with a scuffed brown leather strap. Plain and serviceable. He glanced down, flicked his wrist, and checked the time on Mickey's golden silhouette.

Half past two. Where the hell was she? Didn't she realize the kids were waiting for her?

The door behind him opened and Mitch turned his head just enough to glimpse that it was his own lawyer who had entered. "Is she here yet?"

Wayne Anderson was a button-down type who was more at ease in his own skin when he was wearing a three-piece suit. He dropped his briefcase on the table and took the chair beside Mitch. "Good afternoon to you, too."

"Well?"

"You're not even going to attempt a civil overture?"

Mitch merely shot him a sideways glance, his mouth flattening.

Wayne sighed. "Perhaps pleasantries are overrated. No, she's not here yet." Ignoring Mitch's grunt, he opened his briefcase and pulled out the topmost folder. "You got my message, didn't you?"

"I don't know. What was it?"

"I told Gina that it was very likely that Thea wouldn't be here today. Just her lawyer. I'm sure—"

Mitch held up one hand, cutting Wayne off. "You told Gina?"

"Hmmm. Yesterday, I think. I made a note somewhere of when I called."

Mitch was certain he did. "Yeah, I'll see it when I get your bill." Sitting up, he ran a hand through his hair. "Hell, Wayne, it wasn't Gina you talked to. She hasn't been at the house for days. You should have called my cell. That was Emilie."

"Emilie? Couldn't have been. I think I would have recognized a child's voice."

"Emilie is older than you and me together." It didn't seem like much of an exaggeration. "Body snatching. Mature woman in the guise of a self-absorbed eleven-year-old. I'm pretty sure there's a pod in my basement."

Wayne chuckled. "Sorry." He snapped the briefcase shut and dropped it between the chairs. "I really thought it was Gina. Afraid I just spit out the message and hung up." He started to open the folder, paused, and closed it again. Turning sideways in his chair he looked carefully at his client and friend. "Everything all right with you and Gina?"

There was an infinitesimal pause. "Sure."

Wayne regarded Mitch's carefully neutral expression, searching for a chink in the armor. He let the pause pass. "Glad to hear it. This thing with the kids could throw anyone for a loop."

"This *thing* will be over today." Mitch waited for some reassurance from Wayne. "Won't it?"

"I suppose that depends on how you define 'over.'"

That wasn't what Mitch wanted to hear. His fallback position was wry humor. "You'd think a sharp lawyer like you would know that. Finished. *Finito. Le fin.* The end. History. Does that help?"

Wayne grinned. His broad, craggy features split along the fault line of his mouth. The lines at the corners of his eyes deepened. He tapped the folder with his index finger. "Have you considered a prenup?" At Mitch's blank look, he explained. "A prenuptial agreement."

"I know what a prenup is. What I don't know is why you're changing the subject."

"I'm not. Not really. Have you and Gina considered one?"

"We're not that serious. We haven't even discussed marriage." It was almost the truth. To the best of his recollection, *he* had listened while Gina talked. If he hadn't contributed anything it wasn't technically a conversation, was it? Just a monologue. Maybe a soliloquy. It sure as hell wasn't a discussion. "I have issues."

Wayne smirked. "Issues?"

"Uh-huh. Like Gina doesn't know where she was when Kurt Cobain died."

Whistling softly at the enormity of this chasm, Wayne shook his head. "I knew Gina was young, but—" He made that whistle-sigh again. "I didn't realize she was practically prepubescent. You could be facing charges."

Mitch grimaced. "Very funny. She's twenty-two."

"Ouch." Since Wayne and Mitch had been sixteen when Cobain shot himself, and mourned the event with a candle-light vigil in Buddy Yarbrough's basement listening to grunge rock, there were some significant years separating Mitch and his current girlfriend. "Then she probably doesn't understand the existential subtext of Scooby-Doo either."

Mitch ignored that. "Look, Wayne, I make a decent living, but women aren't after me for my money. I don't have three homes and a lucrative stock portfolio to protect."

"I know, and you should let me give you the name of someone who can help you with that." He held up one hand when he saw Mitch was running out of patience. "Actually I was thinking of Gina. She comes from money. I don't know anything about her personal wealth, but—"

"We don't talk about money."

"Probably a mistake."

"Hey, I'm telling you, there's no marriage in my immediate

future. But if I tie the knot, I promise I'll throw the divorce work your way."

Wayne went on as if Mitch hadn't spoken. "There are also the children. In the event you do get serious, you want to be very clear with Gina that if the marriage goes south, Emilie, Case, and Grant are still yours."

Now Mitch's entire body was engaged in the conversation. He pushed himself completely upright, legs squarely under him, forearms stiffly set on the wide arms of the chair. His fingers pressed the arc of brass upholstery tacks until the tips were white. He had an urge to stand up, walk out, and keep walking. He wondered if the odd fluttering in his stomach was an uncomfortable prelude to an ulcer or because he hadn't bothered eating lunch. "I thought we were here today to discuss that the children will be going with Thea."

"Well, yes. We're here to discuss it."

"But you don't think she'll agree." Mitch had never had a panic attack. Maybe that's what was happening in his stomach. His head was a little muzzy as well.

"There are no guarantees."

"Jesus, you sound like a lawyer."

"I *am* a lawyer. Your lawyer. Don't ask me to be your friend right now. You have enough of those. Me included on my off time. Right now you need a lawyer."

"Right now I need Tums."

Wayne didn't smile. "In my briefcase."

Mitch shot Wayne a skeptical look, realized he was serious, and reached for the briefcase. He let it go with a light thud when the door to the conference room opened. Keeping his eyes straight ahead, he let Wayne turn to see who was coming in. That's what he was paying Wayne for, wasn't it? Someone to watch his back.

Wayne got to his feet as Thea Wyndham stepped into the room, Avery Childers immediately behind her. He nodded once to Avery, a cordial lawyerly greeting that established the rules of engagement. For Thea he had an openly warm smile, accepting her hand when she extended it in his direction.

"Wayne," she said softly. "It's been a long time."

"What? Four. Five years?"

"Five. The last time I saw you was at the twins' christening."

He'd forgotten about that. Was that the last time she had seen Mitch as well? He noticed that Mitch was still sitting in his chair and had made no attempt to get up or even look in Thea's direction. "How about that," he murmured. "Rather prophetic." Thea couldn't remove her hand from his light grasp fast enough. Wayne had felt her stiffen at his words. It did not make him hopeful that Mitch's concerns were going to be resolved in a way that was mutually satisfying. He watched Thea skirt past Mitch without acknowledging him and take the chair Avery held out for her.

Mitch waited until she was sitting before he speared her with a glance. She held it steadily, he'd give her that, just as if she hadn't been trying to avoid a confrontation all along. Without preamble, without any attempt to soften his tone, he asked bluntly, "Where've you been?"

Her lips parted fractionally. God, Mitch thought, if she wet her lips with that little pink tongue of hers, he was going to cry foul. She had a great mouth. Always had. Wide and lush but not with that bee-stung look that screamed collagen injections. What she did was take a short, indrawn breath and catch her bottom lip between her teeth. It was not precisely a foul, Mitch decided, but she was playing fast and loose with the rules.

She let her lip go when his eyes strayed purposely to her mouth. He noticed that she wasn't wearing any lipstick. To get that particular shade of rose she must have been worrying her lip the entire way to this meeting. Good. He hoped her nerves were as taut as his own.

"Well?" he asked again.

Avery broke in. "Mr. Baker. You should address your questions to me."

"Why?" he asked insolently before Wayne could stop him. "Has she lost her voice since she sat down?" Under the table Wayne kicked him. Mitch slumped in his chair, stretched his legs out and away from further abuse. "Go on. You two talk to each other. Thea and I will await your verdict."

Avery had mastered the cold smile. He gave it to Mitch now. "We're not making a judgment, Mr. Baker."

Before Mitch could respond to the other lawyer's patronizing tone, Wayne opened the folder in front of him. "I have copies of the agreement." He passed one to everyone. "This was drawn up shortly after the twins were christened. The same language was used in the will. I know, because I was the attorney for the deceased." He slid a copy of the will across the table to Avery. "Duly witnessed. You can see, Mr. Childers, that both our clients agreed to the terms of legal guardianship in the event of the deaths of Gabriel and Kathryn Reasoner."

Mitch kept his eyes on Thea. He thought she winced but he couldn't be sure. Except for that brief thing with her lips she hadn't given him another sign that she was moved in any way by these proceedings. If he was giving her the benefit of the doubt, he'd say she was still in shock. He'd had a month to get used to the idea that Gabe and Kathy were dead. He'd had to arrange the funeral, attend the viewings, speak at the memorial service, and go to the grave site for the burial. He'd had a month with Gabe and Kathy's children to know how devastatingly final it all was.

Thea? She couldn't be bothered.

Literally.

She'd gone to ground. It was hard to believe that in this day of electronic accessibility, Thea Wyndham had effectively disappeared. No cell phone. No e-mail. No voice mail or answering machine. Until four days ago no one knew where she was, or at least no one would give her up. She reappeared on Monday morning in her offices at Foster and Wyndham, the advertising firm her grandfather had founded, just as her weekly planner suggested she would, vacation over. It was then that she was informed of the deaths of her friends.

Mitch wondered what had gone through her mind. Had she regretted for even a moment that she had been so completely out of touch? Mitch didn't know the answer. The truth was he didn't know Thea Wyndham well at all. There were times he had wished that were different, but not just now. Right now he didn't give a damn.

Something Wayne was saying drew his attention away from Thea. He still watched her, watched her tuck a strand of red-tinted hair behind her left ear, watched her finger the onyx pendant around her neck, watched her keep her expression perfectly still while he studied her, but he finally was listening to Wayne again.

"It's clear Gabe and Kathy's intent was to have Ms. Wyndham *and* Mr. Baker jointly raise the children. The language reflects that decision. I drew up the will and the agreement to their exact wishes."

Avery's eyes fell as he peered at the documents through the lower third of his progressive lenses. He grunted softly, a sound that committed him to neither agreement nor disapproval.

"It's unusual," Wayne went on. "As you know, in most cases the parents assign guardianship to one person. If there are two, typically they're a married couple, more often parents themselves."

Mitch did not miss the faint widening of Thea's almond-shaped eyes. If she'd been a deer he would have already made her a hood ornament. His lip curled at one corner in a smile that was clearly not meant to be one. Thea Wyndham actually flinched.

Refusing to acknowledge the undercurrents between Mitch and Thea, Wayne continued addressing opposing counsel. "You will notice it was duly signed and witnessed. Ms. Wyndham—"

Avery Childers looked up over the top of the glasses. "Didn't you try to talk Mr. and Mrs. Reasoner out of this course of action?"

"I wouldn't characterize it as trying to talk them out of it. I counseled them regarding the potential difficulties. They were convincing in their own arguments, Mr. Childers. They believed that their children needed the guidance of two adults whose values and backgrounds were similar to their own. Mr. Baker and Ms. Wyndham were the two people they trusted with the lives of their children."

"Relatives?"

"Mrs. Reasoner had a maternal great-aunt." Wayne thumbed through some notes he had scrawled on a legal pad. "Mrs. Edna Archer. They were not close. Her age, I believe, is seventy-six. Mrs. Archer has three children and there are assorted cousins in Mrs. Reasoner's generation, none of whom she knew as well as she knew Mr. Baker."

Avery's brows knit. He glanced at his client. Thea nodded slightly, confirming that it was Kathryn Reasoner who had selected Mitch Baker as one of the children's guardians. She had been Gabe's choice.

Wayne continued. "Mr. Reasoner had no one that he knew of. He was adopted by the Reasoners when he was four. He was their only child, and they passed away when Emilie was an infant, a few months apart. He also had no biological siblings, at least at the time of the adoption. Unlike many adoptees, Mr. Reasoner never expressed any interest in searching out his birth parents."

Mitch saw Thea stir. For a moment her mouth had become tight, her eyes distant. Impatience? Discomfort? He didn't know but he found himself irritated rather than sympathetic. Hadn't she taken the time to explain any of this to her lawyer? As far as he was concerned, Wayne was going over information everyone in the room should have known.

Thea stood abruptly. "Excuse me," she said quietly. "I need—" She didn't finish. Rounding the table quickly, she let herself out of the windowless conference room and into the hallway.

The silence didn't last past the door being closed behind her. "What the hell?" Mitch asked, looking at Childers. "That question *is* for you, by the way."

Wayne's attempt to nudge Mitch under the table fell short of the mark. Leaning back in his chair, Wayne surreptitiously looked to see where Mitch had moved his feet. The next time he wouldn't miss his target.

Avery Childers neatly squared off the documents in front of him, running his index finger along the side and bottom to even the stack. "Ms. Wyndham is not the enemy," he said finally, looking up at Mitch. "Neither am I, for that matter, but if you're going to try to intimidate one of us, save it for me. I'm paid handsomely to be impervious."

"My client is not trying to intimidate anyone. For God's sake, he's a *cartoonist*."

Mitch smiled blandly and fought the urge to cup his balls to make sure they were still there. "Think Charles Schulz," Wayne went on. Inspired, he added, "Or Cathy Guisewite."

Avery wasn't having any of it. "He's a *political* cartoonist," he said to Wayne. His tone made Mitch out to be the Antichrist, but it also gave him his balls back. "I've seen your work, Mr. Baker. In fact, I saw it in this morning's *Chronicle*. If I were the speaker of the house, I'd want to sue your ass."

"Careful, you'll turn my head with compliments like that. Anyway, it was a good likeness. Flattering, I thought."

"I was referring to the subject matter."

"Aaah. The pissing contest." Mitch's rendering of the speaker pushing the minority whip out of the way to be first to register for a pissing contest was front and center on the editorial page. "You realize, of course, that in the tradition of the great Thomas Nast, it is symbolic of the struggle for power and suggests a manner in which the struggle could be ended, in what I like to think is a rather whimsical fashion."

"I understood the symbolism," Avery said dryly. "I missed the whimsy."

Mitch sighed, feigning disappointment. "I can only hope that *Newsweek* doesn't. I'm hoping they'll pick it up for their Perspectives section."

Avery pushed his glasses up the bridge of his nose and gave Mitch a level look. "Stop trying to intimidate my client, Mr. Baker. Wayne, if you can't get him to stop staring at Ms. Wyndham like he's measuring her for a noose, this meeting is going to be over when she steps back in here."

"Look here, *Avery,*" Wayne began, gloves off. "My client—" He stopped because out of the corner of his eye he saw Mitch's small negative shake. He wasn't entirely certain what Mitch was trying to communicate until he heard the door handle turn. Thea was just on the other side of the door. If Mitch had really been trying to intimidate Thea before, he was now trying to protect her. Wayne shot Avery a look that said, See?

Avery Childers rose slightly as Thea entered. She waved him back. "I apologize," she said. "What have I missed?"

Mitch didn't hear what was said in response, or who said it. His attention was riveted on Thea's left hand, most particularly on the oval-cut diamond that had almost blinded him when she waved her attorney back in his chair. It took a measure of self-control not to blink. How had he missed it the first time? The diamond was the size of an ice cube. He wasn't certain he could have looked away if Thea had not finally sat down and folded her hands primly in her lap. Mitch half expected to see a band of white light rimming the horizon of the table, rising from her lap like a winter sunrise. He glanced at Thea, but if she was aware of it, she gave no indication. Her head was turned from him in three-quarter profile and she appeared to be listening intently to Wayne. Mitch couldn't imagine that Wayne was all that interesting.

"Both of our clients agreed to this shared guardianship arrangement," Wayne was saying. "It is for us to determine the actual physical custody. Mr. Baker has been taking care of the Reasoner children since the death of their parents. As Ms. Wyndham could not be reached, this only made sense. Now that she is available, Mr. Baker is requesting that a shared custody arrangement be drawn up and presented to the family court judge for approval. I have several proposals for you to discuss with your client. Each of them has their own advantages and drawbacks. I'm afraid there is no perfect solution. Judge Carmody is no Solomon, either. I don't expect that we'll be saved by a particularly thoughtful or wise decision if we approach her without a solution ourselves. She'll appoint a guardian ad litem and order a home study. She may still do that, in any event. I'm sure your client does not want to make the children the subject of a custody battle or pin our hopes for a reasonable outcome on being able to get another judge to review the matter."

Avery let silence settle as if giving careful consideration to this last statement. Then he pounced. Timing was everything. "Then you'll be pleased to hear that Ms. Wyndham is willing to give full custody to Mr. Baker."

Mitch's head snapped up and his internal threat level went from blue to orange, skipping yellow entirely.

"Moreover," Avery went on, "my client does not want to disrupt the children's lives further by devising a visitation schedule in which no one is served. Rather, she is proposing that while the children remain with Mr. Baker, she will visit them as she has always done when the children were with their parents."

Mitch felt Wayne's restraining hand on his forearm. Did Wayne really think he was going to jump up and slug somebody? Wayne's hand should have clapped itself over his *mouth*. "This is a joke, right? Thea? What the hell is he talking about?"

"Address me," Childers reminded Mitch. "Or better yet, leave it to your attorney."

Mitch's nostril flared slightly and a succinct profanity hovered on the tip of his tongue. He held it back, but he saw Thea Wyndham flinch as if he had shouted it at her.

Wayne removed his hand from Mitch. He took a gold Mont Blanc from his jacket and made a few notations on his pad. The scrawl was perfectly illegible to everyone but him. After a moment he looked up at Avery. "This is Ms. Wyndham's idea?"

"Whose else would it be?"

"Her fiancé's."

Mitch had a vision of his head doing a three-sixty. "You *knew*?" he asked accusingly.

Wayne shrugged. "If you had gotten my message . . ."

"Is Wayne right?" Mitch asked Thea. "Is this your fiancé's idea?"

Avery said, "You don't have to answer that."

"For God's sake," Mitch said. "It's a simple enough question."

"You wouldn't think that if you were sitting in her chair. For the full effect you need only add a naked white bulb over her head."

Mitch had the grace to look abashed. His voice gentled. "Thea?"

She answered before her lawyer could cut her off again. "Joel and I discussed it, Mitch. It was a mutual decision."

"Joel?"

"Strahern."

"Strahern Investments? That Strahern?"

"Yes."

As a financial force to be courted and respected, the Strahern banking family was second only to Mellon. "I see," Mitch said softly. He turned back to Wayne. "I suppose there is no sense in not sharing my own news."

Wayne was surprised and wary but neither of these expressions showed on his face. "Perhaps now is not the time," he ventured, feeling his way in the dark.

"I don't see why not. If Ms. Wyndham hadn't been incommunicado this last month, she would know by now."

Avery broke in. "What is he talking about, Wayne? Someone just say it."

"I'm engaged myself," Mitch said. He gave Wayne full marks for the poker face he maintained. It would be difficult facing him in five-card stud again. Mitch had no idea how very good he could be. "To Regina Sommers."

"Congratulations."

"Sommers Real Estate?"

Thea and her attorney spoke simultaneously. There was no mistaking her sincerity or his curiosity.

Mitch nodded, accepting Thea's best wishes and answering Avery's question. Under the table, Wayne had found his foot again and was grinding it with the heel of his shoe. "Yes, well, perhaps I should let Wayne conclude this."

Wayne took the opening given to him but he did not remove his foot. "You'll understand that our proposals were based on the fact that Mr. Baker is also marrying and has raised concerns about whether he can take full custody of the children at this time. It would unduly strain the marriage."

Mitch felt the full impact of Thea's darkening eyes on him. She was searching his face, her own a shade paler than it had been moments earlier. The color left in her cheeks owed everything to Clinique. "You don't want the children?"

It was Wayne who responded. "Mr. Baker is quite willing to share custody. If you will review the proposals, you'll see that they call for him to be a partner in raising Emilie, Case, and Grant."

Avery was scanning the documents. "An unequal partner. He wants to be the part-time custodian. Second and fourth weekends. Every other Wednesday. Here's a proposal that gives you each two weeks with the children."

Thea's eyes widened. "Mitch? You're not serious about that one, are you? We don't even live in the same school district. Their education would be completely disrupted."

Mitch said nothing, finally willing to let Wayne speak for him. Easy to let the lawyer take over when what you felt like yourself was way down on the food chain.

"It's merely one idea, Ms. Wyndham," Wayne said. "The matter of school attendance does present some thorny problems."

"Thorny problems?" Thea said, squaring off her shoulders. "It's lunacy. Gabe and Kathy would never agree to something like that."

It pained Wayne, but he took the hard line. "Gabe and Kathy don't have to agree to it. They put it in your hands. Yours and Mitch's. I don't think it ever occurred to them that you would not want the children."

Thea actually shrank back in her chair and Wayne almost felt sorry for her.

"Let's not throw stones, shall we?" Avery said. He looked pointedly at Mitch. "People in glass houses, after all. Your client is not clamoring to take on the responsibilities of surrogate parenthood himself."

Wayne opened his mouth to respond but Mitch cut him

off. "Leave us," he said without inflection. "You too, Mr. Childers. I want to talk to Ms. Wyndham alone."

"I don't think that's—" Avery stopped when he saw Wayne getting to his feet. He looked at his client. "This isn't a good idea, Ms. Wyndham. Mr. Strahern wouldn't like—" He didn't finish this time because he saw Thea's resolve had been strengthened by the mention of her fiancé. Too late, Avery realized he had blundered by assuming she was in some way subservient to Joel Strahern. "Very well," he said with an obvious show of reluctance. "But I insist that you do not come to any agreements without reviewing them with me."

Thea offered no comment and Avery had to be satisfied with her silence, choosing to accept it as consent. He stood, gathering the papers in front of him, and followed Wayne out of the room.

"He hated that," Mitch said after the door closed.

"Wayne is not entirely happy with you right now."

Mitch shrugged. "He'll give me hell and then we'll go play some hoops. I'll let him win and we'll be back on an even keel."

"No pissing contest, then."

He gave a bark of laughter. "You saw today's paper."

"I saw it. I always look for your work. Your liberal bias is showing."

Mitch looked down at himself. "Where?" He patted his chest with both hands searching for the offending bias.

"There," she said dryly. "Your bleeding heart."

His grin was brief and quirky. By the time Mitch dropped his hands to the arms of the chair it was gone. He studied her for a moment, taking in the things he hadn't wanted to see earlier: the faintly swollen eyelids; the bleak expression; the skin that was stretched tautly over a beautifully sculpted face. "What are we going to do, Thea?"

"I don't know." There was hardly any sound in this admission, as if she could not bear to hear her own helplessness.

He saw her chin wobble. She looked away quickly as tears welled in her eyes, and Mitch was selfishly glad when she managed to blink them back. He remained quiet, suspecting that anything he might say right now would open the floodgates. Comforting Thea was not the reason he'd asked to be alone with her.

Her smile was both regretful and watery as her eyes darted around the room. "You'd think a lawyer's office would have some tissues. They must get lots of hysterical clients."

"Hmmm."

She touched an index finger to the corner of each eye and quickly erased the last vestige of tears. Taking a short, steadying breath, she said, "I had no idea you were getting married. Gabe and Kathy never mentioned you were serious about someone." When she saw his discomfort, she hastened to add, "Not that we talked about you. I mean, things just came up from time to time. Sometimes Emilie would . . ." Thea just let her thought drift away.

"Yes?" Mitch prompted.

Thea shook her head. "Nothing."

"All right. Let's discuss our options." Mitch leaned forward and placed his clasped hands on the table. He didn't think his body language was particularly threatening, but he didn't miss Thea sliding back in her chair. "Am I making you nervous?"

The directness of the question startled her. Her honesty startled her more. "Yes. As a matter of fact, you are."

One of Mitch's brows arched. "Really? What do you think I'm going to do?"

"I don't know. That's what's making me nervous. I know you're angry with me."

Characterizing what he felt toward her as anger was so much less than it was. "Angry? I don't know about that. Disappointed. Resentful. Frustrated. And now that you're telling me you don't want the children, I'm even a little afraid." She actually blinked at this last admission. "If all that comes across as anger, then it does. I'm not apologizing for it."

"I'm not asking you to. I just wanted to understand."

"Well, now you do."

"You think I should have been here."

"I think you should have been able to be reached." Mitch's fingers threaded through his hair. "Why didn't you tell someone where the hell you were going?"

"I did." There was a faint shudder to her indrawn breath. "Gabe and Kathy knew."

Mitch fell silent. Finally, "Aaah, hell."

Closing her eyes for a moment, Thea nodded. "Yeah," she said softly. "Hell." She made another quick swipe at the corners of her eyes and gathered the fraying threads of her composure. "Gabe was my closest friend. Kathy became exactly what I'd imagine a sister might be. I know you think I'm failing them now by not taking their children, but—"

"Emilie, Case, and Grant."

She frowned. "Yes, I know."

"We have to stop talking about them collectively as the children," he said. "It makes it impersonal somehow. This is very personal. You and I made promises to their parents and now we're seriously discussing who is *not* going to take them. Don't you feel the least bit ashamed?"

Thea flushed. Her fingers tightened on the arms of her chair. "Yes," she said quietly. "I'm ashamed. Probably more deeply than you can comprehend. It changes nothing, though. It's not that I'm not taking Em and Case and Grant because I don't want to. I'm not taking them because I can't."

"Can't? Because you're getting married?"

That was the only reason Thea was prepared to discuss. "Yes. Isn't it the same for you? What does . . ." She paused, searching for the name of Mitch's fiancée.

"Gina."

"Thank you. What does Gina think about sharing this responsibility with you?"

There were a lot of ways Mitch could have answered that question. He could have come clean and admitted there were no serious wedding plans, at least on his part. He could have said Gina was too young herself to take on an instant family. He considered pointing out that Gina would do whatever he told her, but it sounded too caveman and he suspected Thea wouldn't buy it. He might have explained that Gina just wanted to please him, but a vision of Thea laughing outright stopped him. He finally came up with "Gina and I haven't discussed that eventuality."

"You haven't discussed—" She stopped, searching his face. "Oh, I see. You didn't discuss it because you assumed I would take Emilie and the twins when I heard what happened."

"Something like that."

"Aren't you the least bit ashamed?"

"That's a fair description."

His easy admission had the effect of deflating her. She took a deep breath and began again. "Look, Mitch, you and I don't know each other very well. We had Gabe and Kathy in common. Later, the children. We've met, what? a half dozen times over the years?"

Ten. They'd met ten times. Mitch did not say this. Instead he shrugged and offered, "That sounds about right."

"My point is that you don't know nearly enough about me to assume that I would be a good mother."

"Gabe chose you. Kathy agreed. They must have thought you could do the job."

"Oh, be serious. They never really thought they wouldn't be around to raise their own children."

"I disagree. If they had only asked us to be godparents, I would say you were right. But they made a point of setting things in motion for us to be legal guardians. I think they did give it thought. A lot of thought. They hoped it would never happen, but they planned carefully for just the opposite."

"Then what about you? Following your logic, they must have thought you'd be a good father. Who's to say you shouldn't have the children in your custody full-time? Why do you think it has to be me?"

"Because you're the girl."

She blinked. "You didn't just say that, did you? I probably misheard you."

Mitch proposed his alternate theory. "Because I'm the boy?"

Thea actually smiled. "I'm going to do you a favor and pretend you don't walk dragging your knuckles. See if you can follow this." Her smile faded as she began presenting her points. "I work twelve-hour days downtown. That's if things are going smoothly. You, on the other hand, have the option of working out of your home and have done that on and off for the last five years. I currently live in Fox Chapel. You live in Connaugh Creek. When I get married Joel and I will be living in one of his condo properties on the North Shore."

"The stadium or the ballpark?"

Thea's lush mouth tightened briefly. It was enough to keep her from taking the bait. "When you get married you'll still live in Connaugh Creek."

"Gina is Sommers Real Estate, remember? We could live anywhere. Even the North Shore."

"You'll live in Connaugh Creek," she said. "Your family. Friends. Everyone is right here. Why would you want to live anywhere else?"

"A good question. Maybe you and Joel could get a home here. I could talk to Gina's dad."

Thea kept going. "If the children are with me they'd have to change schools, make new friends. What about their activities? T-ball. Dance. Swimming. I'm not even certain

Joel and I will have a yard. They've just lost their parents. Another upheaval can't be good for them. With you, they can stay where things are familiar. You saw them regularly. I didn't. I *couldn't*."

"And why was that?" he asked. "It's not as if you lived on the other side of the planet. You're an hour away. Maybe less."

Because you were always hanging around. "Are you taking me to task? Because Gabe and Kathy never did."

Mitch knew he did not want to pursue that. Waving her comment brusquely aside, he pushed his chair back and got to his feet. Increasingly restless, he found himself wishing there was room enough to pace. He walked over to the polished credenza that almost filled the back wall and parted a double stack of accordion folders so he could hitch his hip between them. He stretched out one leg for balance and support. Crossing his arms in front of him, his posture not so much defensive as it was contained, he regarded Thea frankly. "What about this other load of . . . *stuff* . . . that Childers was proposing? It's one thing that you don't want the kids living with you, but not even having them on weekends? I don't understand. How can you not want to see them during summer vacation or on holidays?"

"I never said I didn't want to see them. In fact, I said I would visit them."

"Jesus, Thea. Maybe you don't want to get that close. Are you and Joel afraid they have cooties? I'll send them with a certificate that proves they were deloused."

"Stop it!" She swiped at the strands of hair that had slipped past her ear to brush her cheek. The diamond on her left hand flashed with the movement. "I'm not like that."

"Like what?"

"Insensitive. Cruel."

"Yeah? I didn't used to think so but I'm getting to know you better."

Reeling, Thea forced herself not to show it. She was

rather proud when she could respond with a certain steadiness. "I want to see Emilie and the twins. Don't ever doubt that."

"But on your terms."

She hesitated. "I suppose so." Thea watched Mitch shake his head slowly, something like distaste curling his lip. Distaste might be softening it a bit. More likely it was disgust. She decided she may as well move into the area of complete dislike. "I'm willing to pay child support. Education. Activities. Medical. Whatever they need."

"Fuck you."

Thea's mouth went dry. She could feel a flush stealing up past the scooped neckline of her little black dress by Chanel. Closing the short-waisted jacket wouldn't help. The heat was rising fast, warming the pendant at her throat, climbing to her cheeks and finally making her scalp tingle. Her cropped hair, light and feathery and already a deeply tinted red, threatened to combust. "I see why you chose cartooning," she said evenly. "Words are clearly not your forte."

"You understood me. That's all I was after." Mitch unhitched his hip from the top of credenza and just leaned back against it. He lowered his arms to his side, holding the edge lightly. "I don't want your money." A thought suddenly occurred to him. "Or were you offering Joel Strahern's money?"

"Joel has nothing to do with this."

Mitch didn't believe that for a second but he let it pass. "The kids don't need your money. Gabe and Kathy had a good insurance policy. Triple indemnity for accidents. You'd know that if you'd been around."

"I know about the policy. Avery told me. But most of it will go into a trust."

"That's right. Wayne is setting it up. Ironic, isn't it? Gabe and Kathy were working hard, saving, and still cutting some corners so there'd be no question of the kids going to any college that would have them. One drunk driver later . . ." A muscle worked in his jaw. His nostrils flared as he inhaled deeply. "One drunk driver later and the kids' college fund is secure." Because bitterness served no purpose, he reined it in. "As far as current expenses, the kids are eligible for Social Security. Wayne's already submitted the paperwork to the SSA. In the meantime, I'm not exactly flirting with the poverty line."

"I didn't say you were."

"I don't need your money any more than the kids do."

"I know that. I want to help."

"Who do you think you're kidding? You *want* to salve your conscience. Maybe you even need to. Sorry. Not interested."

Thea was done deflecting his darts. She challenged him instead. "If you weren't prepared to take Emilie and the boys, why did *you* agree to it?"

The pitch of Mitch's voice was like a growl. "For the same reason you did: because I didn't think anything would ever happen."

"So you signed up hoping you'd never be called upon to serve."

"Like I said: same as you."

They both fell silent, each of them looking away. There was enough self-recrimination to go around without any more pointing fingers.

Thea was the first to speak, her voice barely audible. "I can't do it, Mitch. I'm offering exactly what I'm able to give."

"Money and a few hours here and there with your best friend's kids?"

"Yes."

"Jesus, that's pathetic."

"Yes. It is." There was an ache in her throat. Thea swallowed hard, first literally, then her pride. "Please don't throw it back in my face."

Mitch stared at her a long moment, then he sighed. "I

don't get this." She wasn't telling him everything; he was fairly certain of that. He was also thinking that he was unlikely to persuade her to confide in him. He had managed to make himself as likable as Snidely Whiplash was to poor Nell. "What if you took Emilie and I took Case and Grant?"

When Thea didn't regard him with horror-filled eyes he knew it was because she didn't believe he'd ever sanction breaking up the kids. She was right, too. "Okay, it was a bad bluff," he admitted.

"Yes." Thea fingered her necklace. "You have family around, Mitch. A sister. A brother-in-law. Your parents are still young. I imagine your mom is the one watching the kids now."

"A lot you know. They're in school."

"Oh." Her smile was a trifle sad. "Well, there you have it. I don't know much about it. I think some people are born nurturers, Mitch, and some of us . . . that is, some people aren't."

"Yeah? You're squeezing my bleeding heart."

Inwardly, Thea winced. "I'm sorry," she said, her eyes dropping to his chest. "I wish I could do this differently." *I wish I could be different.* "My parents are in their seventies. They travel a lot. So much so that my wedding is scheduled around *their* itinerary." She meant to say it lightly, with a little chuckle in her voice, but it was painfully close to the truth. Mitch didn't smile and her own fell flat. "They're in Florence now."

"I know. We tracked them down in an attempt to find you."

"Oh. I hadn't realized."

"No, I don't suppose you did."

Thea let her hand fall to her lap. "The children wouldn't have the same support with me that they have with you."

"No arguments there. I'm realizing you Wyndhams are a cold bunch. Marrying Strahern is overkill, don't you think? Kind of like frost on a glacier." He saw she wasn't going to deign to respond to that but he was sure he hit the big red bull's-eye. "What about Strahern anyway? He has kids."

"Yes, but they're grown."

"No, I mean—" He stopped, momentarily struck dumb. His recovery was swift, though. "My God, you're not marrying Junior, are you?"

Thea tried not to bristle. "If you mean Joel Strahern II, then no, I'm not marrying him. Jay happens to be happily married."

"His father. You're marrying his *father*." Disbelief was rife in his tone. "He must be in his sixties."

"He's sixty-one. About the same age as *your* parents and if you recall, I just finished characterizing them as young."

"Sixty-one." He whistled softly. "Hell, he probably remembers where he was the day the music died."

"What are you talking about? What does Buddy Holly have to do with anything?"

Mitch realized he had spoken his wayward thought aloud. "Nothing. It's not important. Just something I've been thinking about." He did some quick calculations. He and Thea were only a few months apart in age. "So Strahern's what, almost thirty years older than you?"

"Yes."

"More than a quarter of a century."

"You know, I might have fried a few synaptic pathways trying to come up with that. Thank you for saving my gray matter for really important stuff."

"No problem." *Thea Wyndham was marrying Strahern senior?* He still couldn't quite believe it was true. "So when's the wedding?" Please don't say June. He didn't think he could keep from laughing if she said June.

"None of your business. Our engagement hasn't been formally announced."

"I see." It was still a struggle to keep a straight face,

though amusement wasn't precisely what he was feeling. "Waiting to get it in *Town & Country,* are we?" He held up both hands, palms out, surrendering before she could attack. "All right. I'm sorry. I take that back. I wish you well."

Thea's eyes narrowed, gauging his sincerity. His expression was implacable. She chose to believe he meant what he said. "Thank you."

"I guess it makes it easier to understand why he doesn't want Emilie, Case, and Grant underfoot twenty-four/seven. Em's pretty quiet, but the boys . . . well, they're boys. Snips and snails and puppy dog tails packaged as testosterone time bombs."

The corners of Thea's mouth lifted in a faint smile. It hovered for a moment, then disappeared. "They're doing all right, though?"

He almost asked, *What do you care?* then thought better of it. Maybe she really was doing the best she could. In that case, he should just feel sorry for her and be relieved she wasn't taking Kathy and Gabe's kids out of some twisted sense of duty. "All right? I don't know how to answer that. They're grieving in their own way. Emilie cries when she thinks no one can hear her. I'm not sure the boys entirely understand that Gabe and Kathy aren't coming back. They talk about them as if they're still around, just away. It's still so fresh. I'm playing it by ear, waiting to see what happens. Maybe we'll all do some counseling."

Thea nodded. She pressed her lips together. Her chin wobbled anyway. After a moment she said, "I know someone, if you're interested."

"I'll call you if it comes to that. I'm talking to their teachers, keeping an eye on how they're sleeping and eating, things like that. We'll see how it goes."

"You're doing a good job."

"I'm just doing it, Thea. One of us has to." He almost wished he hadn't said the last. The hurt in her eyes was palpable and somehow he ended up feeling worse for it. "I'll be able to reach you?"

"Yes. I won't be going anywhere without letting you know."

He took a breath and let it out slowly. "When can I tell the kids you'll visit them?"

"I don't know. I have to check m—"

He had suspected it was going to happen; he just hadn't known what would set him off. "Jesus H. Christ! Tell me you weren't going to say you have to check your calendar!" He saw the truth clearly on her face. Mitch leaned forward at the waist, but he kept his hands white-knuckled on the edge of the credenza, only just holding himself back. "Listen, you enter them in when you get a couple or three minutes. Maybe you can call or send an e-card." He saw her flinch and knew she correctly interpreted the homicidal bent of his mind. "You're a hell of a piece of work, Thea Wyndham. You know those times Kathy and Gabe pressed me into asking you out? Right now I'm thanking God you always said no."

Chapter 2

The phone was ringing as Mitch let himself in the kitchen through the garage entrance. He tossed his keys on the counter and watched them skid across the surface and land on the floor while he made a grab for the phone. "Hello."

"Mitchell. This is your mother."

"Mum, you don't have to identify yourself. No one else calls me Mitchell."

"Well, I don't know why. It's a perfectly good name."

"Sissy name, Mum. Dad tried to tell you." Predictably another voice immediately joined the conversation. Trust his mother to have him on speaker.

"I sure did, son. Wanted to name you Max. You'd have been the toughest kid on the block with a name like that."

Chuckling, Mitch went through the contortions of removing his leather jacket without taking the phone from his ear. "I did okay for myself." He hooked the jacket over the back of a chair and went to the refrigerator. "Who else is with you?" He surveyed the contents of the fridge.

"Mitchell, I put a pan of lasagna in your refrigerator."

He grabbed a Corona. "I'm looking at it now. Thanks. The kids will appreciate it. Can you believe it? They're getting tired of pizza."

"They need fruits and vegetables, dear."

"Hey, I ordered pizza with pineapple and green peppers."

Farther in the background another voice chimed in. "That's great, Mitch! You're a credit to your gender!"

Mitch frowned. "Is that you, Amy?"

"Sure is."

"Jeez, Mum, who all is listening in?"

"Just your sister and your dad. Oh, and Mrs. Talbot. She's here with my Avon order. I told her I had to call you before the twins got home from school."

Great, Mitch thought. "Hi, Mrs. Talbot."

"Hello, Mitch. I saw your cartoon today. Naughty, but oh, so funny."

"Thanks. Mum?"

"Yes?"

He took a long pull on his Corona. "Did you have something you wanted to tell me about besides the lasagna?"

"Well, no. I wanted to hear what happened at Wayne's. Was Thea there? Emilie said she might not be at the meeting."

So Emilie had passed Wayne's message along after all, only to his mother. Mitch took another swallow. Apparently there were some glitches with the ponytail express. "She was there. With Avery Childers. He must have cost her a small fortune. His suit wasn't exactly off the rack."

"I suppose you wore jeans."

"Yep." He knew his mother was sighing even if he couldn't hear it over his sister's laughter. "Anything else you want to know?"

"That's not funny."

"All right. But I can't tell you much because the bus will be coming any minute." It was now almost second nature for Mitch to meet the school bus at the corner. A few days after Case and Grant started back to school they forgot about going to Mitch's house and got off the bus at their old stop. No one was used to the new routine, including him. Lost in inking a cartoon, working against a deadline, it was only when Emilie came in the door forty minutes later that Mitch realized the twins weren't around. Admitting that he didn't know where her brothers were was not a position he wanted to be in again, and he knew he *never* wanted to see that look on Emilie's face a second time. Mitch still didn't know if he'd ever be able to make it up to her. It was not an auspicious beginning for them. Case and Grant, though, were none the worse for their experience. They'd found a spare key their parents kept under a terra-cotta pot on the porch and gone inside. The cable hadn't been disconnected yet, and when Mitch and Emilie and the police found them, the boys were watching Nickelodeon. If it had been MTV, Sergeant Wolliver would have probably taken Emilie's complaint that her uncle Mitch didn't know what he was doing more seriously. It was true enough.

"Is Thea taking the children?" his mother asked.

"No."

"That's—" She stopped herself, withholding her opinion. "What do *you* think?"

Mitch was fairly certain his mother was relieved, but he didn't know how he felt about it yet. "I think I'll manage without her."

"Of course you'll manage," she said immediately. "Why wouldn't you? You've done—"

"Mum! The bus is here. I've got to run."

"All right, dear! Call me later!"

Mitch heard a few more good-byes in the background before he hit the Off button. He set the phone down and leaned against the counter. The bus wasn't anywhere in sight and a glance at his watch told him he had a few more minutes. He just couldn't bear to hear his mother offer praise when he didn't think he deserved it. She thought he could do anything, and even though he usually shared her confidence, he wasn't so sure it was warranted just now.

Thea was right about one thing. He wouldn't be taking on the task of raising the kids alone. He only had to go as far as his refrigerator for proof of that. He could probably count on his mother's version of meals-on-wheels at least two times a week. More, if he asked her. Amy would be good for some baby-sitting time. She'd been married three years but she and David were in no hurry to have children. Gabe and Kathy's kids had always been surrogate grandchildren to his parents; but now that he had them in his care, the pressure to reproduce was really off him and Amy. There was no way of knowing how long the reprieve would last.

Mitch finished his beer, rinsed the bottle, and dropped it in the blue recycling bin inside the breezeway. He started out to wait for the bus, felt the chill, and went back for his coat. In the past he wouldn't have thought twice about making a jaunt to the corner without his jacket. Even if he had had to wait there a few minutes he'd have been okay. Now, with the twins watching his every move, and Emilie grading his screwups as mild, moderate, and I'm-gonna-call 911, he tried to make sure he practiced what he preached. Just that morning he wouldn't let Grant go for the bus without snapping his jacket. Mitch couldn't very well go outside now without a coat.

He made it as far as the driveway when he saw Gina's bright yellow Nissan Xterra turn the corner. Case and Grant loved her banana car and were always clamoring for rides. Mitch wished she had chosen another color from the Crayola box. Like black.

He waited on the sidewalk for her to pull up. The street in front of his house was wide enough to permit parking on both sides. Gina stopped the SUV directly beside him and threw it into park. That was another thing that bothered Mitch. She bought a tough little truck-based SUV with an *automatic* transmission. It was some kind of vehicle castration as far as Mitch was concerned. It made him uncomfortable.

"Hey," he greeted her when she fairly danced up to him. "What's up?"

Gina threw her arms around his neck, gave a little hop, and clapped her thighs around his hips, locking her ankles behind him. Scooching around a bit to find a comfortable cradle against his groin, Gina waited for Mitch's hands to cup her bottom. As soon as he did she planted her mouth firmly over his.

Mitch was the first to draw back. "Wow," he said softly. "What's that for?"

"I sold a house today." Beaming, she kissed him again, humming against his mouth so the kiss fairly vibrated.

Out of the corner of his eye Mitch was watching for that other banana ride, the No. 83 bus, and wishing Gina would give him back his tongue. He gently disengaged himself from her mouth and a moment later from the barnaclelike hold she had on his body. "This part of town is zoned residential," he said dryly. "You want to put on a show, we should take this outside the town limits."

Gina caught Mitch's wrists and leaned back against the Xterra. Tugging, she got him to take another half step toward her. "Too bad. I'd let you fuck me right here."

"Yeah?"

"Oh, yeah." She put his hands inside her open jacket and arched just enough to make her breasts an offering. "Go on. You know you want to."

Mitch wasn't certain that he did but his hands seemed to be taking their orders from his other head. He cupped Gina's breasts. Her nipples poked the heart of his palms. "You do pick your moments." He lowered his head and blew lightly on the strands of dark hair that were covering her ear. He felt her shiver; her delicious little body rubbed against him. Mitch nuzzled her neck.

"Hey, Mitch! You wanna getta room? I don't let my kids watch PG-13 yet!"

Tips of his ears reddening, Mitch was still game. He stepped back and called out to Susan Gerow as she walked briskly past him on her way to meet the bus. "I was going for an R here."

Susan turned, never breaking her brisk stride as she walked backward. "Then someone has to get nekkid."

One of Mitch's brows kicked up. "Really?"

"Really!" She pivoted again and continued on, yelling back, "They set the bar so low that *Porky's* would get a G."

Gina was dusting off her behind from where she'd been rubbing up against the SUV. "What's *Porky's?*"

"You never saw it?"

She put her hands on her hips and gave him a sigh that was not entirely exaggerated. "Why do you do that? I just asked you what it was and then you ask me if I've seen it. Doesn't that seem a tad like you're wasting your breath? No, I haven't seen it."

"Think *American Pie* of the eighties."

Regina Sommers graduated magna cum laude from Pitt. She had a bachelor's degree in Business Administration and was accepted for the master's program in the fall at Duquesne. She knew she wasn't exactly a slouch in the brains department, but sometimes she really didn't understand what Mitch was talking about. "*American Pie* the movie, right? Not the song."

"The movie, Regina."

"Now you're being patronizing. Last week we had this big ol' discussion about "American Pie" the *song* and how it was about the day the music died—which was *not,* apparently, about the Beatles breaking up or even Kurt Cobain offing himself—which, by the way, I *apologized* for not knowing where I was even though I was only *six* at the time—and how the song referred to the Buddy Holly plane crash and him dying along with Richie Valens and the Big Chopper."

"Bopper."

"What?"

"It was the Big Bopper."

"Oh." She slipped her arm through his and fell in step as he began walking to the corner. "It's not as if you remember where you were when Buddy bought it."

"It's just about having some sense of the past, I suppose. I admit it's a quirk of mine."

"So, what? I need to watch the History Channel *and Legends of Rock and Roll?*"

Mitch chuckled. "I promise I'll pick up tips from HGTV." He gave her arm a squeeze. Gina leaned into him, all warm and snuggly. She had a lithe, compact body, a nice round ass and hard belly. She was built more like a gymnast than a runner but she ran several times a week, always outdoors. Treadmills, she'd told him, were for pussies. She came from WASP stock on both sides of her family. Mitch believed that somewhere in the past the thin blue-blooded Sommers' line had benefited from the infusion of a little Mediterranean DNA. Gina had thick, coffee-colored hair and eyes, beautiful olive-toned skin, and fairly radiated warmth when she smiled. She liked to touch him when she talked, laying her hand on his forearm or leaning into his shoulder, and she never seemed to be satisfied that she was close enough. Conversation was practically foreplay because Gina could rub herself against him like a cat in heat when they were just discussing where to order takeout. She was excitable and exciting and it was a pretty heady combination. When Mitch considered the breasts that went with all of it, it was damn near intoxicating.

So why couldn't he quite get Thea Wyndham out of his mind?

"If you can control your hormones," he told Gina, "tell me about your sale."

"Later. When the kids are in bed." She gave him an arch

look. "Then I've got a story for you that will make your interest rate soar."

"Sounds good." Mitch felt her stiffen slightly and knew he had not quite mustered the enthusiasm she was looking for. "How late can you stay?"

"I can stay all night."

"Gina."

"Yeah, I know. Not while the kids are with you. You know, you're a pretty old-fashioned kind of guy."

"Their parents were married. I'm just not ready to try to explain a different kind of relationship to them."

She held up both hands. "All right. I can appreciate that. So, tell me about your meeting today. When is Thea taking the kids?"

Mitch loosed himself from Gina's arm and waved to the twins. They were sitting in separate seats on the bus, both of them with their faces pressed to the window, mouths open wide so they could make humid circles on the glass. They saw him almost simultaneously and jumped up as the bus squealed and groaned to a stop. The doors opened and there was a lot of scrambling for position in the aisle. The mothers congregating on the sidewalk stopped their conversations and prepared to pluck their chicks as they descended the steps.

"She's not," Mitch told Gina. He didn't look at her as he dropped the bomb. "She says she can't."

"You're not fu . . ." She remembered herself at the same time one of the mothers turned to give her a sharp, disapproving stare. Smiling sweetly, Gina began again, this time in a much less vocal manner. "You're not freakin' serious."

Mitch rolled his eyes. "You don't need the adjective."

"The fuck I don't." Making an abrupt about-face, Gina stalked off toward the house.

"Hey, Uncle Mitch!"

Case reached him first and Mitch immediately put him in

a headlock and gave him a noogie. "Nice hair, Spike. Did Nonny let you gel it yourself?"

"Yeah! Pap said I'm a lethal weapon. Double-O Jell-O."

"Cool." Since the district only offered half-day kindergarten, the twins sometimes went to his mother's house in the morning so Mitch could work undisturbed. She put them on the school bus at eleven-thirty. "Great secret identity."

Grinning, Case escaped the loose headlock and gave up his place for his brother. "Double-O Poop-O," he said to Grant once Mitch had him securely under arm.

"Hey! Not nice," Mitch said. "I can't keep him here forever." He knuckled Grant's head while the boy struggled to get free so he could pulverize his brother. "Easy, Sport. Case is sorry." He gave Case a significant look which suggested he'd better get sorry fast.

"I was only teasin'." He broke into a high-pitched giggle as he danced around his twin and Mitch. "Poop-O knows that."

"Hmmm. Let's see." He let Grant go and Case immediately sprinted off, his brother hot on his trail. Their book bags bobbed against their shoulders until they both managed to wiggle out of them on the run. Mitch just shook his head, a glimmer of a smile on his lips, and followed at a slower pace.

Susan Gerow and her daughter passed him as he was picking up the book bags. "They'll be friends by the time they reach the door," she assured him.

"Yeah. That's what I'm learning."

She gave him a thumbs-up.

The boys were actually waiting for him at the stop sign on the next corner. It was a rule they weren't allowed to cross without an adult yet, though their spin on it was that they were helping *him* get to the other side.

Grant pointed up the street to where Gina was opening the door to her banana car. "Is Miss Sommers leaving?"

Mitch felt a brief surge of wistfulness and pride each time

the twins and Emilie addressed adults with polite formality. That was Kathy's instruction and Mitch had discovered he liked it. It was what he had been taught as a child but he was finding that many of his friends' children were permitted lots of familiarities, usually by adults who were not their parents. Gina had tried to get them to call her almost anything but Miss Sommers until Mitch gently put his foot down. "It looks like she's getting her purse," he told them. Indeed, Gina seemed to be wrestling with her Sak. "She's probably got the straps caught in her wannabe stick shift." He looked both ways, made certain the coast was clear, and sent the boys ahead to help her. Gina would be so appreciative. They would undoubtedly clamor for a ride in the SUV.

"Maybe later, guys," she was telling them as Mitch approached. By the tone of her voice, Mitch judged it was probably at least the third time she'd said it.

"Just say no, Gina. Believe it or not, they get that."

She slammed the door, slinging her bag over her shoulder. "Sorry, guys. You heard your uncle Mitch. No."

The twins, having perfected the hangdog expression of monumental disappointment, turned on Mitch in unison. He felt the double blow of soulful brown eyes—their mother's eyes—and pouty lower lips. He simply canted his head to the side, indicating they should hightail it into the house. "And take off your shoes in the breezeway!" he called after them. To Gina, he said, "That was low."

She shrugged. "'Just say no, Gina,'" she mimicked. "Isn't that what you told me to do?"

"You know I meant that you should give them a clear answer one way or the other."

"Hmmm." Gina glanced over her shoulder at him as she entered the garage. "Then maybe you're the one who needs to give clear instructions."

Mitch sighed. She really had her back up.

Gina yanked off her boots in the breezeway. "Don't ever

correct me like that again in public, Mitch. I'm not one of the kids."

He bit back the obvious reply—*Then don't act like one.*—and said instead, "The potty mouth has no place around the kids."

"What are you doing, like, reading every parent magazine? You think they haven't heard it before?"

"Not from their parents or mine. I'm trying not to let them hear it from me, and I'd like that they didn't hear it from you."

"They weren't even around yet. You were just worried about the other parents. As if *they've* never said anything like that."

Mitch slipped Grant's book bag onto the same forearm that held Case's. He used his free hand to rake his hair. "Look, I'm sorry, Gina, if I embarrassed or offended you."

"*If?*"

He sighed heavily this time. "I'm trying to apologize."

The arms that were crossed tightly under Gina's breasts relaxed slightly. "Go on."

"That's it. I'm sorry. I'm feeling my way here. I haven't had *time* to read a magazine about parenting. I've hardly been able to read what I have to to do my job. I could use your help, and if you can't give that, I could at least use your understanding."

Gina was silent a moment, studying his face. There was about a snowball's chance that she wasn't going to forgive him. As much as these recent choices of his had inconvenienced her plans, there was a part of her that admired Mitch for taking it all on, almost without blinking an eye. Steady. Decent. Sincere. It didn't hurt that he was handsome as sin either. She took one of the book bags from him, stood on tiptoe, and gave him a kiss full on the lips. "I still want to boink you," she whispered against his mouth.

Mitch wasn't exactly proof against the firm little body

she thrust against him. "Yeah," he whispered back. "Boink works for me, too."

She laughed and grabbed his hand. "C'mon. Before Case and Grant get curious."

No chance of that, Mitch thought as he rounded the corner into the living room. The twins were already sitting cross-legged and catatonic in front of the TV, their jackets only partially unbuttoned and halfway to their elbows. *Disrobing interruptus.* "Guys! Jackets. Hall closet."

Gina smirked when they didn't move. "You've got to turn the TV off or stand in front of it. Even *I* know that."

Mitch chuckled and gave her a kiss on the cheek. "Thanks for the help."

Thea was curled in one corner of the overstuffed sofa in her office when her assistant buzzed her. She looked up from the layout she was only pretending to study and stared just as vaguely at the offending phone.

"Ms. Wyndham? Are you in there?"

It was no use not answering. Mrs. Admundson, a frighteningly efficient holdover from the days when Thea's father still ran the firm, would wonder why she hadn't seen her leave and come in to check. "I'm here," Thea answered, trying for a tone that was neither tired nor impatient and afraid it was both. "What do you need?"

"Mr. Strahern is here."

"Oh. Of course." She pushed the layout to one side. "Show him—" The door was opening before Thea could unfold her legs and make a search for her sling-back Ferragamos.

"Don't move," Joel commanded. "You look all soft and sleepy-eyed. Very sexy." He shut the door behind him and leaned one shoulder against it, just taking his fill of Thea's momentary and unexpected vulnerability here in her office. "Were you napping?"

"Hmmm. No, not really." Thea's smile surrendered to an abrupt yawn. Embarrassed, and not entirely certain why that was, she added, "Though I wasn't doing anything more productive." She found her shoes and slipped them on, coming to her feet in spite of Joel's insistence that she do otherwise. "Come in. Can I get you something to drink?" She started in the direction of the wet bar, remembered herself, and backtracked to give Joel a kiss. What she intended as a peck on the cheek became something more than that when he turned his head and caught her mouth with his own. She returned it but her discomfort was clearly communicated. After a moment, he let her go. "It's just that it's my office," she said, explaining herself for perhaps the dozenth time. "I have to work here and I don't want—"

He laughed deeply, a pleasant chuckle that was at once knowing and indulgent. "I know," he said, cupping the side of her face. "But you can't blame me for trying."

Actually she did, though she felt rather small about it. He was her fiancé, after all. One would think she'd be able to make some allowances where he was concerned. On the other side of the door Mrs. Admundson was probably thinking Joel already had her dress shoved up to her hips and was bending her over the desk. Mrs. Admundson remained thoroughly professional but Thea could see that the specter of some sexual escapade had been raised. It was there in her eyes, in the way she couldn't quite meet Thea's after Joel left. Thea was mortified. When she told Joel, he was amused. He rather liked the idea that the office staff at Foster and Wyndham thought he dropped in for a quickie. That was because she'd never told him about the seltzer-water-with-a-Viagra-chaser jokes that were going around.

He would have screwed her in front of the entire agency just to prove medication had nothing to do with it.

"Water," Joel said.

"Hmm?"

He smiled indulgently. "You asked me if I wanted something to drink? I'll take water."

"Oh." Absurdly, Thea felt herself blushing. What in God's name was wrong with her? She resolutely suppressed the answer that came immediately to her mind as too absurd to be true. Mitchell Baker had nothing to do with anything. Didn't he? Stepping back, she beat a rather hasty retreat to the wet bar. "Lemon?"

"If you have it."

Thea poured Evian into a glass for Joel, added a slice of fresh lemon, and carried it to the sofa where he was now sitting. He had the layout board on his lap and was studying it with more interest than she had shown minutes earlier. "Here." She handed him the glass and indicated the layout with a nod. "What do you think?"

"I think you ad people are a devious and unscrupulous lot. I'd buy this."

"No, you wouldn't. You've never used a cleaning product like that in your life. But thanks for the devious and unscrupulous compliment."

Grinning, Joel handed her the board. "I'm sure Betty would buy it," he said, referring to his housekeeper. "Are you going after the Carver Chemical account?"

"Not with ideas like this, we're not." She dropped the board on a stack of layouts she had discarded earlier. Although there was room beside him on the sofa now, Thea sat in a chair opposite Joel. She crossed her legs and saw his eyes immediately follow the movement. Not for the first time Thea wished she was more comfortable with his overt interest. What was wrong with her that she didn't feel flattered? "Whether or not we can get the account depends on our ability to make their most familiar, tried-and-true, big-yawn products exciting again. With so many competing products on the market, Carver needs to build brand loyalty with a new generation. Betty already buys Shine and Shield. Her daughter probably does, too. But her granddaughter? Not likely."

"Maybe her granddaughter doesn't clean."

Thea's arch look was only moderately playful. "Then we have to find out why, change an attitude, *and* put Shine and Shield in her hand."

Joel regarded her as if he were completely confident in her ability to do just that. "If Satan had hired Foster and Wyndham, his temptation-of-Christ campaign would have been a success."

"Joel!"

His smile was mischievous and youthful. "I'm Episcopalian. We live on the edge."

Thea laughed. Sometimes he seemed so much younger than she felt. It was more than the fact that he wore his sixty-one years so very well. It didn't hurt that his dark hair had just begun to gray and that it was a gunmetal color that perfectly matched his eyes. He kept himself fit playing golf and rowing. He walked the links and his rowing was done on the Allegheny. Machines, he'd told her, were for pussies. Give or take a few pounds, he'd kept his weight at 175 for the last thirty years and except for an occasional cigar, he had never been a smoker. He was still taut in all the right places, firm and toned and vital. At just over six feet, Joel could turn heads, and often did. He worked hard, as hard or harder than most of the people under him at Strahern Investments. He was tough, sharp, and competitive, and he had had plenty of young turks for lunch when they forgot he was ultimately a predator; but when the mood was on him, he could also be boyishly curious and playful. For all his years in business, he'd never attached himself to a cynical life view that did not allow for change or hope.

It was, perhaps, the quality that Thea found most appealing. If not precisely jaded herself, then she was certainly weary.

Joel's eyes settled thoughtfully on Thea's face. Now that she had shaken off her pensive, vaguely distracted mien, signs of tension were visible in the set of mouth and the crease between her brows. "Tell me about the meeting," he said. "That's why I came over."

She thought it had been. "You could have called, Joel."

"I could have. It would have been a tad impersonal, don't you think?"

Thea's small smile acknowledged the truth of that. He had known he couldn't trust her to be quite so honest over the phone. It was not that he thought she would lie about what happened, but rather that she would minimize how she felt about it. "It was . . ." She hesitated, searching for the right word. "Difficult. Mitchell was there with Wayne. Emilie, Case, and Grant were all in school, so I wasn't ambushed by them in Wayne's office."

"You were right, then. You said he wouldn't bring them."

"He's a decent man, even if some of his ideas are from another century."

Joel had no trouble interpreting what that meant. "He expected you to take the children because you're a woman."

Thea nodded. The memory of that particular exchange with Mitch had the power to raise a small smile. "Because I'm a girl, I believe is how he phrased it. Just as if he thought taking Emilie and the twins for life was the equivalent of playing house."

"He's had them for the last month," Joel pointed out.

"I know. But I don't believe he ever really thought I *wouldn't* take them; so in some ways he's been the one playing house." Thea propped her bent elbow on the arm of her chair and leaned slightly to one side, letting her cheek rest against her open palm. "The light he saw at the end of the tunnel turned out to be a freight train."

"He was angry?"

Thea recalled Mitch's words. "Disappointed, he said. And confused." She regarded Joel frankly. "It looked a lot like anger. It was a tense confrontation at times."

"Avery likes it tense. That's his element."

"Avery and Wayne were out of the room for most of my meeting with Mitch."

One of Joel's brows lifted. "The idea behind having an attorney is having the attorney present."

As reprimands went, it was a mild one. Avery Childers had much stronger words for her on their way back to town. Thea simply accepted the disapproval from both men without trying to defend her decision. Even now she didn't know if she had had a chance to do the meeting over again if she would do anything different. There was no point in explaining that to Joel, not when what she had to tell him was so much more important. "I'd like to have the children with us sometimes. Once a month, perhaps. For a long weekend."

Joel rolled his glass between his palms, saying nothing, just staring at her. Finally he stood and walked to the wet bar. He poured out most of the water into the small sink, removed the lemon slice, then added a couple of fingers of Dewar's to his glass. He took a long swallow before he turned to face Thea. "I thought we had an agreement."

"We did." She added softly, "We do."

"I'd prefer not to rehash this, Thea. You shouldn't have talked to Baker alone. That's what Avery was there for. To protect you."

She bristled a little at that. Her head came up and she dropped the hand that had been supporting it into her lap. "I didn't require protection. I kept up my end and I never wavered once. Mitchell would be surprised if he knew I was suggesting this to you now."

"I don't care if he's surprised. *I'm* surprised. We discussed this. I don't want the children in our lives, Thea, and you said yourself that you're not ready."

"I'm not ready . . . not now . . . but someday, Joel . . ." She fell silent when she saw his features go rigid and his gunmetal gray eyes frost over.

"I've raised my family," he said flatly. "Three children. Seven grandchildren. I want something different. I don't want a second go-around at this stage of my life."

"I'm not talking about raising Emilie and the twins. I'm talking about having them on a weekend once a month. Taking them to a play or the Science Center. Going out to Oakland to the museum. Making tents out of blankets and a cardboard table and reading stories by flashlight."

"And I'm talking about being able to fly to New York or the Vineyard at a moment's notice. Going to the islands for a long weekend just because we want to and because we can." He finished his drink and set the glass behind him. "What about my own grandchildren?"

"What about them? I always imagined we'd do things with them. We do now."

"But not as a matter of structure or routine or, God forbid, a court order. I like it that way. I can have them anytime I want them."

"On your terms."

"Yes. And I'm not apologizing for it." He pushed away from the wet bar and closed the distance between them. Hunkering down in front of her, he said, "You can ask my children, Thea; they'll tell you I wasn't an absent father. I couldn't get to everything they were involved in—Nancy, even when her health was good, couldn't manage that—but I knew what they were doing. I didn't work at home at night or on weekends. I enjoyed myself with my kids. Now I want to enjoy myself separate from them." He searched her face. "With you," he said softly. "I want to be with you."

Thea said nothing. There was a sense of building pressure against her chest, but when she looked down there was only her own hand over her heart and her fingers twisting the onyx stone at her neck. His declaration was meant to compliment her, or at least there was a time she would have accepted it as such. Now she saw he was only expressing his own needs. She didn't fault him for the inherent selfishness of his position, but she was less certain that it reflected what she wanted for herself. Before she could put her thoughts into words, Joel came to his feet. He did not step back but stood his ground over her. Thea looked up at him, knowing all the while she didn't have the defenses yet to brace herself for what was coming.

"You're not ready, Thea. You said so yourself. If you're having doubts then perhaps you should call someone who can help you think this through. Forget about what I want and think about what you need. Those children are precisely the sort of responsibility you shouldn't be taking on at this time."

"Emilie, Case, and Grant," she said quietly.

"What?"

"The children have names. Emilie, Case, and Grant." Tears welled in her eyes and she made no effort to blink them back. This was Joel who was with her now, not Mitchell Baker. Joel loved her. Surely it was safe to share her pain with him. "I'm afraid, Joel. I don't know—" Thea's vision blurred so completely for a moment that she wasn't aware of Joel bending over her until she felt his hands under her elbows. With surprising little encouragement, he brought her to her feet and into the circle of his arms. She rested her head against his impeccably tailored suit, and to his credit he never once said that he gave a damn about the wet spots. "I feel as if I'm abandoning them," she whispered. "I have to see them sometimes. You can't expect that I won't ever see them." Thea felt him stiffen slightly. She tried to raise her face to look at him but the hand at the back of her head increased its pressure and she remained where she was.

"Is that what you told Baker?" Joel asked. "That you'd visit them?"

She nodded. "I know I said I wouldn't, but—"

"But you made Avery leave."

"I didn't make him leave."

"You told him it was all right for him to be out of the room while you talked to Baker. That's making him leave in my book."

Now Thea did push hard enough to free herself, first from the hand cradling her head and then from the one exerting pressure against her back. "You knew all along," she accused him. The tears, she noticed, were gone now. She swiped at her damp cheeks and felt the heat of righteous anger flushing her face. "You spoke to Avery before you came here."

"Thea."

"Don't say my name as if you're talking to an unreasonable child. You sound like Avery now."

Joel sighed. He took a step back, and then another. Finally, in what he knew was tantamount to entering a guilty plea, he went to the sofa where he perched on the wide curving arm. He wished they were having this out anyplace but in Thea's office. It was more of a sanctuary to her than her own home. This was where she felt comfortable and confident, and where she could best express both. On the wall behind him was a Warhol print Thea's father had commissioned in the early sixties for an ad campaign. Wyndham had never liked the finished piece, never used the print, and it was left to gather dust in storage even after the Pittsburgh native's fifteen minutes of fame ran the course of three decades. Thea rescued it when Foster and Wyndham moved to their new offices on Sixth and Smithfield and gave it a place of prominence in her suite. It was not so much that she liked the silkscreen, she'd told him once, but that it served to remind her that she was not her father's daughter.

"What do you want me to say, Thea?" Joel asked. "Do you want to hear that it won't happen again?"

"I know it won't happen again. I'm firing Avery Childers."

Joel didn't try to change her mind. She was every bit as stubborn as her father. No matter what she thought, the apple didn't fall far from the tree. "What about seeing the children? Are you firm on that?"

"Yes. I told Mitch that I would visit them in Connaugh Creek. I never suggested more than that, Joel. I'm sorry if you think I went back on our agreement by offering that much of my time to Gabe and Kathy's children, but I made a promise to them, too. That means something to me."

He held up one hand, palm out. "All right," he said quietly. "I can accept that."

Thea bit her tongue to keep from having the last word. There was nothing to be gained by telling him he'd *have* to accept it. She didn't even know if it were true. Walking over to the wet bar she withdrew a bottle of water from the refrigerator and opened it. She drank enough to ease the dryness in her throat and then set the bottle down. There was nothing worse than not even knowing her own mind. Joel was probably right: she would have to call someone to help her. She couldn't do this on her own.

Joel recognized that it was time to change the subject, at least until he was on firmer ground. "I have tickets for the symphony tonight." He reached in his inside jacket pocket and withdrew them, fanning them open so she could see both. *"Water Music."*

Thea felt herself being drawn into that beautiful smile that was no longer entirely confident of her answer. She was careful to make sure he understood that it wasn't their disagreement, or even him going to Avery before speaking to her, that was guiding her answer. "I can't. I have a brainstorming session with the Blue Team in"—she checked her watch—"five minutes ago. It will last until at least six. And then I have a meeting." She held her breath, waiting for him to ask her to skip the meeting, even though he promised her he wouldn't do that. He didn't, but she didn't miss that the thought had crossed his mind. She tried not to blame him for that. "I think I need to go home after that, Joel. Alone," she added in the event he thought he should come out to her house after the symphony. "Why don't you meet Barbara at Heinz Hall? She loves the symphony and Jay never wants to go."

Joel considered that a moment. His daughter-in-law would drop everything to come into town for the evening. He'd break the news to his son when he got back to the office. "Good idea. You know, you should really try working somewhere where they expect good ideas nonstop. I bet you'd be excellent at it."

Thea heard her laughter and knew it wasn't completely forced. She felt the tension of the last thirty minutes slowly seeping out of her. "I'll think about that." She stayed where she was as Joel rose to his feet. When he hesitated, uncertain of the reception he might receive if he tried to kiss her, Thea relented. She went to him and raised her face to his. "I don't like fighting with you," she whispered.

"That wasn't a fight. Nancy and I fought. That was a skirmish."

"In my house that was a fight."

"I'll remember that." He bent his head and kissed her softly on the mouth. "I love you, Thea. Please say you know that."

She nodded. "I know. Even when I'm not certain of anything else, I know that."

"Good." He kissed her again, briefly this time, but hard, leaving the imprint of his mouth on hers. "Think about me."

Thea found herself inclining toward Joel as he backed away, her smile slightly bemused. "I have to think about Shine and Shield."

Joel chuckled. "Of course you do." He opened the door and started out, only to poke his head back in and tell her, "It's all right. Mrs. Admundson is thinking about me."

Shaking her head, Thea waved him out. She gave herself a few minutes to collect her thoughts before she pressed the intercom. "Tell the Blue Team to come in, Mrs. Admundson." She'd given them ten extra minutes. They had better be brilliant.

Thea hit the mute button on the remote just as the commercial voiceover began. It was an unusual move for her. She was more in the habit of silencing the program and listening to the ads. Tossing the remote on the floor beside the couch, she let her head fall back on the cushion and closed her eyes. Blessed silence and complete darkness. It didn't seem to help. She still felt restless and unsettled.

She wondered if she should have just stayed at the office. Her sofa unfolded into a relatively comfortable bed and she had long ago stocked her private bathroom with all the important amenities. In addition, the closet held several choices in day and evening wear with shoes to match. It was difficult to stop second-guessing her decision to drive home. She had made a promise to herself to spend less time in the Foster and Wyndham headquarters. She also made a promise that she would not keep running on empty, in the figurative sense of the phrase. Well, she was out of the office, but the thirty-five minute drive home had left her with no purposeful energy.

What she felt now was just edgy.

Thea stood, cinched her robe around her waist, and padded softly to the kitchen where the phone was. Except for the flickering images from the TV, the house was dark. She hovered beside the base unit for a moment, staring at the phone as if she didn't know quite what to do with it. Joel would still be at the symphony so there was no point in calling him. She tapped her index nail against the smoky granite countertop as her mind raced.

God, she hated this feeling! Arching her back, she stretched so that her vertebrae popped. She rolled her neck, first clockwise, then counter. The refrigerator captured her interest briefly but when she opened the door and saw that her choices were rancid orange juice, an assortment of condiments, something green that might have been a dairy product, and congealed Chinese takeout from better than a month ago, she closed it again.

Where was her phone book? She absolutely needed to make the call and she realized she shouldn't have put it off until she was practically unhinged. Why hadn't she asked for the number when she had a chance? Now she thought she would be lucky to find it.

Hands shaking, Thea found the directory in one of the cabinets and dropped it on the breakfast bar with a resounding thump. She opened it randomly and began flipping through the thin pages, softly reciting the alphabet song as she made her search. She had no clear idea of how long she spent on this task before she was forced to conclude the number wasn't there.

Thea shoved the book away. It was so heavy that it didn't go very far but the act of pushing it, the pent-up violence inherent in the movement, frightened her. This is not the way she wanted to be.

She took a deep breath and let it out slowly through her nose. On the second inhale/exhale she closed her eyes. The simple relaxation technique actually worked and she wondered why she had always resisted these little tricks when they were suggested to her. With the third breath she didn't think about it anymore and tried to clear her mind instead.

For a few brief moments calm embraced her. Thea felt it like something thick and heavy and liquid that slipped over her skin and then was absorbed by it. It was an uncertain state but while it lasted Thea learned that she had the capacity to appreciate it. She had not known that about herself.

Picking up the phone, Thea walked to the sliding glass doors that opened on the rear deck. She spent a minute contemplating what she was going to do before she stepped outside. It was cold and she was barefoot, but the moon was full and the outdoors were better lit than the tomb she'd allowed her home to become. Holding the phone so she could make out the touch pad, she punched in directory assistance. It didn't take long to get the computer-generated voice to give her the numbers she needed.

Thea sat down on one of the Adirondack chairs that she had never bothered covering for winter and pulled her feet up under her. It was a balmy night for February, but it was not exactly deck weather. She pressed the numbers before she lost her nerve.

"Hello?"

The phone was picked up so quickly Thea wasn't prepared. The fact that it was picked up by a woman also caught her off guard.

"Hello?"

The voice was impatient this time. Thea cleared her throat. "I think I have the wrong—"

"Mitch! I think this one's for you!"

In the background Thea could hear Mitch calling back, "Take a message." There was some grumbling about getting caller ID and then the woman's clear voice was back on the line again. "I'm sorry," Gina said. "Were you calling for Mitch?"

"I . . . this was a mistake," Thea said. "I didn't mean to

disturb—" She hung up before she said anything else. In spite of the cold, her palm was sweating. Thea practically launched herself out of the chair and into the house. She was putting the phone back in its base when it rang. Startled, she almost dropped it. Her thumb reflexively hit the talk button before she was certain she wanted to have a conversation with anyone.

"Hello?" she asked.

"Thea?"

It was Mitch. Thea had no difficulty recognizing the pleasantly deep, slightly gritty timbre of his voice. She could picture him standing with the phone in one hand, the other making a raking motion through his hair. "Er, yes. It's Thea."

"Did you just call me?"

"Umm, yes. Yes, I did. How—how did you . . ." She sighed, impatient with herself for this hesitancy and stumbling. "It's just that the woman who answered the phone said something about you needing to get caller ID."

"It's on the to-do list. Mostly I use my cell," he said. "I took a guess." He paused a beat, then added, "Actually, I hit star sixty-nine."

"Oh. Then I'm glad I didn't lie."

Mitch caught himself before he let his smile seep into his voice. He'd called her back out of curiosity, not because he was feeling in a particularly forgiving mood. "What do you want?" he asked bluntly.

At her end, Thea started. His initial friendliness was gone. It was not even that he was wary; just that he was cold. "I was wondering . . . that is, you mentioned that I might be able to . . ." She realized her heart was hammering in her chest and there was a softball-size lump in her throat. "I'd like to visit the children," she said in a rush. "I thought I might come out. I could be there in under an hour."

Mitch blinked. He held the phone away from his ear and stared at it a moment, not quite believing what he'd heard.

Slowly, he returned it to his ear. There was silence on the other end. "You still there, Thea?"

"Yes . . ."

"Do you have a clock nearby?"

She glanced at the one on the microwave. "Yes."

"You can read it, can't you? Big hand. Little hand. If it's digital it should be—"

Thea hung up. She was walking away when the phone started ringing. She let it go. If it was Joel, he'd think she had gone to bed. If it was Mitch, he'd learn soon enough that she had no intention of talking to him. Whoever it was gave up by the time Thea reached her bedroom. She turned on the bedside lamp long enough to turn down the covers and remove her robe. When she lay down she knew immediately that sleep was not going to happen without help. This is what she had been afraid of all day. Thea looked toward the bathroom. The door was open and she could see the reflection of her medicine cabinet in the mirror above the sink.

She picked up the phone instead and scrolled the database for the number she needed. This time when a woman answered, she expected it. "Hi," she said softly. "It's Thea."

"Hey. When I saw you tonight I thought you might be calling."

"You should have told me. It took me a long time to figure it out."

"You got me now."

"It's not too late?" Thea recognized the pause in the conversation as Rosie looked around for a clock.

"Hell, it's only a little past ten. Early in my book. What's up?"

Thea took a deep breath. Her voice shook slightly when she spoke again. "I'm exhausted and wound up at the same time. I don't think I'm going to be able to sleep on my own."

"Go make yourself a cup of tea. I'm on my way."

Chapter 3

Thea's cell rang as she was merging into rush hour traffic on Route 28. She had little patience for the intrusion, but it was her weakness that she was as well-conditioned as one of Pavlov's dogs. Her car came with Bluetooth, and she was almost helpless to keep from answering when she heard a ringtone. She waited until she was safely in line before she began talking. "I'm here. What do you need?"

"It's Joel, sweetie."

Her voice softened. "I thought you were someone from the Blue Team."

"I take it they weren't exactly on their game yesterday."

"That's an understatement. Where are you?"

"On Greentree Hill, crawling toward the tunnels. You?"

"Ready to grind to a halt on 28." She applied the brake as she was speaking. "I should have left earlier."

"How did you sleep?"

Thea knew that's why he had called. "It was tough at first. I had to call Rosie." Joel's silence let her know he wished she had called someone else. "She helped me, Joel. I don't think it would have been a very good night without her."

"Well, that's all right, then."

"You don't like Rosie, do you?"

"I don't really know her."

Thea eased on the gas as traffic started to move. In the rearview mirror, she caught the disapproving look of the driver behind her. He looked as if he wanted to report her to the phone police for driving under the influence of conversation. If they had been going more than ten miles an hour she wouldn't have blamed him. "That's right," she said. "You don't really know her. She's a very nice person."

"You hardly know her yourself."

"That's going to change, Joel. Last night wasn't the last time I'll be calling her."

"I just wish—"

"What?" She glanced in the mirror again and saw the driver behind her was picking his nose. Now *there* was a reportable offense. Shaking her head, she let someone slide into the lane in front of her just to piss him off.

"I wish you had found someone more like . . ."

Thea waited for him to finish the sentence, afraid she'd lost the connection. "Like whom, Joel?" she prompted.

"Well, like you."

"Rosie *is* like me."

"You know what I mean."

Thea did, but she wouldn't admit it. Rosie wasn't terribly sophisticated and that was putting it in a very flattering light. She was brash, large, and spoke with such a heavy Pittsburgh accent that to an outsider she would sound like she had a speech impediment. "I think she's the perfect right one for me, Joel. She makes me laugh."

"Just so you don't make her your maid of honor."

Thea couldn't tell if he was serious or not. She was afraid he might be. "You're a snob, Joel Strahern. Did you know that?"

"I don't mean to be."

"I have to go. The man tailgating me in his BMW is making a sexual proposition." She smiled sweetly so the driver would know she had seen him flip her off. "I'm ending this before there's road rage. I'll call when I get to work. I want to hear about the symphony." She disconnected before Joel could reply and turned on NPR.

A seven-story atrium was the centerpiece of the renovated office complex that Foster and Wyndham called home. Formerly a department store, the site was now the Heinz 57 Center, home to the headquarters of Heinz's U.S. Consumer Products and Foodservice businesses. In addition to Heinz, a variety of other firms—accountants, real estate developers, attorneys, medical practitioners—rented the spacious floors while retailers on the ground level brought in pedestrian traffic.

Thea passed on the elevators and walked up three flights, her heels clicking lightly in the empty stairwell. There were already more than a dozen people working when she walked into the lobby at Foster and Wyndham. An inflatable beach ball sailed out of one of the small conference rooms as she passed. She automatically batted it back and heard someone call, "Way to go! Three points!" Smiling, she walked on. It was a whatever-helps-you-think working environment that was first cultivated by Alvin Foster and suffered by his founding partner William Wyndham. Thea's own father had been only a little more tolerant than his parent but the Fosters still liked to have a good time on their way to triple bypass surgery and stress-related breakdowns. Thea's position was more practical: if inflatable beach balls were what it took to make the ideas flow, she didn't have a problem. She shared her partner's need to see results at the end of the day.

"Good morning, Hank." She stuck her head through the open doorway to Hank Foster's office. The CEO was tipped so far back in his chair that he was practically reclining. His hands were folded behind his head and his feet were propped on one corner of his desk. Thea couldn't tell if he was sleeping. He was wearing a pair of sunglasses with blue jewel-toned frames and mirrored lenses. "Nice shades. Indisposed or incognito this morning?"

"Indisposed," he said. "I was with clients at Rosebud last night."

"Drink too much, did you?"

He shook his head. "No, we ended up at Primanti Brothers at three in the morning. I had a cheese steak with fries and coleslaw."

Thea knew the fries and coleslaw weren't served on the side. They were *on* the sandwich. "Yum." She meant it; it was a terrific sandwich. Primanti Brothers was a Pittsburgh institution and a must-visit for clients who wanted a taste of the city's blue-collar cuisine. "You need some Pepcid?"

"I need a stomach transplant." He patted the offending portion of his anatomy which, even in his almost prone position, was distended above his belt line. "How can something I love so much do this to me? It's not right." He moved his feet gingerly off the edge of the desk and sat up slowly, pushing the garish sunglasses past the bridge of his nose until they rested against the blunt slope of his forehead. Now he regarded Thea with what looked like four eyes. "You have any luck with the Carver Chemical stuff?"

"No. We were here until almost seven."

"Go easy, Thea," he said lightly. "Your vacation will have been worthless if you come on like gangbusters." When she didn't respond, he went on. "What's the word on your friends' kids?"

"Mitchell is going to keep them."

"You're kidding." Between the pairs of eyes his brows arched in surprise. He studied her for a moment. "You all right with that?"

She nodded. "Sure." Thea backed out the doorway. "Let

me know about the Pepcid." She was gone before Hank, who knew her just about as well as anybody, could guess that maybe she wasn't as all right with it as she had been yesterday.

In her own office Thea kicked off her shoes and put her purse and coat in the closet. She twisted the buttons on her black Donna Karan jacket so it opened casually to reveal a white silk shell. Once she was sitting behind her desk, Thea picked up the pink message slips that Mrs. Admundson had placed on her blotter, and swiveled to face the windows while she read them. Most of the employees had voice mail but Thea hated it and preferred callers leave their messages with a real person. Mrs. Admundson almost qualified.

There was one from Joel this morning, before he reached her on the cell phone. He must have guessed that she had spent the night at the office. Thea crumpled it and tossed it over her shoulder onto the desk. There were two from locally based corporations, one an Internet firm, the other a health maintenance organization. She would return those quickly then set them up with Hank if they were looking for consultation. He would bring her back after he had some idea of how serious they were about changing advertisers. In the meantime she would put the creative teams to work developing something interesting for them to consider.

There was a message from the secretary of one of the local family service organizations where she sat on the board of directors, reminding her there was a luncheon meeting on Thursday. Yes, she thought, wouldn't she feel like a complete hypocrite attending that function? She slipped it in her pocket.

Flipping through the rest of the stack she saw that a colleague at another firm had called. There was a message from a Carolyn Schafer in human resources at Dwight Ennis, Inc. requesting a reference check, which meant that someone at Foster and Wyndham was jumping ship, and either he hadn't told Hank or Hank had forgotten to tell her. There was a message from Avery Childers and the *Chronicle* called and . . .

Thea's fingers stilled. It wasn't the paper specifically that had called, but Mitchell Baker. Mrs. Admundson, always playing her cards close, had pretended not to know his connection to Thea and had asked where he worked. Thea saw her assistant also made a note in red that there had been three calls. One of Thea's brows lifted. All of them were before eight o'clock. She looked at the number and saw it was the local exchange. He was in town, then, not at home.

She stared at the pink slip a long time before she made a tight fist around it. Turning ninety degrees in her chair, Thea sent it sailing toward the wet bar where it fell in the sink. She threw up her hands and made crowd noises. "And the fans go wild!" Finishing the turn so she faced her desk, Thea picked up the phone and called Joel. She listened while he told her about the concert. He passed on his daughter-in-law's thanks for thinking of her as a replacement and then they broke away, each with their agendas for the day in front of them.

Thea spent the next hour on the phone with the Net firm and the HMO. Then she initiated a few calls which took another hour. The call to Avery took longer than expected. The attorney didn't want to hear that she was firing him. During all the calls, the earbud let her move around the office. She dallied in front of the window, looking down on Smithfield Street while she talked and watching the pedestrians jostle for position on the sidewalk and dart willy-nilly between the moving cars. She watered her plants, pulled the dead leaves, and straightened the books on her shelves. For a while she walked on the treadmill, stopping short of glowing or labored breathing. It hardly qualified as exercise, but it was better than nothing and she didn't want to beat Hank Foster to that first bypass.

When she finished with business calls she made one

more personal one. She got voice mail. *"Hey there. Unless you're new to the planet, you know what to do."* Thea smiled. That was pure Rosie. "Hi. It's Thea. Just checking in. Thank you for last night. It helped." Thea almost asked if she wanted to be a bridesmaid but managed to stop herself. "I'll be in touch." She ended the call, removed the earbud, and put on her shoes. She left her office to pass out assignments to the Green and Yellow Teams and round up the Blues.

When Thea didn't call by eleven-thirty, Mitch decided she wasn't going to return his call at all. He didn't blame her. He knew he'd been a first-class ass last night when she'd phoned unexpectedly. In her sexy Ferragamo sling-backs, he wouldn't return his calls either. Clearly some act of contrition was in order.

The *Chronicle*'s building was across town from Foster and Wyndham, but the nice thing about Pittsburgh's golden triangle was that virtually everything was within walking distance. Mitch finished his meeting with the editor of the Sunday Forum section in record time, grabbed his jacket, and hurried out of the building. He stopped for flowers, bagel sandwiches, and Godiva chocolates, and still managed to make it to the ad agency by twelve-twenty.

Mitch thought the receptionist regarded him and his bribes with something akin to pity when he told her whom he wanted to see, but she lifted the phone and called through to Thea's office anyway.

"I think she's still in a meeting with the Blues," she said. "You can have a seat and wait if you'd like. I'll let her know you're here as soon as she comes out. I can't interrupt her, though."

"Couldn't I wait in her office?"

She hesitated. "I don't think that's a good idea." She looked from the flowers to the chocolates and then to him again. "I know I look young and impressionable right now, but I'm grooming for the office-dragon position."

Both of Mitch's brows lifted. "They have one here, too?"

"Yes, and she's Ms. Wyndham's admin assistant. So, even if you got by me with this sorry Hail Mary pass you're attempting, she wouldn't let you into the inner sanctum." She pointed a bloodred acrylic-tipped nail at the chairs against the wall. "I promise I'll tell—"

"Hey, Tamika. Who's this?"

The beadwork in Tamika's hair clicked softly as she swiveled in her chair and looked up. "Nice shades, Mr. Foster."

"Thanks." He pushed them up a notch so they went from his forehead to the forefront of his receding hairline. "Your boyfriend?" he asked. "You need a long lunch?"

"No, but that's a nice offer. This is Mr. Baker. He's asking to see Ms. Wyndham."

Mitch thrust the bagel bag into his left hand and held out his right. The flowers and chocolates were squeezed in the crook of his arm. "Mitch Baker," he said. "I'm a . . ." He hesitated, not certain how to describe himself in relation to Thea Wyndham. His eyes darted to the gold Godiva box and then back to Hank Foster. "I'm a penitent."

Foster laughed. "Then I hope you have shoes in that bag because flowers and chocolates aren't going to cut it." He put his hand in Mitch's and gave it a firm shake. "Come on back. It's all right, Tamika. I know who Mr. Baker is. I'll show him to Thea's office."

Mitch started to follow, paused, and planning for a future of needing favors from the dragon-in-training, he placed the flowers in her arms. Her smile was beatific.

Watching the exchange, Hank Foster shook his head. As he led the way to Thea's office, he confided, "You've done it now. Upset the delicate balance of power around here." He pointed to the aging Valkyrie at the copier. "See her? That's

Mrs. Admundson. She's been here longer than I have. This is her desk." He tapped it as they passed.

Without missing a beat, Mitch placed the gold Godiva box at the center of it.

"Good. Détente is achieved. What do you have in the bag?"

"Bagel sandwiches."

"Better give those to me. They're pretty unimpressive without the flowers and the chocolates."

Mitch's eyes darted to the wrinkled brown bag he was still clutching. It was hanging from his left hand like a game pheasant he'd shot down in the wild. He held it out to Foster who snatched it up before he could change his mind.

"Thanks." The CEO peeked in the bag. "I'm sure these will be great."

"No problem." He stepped into Thea's office empty-handed. "You think shoes would have been better?" They seemed too personal . . . worse, cliché.

Foster didn't hesitate. "Six and a half, narrow. They have the added advantage that no one else around here can use them." Grinning, he pushed the sunglasses back to the bridge of his nose. "Make yourself at home. She won't be long." He stepped out, shutting the door behind him.

Rocking slightly on the balls of his feet, Mitch glanced around Thea's office, eyeing the forest green leather sofa and chairs for comfort versus style. The top of her desk was clear of the detritus of the workday. There were no Post-it notes sticking to the blotter. No message slips impaled on a spindle. No uneven stack of reading to get through. It was also devoid of personal items. No picture frames. No business cards. No crystalline paperweights or executive toys. For Mitch, who hadn't seen the wood grain of his desktop for several years, this barren landscape was a little frightening.

Clearly, Thea Wyndham, the neat freak, had a seriously disordered mind. In the event she dusted for fingerprints,

Mitch thrust his hands in his jeans when he began his tour. He looked over her bookcase but found most of the material was work related: designer and graphics magazines that he, in some cases, also subscribed to. There were large volumes of photography by Annie Leibovitz, Mary Ellen Mark, and Richard Avedon and collections that included Alfred Stieglitz and Pittsburgher Charles "Teenie" Harris. He marveled that her plants were all healthy and well tended. He wondered what she could do with the crinkly brown thing in the corner of his office that he kept watering out of a sense of duty.

She had the latest generation of Apple's MacBook Pro, but the lid was closed and he doubted she had any good games. He was tempted to try out the treadmill and relieved when the urge quickly passed.

Except for some aromatic candles on a silver tray, the surface of her credenza was clear. When he leaned forward he could actually see his reflection. Amazing. He resisted a powerful urge to place his palms firmly on the polished top just to leave signs of life.

He nudged one of the sliding doors below open with his knee. Hunkering down, he realized he'd hit pay dirt. Her sound system was a thing of beauty and her iPod was resting snugly in its dock. Mitch didn't even try to resist. His hands were out of his pockets before he could consider any other course of action.

Plucking the iPod from its nest, he began scrolling Thea's playlists and discovered Ms. Wyndham had eclectic listening tastes: jazz, classical, country, rock, zydeco. Almost every musical genre was represented in her collection. She also had some guilty pleasures, else how could one explain Duran Duran and the show tunes? Mitch opened the On The Go playlist and found her exercise tunes. She'd downloaded or copied five decades of pop tunes, chosen it seemed for their relentless beat, not their lyrics, and certainly not their subtlety. Who *was* this woman?

Mitch scrolled down to "Smooth Criminal," set the iPod back in the dock, and hit play. In moments, from unobtrusive speakers throughout the office, Michael Jackson was asking Annie if she was okay. Grinning, Mitch slid the door to the credenza closed.

Taking Hank Foster's advice to make himself at home, he explored Thea's wet bar, took a bottled water, and just as he was turning away, caught sight of the crumpled pink message slip in the sink. He would have left it there if he hadn't seen the creased letters in his own name. Smoothing it out revealed that Thea had indeed received his messages. Circled in red ink was the notation that he had called three times. The fact that it had been relegated to the sink told him what she thought of it.

Mitch's fingers were in the act of closing over it when Thea Wyndham opened the door to her office. He noticed immediately that she didn't stare at him in disbelief. That would have been a compliment. No, she stared at him as if he'd just managed to meet every one of her low expectations.

He held up the wrinkled pink slip. "Checking out your unique message filing system." He dropped it back in the sink, then casually raised the bottled water to his mouth. "Should I put this where I found it?"

Thea stepped inside and shut the door behind her. Michael was singing. She wished he would ask if *she* was okay. "Would you mind turning that off?"

"No problem." Mitch opened the credenza and deftly returned the office to silence. Glancing over his shoulder, he asked, "Better?"

Thea merely nodded. Walking over to her desk, she placed the portfolio of sketches and copy ideas she was carrying on one corner. She turned to face Mitch, her arms crossed in front her, a posture that was not defensive but demanding. One brow lifted in a perfect arch. "You're here because . . . ?"

"Because you didn't return my calls."

"Most people would understand that meant I didn't want to talk to them."

He shrugged. "There are alternate explanations, you know. Like you could have a head injury and forgot how to work a phone. Or been abducted." His dark green eyes slid over her from head to heels. "It's good to know neither of those things happened."

Thea felt a slight pressure along her jawline and realized she was actually grinding her teeth. There was probably a muscle twitching in her cheek.

"Would you like something to drink?" asked Mitch. "There's all kinds of bottled water here. Unless you'd like something with a little bite? Then I can pour a glass from the tap. No?" He took a swig from his bottle. "Scotch? Gin and tonic? Do people still do martini lunches?"

"I don't know about other people," she said with credible calm. "I don't."

"Hmm." Mitch's eyes dropped to the silver-plated letter opener lying perfectly parallel to her blotter. If only she would pick it up and plunge it in his throat. He wasn't sure there was any other way to keep him from making more of an idiot of himself. She looked great; there was no getting around that. With her red hair and brilliant green eyes, she didn't require extraneous splashes of color. She had an artist's eye for style and a way of carrying herself that would make her look runway ready in a sweatshirt and jeans. The black designer suit she was wearing could have been a ball buster: long jacket, short skirt, and tailored for testosterone, but on Thea it just seemed casually feminine. The silky thing she had on underneath had the iridescent quality of mother-of-pearl. It had shimmered when she walked to her desk. Now that she was standing perfectly still, Mitch had to wait for her to take a breath to get the same effect. Figuring there was no sense in holding his own breath waiting for her, Mitch's eyes went lower. It was a mistake. Thea Wyndham had a lot of leg and most of it was a silhouette in sheer black stockings. He tried not to think about what was holding them up, but that was all he needed to get the various possibilities firmly in focus. Thigh-highs? Panty hose? Garter belt?

His mouth actually went dry. He took another long swallow from his water bottle before he set it down behind him. "Nice shoes."

Thea looked down at her feet. Except for an edge of patent leather piping around the vamp, this pair of black heels was very plain. Her eyes returned to Mitch and in spite of wishing that it were otherwise, she knew there was a trace of a smile on her lips. She leaned one hip against her desk. "Tell me again why you're here," she said. "The truth this time."

"I haven't had ample opportunity to be a jerk today. Thought I'd come here and get it out of my system."

"I see." Thea regarded him thoughtfully. "'Jerk' is putting it mildly."

"I was trying not to be vulgar."

"Don't hold back on my account."

"It's not entirely for you. I'm practicing because of the kids."

"Good idea."

Mitch sat on the edge of the credenza and stretched his legs in front of him. Picking up the empty water bottle, he rolled it lightly between his palms. "I'm sorry about last night, Thea. I shouldn't have made that crack about the clocks and—"

She lifted one hand just enough to cut him off. "I shouldn't have called. It was stupid. I never thought about what time the kids would be in bed."

"The twins go down at eight-thirty," he told her. "Emilie collapses between nine and nine-thirty."

"I'll remember that," she said quietly.

Mitch nodded. He watched the water bottle he was still rolling absently for a moment. "I told them at breakfast that you called last night. They were pretty upset with me that I didn't wake them up so you could talk to them. Case called me a butthead. Grant said I was a *real* butthead. Emilie told me I was a dicksmack."

Thea's eyes widened. "A dicksmack?"

"Pretty descriptive, don't you think? I don't know where she picked that up. I don't think she's considered what it means in the literal sense, at least I hope she hasn't, but she managed to use the term in the right context." Mitch's expression conveyed a little of his sense of being overwhelmed. "I tried to correct her and not make a big deal about it at the same time. The twins were hanging on my every word."

"Uh-oh."

"Yeah. Tell me about it. One of them is going to call the other a dicksmack today in school, and *I'm* going to get called to the principal's office. Mrs. Leone never liked me either."

Thea felt the corners of her mouth lifting again. "You might want to compliment her shoes," she said softly.

Mitch's quicksilver grin touched his eyes. "That works?"

"You're still here."

He chuckled and actually felt a lightening in his chest. "Do you think you'll come out this weekend? Maybe I shouldn't have told the kids about your call. It raised their hopes."

"It's all right. I want to see them. I would have called you tomorrow. I had designated today for being disagreeable and self-righteous. It generally takes twenty-four hours for me to get over myself."

Mitch pushed away from the credenza. He took the water bottle to the sink and set it down there. He saw the crumpled pink slip in the stainless-steel basin and smiled to himself. He was actually glad she hadn't returned his calls. Some things were worth doing in person. Mitch turned back to her. "What time can you make it?"

"Three? Four? I was thinking of just hanging out, then maybe dinner and a movie."

"That'd be great. Saturday, right?"

"Yes."

"They'll love it. And they've been wanting to see *Easy Kills It.*"

A small vertical crease appeared between Thea's brows. "I don't think I'm familiar with—" Then she saw that Mitch was just a bit too serious, his mobile mouth a tad too straight. And surely those green eyes had never been so solemn. "This is a test, right?"

"Something like that."

"I wouldn't take the twins and Emilie to see something called *Easy Kills It* even if it did exist."

"Just checking."

Thea couldn't work up to being offended. "Probably a good idea. As last night indicates, I'm likely to do lots of dumb things."

Mitch felt an unexpected surge of sympathy for her. Thea hadn't made a casual, self-deprecating comment offered to elicit a laugh. She really seemed to mean it. "Kathy and Gabe should have given us a test."

Thea offered him a small smile. "It's kind of you to include yourself, but I have a feeling you're a natural at this parenting stuff."

"Are you kidding?" He rubbed his chin with knuckles. "This morning, I was a dicksmack." Mitch saw Thea's smile broaden slightly but he had the odd sense it was forced, as if she were already wondering what words the kids would find to describe her. "It'll be fine, Thea."

She unfolded her arms and let her hands fall to her sides. Her gaze was direct but she could not quite keep the uncertainty out of her voice. "You're not expecting anything to come of this . . ." She saw him frown and let the end of her thought just drift away.

"What do you mean?" he asked. "Expect what?"

"I mean, if you think that encouraging me to visit will alter my decision to take Emilie and—"

"Stop right there. We were having a decent discussion. Let's not ruin it by taking up that topic."

"I just want to be clear that—" She stopped because he sighed. He jammed his hands in the pockets of his comfortably worn, brown leather jacket and simply sighed. His expression was almost wistful. "You're right," she said. "Let's not ruin it."

One of Mitch's brows lifted. The look he gave her was clearly skeptical.

"I mean it," she said. To prove it she changed the subject. "Have the children been back to the cemetery since the burial?"

"Twice." There was a note of caution in his voice. "You weren't thinking of taking them there, were you?"

"No!" She repeated the denial more softly. "No. I wouldn't do that."

"It's all right, if they ask," he said. "But you have to be prepared for the fallout. My mother took them once after Case and Grant drew some pretty terrific pictures at school and wanted to *show* them to their parents. It was more of an emotional roller coaster for my mother and Emilie than for the twins—that is until Case and Grant saw their Nonny and sister crying." Mitch worked the words out past the lump in his own throat as he remembered how quiet the kids had been when his mother returned them to the house. Feeling helpless and lost himself, he'd cursed Gabe and Kathy for running out on their children, just as if they'd had a choice in what happened. It was even harder when the twins seemed to sense his distress and crawled on the couch beside him, offering the comfort and warmth of their squirmy little bodies, while Emilie, solemn and adultlike prepared him hot tea in the kitchen. "I took them down this past Sunday after church. They had fresh flowers for the vases. There were some tears but a lot of laughter, too. I'm playing it by ear."

Thea could have said that was all very well for him, but she was tone-deaf. She remained silent, though, transfixed in part by the momentary brightness of his eyes. It might have been a trick of the light as he turned his head, but she didn't think so. Her heart gave a peculiar lurch and then Mitch was going on and she listened hard to what he was saying so she didn't have to think about the other.

"You know Gabe and Kathy have plots in the Allegheny County Cemetery, don't you? Not in Connaugh Creek. I don't know why they chose there, but that's what was in their papers."

"Gabe bought the plots just after he and Kathy were married." She shook her head, disbelief and tenderness softening her voice. "Who else does that? He was the ultimate Boy Scout, prepared for every eventuality. Do you own a plot?"

"No. Do you?"

"Not my own."

"What does that mean?"

"There's the family plot. In the mausoleum. I don't think I want to end up in a drawer." Or beside my parents, she almost added. "I went out to the cemetery yesterday," she said. "On the way to our meeting. Avery took me and showed me the graves."

Mitch remembered her slightly shell-shocked look, the swollen eyelids, and hint of redness. "I didn't know."

She shrugged. "There was no reason that you should."

They both fell silent. It stretched long enough to become awkward and uncomfortable. Mitch finally broke it, shifting his weight as he spoke, "I'll see you Saturday, then."

Thea's eyes returned to his. "Yes. Fourish."

"Great." Mitch pulled his hands out of his pockets. He tipped his head toward the door. "I have to be going." He saw her start to move in anticipation of showing him out and he waved her back. "Don't bother. I can find my way."

Thea relaxed. She wasn't certain she wanted to be seen walking with him to the entrance of the firm. She envisioned twenty pairs of eyes following her progress, one pair in particular hiding behind garish sunglasses. "Do you have a deadline?"

"Not at the paper. The afternoon bus." He grinned suddenly. "I have a standing date with five other mothers on the corner of Second Avenue and Porter Street."

Lucky mothers, Thea was thinking as she watched him go to the door. He paused on the threshold and she half expected that he would say something. When he remained quiet for a full beat, she said, "Thank you for coming."

He glanced over his shoulder, unable to hide his startle reflex. He knew it wasn't flattering for him to be surprised by her appreciation, but there it was. "Thanks for not throwing me out."

She smiled. "Good-bye, Mitch."

He shut the door quietly behind him.

Thea's knees went wobbly the moment she heard the latch click. She got around her desk and let herself just fall into her chair. There was a soft *poof* as the leather gave to accommodate her shape and weight. "Oh my," she said under her breath.

Her body filed a status report to her brain. Racing heart. Noodlelike limbs. Metallic taste in her mouth. And when her stomach finally uncurled there was the faint sensation of nausea. Thea found none of it encouraging and all of it a little frightening. She was familiar with the aftermath of an adrenaline rush, but having one in response to a person who meant her no harm was outside of her experience.

Even as she thought it, Thea recognized that it wasn't entirely true. She had made a point of avoiding Mitchell Baker for years. If she was going to be honest with herself— and apparently she was—her behavior had been due in part to some not fully realized understanding that he made her uncomfortable. Or more factually, that he made her uncomfortable in this heart-stalling, jelly-kneed, short-of-breath way.

Thea swiveled in her chair so she was facing the wet bar where Mitch had been standing. She resisted closing her eyes as too juvenile a response. As it turned out, she didn't require a blank screen to recreate his image in her mind's eye. Almost instantly all six-feet-two of him was leaning casually against the wet bar, his shoulders hunched a little in the gently scarred leather jacket. He wore jeans and a pale blue Oxford shirt. There was no tie. A crosshatch of brown and blond, Mitch's thick hair was wind-ruffled and finger-combed and neither effect was unappealing. He flashed a smile suddenly and Thea actually blinked. It was a killer smile, just a kilter off from being male-model perfect. Each time he turned it on his eyes brightened to a shade of green that seemed to be outside the standard spectrum. Amused or serious, he conveyed interest and intelligence in his glance.

There was another look, one with his eyelids at half-mast that was both watchful and intense, that Thea would not let herself dwell on. The image in front of her flickered and she stamped Mitch's features with the mischievous grin, the one that made him seem no more dangerous than Case and Grant.

"Ms. Wyndham?"

Thea was torn out of her reverie by the disembodied voice of her assistant. She turned to the phone. "Yes?"

"I'm here, Ms. Wyndham." Jane Amundson's voice came from the doorway. She had a pad and pen in hand. "Some of us are ordering out for lunch. Jim is going to pick it up. Would you like a sandwich?"

Thea looked at her phone for the time. "I have to be leaving for a meeting." She saw Mrs. Amundson's frown, obviously trying to remember what she had downloaded from Thea's e-planner. "It's not on my schedule. Something that I arranged just last night. I'll be gone about an hour and a half." Thea pretended to misunderstand her assistant's disapproval. "Don't worry that I won't eat. I'll pick up something on my way back. Thank you for asking." It was an effective dismissal, and Mrs. Admundson only hesitated another moment before stepping back into the outer offices.

When she was gone Thea picked up the receiver on her phone and punched in Rosie's number. Smiling to herself as voice mail picked up again, Thea left a brief message. "Mitch was here," she said. "I'm going to see the kids on Saturday. I'm on my way to a meeting now but I'll be back around two-thirty. You can call me at the office if you want. I could use some movies-suitable-for-kids ideas." She started to lower the receiver, then the streak of honesty that had been plaguing her of late compelled her to state the real reason she had called. She added softly, "A pep talk wouldn't be unwelcome."

Thea worked until almost eight. The meeting and Rosie's return call had put her behind in her work. She regretted neither but she also didn't want to haul projects home with her. The alternative was to stay late and greet the cleaning staff. The last month notwithstanding, they were used to seeing her, and she was vaguely discomfited by the realization. It registered with Thea quite suddenly that this was progress of sorts. Not so very long ago she wouldn't have been aware of that feeling at all, or known what to do about it if she had been.

On the way home she stopped at the supermarket and picked up a cartful of staples and essential favorites. She was so used to eating out that she experienced something akin to sticker shock when the clerk gave her the final total.

Later that night, however, when she was ladling homemade potato soup into a bowl, she knew a sense of satisfaction that was almost out of proportion to her accomplishment. It hardly mattered that she was eating dinner at ten-thirty or that there was a mess in the kitchen. The soup was creamy and warm and every last bit of it went down like a liquid hug.

Thea fell asleep on the couch, holding the empty bowl in her hands.

Mitch was not fully awake when the phone rang. He made a halfhearted attempt to reach it but let his hand slide from the nightstand and dangle over the edge of the bed. It rang two more times before it stopped and he grunted softly with approval, believing the caller had given up. A moment later he found out he was wrong.

"Uncle Mi-itch!"

It was Emilie. There was no mistaking that singsong emphasis in her voice as it floated up from the bottom of the stairs. He had ceased thinking of his name as a single syllable.

"The phone's for yoo-oooo."

He made another stab at reaching it and succeeded in knocking it off the stand. "Find out who it is." It was amazing, he thought, that he didn't have to raise his voice at all for Emilie to hear him, yet she remained firm in her opinion that shouting improved communication. For a while he enjoyed the relative silence while Emilie did as she was told.

He could hear the muted sounds of the TV in the living room—Case and Grant rose at the obscene hour of six, even on Saturdays—then Mitch recognized the Nickelodeon theme in the background and knew a sense of relief. Good boys, he thought sleepily. TV-G.

His eyes opened wide. Glancing at the clock he saw that more than fifteen minutes had passed since Emilie had called to him. He lurched out of bed and grabbed the phone off the floor, straining a muscle in the small of his back as he did so.

"Aaah, dammit!" His thumb pressed the Talk button at the same time he swore. Holding his back with one hand and the receiver with the other, he raised the phone. "Hello?"

No one spoke. Mitch thought Emilie must have turned the caller away before he realized he wasn't hearing a dial tone either. "Hello?" he repeated. "Emilie? Are you on the line?"

There was a soft click but still no dial tone.

Thea said, "I think you scared her off."

"Thea?"

"Uh-huh. It's me."

"Oh. Sorry."

"I'm not offended," she said. "But you'll probably have to apologize to Em."

Mitch rubbed his back and tentatively tried a lateral stretch. "Yeah. I'm getting to be a real pro at that. Who knew eleven-year-old girls were so sensitive?"

I did. Thea didn't offer any response to his rhetorical question. "What happened?" She listened as he told her about his lurch for the phone and try as she might, could not imagine him as graceless as his description. Mitch Baker didn't have a false move. "I didn't mean to wake you," she said.

"Not a problem. I needed to be up."

It occurred to her that he was standing in his bedroom,

disheveled and loose-limbed, and quite possibly naked. Immediately she put briefs on him, changed those to boxers, changed those to sweats, and finally covered him up in a long nightshirt with tails that flapped around his calves. She'd never actually seen one of those on a man, but there was an illustration in a childhood book that she remembered and liked. The man had worn a striped stocking cap as well. It didn't look good on Mitch.

"You still there?" asked Mitch.

"What? Oh, yes. I'm here." She removed that stocking cap quickly. "I was wondering if I should bring something for the kids when I come out this afternoon. What do you think?"

Mitch rubbed his chin, felt the stubble, and padded into the adjoining bathroom. He absently scratched his bare chest while he looked in the mirror. The face staring back at him was vaguely disreputable, and not in a sexy way. "I don't know, Thea. What were your thoughts?" He started running cold water and picked up his toothbrush.

Thea placed an orange half in the juicer and squeezed. Her mouth watered instantly. "I used to bring things with me when I came to visit. Nothing big, you understand. Puzzles. Games. Maybe a DVD they didn't already own. Kathy usually had suggestions when I asked. But this is different now. I don't know how to do it. It's a visit, but more than a visit. At least it seems that way. I don't know what they expect from me." *Hell,* she thought, *I don't know what I expect from myself.*

"You were talking to Emilie, weren't you?" Mitch managed to keep the phone in the crook of his neck and shoulder while he put toothpaste on his brush. Multitasking, he thought. It used to be walking and chewing gum was the benchmark for coordination. He was really pushing the envelope here. "Did you ask her?"

"Ask her what?"

Mitch jammed the brush in his mouth. "What she expected."

Thea frowned at the odd slur in his speech. "Mitch? Are you all right? What are you doing?"

"Brushin' ma tee."

"Oh." Thea wrung the juice out of another sweet orange. "You mean I can actually ask her that?"

"Sure." He got his crown molars, the back of his incisors, and his tongue. "Jus a min-ute." Mitch spit and rinsed his mouth. He spit again. "That's better."

Maybe for you, she thought. Thea felt like she was sharing a bathroom with him. If she heard the toilet next, it wouldn't be the only thing flushing. "What would I say?"

"I don't know." He considered it a moment, running his hand through his hair. "Just maybe ask her if there's anything she needs from you. She'll give you some concrete stuff at first, like neon pink fingernail polish and a tongue stud, but I'm pretty sure with a little prompting she'll get the idea of what you really mean."

Thea's voice was tentative. She paused in pouring her orange juice into a glass. "Umm, about the other two things. I should say no to those, right?"

Mitch smiled. "Neon pink's okay. I'm boycotting black even though she says it's a mourning color. Emilie can be very dark at times and she doesn't need nails to match. No on the tongue stud, though, otherwise I won't know what to get her for her sixteenth birthday." Silence. "I'm kidding about the birthday present."

"Oh, yes. Of course."

Mitch could only shake his head. Even Emilie had gotten the joke quicker. Maybe the phone wasn't a good medium for his half wit. "If you want to bring something with you, I don't really see the problem. Just make it something you can do with them."

"All right."

"And, Thea?"

"Hmmm?"

"Thanks for asking." He fumbled with the opening on his boxers. "I've got to go now." He hadn't meant it as a literal description of his current bodily needs, but the alacrity with which the phone went dead told him Thea had taken it that way. Heat crept into his cheeks as he set the phone on the sink top. "You're smooth, Mitch Baker. Real smooth."

Thea pulled up to Mitch's redbrick Colonial and parked on the street behind a bright yellow SUV. Feeling decidedly unhip for herself and her classic Volvo, Thea patted the dashboard lightly. "It's okay, baby. You're safe."

Inside the house the curtains in the living room fell back into place. Case flopped dramatically onto the sofa. "Aunt Thea's here!" With the gap in his front teeth, he was announcing the arrival of someone named Anthea. "And she's talkin' to her car!"

"Go open the garage door, Mega-mouth," Mitch told him. "Let her in." He gave Gina a nudge off the arm of the chair he was sitting in so he could get up. Emilie and Grant had already dropped the Wii game controls and were running after their brother.

Gina flicked her wrist and looked at her watch. "Well, she's on time. That's something."

Mitch shot her a glance. "Be nice." He hadn't missed the fact that Gina had been edgy since she showed up. He didn't even want to think what that was about. Taking her hand, Mitch gave a tug. With only minimal resistance, Gina let herself be pulled along. By the time they reached the garage, she was practically curled around his arm.

Thea dropped the box she was carrying as the twins and

Emilie launched themselves at her. To keep from getting bowled over, she fell to her knees in the driveway. Case and Grant were like frisky puppies while Emilie got an arm around her torso and held on.

"Goodness," Thea said. "What a welcome!" She managed to close in on all three and squeezed. Over the top of Emilie's dark head she saw Mitch walking out of the garage sporting a stunning young woman where his right arm used to be. She closed her eyes against that feline smile. "Ooooh! I've missed you guys." They loosened their grips enough so that she could get a good look at them. "Should I pinch cheeks?"

Grant gave her an impish smile and patted his behind.

"Grant Reasoner!" Thea exclaimed. "Don't tempt me." She made a play for his bottom but he scampered backward, almost falling on it in his eagerness to get out of reach. "That would have served you right." She looked at Case who was shifting his weight in anticipation that she would go after him. Loath to disappoint, Thea reached around Emilie, her fingers and thumb curled like pincers. Case laughed and danced away. "What happened to your tooth? Did your brother knock it out?"

Both boys thought that was funny. Emilie just shook her head at their laughter. "They're being stupid," she confided to Thea. "Uncle Mitch says it's what they do. Like it's their job or something."

Thea nodded solemnly. "I'm afraid he's right."

Emilie had already perfected the long-suffering sigh. She used it to great effect now.

Thea captured Emilie's rounded chin in her pincers and held on. Unlike the boys, Emilie didn't try to get away. She stared back through great, dark green eyes, the centers so wide at the moment that Thea could almost see herself mirrored there. Here was beauty ripening, Thea thought. Not that Emilie would necessarily know that yet. She probably couldn't see past the layer of baby fat that gave her features a marked lack of definition. But there were some very good bones under there and they would eventually shape her face with the perfect symmetry that the human eye found so pleasing. "Emilie Reasoner, I think you are an actor. But try not to chew the scenery." While Emilie was puzzling over what that meant, Thea got to her feet and brushed off her jeans. Raising her head, she greeted Mitch.

"Hi. They look wonderful. You're feeding and grooming them beautifully."

"Anthea!" Case darted around her. "We're not dogs!"

As if on cue, Grant growled and began chasing his brother. "Aunt Thea! Aunt Thea!" He was not calling for Thea but taunting Case for his gap-toothed mispronunciation.

Mitch nodded to Thea. "You found us. It occurred to me that you never asked for directions so I assumed you knew where I lived."

"Kathy showed me once." More like a dozen times, but Thea had no wish to share that.

No one but Thea was wearing a jacket so Mitch started motioning the children toward the garage entrance with his free hand. "Inside. Now. Go." Out of the corner of his eye he saw Thea trying to tamp her smile. "I've discovered that one-word commands are effective."

"Yes." She didn't point out that the twins were not only still chasing each other, but that Emilie had joined them. "Try barking them next time."

Mitch laughed, freeing himself from Gina. "Roundup time. Thea, this is Gina. Gina, Thea. If you go inside, I have a feeling they'll follow." He started after them. "Get along, little doggies!"

Thea smiled. Doggies. Dogies. Mitch thought he was

pretty funny. She walked up to Gina and held out her hand. "Thea Wyndham. It's very nice to meet you."

"Regina Sommers. Reggie, really. No one calls me Gina but Mitch. It's like a pet name."

Meow, Thea thought. Mitch's sex kitten had teeny-tiny claws.

Chapter 4

Thea picked up the game she bought that morning for the kids and followed Gina into the garage. Behind her she could hear one of the twins squealing because Mitch had scooped him up and was threatening to bounce him on his head. There wasn't a lot of room in the garage to pass through. Thea secured the board game under her arm so she wouldn't bump into paint cans or knock over the aluminum ladder. Mitch's Indian motorcycle and a restored 1953 cherry red Chevy truck took up most of the floor space. There were also four bicycles, a wagon, garbage cans, enough wood to build an addition, and a workbench with every imaginable tool cluttering the top and not one hanging from the white pegboard on the wall behind it.

Stepping into the breezeway, Thea automatically removed her shoes when she saw the small pyramid of footwear just inside the door.

"You don't have to do that," Gina said. "It's for the kids."

"I don't mind." Thea pushed her Nikes into the base of the pyramid. The size tens they rubbed against certainly didn't belong to the children, but she noticed Gina kept hers on. Thea searched her mind for an icebreaker and came up with "I was glad when Mitch said I could come out today."

"I'll take your jacket." Gina held out her hand. "There's room in the hall closet." She kept on going, expecting Thea to follow. "Yeah, we were both happy that you wanted to spend time with the kids. Mitch and I haven't had a moment to ourselves since . . . well, since his friends died." She opened the closet door and withdrew a wooden hanger. Gina recognized Thea's short-waisted gray leather jacket as Halston before she saw the label. It was exactly the sort of thing she wished she could wear and thought she didn't have enough leg to carry it off. That was not a problem Thea Wyndham knew anything about. She was leg from the neck down. Gina considered scratching her eyes out on mere principle. "I suppose I should say *your* friends. That's right, isn't it? The Reasoners were your friends also."

"Yes, that's right. Gabe and I were friends before we started school."

"College, you mean?"

"No. Kindergarten."

Gina closed the door and regarded Thea with interest. The hair was great, too: cropped short, but stylish; feather soft and deep red right down to the roots. Maybe it came out of a bottle but Gina wasn't hopeful. "I don't think I have any friends that go back that far."

And it wasn't even so very long ago, Thea thought. Exactly how many minutes had this girl been out of high school anyway? *Meow. Pffft.* She wondered what she'd done to put Gina's back up and consequently her own. Politely she said, "Gabe is the only friend I have like that." The tense brought her up short and she corrected herself softly. "Was. Had. It's going to take getting used to."

The change in Gina was immediate. Her dark eyes went liquid and her expression was not only sympathetic, but sincerely so. Reaching out, she touched Thea's arm at the elbow. "It must be strange for you. I mean, to have the funeral a little more than a month now in the past and you just finding out about it all on Monday. Not even a week's gone by for you."

"It *is* strange. I feel out of step with Mitchell and the children." Thea found it odd that she was making this admission to Mitch's fiancée. She hadn't explained it so clearly to Joel. "I suppose time will ease that."

"I'm certain it will."

Thea couldn't imagine what Regina Sommers knew about it, yet she didn't doubt the words were most heartfelt. To say that Mitch's fiancée was something of a surprise was putting it mildly. Her age had brought Thea up short immediately, until she remembered her nearly thirty-year difference with Joel. On a very subjective level, Thea made the observation that the ten or twelve years separating Gina from Mitch yawned more widely than the span between her and Joel.

Once she moved past Gina's age, it was easy to see what had attracted Mitch. Her dark chocolate eyes, olive skin, and pouty mouth lent her an exotic look, and if Thea hadn't failed to miss the taut and toned body that carried it off, she was certain Mitch hadn't either. Less obvious as a first impression was the way Regina Sommers radiated warmth. After she had marked her territory and determined that Thea didn't pose a threat to her, she fairly glowed. Through the fine wool threads of her sweater, Thea could still feel the heat of Gina's touch just below her elbow.

The noisy approach of Mitch and the children forced Thea into another line of thought. "What's the movie?" she asked when they all skidded to a halt in their stocking feet.

Emilie answered, "We want to see *The Boy Who Played with Food*."

"Is that okay with you?" Mitch asked Thea.

"Sure. Sounds fun."

Mitch nodded. "Come on into the kitchen and I'll show you where everything is."

Not willing to admit to any bewilderment, Thea gamely followed the troops into Mitch's large kitchen. Gina stayed behind and Thea heard the hall closet door opening and closing again. Something niggled at the back of her brain, a stray thought she could not grasp, but knew was important for her to remember. "What time is the movie?"

"There's one showing at five-thirty and another at seven-fifteen. Either one's okay depending on when everyone wants to eat." He pointed to the phone on the wall above the microwave. A bulletin board tacked full of notes in a rainbow of colors hung beside it. Mitch showed her the Things I Have To Do list that had been composed using a neon pink gel pen. Thea judged by the handwriting that Emilie had been given the task of compiling the data. "These are all the phone numbers you might need: Mum's, 911, my cell phone, Gina's cell phone, the restaurant where we'll be in case there's no signal, my sister's, and three places that deliver, in the event you decide to eat here."

Thea blinked. The numbers swam on the paper as her stomach began to agitate the remains of her last meal. Emilie was leaning into her and Thea's arm slipped around the little girl's shoulders. It was a toss-up as to who was supporting whom at the moment. She stared at Mitch, her mouth completely dry. "You're not going with us?"

"Well, no. I didn't realize—"

Thea was mortified. His surprise was completely genuine. He had had no idea that she wasn't expecting to take the children on her own. Pride and fear warred and while pride won out, it was a narrow thing. She forced a smile, a dim twenty-five watts compared to the sunbeam that Gina flashed as she walked into the kitchen.

"You ready, Mitch?" Gina held up his jacket. "We should be going."

"Just a minute." Frowning slightly, he regarded Thea's pale face. "Are you all right?"

"I'm fine." As long as Emilie didn't squirm out from under her, she'd be okay. At least she wouldn't fall, she amended. There was no chance that she was going to be okay. "Really, it's nothing."

Mitch was still watching her through narrowed eyes. "I thought you would want to be with the kids by yourself."

"Oh, yes," she said quickly, too quickly.

Emilie sighed. "I told you we make her nervous, Uncle Mitch. You didn't believe me."

One of Mitch's brows kicked up. "You didn't tell *me* that."

"Maybe I told Nonny."

Mitch's watchful eyes returned to Thea. She didn't look nervous; she looked frightened. "Look, if it's a problem, Gina and I can—"

Gina came around the tight gathering and thrust Mitch's jacket at him. "No, Gina and I *can't*. You promised me, Mitch. We're going out *alone*."

"Of course you are," Thea said. "I'll manage. I don't know why Emilie thinks I'm nervous around her and the boys."

"Mom said you were," Emilie said simply. "That's why she said you never took us anywhere by ourselves."

As a child Thea had imagined living life on a stage where trapdoors could be made to open and swallow her whole whenever she made a misstep. She wished she was standing on one now. "That's not why," Thea objected. Too late, she realized her second misstep. This was worse than the first, because now she had called Kathy's veracity into question. She felt Emilie pulling away and knew an immediate sense of loss and something more devastating, like betrayal.

Emilie's hands went to her hips and her chin came up. "That's what Mom told me. She wouldn't lie."

"Emilie." Mitch's voice was firm. "I don't think that Thea meant your mother wasn't telling the truth, but just that she didn't really understand Thea's reasons."

Chin wobbling ever so slightly, Emilie looked from her uncle Mitch to Thea. Her green eyes were soulful, wanting to be convinced. "Is he right?"

Thea realized that even the twins had fallen quiet. Their chatter was no longer part of the background noise. "Yes," she said softly. "He's right."

"Then why didn't you take us anywhere alone?" Emilie challenged. "Uncle Mitch did. Sometimes he took just me to the movies or shopping."

"Or us," Case said.

"Yeah. Swimming," Grant added. "And go-carts."

Mitch held up his hand. "Guys. Enough. I think Thea gets the idea." He reached out to Emilie and gave her hair an affectionate tug. "I live right here, Em. Thea doesn't. I saw your parents and you all the time so I could pick and choose our outings. When Thea came to visit she wanted to see everyone. She would have always felt like she was leaving someone out if she had taken you without your mom or dad along."

Under Emilie's skeptical scrutiny, Thea nodded slowly. She didn't dare glance in Mitch's direction, afraid the gratefulness she felt would be too easily seen and correctly interpreted by all three of the children.

"Oh." Emilie's chin lost its wobble and her mien became frighteningly adult. "You should have told Mom that, Aunt Thea. She worried about you."

Thea knew that was true. What she said was, "I wish I had." When she was certain her expression could remain unrevealing, Thea turned back to Mitch. "I hope you and Regina have a very nice time this evening. Don't give us another thought. Right, guys?"

"Right," the twins said simultaneously. Emilie responded a beat later with the same affirmative.

"See? We'll be fine. I know where the Cineplex is. I

know who wants their popcorn swimming in butter. It's under control." She could see that Mitch wanted to be convinced. "I have enough seat belts for everyone. I drive a Volvo. There's a first-aid kit in the glove compartment. I carry a cell phone in my purse. I know how to do the Heimlich maneuver and I can change a tire." Actually she would call Triple A for the last, but he didn't need to know that. "I have my credit card in the event they all want surf and turf for dinner."

"Surf and turf?" Grant whispered to his brother.

Mitch answered the aside. "She means lobster and steak," he said. "A very expensive meal."

"Lobster!" Grant made a face while Case held his stomach. A second later they were pinching each other. When Mitch pointed to the living room they escaped there on a run to continue playing.

"I don't think you have to worry they'll take you over your credit limit at dinner," Mitch said dryly. "Something more than pizza, though."

"But not Quaker Steak and Lube," Gina interjected. "That's where we're going."

That niggling thought came back to Thea, and she captured it this time, finding complete clarity: *Mitch and I haven't had a moment together since . . .* Who was Gina kidding? Thea wondered. She wasn't going to let Mitch out of bed. "We'll be certain to pass on that," Thea said, straight-faced.

"They have great wings," Mitch said.

Thea found her lips were twitching. He seemed genuinely clueless about what Gina had in store for him. "Enjoy."

Mitch folded his jacket over his arm instead of putting it on. "Since it's Saturday, bedtime is ten o'clock for Emilie. Case and Grant will drop like stones before then. Don't worry about baths."

Thea hadn't even *thought* about baths. "If you're sure," she said gamely.

"Oh, I'm sure," said Mitch. There was a subtle warning in his tone not to press her luck. Gina had slipped her arm through his and was nudging him to leave. "I think that's everything." He used his thumb to point to the bulletin board. "My mom is good for just about every emergency that doesn't require hoses and ladders."

"Right," Thea said. "I've got it. First number on the list. Three exclamation points."

"That was my idea," Emilie said. "Uncle Mitch just asked me to underline it."

"Nicely done. It stands out."

"It's also number one on the speed dial," Emilie said.

"Well, then, I'd say we have a very large safety net. Go get your brothers. We'll hang out at the strip mall before the movie if we're too early." She waited until Emilie took off. "It'll be fine, Mitch. You and Regina should go."

Mitch reached in the pocket of his jacket and pulled out a ring of keys. He removed one and gave it to her. "For the front door. You won't be able to get back in through the garage and I don't have a key for the breezeway anymore."

Thea dropped it in her jeans pocket. "We're set." If he didn't move soon Gina was going to pop his shoulder out of joint. "Are you taking the bike or the truck?"

"Too cold for the bike. And Gina doesn't like the truck. We're taking the banana car."

Gina gave him a quick jab in the stomach with her fist. "Stop calling it that."

"The SUV I parked behind?" asked Thea. "That's yours?" She nodded. "I love it."

It was the cue Mitch needed to get him moving. Before he got into an argument over the merits of manual versus automatic transmissions, he headed toward the garage. Emilie was getting coats for the boys and no matter what Thea's parenting skills were, Em would mother them. He felt better, though he wasn't sure he should.

Everyone ended up on the sidewalk at the same time. Thea shrugged into her jacket while she opened the doors. "Everyone in the back," she told them. "I have a passenger side airbag. No kids." That should impress Mitch, she thought. She didn't have to tell him that her knowledge came from an aggressive ad campaign she headed up for Honda and the National Transportation Safety Board. The agency even won a Clio for it. "I'll be your chauffeur. This is the one time you can tell me where to go." The kids giggled and climbed in. There was some arguing about window and middle seats but Thea was patient, didn't get involved, and let them work it out. That was something she had seen Kathy and Gabe do. It seemed to work for them; at least they didn't end up being angrier than the kids. "Buckle up." She leaned in, helped Case with his strap, then walked around to the driver's side. "You're not going to follow us, are you?" she asked Mitch.

"I'm driving," Gina said. "Otherwise you'd have a tail."

Mitch shrugged, unapologetic. "I can't help it. This is the first time they've been out of my sight with anyone but my family or the school." He leaned down, waved through the window. They made faces back. "Okay," he said, straightening. "You're good to go." He tapped the hood with the flat of his hand. "You have enough gas?"

"Mitch!" Gina and Thea both responded with exasperation.

"Take him," Thea ordered Gina.

"I'm taking him," Gina said at the same time.

Thea slipped behind the wheel and automatically locked all the doors, a safeguard against Mitch trying to get in. She pressed the ignition button and the engine caught. "All set?" she asked her crew.

"Set!"

Thea backed up a few feet to clear the Xterra when she pulled out into the street. "Everybody wave to your uncle Mitch. Case, see if you can't make that monster face again. He seemed to really like that." They started down the block. "And don't think you're all going to slouch down back there so you can't be seen by other drivers." Of course that's exactly what they did most of the way to the Cineplex, thus making sure it looked like Thea was talking on the phone or having an animated conversation with herself.

Gina waited until the Volvo was out of sight before she started the car. "Where to?" she asked. "The Hampton or the Fairfield? Or maybe you want to just go back in the house?" Her hand slid off the gearshift and onto Mitch's thigh. She ran her fingertips right up the inside to his groin and cupped him through his jeans. His response was immediate and not the one she expected.

"Gina!" He moved her hand back to the shift.

"What?"

He knew he'd hurt her feelings. God, he thought, all he seemed to do lately was apologize to women. "Sorry," he said. "I need a little time."

Gina said nothing. She put the SUV into drive and pulled out, keeping her eyes straight ahead. Beside her, she was aware that Mitch was equally focused on the road. She doubted he was seeing anything related to the traffic. "Maybe we could stop at the bookstore first. Pick up an early edition of the Sunday paper or something. Get a cup of coffee." She glanced over in time to see him shrug. "What the hell is wrong with you?"

"I don't *know*." The words came out like a growl, equal

parts frustration and annoyance. Neither of those emotions were directed at Gina. Mitch meant them for himself. He sat up suddenly. "This isn't going to work, Gina."

Panicked, her knuckles bleached of color as she gripped the steering wheel. She stared at him as long as she could and still keep the SUV from crossing into the passing lane. Finally she got the nerve to ask, "What isn't going to work?"

"Tonight. Going out. I'm not going to be good company."

Gina's relief that he was not breaking up with her was so immense that she put aside how much she had been looking forward to these hours alone. "Then we won't do anything right now. What if I just drive for a while?"

It wasn't a bad idea, but Mitch also knew that Gina's idea of driving aimlessly had a lot in common with house hunting and property searches. "That's fine," he said. "Lead on."

Over the next hour and a half they covered enough of three townships to get a flavor of the communities. Mitch concluded there wasn't much in the way of pasture left in this corner of the county. Houses were sown here instead, rising out of furrows in the hillsides, or where woods were cleared to make the land barren and suitable for nothing but topiary inspired by Dr. Seuss. The sameness of the homes was depressing. There were no two alike and yet they were difficult to tell apart. Redbrick. Pink brick. Yellow brick. Two stories, five bedrooms, four baths. Windows the size of garage doors. White shutters. Black shutters. A deck a helicopter could land on. What grass was left on the quarter-acre lots after the driveway was poured was fenced in like a stockade. No one seemed to find any contradiction in cathedral-like windows that invited public viewing and privacy fences that fairly screamed no peeking. It seemed to Mitch that all the good stuff must be going on in the backyard.

Gina loved all of it. She made Mitch take out her phone and make notes about locations and lot numbers. He did it because it helped him keep his mind off Thea and the kids.

It was easier to take info on mortgage hell than it was to remember he had already passed up one chance at athletic sex
with Gina—and that happened because he'd been thinking
he should be at a cartoon movie for kids, about kids, with
kids. He *was* a dicksmack.

It was dark when Mitch tossed the phone down. "Let's go
get something to eat," he said.

Gina nodded and shot him an encouraging smile.
"Quaker Steak still okay?"

"I was thinking of somewhere with room service."

Thea unlocked the front door and pushed it open. The
twins barreled inside. Emilie followed more sedately.
"Shoes!" Thea called after them. She kicked her own off as
soon as she stepped on the carpet. "Come on, guys. A little
cooperation." Emilie's thick-soled shoes thumped to the floor
then she went off to corral her brothers. Thea had to admit
the twins had been very good at the movie and the restaurant,
even subdued. They had come alive on the ride home,
making up for every quiet moment that had come before.
"Just add water," she said under her breath. "Insta-boy." She
hung up her jacket and then put out an arm to take the children's coats.

"Anthea?"

"Yes, Case?" She turned away from the closet and took
the foot he held out and untied the laces.

"You're talking to yourself."

"Was I?" She dropped the sneaker on the carpet. Case
braced himself against the wall and offered her a second
go at the other foot. "I live alone. Who else am I going to
talk to?"

"Mom used to talk to herself and she didn't live alone."

Grant stumbled in, pushed by his sister, and caught the

gist of the conversation. He backed up to the wall like his twin. "She said we made her crazy."

"I don't believe it," Thea scoffed. She wrestled Case's shoe off him and started on Grant's. "Your dad made her crazy. The three of you were her absolute joy." Impulsively she hugged Grant to her. He suffered it while his brother laughed. In the face of his stoicism, Thea found herself blinking back unexpected tears and unable to trust her voice. She knelt down quickly, bending her head to get Grant's right shoe. The knot was tight and her blurred vision didn't help. She felt a small hand come to rest lightly on the crown of her head. She wasn't sure who it belonged to until she heard her name.

"It's all right, Anthea. We miss her, too."

"And our dad," Grant added in a perfectly natural tone.

For a moment Thea simply couldn't breathe. She fought with the shoelace, making the knot tighter instead of unraveling it. "Damn," she swore softly. "Damn. Damn. Damn."

"Aunt Thea," Emilie said, "you're swearing. You'll have to put money in the jar."

"I'll get it," Grant offered. He wriggled free of Thea by somehow wiggling out of that knotted shoe and ran to the kitchen.

Thea held up the sneaker and stared at it, realizing her vision had cleared. That fast a minor crisis had been averted; she had not wanted to cry in front of the kids and have them comfort her. "Hey, Houdini, how about the other one?"

"Who is Dini?" Case asked. His hand had dropped from Thea's hair to her shoulder.

"Houdini," she said. "Harry Houdini. He was a great magician and escape artist. He'd have himself handcuffed and tied up and then he'd escape out of tanks filled with water and chained boxes. Stuff like that."

"Like David Blaine," Emilie said helpfully. "Remember,

Case? We saw that video where he was buried in a box, like, for a week or something."

Case's memory was jogged. His eyes grew round. "Yeah! That was cool." Within the space of a heartbeat his expression changed and became contemplative. "Do you think Mom and Dad could do that? They saw the video."

Emilie's response was scornful. "They're dead, stupid."

A siren went off in Thea's head. Red alert! Incoming! Phasers on stun! Emilie clamped a hand over her mouth, hiding half of her stricken face. Thea dropped the sneaker, holding out one hand to Emilie and blocking Case's attempt to headbutt his sister. Emilie was just outside her reach, and she backed up rather than come closer as Thea held on to Case. Before Thea could move, Emilie spun around and was running full tilt toward some predetermined refuge. Grant came around the corner, jangling change in the cussing jar, and was almost upended by Emilie's charge to the stairway.

"What's wrong with Em?" he asked. His eyes fell on Case squirming in Thea's arms. "You guys wrestling?"

"Not exactly," Thea gritted as she restrained Case's flailing arms. "Case, come on. You know Emily's sorry. She ran away because she feels so bad."

"She called me stupid!" He twisted his head around and caught Thea on the chin. Had her jaw not already been clenched, it would have hurt more. "Ow!" Tears sprang to his eyes, more from frustration than pain. "I'm *not* stupid! I know they're dead! Everybody knows that! But maybe they *could* get out of the boxes."

Thea held him close as his body went limp. A second later he was crying softly against her sweater. Over the top of his head she could see Grant was perilously close to tears himself, ready to dissolve because his brother was hurting. She motioned him to come closer and cuddled him when he dropped to the floor beside her. "They did get out," she said quietly, rocking Case, sheltering Grant. "That's what God promises. You learned that in Sunday school, didn't you?"

"B-but they're n-not here now."

Thea took a steadying breath. "Not that you can see them, no. But when I look at you and your brother, I see so many things that remind me of your mom and daddy that it doesn't seem they're so very far away. I like to think they're still watching you and that they always will be."

Case sniffed loudly. "Then they know Emilie called me stupid."

Thea realized she was a becoming a big fan of concrete thinking. The abstract, existential processes were years away and maybe she could leave it to Mitch to debate the finer philosophical points when Case reached that stage. "Yes, they know Emilie called you stupid. Does that make you feel better?" She wasn't surprised when he nodded. "They're not angry at her, though. They know she only said it because her heart is hurting, too."

"Yeah?"

"Yeah."

Case remained where he was while Grant scooted away, leaving the cussing jar behind.

"Where are you going, Grant?" asked Thea.

"To get Em somethin' for her heart."

Thea didn't even try to stop him. She asked Case, "How much do I owe the jar?"

"Uncle Mitch puts in a quarter every time he swears."

Glancing at the jar, which was only about about a fifth full, Thea thought he wasn't doing too badly. She slipped her bag off her shoulder, found her change purse and gave it to Case along with a tissue. "You put in what you think is fair. I'm going to check on Emilie."

Grant was standing outside his sister's room holding a tin of plastic bandages decorated with superheroes. "Great idea," she said. "I'll take them in and tell her they're from you. Go on downstairs. You and Case can set up the game I brought."

Grant didn't require more prompting. He thrust the tin at Thea and started off. "She locked her door," he called back.

"I can handle it," she assured him. "Go on."

Thea rapped lightly. "Em? It's Thea. Can I come in?" *Please, Emilie. I'd rather not use a bobby pin and I'll be damned if I'm calling one number on Mitch's list.* With one ear, Thea listened for sounds that Emilie was going to cooperate, with the other she tried to hear what the boys were up to. The cussing jar was still jangling so they hadn't moved on to the game yet. She rapped on the door again. "Please, Emilie."

The knob turned and the door opened a crack. Thea pushed it wide enough to put her head through. When she saw Emilie was already retreating toward the bed, she stepped inside.

Emilie flopped on the bed on her stomach, face hidden in the crook of her arm. "Shut the door."

"I can't," Thea said. "At least not completely. I have to listen for the boys." She carefully closed the door so that only a two-inch opening remained. "May I sit on your bed?"

"I don't care."

In the vernacular of an eleven-year-old, Thea remembered "I don't care" was practically an engraved invitation. She walked around the canopy bed to where there was some space on the other side of the double mattress. Sitting down, she looked around the room. It was not so different from the room Emilie had when she was living with her parents. Thea realized Mitch must have brought a lot of the kids' personal things, including furniture, to his house. She wondered if she would have thought of doing something like that. Thea's fingertips smoothed the quilted coverlet. "You still like pink, I see."

Emilie didn't turn her head. "It's okay."

It was everywhere, is what it was. The canopy and spread, the pillow shams, the throw for the chair, the wastepaper basket—even the stapler on Emilie's desk—were all pink. "It's your signature color," said Thea.

Emilie's head lifted fractionally but she still didn't turn. This time, though, her words weren't muffled by an arm over her mouth. "What's that?"

"It's a little like a personal trademark. Something people will associate just with you. McDonald's has the golden arches. Target is all about red. You've embraced a color. Which also happens to look great on you, by the way." Thea paused. She reached tentatively for one of Emilie's half-hidden hands. Lightly stroking the part that was visible, she said, "Maybe later, when the boys go to bed you'll let me do your nails. I picked up a bottle of this pink polish that practically glows in the dark. It doesn't work with my hair, but I bet it would be a good color for you."

Emilie shifted her body so she was lying on her side facing Thea. Her look was faintly accusing. "You're bribing me."

Thea considered that. "Have I asked you do something in exchange?"

"Not yet."

"Oh my, Em. You are wise to the ways of the world." Thea's hand touched Emilie's hair, smoothing the heavy lock that came just under her chin. "I suppose it is a little bit like a bribe. Here's another one." She raised the tin of bandages. "Grant was bringing these up to you. I told him your heart was hurting. He thought one or all these would help."

When Emilie closed her eyes this time tears were squeezed out of the corners. She immediately buried her face again. "Boys are so stupid."

Thea's voice was gentle. "Sometimes they are. Just like girls can be stupid. But I thought this was sweet. He's only five, Emilie, but he knows he doesn't want his sister hurting." She rubbed Emilie's back. "You and I know it doesn't change anything, but Grant's offer is genuine. Won't you take one?" Thea opened the tin and began looking through it. "Here's Wonder Woman. Do you want that one?"

Emilie shrugged.

"You know who she is, don't you?" There was a small negative shake this time. Thea's response was something between a choked laugh and a sigh as she realized the truth. "These are Mitch's." At Emilie's nod, Thea simply shook her head. "Boys *are* stupid."

Giggling, Emilie turned on her back, her smile a trifle watery. She took the bandage that Thea was dangling over her head and peeled back the paper.

Thea reached for the pink tissue box on Emilie's nightstand. "You're going to wear it?"

"Right here." She pointed to her forearm which was covered by the long sleeve of her pink tee. "Isn't that right? Don't some people wear their heart on their sleeve?"

Thea used the first tissue out of the box for her own damp eyes.

"What time is it?" Case asked for the third time in three minutes.

"Nine-seventeen," said Emilie. She picked up a card, read it, and moved one of her men into the red safety zone. "Your turn, Grant."

Grant didn't pick up a card. Instead he looked at Thea across the table. "Why isn't Uncle Mitch here?"

"I suppose because he's with Ms. Sommers," Thea said. She'd already made the error several times of calling Gina by her first name. The kids had been quick to correct her. "They're on a date. You know what that is, don't you?"

"Sure," Case said. He put the back of his hand to his mouth and began kissing it in earnest.

Thea laughed. "All right. That's enough. So you know

something about it, big shot. Grant, take your turn. Emilie, did your uncle Mitch tell us what time he was coming back?"

Emilie shook her head. She helped Grant move his token since it was closer to her side of the board. "I think it's going to be late."

That was Thea's take on it, too. Mitch had told her the kids' bedtimes for a reason, that reason being that he expected to return sometime after they were asleep. Grant and Case, contrary to his prediction that they would drop like stones, were battling hard to stay awake. Thea wasn't fooling herself that it was because they were enjoying her company or the game. They were worried about Mitch, wondering where he was and if he was all right. Emilie, too, was becoming a little agitated, glancing frequently toward the door, shifting in her chair, suddenly alert when a car drove up the street. The car accident that had killed Gabe and Kathy had happened in the evening. Thea had no doubt they were thinking about that now, whether they said it or not. She certainly was.

"Maybe we should just put the game away for now," Thea suggested. This was met with a chorus of no's and against her better judgment, she relented. Therefore, she had no one but herself to blame when the game deteriorated into a fractious, no-win, name-calling match in which every token and most of the cards ended up on the floor.

Thea stared at the mess, then at the children. They were all subdued now that there was nothing left to shove and throw. "Well," she said finally, "I don't even know what to think about that. What happens now?" There were some accusing glances exchanged but they remained silent. "Then I suppose I'll have to come up with something on my own. Do you want me to do that?"

"We should go to bed," Emilie said quickly.

"Oh, yes," Thea said. "Definitely. Before or after you and

your brothers pick up everything?" There were some mixed opinions voiced so Thea announced they would have to do it after the pickup. "I'll help, but I won't do it all."

It took the chain gang five long minutes to collect everything and put it back in the box. When they dawdled, she stopped helping. Thea pointed to the stairs, and they shuffled off while she folded the game board and placed it inside the box. "I'll be up in a minute," she called after them. "I have to make a phone call." She saw them all stop in their tracks. "What is it?" she asked.

Emilie was the trio's spokesperson. "Are you calling Uncle Mitch?"

"No. Do you want me to?" Judging by their expressions, the twins were in favor of it, while Emilie was firmly against it. The problem for Case and Grant was that they had already abdicated their right to have an opinion as far as their older sister was concerned. She hustled them out of sight. Thea wouldn't have been surprised if she bound and gagged them when they got to their room.

The phone call to Joel was brief. He was mildly irritated that she hadn't called earlier in the evening and had expected her to be on her way home by now. Thea assured him that she wasn't spending the night and would be leaving as soon as Mitch arrived. She turned down an invitation for Sunday brunch, saying she simply wanted to spend the day in her bathrobe with the crossword puzzle and green tea. As gently as she was able, she rebuffed his hints that he wanted to come out to her house. He did not take it well, and their good-bye was awkward and strained as a result.

Thea turned off her phone and put it back in her purse, vaguely unsettled by the tone of the call. Had Joel always been possessive? she wondered. Was that even what it was? She'd never noticed before, but then she had never had anything that diverted her attention from him. Nothing except work, she amended, and Joel certainly understood about work.

All was quiet when Thea reached the upstairs hallway. She shook off the residual discomfort from her conversation with Joel and checked on the children. The boys weren't in their room so she went to Emilie's. She found them huddled under the covers with their sister, engaged in some kind of foot wrestling contest that made the pink quilts bounce and jerk like the alien in John Hurt's chest. Thea made a face at the unpleasant image she'd created. "You're all going to sleep in here?"

"Can we?" Grant asked. "Emilie doesn't want—"

"It's not me," Emilie said. "Case is a ba—"

"Am not," Case interrupted. "Grant's the ba—"

The timing of the phone call was impeccable. Thea looked around Emilie's room for an extension.

"I'm not allowed to have a phone yet," she told Thea, pointing down the hall. "There's one in Uncle Mitch's room."

Thea found the master bedroom at the end of the hall. She flipped the light switch, saw the phone on the nightstand, and picked it up on the same ring that the answering machine kicked in. "Just a moment. I'm here. I can't—"

"It's Joel, Thea. Listen, I don't like the way we left—" He broke off when he heard a click on the line. "What was that?"

Thea sat on the edge of Mitch's unmade bed. She was unexpectedly brought up short by fragrance of him that lingered on the sheets. "The answering machine stopped recording. What is it, Joel?" Her voice was shorter than she meant it to be and she knew he couldn't have missed it. Thea felt her stomach churn. "I'm sorry. I'm trying to get the kids to bed. Can I call you back?" Out of the corner of her eye she saw something move in the hallway. Training her gaze on the door, it was only another moment before she caught sight of three heads bobbing around the doorjamb. She could not find it in herself to be annoyed with them. No doubt they were hoping it was Mitch on the line, and damn him, she thought, for *not* being the one she was talking to.

Waving the kids in, she spoke softly into the receiver. "It's all right. They're here now."

"Mitch and his fiancée?"

"No, the children." She covered the bottom of the phone with her hand. "It's my friend Joel," she told them. "Not your uncle." Their disappointment was tangible. Case was already climbing up beside her and he stopped, half on and off the bed. She grabbed him by the seat of his NASCAR pajamas and pulled. "Come on. All of you. It's okay. We'll have a slumber party here." Thea bounced, almost losing her grip on the phone as Grant and Emilie threw themselves onto the king-sized mattress. She reached behind her and gave somebody's bottom an affectionate whack. "I'm back, Joel. What do you need?"

"You." Greeted by her silence, he added, "It's not an unreasonable request."

Thea realized she had set him up for that response. "You have me."

"You know damn well what I mean. I haven't had you since you've been back. And I didn't have you for a month before that. Don't pretend that I'm only talking about sex, because you know I'm not. I was prepared for you to be away, but now that you're back, you're still away. I don't like it."

"I'm sorry you don't like it." *Was he pouting? He was sixty-one years old. Wasn't there some cut-off for pouting?* Thea stood and walked to the light switch. The children had more or less nestled into one big mound at the center of Mitch's bed. She indicated she was going to turn off the light and they nodded that they were ready. "But I'm fairly certain this isn't a good time to talk about it. I don't think I should tie up Mitch's phone. He might be trying to get through. What made you call this number anyway? I have my phone with me."

"You turned it off. You're the only person I know who turns it *off*."

"It's a coping strategy that was suggested to me. Reduce stress. Anyway, the battery's low." It sounded lame to her own ears. There was a long pause at the other end of the line and Thea could hear the faint chords of a piano concerto playing in the background. Joel was listening to Chopin. Thea returned to the bed and sat down. She drew her feet up beside her and pulled one free corner of the comforter over the lower part of her legs. "It's nice," she said softly. "What you're listening to."

"Chopin."

"Mmm. *Polonaise.* I recognized it. Do you have a fire?"

"A small one now. I'm letting it burn down."

"Did you warm a brandy?"

"I'm holding it."

She sighed. "It sounds lovely."

Another pause, then, "I miss you, Thea."

"I'll call you tomorrow, Joel. We'll make plans." Her eyes slid to the engagement ring on her left hand. She wiggled her fingers. There was just enough light from the hallway to make the diamond clearly visible. It was a beautiful stone in an elegant, sophisticated Tiffany setting, but not something she would have chosen if Joel had allowed her to be part of the purchase. She felt churlish having these thoughts. It had been important to him to surprise her, and she wanted to appreciate his effort even though surprises unsettled her. They'd flown to New York in his Cessna, Joel at the controls. After landing: dinner at Craft in the Flatiron District, a play, and a proposal at breakfast in their room at the Waldorf. He had thought this surprise would be different, and Thea didn't have it in her to tell him he had been wrong. She'd gone on emotional autopilot the moment he told her he had something special planned. "I promise we'll get together early in the week."

"I'm flying to New York Tuesday afternoon."

Had he mentioned that before? she wondered. Thinking of the work she had left at the office so her weekend would be clear, Thea did not want to be pressed into doing something with him on Monday. "When you get back, then." Joel's silence told her exactly what he thought of that. "Please, Joel. Please, don't press me right now."

"Thea . . ."

"Please, Joel."

There was a long exhale. "Call me tomorrow when you get home."

"Of course." Thea realized she wanted to get off the phone before their conversation ended with a rote exchange of I love you. "Good night, Joel." Her thumb poised, she clicked off and replaced the phone on the nightstand. She sat quietly for more than a minute, not so much thinking as calming herself. By slow degrees she became aware of some oddly rhythmic breathing behind her, punctuated by little whistles, sighs, and exaggerated snoring sounds. "All right, you guys, you asked for it!" She raised the comforter, slid beneath it, and attacked three giggling, wriggling bodies with tickle fingers.

Mitch stood in the driveway and waved Gina off. He watched the SUV to the end of the block before he pressed the garage door opener he was carrying with him. The light came on inside the garage and Mitch tossed the opener on the front seat of his truck before he entered the house. Except for the eerie blue glow of a few night-lights, the house was dark. He expected to find Thea in the living room, perhaps crashed on the couch, but it was empty. Out of habit, he checked the front door and found it unlocked. He nearly tripped on the pile of shoes half blocking the entrance, and as he was catching his balance his foot hit something that overturned, bounced, and rolled. For a moment he thought he'd broken whatever it was, then he recognized the sound of change spilling onto the floor. The cussing jar. Remembering Thea's almost compulsively neat office, as well as her disapproval of his frank language, Mitch had to grin. Apparently she'd had a revision of standards.

Mitch went to the kitchen, checked the patio doors, and put the ball of his foot on something hard and round that had him hopping on one foot until he could get at it. Once he had it in hand he recognized the plastic game token for what it was. He set it on the table on top of the game box and for a moment he didn't move, afraid of what other booby traps they'd set for him. He had also made plenty of noise to get Thea's attention, but he'd yet to hear anyone stirring upstairs.

The blinking light on the answering machine caught his attention. Mitch shuffled toward it and hit the button. He recognized Thea's voice: *Just a moment. I'm here. I can't—* Then a man's clear baritone, *It's Joel, Thea. Listen, I don't like the way we left—* Mitch let the machine reset and considered what he'd just heard, or more correctly, overheard. Joel Strahern. So Thea's fiancé had called, and not much more than an hour ago if the machine's time was accurate. The truncated message was too cryptic to analyze. To keep himself from speculating, Mitch shrugged out of his jacket, tossed it over a kitchen chair, and went in search of Thea and the kids. No doubt she'd stretched out with one or two of them and had fallen asleep herself. He knew firsthand how simply that could happen.

Mitch peeked in Emilie's room first and found it empty. The twins' bunks were also vacant. There was only one place left they could be since the guest bedroom was now a giant storage closet. Mitch padded down the hallway and soundlessly entered his own bedroom.

He could have set off an M-80 and not shaken the quartet sleeping in his bed. The children had rooted around Thea like a litter of kittens looking for sustenance. The down comforter and sheet were more off than on, but the combined heat of their huddled bodies kept them from missing the twisted covers.

He stood beside the bed, taking in the scene, and found

himself oddly moved by it. One of Thea's arms was curved around Case's small shoulders. Grant was pressed to her back. Emilie was on the other side of Case, her chin just above his head so her face was very near Thea's. *Serene* was the only word that came to Mitch's mind to describe them, and he knew a certain sense of loss that he had no right to join them. Plus, Case's face was burrowed just about where Mitch wished his own was.

He was such a guy, he thought. Dragging his eyes away from Thea's breasts, they fell on her face. He could make out her fair profile against his navy blue sheets. Feathery threads of her deeply red hair lay lightly against her forehead and cheek. Her lips were slightly parted, her breathing sound-less. The darker shadow of her lashes was like a smudge he should have been able to wipe away with the pad of his thumb. Mitch thrust his hands into his pockets.

Having spent just long enough at his bedside to feel like a voyeur, Mitch retreated to the hallway and shut the door gently. The kids would be fine there even if Thea woke and left them.

Mitch would have preferred to sleep in the twins' room—it at least had some traditional manly stuff like race cars and plush carnivorous dinosaurs in it—but the bunks also had foot and headboards that made it difficult for Mitch to stretch out all seventy-four inches of his frame. That left Emilie's Pepto-pink room or the living room couch. Comfort was the deciding factor. He opted for Em's ruffled canopy bed and hoped he did not have man boobs by morning, even though it would serve him right.

Thea woke disoriented. Sunshine slanted across the room and a beam fell on the back of her hand as she raised it to her face. She blinked and resisted rubbing her eyes, brushing back the hair on her forehead instead. Reaching to the left side of the bed, she searched for the bottle of wetting solution she kept there. With her contacts her vision was always blurry first thing in the morning. She groped, couldn't find it, and allowed a wide, lazy yawn to erase her puzzled expression. And then it came to her. She bolted upright, clutching at the covers and then patting them down for evidence of smaller bodies. She was alone.

Alone in the middle of Mitchell Baker's king-sized bed with no children in sight.

From downstairs she heard voices that were muffled by the closed bedroom door. Outside a car door slammed. Swearing softly, she swiveled her head and squinted at the bedside alarm. Her voice was something between a whisper and a groan. "That can't be right." But she knew it probably was. Nine o'clock. She couldn't remember ever sleeping so long or so late and feeling rested at the end of it. Now, she jumped out of bed and hurried to the window and found it a remarkably easy thing to do.

Looking out the double-hung window on the driveway below, Thea saw a maroon sedan blocking the entrance. The twins' christening had been the last time she had seen the woman standing beside the car, but Thea recognized her as Mitchell's mother. There was no mistaking the energetic hand waving and animated features that were Jennie Baker's calling card. A black felt hat with a rolled, upturned brim covered her chestnut hair. "Steamy cappuccino," she'd confided in Thea at the christening. "That's what my hairdresser tells me. Now, I ask you? Am I the steamy type?" Thea could not remember her own response, but she remembered Jennie throwing back her head and laughing with full-throated enjoyment.

The children were hurrying down the driveway to the car, encouraged by Jennie's broad, welcoming smile and the sweep of her arm. Her trim figure was shown off nicely in a lined and belted raincoat. She had a kiss for each child before she ushered them into the back seat of the car. From Thea's vantage point, she couldn't see the driver, but she assumed it was Mitch's father behind the wheel. Nonny and Pap, she thought, come to take the children to Sunday school.

Thea held her breath, waiting for Mitch to amble out and join the family. He ambled, all right. That slow, rolling, sexy gait moved him from the garage to the car, but Thea knew almost at once he wasn't going to church with the rest of them. Jennie Baker wouldn't have let him in the car in the jeans and wrinkled Oxford shirt that he had had on since yesterday, not when the destination was Sunday services.

Thea watched them converse: Jennie, lively and high-spirited; Mitch, enjoying himself, but infinitely more contained. She knew the exact moment when the conversation turned to her. Jennie's attention shifted to the Volvo parked in front of their car and she pointed to it. Thea could almost hear the question that followed. Mitch began talking—making explanations, Thea was certain—and then she caught the change in their posture, that small movement of shifting weight that signaled they were ready to look back at the house, quite possibly up at the window. She drew back quickly, flattening herself against the wall so if they looked, there was nothing for them to see.

Okay, the fact that she was still holding one panel of the tab curtains in her hands was probably a little damning, she decided. Uncurling her fingers, she let the curtain fall back in place.

Thea let out the breath she was holding slowly. Two car doors closed in quick succession, the sedan pulled away from the curb, and a few moments later there was the sound of the garage door sliding shut. It wasn't long before she could hear Mitch entering the house and moving around the kitchen.

At first she thought he was talking to himself, then she realized he was actually singing. It didn't matter that she couldn't make out the words or the tune, Mitch's message couldn't have been clearer. She didn't know if he was dia-bolical, maniacal, or just plain idiotic, but she was certain he meant for her to know it was time to face the music.

Chapter 5

Thea had a grab-and-go bag in the trunk of her car that was absolutely of no use to her now. Filled with the kind of essentials she might expect to use on a last minute out-of-town jaunt, she discovered she actually missed her toothbrush the most. Squeezing paste on her index finger and smearing it over her teeth was not what the ADA recommended. She found some mouthwash in Mitch's medicine cabinet, checked the contents, then swished it between her teeth to good effect.

Thea looked around for products that Gina might have left behind: face cleanser, moisturizer, a pot of lip gloss. There was nothing. She washed her face with a slim bar of what could have been any soap and turned out to be the deodorant variety. After the chemical face peel, Thea spritzed her hair with water and combed and fluffed it with her fingers.

She regarded herself critically in the mirror and decided she looked exactly like what she was: a thirtysomething woman who was still wearing yesterday's underwear.

In the hope of garnering a casual, unconcerned look for herself, Thea pushed the sleeves of her sweater up to her elbows and did a Scarlett O'Hara on her cheeks and lips. "Ow!" She made a face at her reflection and examined the lower lip she had just bitten too hard. Obviously there were limits to how much rosy color you could raise without bruising.

Thea made Mitch's bed then sat down at the foot of it to compose herself. At least he had stopped singing. It was quiet downstairs; the proof of life below was in the fragrance of brewing coffee that wafted up from the kitchen and slipped under the door. She took a slow, deep breath and became a believer in aromatherapy.

Thea didn't leave the bedroom until she felt prepared to make light conversation and an effortless good-bye. She did not want Mitch to think she was beating a hasty retreat, which of course, was exactly what she was doing. God, she thought, descending the stairs, how insane would she be if she had slept with him instead of three kids?

Thea came up short when she stepped into the kitchen and found it empty. The remains of the children's breakfast were still scattered on the table and by the sink. Her eyes strayed to the under-the-counter coffeemaker with its glass carafe still being filled.

"Pour me a cup, will you?"

Starting, Thea spun around looking for the source of Mitch's disembodied voice. She saw an open door off the rear of the kitchen that she had assumed was a pantry area last night. Now she walked toward it and caught sight of Mitch sitting on a high stool at his drafting table. His heels were hooked on a rung and he was leaning forward, sleeves rolled up, forearms resting on the slanted white laminate surface of the table while he studied his work. A bright red lamp clipped to one corner put the drawing in front of him in a spotlight.

Sensing Thea's presence on the threshold, Mitch looked up. He smiled easily and gave his glasses a slight nudge up the bridge of his nose. His hand lifted higher as he ran it through his hair. "Hi."

Thea's preparation was for nothing. The glasses threw

her. He looked so damn appealing in them: contemplative, cerebral, and hot. He was wearing the same underwear, wasn't he? It wasn't fair.

Mitch looked down at her empty hands. "Coffee?"

Realizing she was hovering, Thea ducked out of the doorway and went in search of a mug. "How do you take it?"

"Cream. It's in the fridge." Mitch picked up his pencil and made a few strokes on the cartoon he was working on, better defining the president's ears. With his own, he listened to Thea moving in his kitchen. "Did you find everything you needed?" he called in.

"The cream was behind the—"

"No, I mean in the bathroom. There's a little basket of toiletries—soaps, toothbrushes, shampoos—mostly stuff I've collected at hotels. The towels are mine though," he added as an afterthought. "The basket was behind them in the linen closet. Did you find it?"

"Oh, yeah. Great idea, that basket." *Lousy place to put it.* She came back with his cup of coffee.

"You're hovering again." He put down his pencil and held out his hand. His fingers made a curling motion, inviting her in.

Thea hesitated, her eyes darting from Mitch's extended hand to the cluttered landscape of his office. It was difficult to take in the totality of the disorder. In addition to the drafting board, there was also a desk, the wide expanse of its surface barely visible because of a cityscape of towers built from sketchbooks, magazines, CDs, books, newspapers, and old calendars. One tower had been shifted from its foundation to make room for the cussing jar. Now the uppermost part of it leaned precariously over the edge of the desk, defying gravity and making Thea want to hold her breath in anticipation of its collapse.

Following her gaze, he grinned. "Not quite what you're used to."

She couldn't disagree. Stepping up to his drafting table, Thea handed him his coffee, carefully avoiding the light-board. "You must have hated my office."

Mitch shrugged. "Let's just say it wouldn't work for me. Go on, look around. I don't mind. It's all right to touch, but don't move anything. I won't be able to find it again."

Expecting to see humor pulling at the corners of his mouth, Thea shot him a skeptical sideways glance. He was perfectly serious. She could have told him she had no intention of touching anything. That's how the spider caught the fly. Thea made a point of keeping her hands at her sides as she wandered around the Federally unrecognized disaster area.

Mitch's studio had been created from an existing utility room which had been expanded several feet so that it jutted at a right angle into the backyard. Now he had what was essentially a sunporch as his workroom. There was plenty of natural light coming in from two skylights and a pair of sliding glass doors. In theory the doors led to the flagstone patio. The reality was they couldn't be reached because of the array of equipment spread out on a long table in front of them. Cords from the computer, copier/printer/scanner/fax, ethernet, and phone had been gathered up into ribbed plastic pipes in an attempt to confine the technoweb, but Mitch had never gotten around to doing the same with the thirty-two-inch TV, DVR, DVD, iPod dock, CD player, and stereo receiver that crowded what remained of the available surface area. The cords to all that equipment dangled over the edge of the table like a waterfall of black snakes. Ugh.

At her sides, Thea's fingers twitched. She moved on before she began untangling the mess. Still, her hand trailed over the back of the Aeron chair that was positioned near the table but not quite under it. She gave it a light push so it rolled into a less obtrusive space.

Watching her, Mitch smiled. He supposed he would be able to find the chair again. "You didn't want coffee?" he asked.

Thea didn't look at him. She was studying the stiff brown contents of a terra cotta container. "I don't drink it as a rule," she said.

It figured that she had rules. "Can I get you something else? Orange juice? Tea?"

"I'm fine," she said absently. Thea lost the battle with herself and picked up the pot. She could feel moisture through the clay and the saucer was damp. He actually watered this thing. "What *is* this?"

Mitch leaned against the back of his stool and asked cautiously, "What do you think it is?"

Now she did look at him, one brow lifted in a perfect arch. "Dead."

"Really?"

"Really." Shaking her head, she set it back in the saucer. "You can stop watering it. How long has it looked like that?"

Mitch considered the question. "Well, my mother gave it to me when this addition was finished. Sort of an office-warming present. I guess that was three, three and a half years ago. It looked like that about two months later. You do the math." He paused. "You're sure there's nothing I can do? Feed it maybe? Turn it?"

"Bury it," she said flatly. "And the next plant someone is foolish enough to give you, keep out of the direct sunlight, or at least move it around. You burned this one."

"Ouch."

Thea hid her smile and moved to one corner of the studio where Mitch had what looked like a sculpture in the making. On closer inspection she recognized old computer monitors, keyboards, cables, motherboards, hard drives, cell phones, and mice, all of them glued together in what was actually a pleasing-to-the-eye arrangement. "You don't like to throw anything away?"

"Those are artifacts."

It was an interesting view of junk. She held up her hands,

surrendering before he could expand his defense. "It's your place. I prefer to visit the Smithsonian. Do you have a name for this piece?"

"Meltdown."

She nodded approvingly, then felt herself seized by hesitation, wondering where to go from here. "May I see what you're doing?"

"Sure." He lifted the long aluminum clip that held his paper in place and tilted the drawing in Thea's direction as she approached. "It's a work in progress. I'm just in the pencil sketching phase. Still playing with the idea."

The idea was to show the president proposing deep tax cuts with one hand and stuffing money into the pockets of wealthy supporters with the other. The wealthy supporters were fat cats. Literally. "It makes your position clear."

Mitch cocked his head to one side and studied the drawing. "That's the problem; it's not really my position. It's my take on what I think the reactivity to the cuts is all about. I'm actually pretty neutral about it." He slid the sketch back into place. "I need to take a break. When I'm having this much trouble with the man's ears, it's time to leave it alone." He set his pencil in the tray and slid off his stool. He had a sense that Thea was trying very hard to stay her ground when he came to his feet inches from her. "Come on. You've seen enough of the inner sanctum to be rightly concerned about my mental health. Let's go in the kitchen and I'll make you some breakfast. I want to hear about your evening with the kids."

"I really have to be going," Thea said quickly, pivoting to follow Mitch's progress to the door. "I didn't expect to sleep in . . . that is, I didn't expect to sleep at all."

Mitch had already cleared the doorway, but he backed up enough to put his head and shoulders into view. "I'm kind of interested in that part," he said, and disappeared again. He called back from near the stove. "You get a good night's rest?"

Thea pressed the narrow bridge of her nose between her thumb and forefinger, closing her eyes briefly. "I slept fine," she said.

"What? You'll have to come in here. I can't hear you."

Try as she might, Thea just couldn't work herself up to the level of annoyance she thought it would take to fight him. She walked into the kitchen. "I said I slept fine."

"Great." Mitch's voice came from the bowels of the refrigerator. He held up a carton of orange juice over the edge of the open door. "One of the kids put this back empty. My mom lives to hear stuff like that. But I have oranges. You want to make some fresh-squeezed?"

"Why not?" Thea's humor came to the forefront. "I could use the workout."

Chuckling, Mitch pitched the carton over his shoulder. His blind toss still made a clean landing in the sink. He straightened, arms filled with about a half-dozen oranges, and stepped back from the fridge. He used the toe of his bare foot to shut the door. "I don't have one of those little droid juicers," he said, dropping the oranges on the countertop, then scrambling to keep them from rolling to the floor. "You'll have to use this." From the cupboard above the toaster, Mitch pulled out an old-fashioned glass juicer. This one required more in the way of manual labor than the one-armed mechanical variety. "You know how to use it?"

"I'll figure it out," she said dryly.

He pulled out a cutting board, laid a knife on top of it, then retrieved two tumblers out of the glassware cupboard. "All yours."

Thea regarded him suspiciously. "Before I start white-washing the fence, Tom, what exactly will you be doing?"

Mitch's grin was appreciative. "I'll be making French toast." He saw her eyes narrow another fraction. "Thea Wyndham, you're a cynic. This is the same honest-to-God, bread-in-the-batter, cinnamon-and-sugar French toast I made for the heathens this morning." He opened the refrigerator door again and pulled out a covered glass bowl. "I saved the extra to entice you."

He could have probably had her with a toaster waffle, but it was nice that he wanted to tempt her. To hide the absurd surge of pleasure she felt, Thea went to the sink and began washing her hands. For the next twenty minutes they moved around the kitchen, and around each other, with ease. Thea sliced, squeezed, and poured the orange juice, and then cleared the table and reset it for the two of them. Mitch stood at the stove and with an economy of motion that spoke of his familiarity with the task, soaked thick slices of real French bread in the batter, and then tossed them, dripping, onto the hot griddle. While they fried, he heated syrup in the microwave and sliced a kiwi. When the bread was done, he used a sifter to sprinkle powdered sugar on each slice, and finally placed them on plates he had warmed in the oven.

"You sure you don't want some coffee?" Mitch asked as he poured himself another cup. He added cream from the carton. "Or I can put the kettle on for tea."

"OJ's fine."

"I can get you water. It's safe." Like many of the residents of Connaugh Creek, he had a water cooler in his kitchen. The town's place at the epicenter of thousands of acres of farmland, and the creek's meandering through the bucolic landscape, had a downside. Chemical fertilizers for crops and cattle had left the creek the polluted source of every home's tap water. It was all right for bathing and washing clothes, but there were regular warnings about dangerously high nitrate levels that left the residents with little choice but to purchase their drinking water. "Or you can get your own," he said, setting his mug down and pulling out the chair at the head of the table.

"Yes." Her mouth curved in a slim smile. "I can do that."

Mitch sat down and regarded her for a few moments before he picked up his fork. "So," he said, "why *did* you never say yes?"

Thea's hand froze halfway to her mouth. Syrup dripped from the triangle of French toast on the end of her fork. Was he really asking why she'd never gone a date with him? "Pardon?"

Mitch considered her response for a lot longer than she considered his question. "Never mind," he said finally. "Go on. Eat. If you know the answer, I don't think you're prepared to tell me."

"Perhaps if I knew what you were talking about." She finished raising the forkful of food to her mouth. With the first bite she closed her eyes and made a little sound of pleasure as her taste buds celebrated. "I think this must be ambrosia. I have a very happy mouth right now."

Mitch's lips twitched. "Happy, huh?"

Thea saw she had amused him and was oddly pleased by that. "Ecstatic, really."

Chuckling, Mitch cut a corner from his own bread and popped it in his mouth. "Not bad."

She ignored his modest comment and applied herself to her own plate. Every bite melted on her tongue. She hadn't known breakfast could be such a sybaritic pleasure.

Mitch observed her over the rim of his coffee cup. He would have agreed right there on the spot to make her French toast for a lifetime just to watch her eat it. And if she let him taste that dollop of syrup clinging to her bottom lip with his own tongue, he'd have a happy mouth himself. "Tell me how it went with the kids," he said. "Was the movie okay?"

"Surprisingly good, actually." Her eyes met his. "Both things, I mean. How the evening went and the movie. Didn't they fill you in this morning?"

"I got a frame-by-frame account of the movie, a soup to nuts version of their dinner at the restaurant, and a highly edited story of the rest of the night. I admit to being suspicious."

Thea set down her fork and took a sip of orange juice. Her gaze shifted to the front door as she considered all that had happened once they arrived home. "Oh!" She straightened in her chair, frowning as she thought back and realized what she hadn't done. She started to get up. "I forgot to lock the door after we came in."

"It's all right. I got it."

It took a moment for Mitch's words to penetrate. Even when they did, Thea was slow to relax. "I'm sorry," she said, her eyes returning to his as she sat again. "Oh, I'm so sorry."

"Thea, it's all right. This is Connaugh Creek. It's not exactly a high crime area. I took care of it."

"But I—"

He reached across the corner of the table and laid his fingers lightly on her wrist. "It's all right," he repeated.

She was startled by the warmth of his hand. He'd been holding his coffee mug between his palms and she thought that must account for it. Thea did not want to consider the possibility that the heat in this contact was only in her mind. With her free hand she reached in her jeans pocket and found the key he'd given her. She pushed it toward his plate. "Here," she said. "You don't want me to drive away with this."

Mitch didn't comment on that. He left the key where it was but removed his hand from Thea's wrist. "I found the cussing jar by the door," he said, leaning back in his chair. "What was it that did you in? Snagged zippers in the parkas or Gordian knots in the sneakers?"

"The knots," she admitted. She felt herself being able to take a full breath now that her chest was less tight, but nothing had changed the deep, abiding tension twisting her stomach. He shouldn't have trusted her with the children, she thought, not when she couldn't remember to do something as fundamental for their safety as locking the front door. Her mind started to spin again as she considered other possibilities. What else had she forgotten to do?

"Thea?"

The sound of her name only garnered her partial attention. "Hmmm?"

"You're drifting." He tapped the stem of her fork so that it jangled against her plate. "And your ambrosia is getting cold."

She looked down at her meal, surprised to find so much of it remaining. There was a fine tremor in her hand when she picked up her fork. "I didn't make them bathe," she said.

"I told you to forget about baths. That was all taken care of this morning."

Thea worried the inside of her lip as she nodded. "I didn't hear them get up."

"They're sneaky. It's a kid thing." He tucked into his own breakfast again. "Besides, they found me and took a great deal of delight in making sure I knew they were awake."

"You slept down here?"

"No. In Emilie's room." He didn't miss the faint lift of one corner of her mouth and the frank surprise in her eyes. "I know," he said. "All that pink. Now I understand how Ken feels when he sleeps over at Barbie's."

"Emasculated, you mean?"

Mitch gave a bark of laughter. "Yeah, I worried about that. I've seen Ken nekkid. It's kind of scary, especially if you have a sister who says the same thing can happen to you."

Thea's smile widened. She felt a crumb on her lip and caught it with the tip of her tongue. That small action seemed to arrest Mitch's gaze. Thea quickly tore the napkin from her lap and applied it to her mouth in a self-conscious manner. She imagined her lips smeared with butter, powdered sugar, and syrup and hoped she didn't have little black kiwi seeds between her teeth. From behind her napkin, she asked, "What time did you get back?"

"Gina dropped me off a little after eleven," he said. "I wanted to explain about that. I meant to—"

Thea put her napkin down and held up one hand. "You don't have to explain yourself—"

Mitch cut in. "I know I don't. I *want* to." When she merely regarded him politely, Mitch sighed. "You must have wondered what happened to us."

"I figured I knew," she said. There was no accusation in her voice. "Gina told me that you and she had not had any time alone. The children, though, were worried."

"They were?"

"I suppose that's why their account of last night was abbreviated. They got rather fractious as the evening wore on and you didn't appear." Thea could see he was genuinely surprised by this. "Didn't you suspect they might get anxious about whether you were coming back?"

"Not coming back?" His brows lifted. "How could they think—" Mitch stopped himself. He removed his glasses and set them on the table, then rubbed the area at his left temple while he stared at his plate. "Jesus," he said softly. "I never thought they wouldn't know I was coming back."

"When you consider it from their perspective . . . their recent experience . . ." Thea's voice trailed off. She laid her hand over his forearm, mirroring the comforting gesture he had extended earlier to her.

"Jesus," he said again.

Thea watched him slip his arm out from under her touch and stand. He was like a sleepwalker as he left the table and disappeared into his studio. When he reappeared he was holding the cussing jar. Still without expression, he placed it on the counter and dug in his pocket for some change. He came out with a couple of bills and stuffed them in the container, establishing credit for what was coming next.

His voice was hardly more than a whisper. "Fuck me." He leaned back against the counter, shaking his head slowly. "Why didn't I anticipate that? I drove Gina a little crazy worrying about them, and here I was worrying about all the wrong things."

"Well, that's easy enough to understand," she said. "You were entrusting them to me."

His glance was sharp and unamused. "Stop it. You left a door open. Big deal. I left them afraid."

"Hey," she said quietly. "You didn't leave them alone. We muddled through, Mitch. There were tears, but we had plenty of tissues to go around and superhero bandages for the really big wounds." Thea saw that puzzlement had slightly softened his expression and she explained the events of the early part of the evening to him. "After that was over, we played a board game for too long, ate too much junk, and ended up with some unsportsmanlike conduct that needed a referee. I phoned Joel for a personal time-out after we finished cleaning up the mess and the kids went up to bed. Someone called a cuddle and we fell asleep in the middle of it."

"In my bed," he said.

Not for the first time Thea wished her complexion was not so fair. There was nothing she could do to hide the wash of color in her face. It wasn't embarrassment that gave rise to this flush, but discomfort. She had no desire to explain the distinction to Mitch, though she disliked the idea that he would think her absurdly disingenuous. She was thirty-two, engaged to be married, and knew something about being in a man's bed. "Joel called back," she said coolly, "and I had to go to your room to answer the phone. Emilie and the twins followed me there, I suppose because they hoped it was you." Thea saw Mitch wince slightly around the eyes as she said this last. "I'm sorry. That sounded as if I was blaming you. I didn't mean to. I could have called you myself when I realized the kids were getting uneasy. I think the boys wanted me to, but Emilie was determined to tough it out. I probably made the wrong decision."

Mitch ran a hand through his hair. "Right. Wrong. Who knows? There probably is no such thing when it comes to stuff like this. I meant to be back before ten. I thought I'd catch Emilie before she conked." He pushed away from the counter and picked up his coffee mug. He took one swallow, made a face, and got up again to put the mug in the microwave. "Since Gina drove, she had the car keys and when I told her I wanted to get back to the house, she was . . . well, she was . . ."

"Less than thrilled?"

"Young," he said. "I was thinking she was just young."

"Oh."

Mitch shrugged. "She didn't get it. We ended up having an argument."

"I'm sorry." It made Thea think of the awkwardness of her own conversation with Joel, and she felt a little guilty for not giving it much consideration before now. "I know how that goes."

One of his brows lifted. "You and Joel?"

Thea nodded. "He doesn't know yet that I spent the night. I think he's going to be . . . well, he'll be . . ."

"Old?"

Thea gave a small laugh. "Old? Joel Strahern? You don't know him at all, if you think that. Let me just say that he'll be less than thrilled and leave it there."

The timer on the microwave went off and Mitch popped open the door and took out his steaming coffee. He played hot potato with the mug, passing it gingerly back and forth between his hands until he got it to the table. Sitting down again, he regarded Thea with interest. "So Strahern's not even a little old-fashioned?"

"Only in the way that recalling the love-ins of the sixties makes him long for that simpler time. Pre-disco, rap, and hip-hop. Pre-HIV. Pre-AK47s in the workplace and our schools. Things like that."

Mitch found himself chuckling. "I'm not sure I disagree with him."

Smiling, Thea said, "We'll work it out. What about you?"

"The same, I suppose."

Thea could not hear any hint that he was invested in the outcome. "How long have you been engaged?"

Mitch brought his coffee up too quickly and almost burned his mouth on the lip of the ceramic mug. "About our engagement," he said slowly. He blew on the coffee, making the dark surface ripple, added cream, then took a tentative sip. "Gina and I . . ."

"You're not really engaged," Thea finished for him.

Mitch had the grace to duck his head. It was a small gesture for the amount of guilt he felt. "Thanks. I was having trouble saying that."

"Why say so in the first place?"

He regarded her frankly. The truth was hardly going to cast him in a good light. Mitch said it anyway. "I was feeling caught and looking for a way out. You seemed to be saying that your impending marriage was reason enough not to take the children. I wanted the same excuse to level the playing field."

Thea nodded, no longer meeting his eyes. "I suppose it seemed that way. There's more to it than that."

"What more?"

The full line of Thea's mouth thinned as she pressed her lips together. When she finally spoke it was to deflect his question with one of her own. "Does it matter? You don't really want to give up the children, do you?"

Mitch was a long time in answering. "No," he said at last. "I don't want to give them up." Not knowing quite what to do with himself in the face of the enormity of this admission, Mitch stood and began clearing the table. "It doesn't mean that I don't want or need your help, Thea."

She simply stared at his back as he scraped and rinsed the dishes at the sink. "What would I do?" So much silence followed that Thea was not certain he'd heard her. "Mitch?"

Turning, he picked up his glasses and put them on again. "Put the syrup in the fridge, will you? Do you want the rest of your orange juice?" Thea took her tumbler out from under his hovering hand, giving him her answer. He picked up her plate instead. Only a smear of syrup remained. "You'll do what you can do," he said. "Call a cuddle. Pay the cussing fines. Get the knots out. And above all, let me know when I'm screwing up."

Thea was already shaking her head. "Oh, Mitch, I don't know. Especially about the last. I don't think I have that right."

"Kathy and Gabe gave you that right," he said flatly. "I'm making sure you know I know it. We might live apart, Thea, but we have to figure out a way to raise these kids together."

"It's like we're divorced."

Mitch was thinking the same thing. "Yeah," he said softly. "Just like that."

Thea got up slowly, carrying the syrup and her glass of juice with her. "Do you think it's an advantage or a disadvantage that we never had a marriage?"

Mitch watched Thea open the refrigerator door, put her orange juice inside, and absently lift the plastic syrup bottle to her lips. She caught herself before a fat dollop of distilled maple sugar landed in her mouth. He laughed as she flushed to the roots of her hair and ducked into the refrigerator again to make the exchange. "I don't know," he said honestly. "My guess is that there's an equal number of pros and cons. It's more to the point that we don't know each other, in or out of a marriage. We should probably do something about that."

"Like what?" She finished off her orange juice with the desperate gusto of throwing back a shot. *If only.* That thought brought Thea up short. She had almost missed it. It was a reminder that she could not afford to get too comfortable. Handing Mitch the glass to rinse, she opened up the dishwasher and began loading it.

"Well," he said, "like talking a couple times a week. Not just about the kids but about what we're doing. That couldn't hurt."

Thea considered that. "I suppose not, though I'm pretty boring."

"Then I'll call you before I go to bed," he said. "And you can put me to sleep."

There was nothing about that image that helped slow Thea's racing heart. She laughed and hoped it wasn't as unsteady as it sounded to her own ears. "Maybe it would be a good idea if you met Joel," she said. *Okay, where the hell had that come from?* This is what happened when anxiety caused a disconnect between her mouth and her brain. Mitch was probably wondering how she'd made a career of thinking on her feet with sound bites like that. Wouldn't the creative teams at Foster and Wyndham be yucking it up now? "What do you think? You and Gina and me and Joel?" *It was* still *happening.* Thea looked past Mitch to the stove. It was gas. She considered doing a Sylvia Plath until she realized that an automatic pilot light made that a no-go. "Dinner some night? We could come out here or you could come into town."

"Great idea. I think Gina would like that." His voice dropped to confidential tones. "Frankly, I think she was a little worried about you."

"Worried?" It was a relief to Thea that the single word was uttered in a casually interested tone. She was still reeling from his "great idea" comment. "Why would Gina be worried about me?" To give herself something to do, Thea began rearranging some of the plates and bowls in the dishwasher to maximize space.

"She knows I've asked you out before."

"Then she knows I said no. All four times."

"Five."

Thea frowned and glanced up. "You're not counting Kathy and Gabe's fire hall wedding reception, are you?"

"That was the first."

"You were the best man, stupid with alcohol, and invited me to go neck with you in one of the fire trucks."

"You looked great in that dress."

"There were two other women wearing gowns in the same awful shade of lilac with tiny capped sleeves and sweetheart necklines. You couldn't tell us apart."

Mitch pretended to consider this. "Well, if that's true, all three of you turned me down."

Thea couldn't help herself. She laughed. It occurred to her that in the little time she'd spent in Mitch's company, she'd been doing quite a bit of that—at least when he wasn't making her crazy. "I can talk to Regina, if you like," she said. "Let her know you're safe with me."

Once Mitch got past the feeling that he'd been insulted, he was able to respond with a certain wryness in tone. "My suspicion is that would be like waving a red flag. I think if she sees you and Joel together, it will be enough. But thank you for the offer." He paused and then plunged ahead. "Although it begs the question: Do I *want* to be safe from you?"

Thea's head snapped up. "That's a rhetorical question, right?"

"If you like."

"I like."

Mitch did not press. A shutter had closed over Thea's green eyes, leaving them dark and expressionless. He stared at the crown of her head as she bent over the dishwasher rack again. "Don't worry about that," he said. "I have to run it anyway so there will be room for dinner dishes."

"Sure. I didn't realize." She slid the top and bottom racks into place. "Where do you keep your detergent?"

Mitch opened the cupboard under the sink and got out the bottle. He filled the dispensers, closed the door, and put the detergent away. He ran water in the sink for about thirty seconds until it was hot before he told her to start the washer. Her response was as stiff as his words.

With the dishwasher door closed, the space between them seemed to have narrowed. Thea took a step backward and found herself squarely in a corner. "I have to go." She didn't move and neither did Mitch. "I never meant to spend the night."

"So you said. Maybe I can talk to Joel. Let him know that three kids gave you all the protection you needed."

The shutters over Thea's eyes slipped and for just a moment she pleaded with him. "Don't, Mitch."

"It's always been there, Thea, whether you admit it or not. Why not admit it?"

There seemed to be no way to respond to that without confirming exactly what she was trying to deny. "I'll call you this week after I talk to Joel. We can decide then where we want—"

One step closed the distance between them. Mitch placed his palms on either side of Thea's shoulders, flat against the pantry cupboard at her back. He made no move to touch her, simply studying her face for some acknowledgment, no matter how fleeting, that he was not acting against her will. It came in the breathy little sigh and the sweet parting of her lips. Mitch bent his head and touched her mouth with his own.

As kisses went, this one was brief. Cool. Dry. And packing about a thousand joules of electricity. Mitch rocked back on his heels, dropping his hands to his sides. For Thea, there was nowhere to go. They stared at each other. It was all Thea could do not to press her fingers to her mouth. Mitch wanted to lay one palm on the back of his neck and flatten the hairs that were standing on end.

"Well," he said softly, "now we know."

Thea said nothing.

"Do you want to borrow some change?" he asked. When she frowned, he added, "For the cussing jar. You look like you have a few choice words."

She didn't smile at his attempt at humor. "You don't have enough money."

Both of Mitch's brows lifted slightly. "I see." He took one step back, then another. He turned his right hand over and lifted it in a small sweep, ushering her out of the corner.

Thea went to the hallway and opened the closet. Removing her jacket, she put it on, and then retrieved her purse. She picked it up and slung it over her shoulder before she pushed her feet into her shoes without untying them.

Mitch came into the living room. He struck a casual pose while he watched her, arms crossed, one shoulder leaning against the wall. "Thea. Don't leave angry. Do you want an apology?"

"Do you want to apologize?"

"No."

She shrugged. Her hand twisted on the doorknob but the door didn't budge. Frustrated, she yanked harder. She was going to have a tantrum, she thought. She was going to kick it and punch it and throw her shoulder into it if it—

"Flip the dead bolt," Mitch said calmly from behind her. "Then twist the lock in the knob."

Thea did both and the door opened as though she had whispered the magic words. She stepped onto the porch. The door caught when she tried to close it, and she realized belatedly that Mitch had followed her and was blocking her attempt with his foot. When she let go of the knob, he stepped onto the porch after her.

"Listen, Thea." He saw her go rigid at the edge of the

steps, her shoulders braced. Perhaps it wasn't the best overture he'd ever made but at least she'd stopped. She *was* listening, or pretending to. "Don't you want to yell at me or something? I wouldn't like it much—I might even yell back—but it would be better than you leaving here mad at me."

She didn't turn, so he couldn't see her face, but Mitch had no trouble making out her words. "What makes you think," she said, each word resonating clearly, "that I'm mad at *you?*"

Thea was still calling herself five kinds of stupid when she got home. A soak in the tub was of marginal help. The call to Rosie twenty minutes later did a lot more, and by the time Thea got off the phone she was feeling better, or at least she was prepared to cope. She didn't notice the light blinking on her phone until she was making tea. She decided she didn't want to check messages. She was getting pretty good at ignoring them.

In the late afternoon, it started to snow. Thea already had a fire going and she opened the drapes at the picture window to enjoy the view from her living room sofa. She sat comfortably curled in one corner, wearing her chenille bathrobe and thickest socks, with the *Times* Sunday crossword on her lap. She played with the puzzle for a while, but when the answers didn't come easily, Thea absently filled in the squares with doodles and diagonal lines.

It shouldn't have been such a big deal, that kiss. It wasn't as if he had never touched her before. In their long history of being best friends to mutual friends, it was inevitable that they would meet from time to time. Gabe and Kathy's wedding was the first. On that occasion he had danced with her through all the obligatory wedding party numbers. There was some flirting, a little teasing, and even a kiss on the cheek, but nothing had jump-started her heart the way that kiss in his kitchen had.

"That's because you wouldn't let it." Thea pushed the newspaper off her lap and tossed her pen on top. Great, she was talking to herself. She reframed this immediately in her own mind as thinking out loud. "Good for you," she said under her breath. "Another helpful rationalization."

Groaning softly, Thea let her head fall back on the sofa. She wondered how different things would be if she had taken Mitch up on his fire truck invitational during the wedding reception. He'd frightened her a little even then, which is what made it so easy to turn him down. Instead of disappearing into the garage where the fire trucks were parked, Thea had fastened herself to the side of her date for the rest of the evening, knowing with absolute certainty that she could control Timothy Martin's frisky overtures in a way she could never have Mitchell Baker's.

They'd met again at various functions that included both Gabe and Kathy. There was Emilie's birth, her christening, a housewarming when Gabe and Kathy stopped renting and became home owners, the birth of the twins and their christening, and the occasional party, usually something at Halloween and the Fourth of July. It wasn't that Mitch hit on her. Thea thought she might have handled that better. He was invariably polite, attentive, and almost always with another woman—someone, in Thea's mind, who was her polar opposite. Which is why it confused her when he'd invariably call several days after seeing her again and ask her out. She could only imagine that Kathy or Gabe put him up to it. They denied matchmaking, but there were also these odd glances exchanged between the two of them that supported Thea's suspicions.

Over the years, it became easier to avoid Mitch than it was to face the inevitable and awkward obligatory date request. She'd stopped attending parties, even ones for the kids, just because she knew he'd be there, and made her own arrangements to see them when he wouldn't be around. "Coward," she whispered to herself. "It wasn't only about him asking you out. You can't even admit that it was just easier to avoid him. Period." So *there,* she thought, satisfied she'd tricked herself into saying it out loud. The thing she couldn't give sound to was the fact that Mitch had always set her nerves humming, when what she had convinced herself she needed was comfort and control. Thea was left with the niggling and unsettling suspicion that she needed to rethink that conviction.

Leaning over the couch, she picked up the phone and called Joel. "Hi. I'm home."

"Where have you been?"

Thea knew she should have expected both the question and the terse delivery, but she was unprepared for both. "Should I call back, Joel?" she asked quietly. "It would give you some time to find a good cop for your interrogation."

"Do you think this is funny, Thea? I left two messages on your home phone, your cell's still off, and it's snowing now. I didn't know what the hell happened to you."

Thea drew in a slow breath, wondering why she didn't feel more contrite. It was probably not a good sign of where this relationship was heading. The thought of what that might mean was like a fist closing over her heart. "I'm sorry," she said. "I haven't been home so very long."

"How long?"

"A few hours."

"And you're just calling now." Joel's disappointment was palpable. "That speaks volumes."

"I told you I just wanted to lie around today," she said. "Alone."

"Oh, I understood that part. What I don't understand is where you've been."

"I spent the night with the children."

There was a long pause, and finally, "They live with Baker."

"Yes, I stayed with them at Mitch's."

"He was there, then."

"At some point," she said. "I don't know when he came in. I fell asleep with the children and didn't stir again until this morning."

"That still should have put you home before my second call."

Thea covered the mouthpiece with her hand so her sigh couldn't be overheard. "I slept in," she told him.

"You never sleep in."

"I did this morning."

"Thea, I don't—"

Guilt, as well as a desire to end the conversation, made Thea rush in. "Can you come out, Joel? The roads aren't bad, are they?"

"It wouldn't matter."

The way he said it made the fist around Thea's heart tighten. "How long?"

"About forty minutes."

"I'll start dinner."

Thea woke alone Monday morning. Guilt might have prompted her invitation to Joel, but it also worked to keep him out of her bed. He didn't press her overmuch though she knew he was dissatisfied as well as frustrated. For herself, there was initial relief, a restless night, and enough self-blame by morning that she compensated for by spending the first three hours in her office making personal calls to update her wedding arrangements.

She ended up working until almost eight, missed a meeting she didn't have in her schedule, and forced herself to drive home in spite of the fact that it would have been easier once again to spend the night at the office.

Rosie Flaugherty was waiting for her in the driveway. She hopped out of her car when Thea opened the garage door from the street and was shaking off flakes of snow inside by the time Thea got out of her car. Rosie swept back her hood to reveal hair that was aggressively big and blond.

Thea gave a start. The last time she had seen Rosie, her big hair had been bottled auburn. "Time for a change?"

"Yeah. Whaddya think?"

"It's bright."

"That's what Robby thinks. He likes it, though. Sez when I change my hair it's like he's sleepin' around without the hassle of tradin' zodiac signs at the bar."

Laughing, Thea opened the door to the house and stepped inside. "It sounds like it's been a while since Robby took that line out for a test drive."

Rosie snorted. "I better be the last woman he asked, 'So, what's your sign, sweetcheeks?' We've been married twenty-four years." She took off her parka, gave it to Thea, and slipped off her boots. "You haven't asked me why I'm here."

"You don't need a reason to drop by."

"Right," she said flatly. "Like you want me hangin' out at the country club."

"You're confusing me with my parents." Thea hung up their coats and then motioned Rosie to have a seat in the breakfast nook of the kitchen. "I'll take you to lunch there some Sunday."

"I bet your boyfriend would love that."

Thea didn't respond to that. "Have you eaten? I was going to make some *aglio e olio.*"

"What's that?"

"Pasta with garlic and olive oil. It will take about twenty minutes."

"Sure. Sounds good. Anything I can do?"

"Keep me company."

"You got any pop?"

Thea opened the refrigerator and found Rosie a Pepsi. "Just for you," she said, snapping back the tab. She poured it into a glass, added ice, and slid it to the far side of the table. "Talk to me."

Rosie leaned back in her chair while Thea returned to the counter. "I just had a feelin'," she said, "that maybe you could use a visitor."

"Good call." Thea filled a five-quart pasta pot with water and set it on the stove. She turned the flame on high and added a lid to bring it to a boil faster. "How did you know?"

"I was talking to Rachel. She didn't see you at the meeting."

"Were you checking up on me?"

"No, that's what I'm doing now. Then, I was talking to Rachel. She mentioned it; I didn't." Rosie's thick acrylic-tipped nails tapped her glass. She wore rings on every finger, including her thumbs, and the synthetic stones flashed just like the real ones. "So what happened?"

Thea shrugged. "I got caught up in something else and Mrs. Admundson didn't remind me."

Across the kitchen, Rosie's eyes narrowed as she went into full bullshit alert mode. Thea didn't have a knife in her drawer as steely or as sharp as what Rosie turned on her now. "Doesn't sound like Mrs. A.," she said, taking it slow, feeling her way. "Thought she was one of those anal types who never forgets where her car is parked—or yours."

"I didn't have it in my calendar."

"So you haven't told her."

"No. It's none of her business." Thea pressed garlic into a sauté pan then added extra virgin olive oil. Her back was to Rosie but it didn't stop her from feeling the strength of the other woman's stare. "Say something."

"We've talked about it before," Rosie said casually. "You don't have to take out a full-page ad or anything."

"But you think Mrs. Admundson should know."

"If you can't remember on your own, I think you damn well need to get it into your calendar, Thea, so someone can remind you."

Thea half turned away from the stove so she could see Rosie while she slowly pushed the garlic through the olive oil with a wooden spoon. She hadn't been wrong about those blue eyes boring into her. "What about you? Can't you call me?"

"I'm not a nursemaid. You have to take some responsibility for yourself."

"And how is having my assistant remind me making me responsible?"

"Because you depend on her to remind you about lots of other things. I don't see how this is any different. It's part of your life now—or it's supposed to be. Unless you're changing your mind about that? Like maybe you're thinkin' you can do it all on your own."

Thea smacked the side of the spoon against the pan. Droplets of warm oil splashed on the back of her hand but she gave them no notice. "I just missed a meeting, Rosie. One meeting."

"Two. Unless you went yesterday."

"Yesterday was Sunday. I didn't know there were meetings on Sunday."

"Honey, there's always a meeting somewhere. That's why it's ninety days/ninety meetings. Or did you think that was just a slogan?" Torn between exasperation and sympathy when she saw the truth in Thea's startled expression, Rosie simply shook her head. "Well, now you know." Her eyes dropped to the stovetop. "You better lower that flame. Somethin's startin' to smoke."

Chapter 6

"Rosie thinks I should tell Mrs. Admundson," Thea said. She glanced over at Joel when he didn't say anything. His strong jaw was set tightly and the line of his mouth could only be called disapproving. Thea turned her eyes back to the road, wishing she had not volunteered to drive him to the airport. Traffic was heavy, they were running late, and Joel had already pressed the phantom brake on his side of the car three times.

"That Buick is slowing down," he warned her.

Thea strove for patience as she lightly tapped the brake. "Thank you." She turned on her signal light, checked the mirrors, then whipped into the passing lane. "So what do you think?"

"About your driving?"

"I know what you think about that. What about telling Mrs. A.?"

"I've told you what I think about that, too." He fell silent a moment, then said, "Just how many people have to know about your condition before that woman is satisfied?"

Thea tried not to bristle at his faintly accusatory tone. "At least one more than you, Joel."

"I don't understand. You go to those meetings. There are,

142	*Jo Goodman*

what? Twenty? Thirty people there? They all know. Isn't that sufficient?"

"Rosie says it's not the same, and I'm inclined to agree with her. The Hi-my-name-is-Thea anonymity serves its purpose but I could use some help outside of the meetings. I'm a substance abuser. An addict. It's not exactly a condition."

"If there's a problem, it's because your doctor overprescribed medication. I think you have a malpractice case. So does Avery."

"That isn't helpful. Don't find excuses for me, Joel. I'm good at finding them for myself."

Joel found the button that adjusted his seat. He pushed it so the back slanted a few degrees more toward the rear of the car. He rested his head on the support and closed his eyes. "Let me know when we're there."

Thea was not sure whether he took that position to avoid conversation or because he hated her driving. It worked on both counts. They didn't speak again until she was pulling into the passenger eject lane at Pittsburgh International.

"Will you at least wait until I get back before you say anything to Mrs. A.?" asked Joel. "A few more days can't hurt. We can both think about it. There could be consequences you haven't considered."

That *she* hadn't considered. Thea hadn't missed that part. It was Joel's way of telling her he knew them all. "Very well."

Joel frowned. "That was too easy," he said. "Do you have a bomb you want to drop?"

"More like a hand grenade." She pulled the trunk release but neither of them made a move to get out of the car. Thea turned slightly in her seat. "I want us to have dinner with Mitchell Baker and his girlfriend when you get back. I was thinking of Saturday night. Will you do that for me?"

"I think that's a great idea." Joel leaned across the console. The kiss he gave Thea was both lingering and hard, and when he pulled back they were both a shade out of breath. "I'm going before we get cited."

Thea saw a uniformed officer walking toward the car. He looked as if he had no patience for public displays of affection and was prepared to give them a dressing-down before he waved them on. Joel pushed his door open and hopped out of the car. "I'll call you tonight." He got his carry-on and garment bag out of the trunk and closed the lid, tapping it twice to indicate he was done.

Thea watched him walk up to the door. He turned once and gave her a little wave. She waved back, a small frown pulling her brows together. She saw the officer motioning her out with his thumb, and she pulled away from the curb without looking. "That was too easy," she said under her breath.

She wasn't talking about her merge into traffic.

Prior to Saturday evening Thea's contact with Mitch was limited to two brief phone calls, the first to suggest the day, restaurant, and time, and the second to confirm that he and Gina could make it.

Joel had arrived back in town only the previous night. Thea met him at their favorite Italian eatery in the Strip District a half hour early so they could have a few private moments before being joined by their guests. Joel ordered a bottle of red before he remembered Thea wouldn't be joining him.

"You're not a drunk, Thea," he said quietly. "One glass wouldn't be out of line."

"I suppose this means we're done with the amenities," she said. She deliberately squeezed her lemon slice into her water and took a sip. She held up her glass to the candle-light. "Light. Zesty. The bouquet is suggestive of lemon-scented Shine and Shield, but not unfriendly."

"Stop it. You've made your point."

Thea reached under the table and touched Joel's thigh. "Are we going to fight? I don't want to do that."

"What do you want, Thea? I'm not certain I know any longer. I don't seem to be able to do anything right since you came out of rehab."

She removed her hand and smoothed the edge of the white tablecloth with her fingertips instead. "It's not rehab," she said. "Or it's not only rehab. I have the children to think about." Thea lowered her voice. "My lifelong friend and his wife were just killed, Joel. How can you not understand that some things have changed for me?"

Joel Strahern did not lack compassion. He saw Thea was hurting and knew he was, in part, responsible for it. He laid his hand over hers, rubbing the back of her hand with the ball of his thumb. "Can you appreciate," he said softly, "that I don't want to lose you? Things I thought we understood, you're asking me to change. And each time I restate my position I wonder if you'll end it." He gave her hand a slight squeeze. "You look great from behind, Thea, but I dread that view if it means you're walking out on me."

Thea's small smile was shaky. "I didn't mean to get into this tonight, Joel. I really didn't. I wouldn't have met you early if I thought this was going to happen. Perhaps there is no good time to tell you that time is exactly what I need." She watched his face go very still and felt his hand leave hers. Thea waded on, feeling the water get deeper and colder. "No one has to know anything's changed between us, if that's the way you want it. It's not as though our engagement's been formally announced. People who have seen the ring will think we're just trying to be quiet about it. People who haven't, won't know differently."

"Obviously you've given this a lot of thought."

It was almost all she had thought about since dropping him off at the airport. She nodded faintly because she owed him the truth. "I'll understand if you don't want to see me," she said. "But that's not what I'm asking for. I want the freedom to be with the children more without feeling as if I'm being pulled in another direction by you. I don't think you can give me that yet, and I don't blame you for it. I know one of the things that attracted you to me was the fact I wanted no children of my own. You were always honest about that."

"So were you," he said bitterly. "Or so I thought."

Thea felt her face warm. "I was honest," she said. "I didn't know what I know now. The circumstances of my life have changed, and I owe it to Emilie and the boys to do my very best by them."

Joel raised his wineglass, took a long swallow, then regarded her over the rim. "Then you're going to ask for full custody?"

"No." Reluctantly she admitted, "It's occurred to me, but you can't know how unfair and cruel that would be to everyone."

"Including Baker."

Thea nodded.

"I thought he didn't want them. Didn't he try to pawn them off on you only a couple of weeks ago?"

Joel's choice of words made Thea stiffen, but she answered calmly enough. "He panicked, Joel. He didn't know how much he wanted the children."

"So now you're going to help." His voice was flat and unflattering. "Who do you think you're kidding, Thea? This is about Mitchell Baker, not the children."

She shook her head. "I can't help it if you think that. It's not true, not in the way you seem to think it is. He's one of the good guys, Joel, and he's asked for my help. I want to give him that."

"Deputy Mom," Joel said against the rim of his glass before he drained it.

Thea drew in her lower lip as she watched Joel pour a second glass of wine. He correctly read her concern and shrugged, the curve of his mouth faintly derisive. With a small, defiant salute he raised his glass and drank again. Thea maintained a stoic silence, glancing at Joel's Rolex as he lifted his arm. He caught the direction of her gaze, looked at the time himself, and commented, "Seems the posse is runnin' a bit behind schedule, ma'am."

"Maybe we should order something," she suggested. "I wouldn't mind an appetizer. I haven't eaten since breakfast."

Joel put his hand over Thea's menu as she began to open it. "I think we should wait. It would be rude to start without them."

Rather than struggle with her menu, Thea removed her hands to her lap.

"I'll behave," Joel said. He touched her chin and applied only minimal pressure to get her to look at him. "I promise."

She searched his face, saw that in spite of the blow she had dealt him and the pain he was in, he was sincere about this. She nodded slowly.

Joel lowered his hand and pushed his wineglass to the side. "Do you want to call him? I have my phone if you don't have yours."

Thea looked around the crowded restaurant. Candlelight was reflected warmly in the darkening windows as night had long since closed around them, but intimacy was an illusion. Privacy was suggested, not ensured. "I don't want to make a call from here. I don't like it when other people do the same thing. Let's just wait them out."

"All right." Joel's eyes followed the progress of a waiter coming toward them with a basket of warm chunks of bread. He picked one out as soon as the basket made a landing and dipped it in a shallow pool of seasoned olive oil. "I'll start with this."

Smiling, Thea chose one for herself. "I'll join you."

There was no bread left by the time Gina and Mitch arrived. Their waiter swept away the evidence of Thea and Joel's head start and replaced it with a new one. Thea made the introductions and watched closely as Joel and Mitch sized each other up. As macho posturing went, it was a fairly mild demonstration, and Thea had the sense they did it more in response to her expectations than out of any real desire to mark their territory. Interesting.

Joel ordered another bottle of wine and poured what remained in his bottle between Gina and Mitch.

"Thank you," Gina said. "But this will have to last the evening. I'm the designated driver tonight."

Joel smiled. "So is Thea."

Thea supposed that was a discreet, if mildly dishonest way to describe her abstinence. "You have the Xterra?" she asked.

Gina nodded. "I refused to climb in and out of his truck in this dress."

Since she was wearing a Slinky, Thea didn't see that it mattered to what heights she climbed. And a leg up on the Chevy couldn't have been much higher than the one she had to make into the SUV. Her comment, though, effectively brought everyone's eyes to the skinny red dress. "Vera Wang?" asked Thea.

"Yes," Gina said. "It is."

"Gina sold another monster house a few days ago," Mitch said. "I think she spent her entire commission in one shopping spree."

Gina rolled her eyes. "He's never understood shopping."

Joel tilted his head to regard Gina and the fabulous red dress. "And the way you go about it, it's obviously not for the faint of heart."

Gina's scarlet lips parted in a brilliantly appreciative smile and her matching nails tapped Joel on the sleeve of his jacket. "You are so right. Shopping is a blood sport."

Thea stared at Joel as he gave a small, spontaneous shout

of laughter. Out of the corner of her eye she saw several diners turn in the direction of their table and smile. It was the first Thea had heard him laugh all evening, and when she thought back, she realized with some dismay that it was the first real laugh she'd heard from him in weeks.

"What's wrong?" asked Joel.

Thea was slow to understand he was speaking to her. She blinked. When he continued to stare at her, a question in his eyes, she came around. "Oh, it was just . . ." Her smile was a shade wistful. "It was just so nice to hear you laugh." Impulsively, Thea reached for his hand and gave it a squeeze.

Over the rim of his wineglass, Mitch regarded his dinner companions with mild disgust. Gina had her True Blood nails pressed into Joel Strahern's jacket and Thea had her hand clamped over his fingers. The sixty-one-year-old investment banker was the hotdog in a girl bun. Mitch tipped back his glass. It was going to be a very long night.

The waiter came by to recite the specials and take their orders. Without discussion, they had all chosen the same salad: roasted red beets, fresh apples, and goat cheese in a red wine vinaigrette. Thea and Gina asked for the salmon *alla griglia,* while Joel ordered the lasagne Bolognese, and Mitch, because he found himself dithering uncharacteristically, selected one of the specials, an endless trio of fresh pasta stuffed with seasonal fillings.

"Tell me about this house you sold," Joel said to Gina when the salads arrived. "Quite the coup in this market. In town or out?"

Mitch caught Thea's eye, smiled blandly, and then started on his salad as Gina began to regale them with the gory details of her second favorite blood sport. She gave a good account of real estate skullduggery that kept Joel entertained, Thea politely interested, and Mitch drinking until his pasta trio arrived.

"So what is it about this truck of yours, Mitch?" Joel asked. "The one that Regina won't ride in."

"It's a '53 Chevy."

Joel didn't have to feign curiosity. "You restored it yourself?"

Mitch nodded. "I worked on it for years on and off."

"We had a Chevy truck when I was kid. A '55, I think. Powder blue. We had a farm out on McKnight before all the development. My dad ran that Chevy all over the countryside, used it for everything."

Straherns? Farmers? They raised capital, not cattle. Their idea of a cash crop was, well, *cash*. Mitch wasn't buying this tilling-the-earth version of Joel's childhood, though he hadn't meant to communicate his skepticism quite so openly that it elicited a response.

"Every man's got to have a hobby," Joel said. "My dad liked farming, even if he only did it on the weekends. I think he always regretted selling the place. He didn't have the retirement he imagined without it."

"What about your hobby?" asked Gina.

"Woodworking."

The immediate image in Mitch's mind was of Joel Strahern bent over a cross section slab of oak, burning pictures of deer and fish and ferns into the wood with a red-hot soldering pen, acrid smoke rising from the surface. He actually smiled.

"Joel's cabinetry is art," Thea said. "He does special pieces for friends. He made an exquisite walnut credenza for my office."

The corners of Mitch's mouth flattened. He remembered the piece very well. There were no engravings of deer and fish and ferns anywhere on it, only the smooth grain of excellent wood, a polished, reflective surface, and beautifully beveled edges.

"Really?" asked Gina. "I made a bookcase once out of two-by-fours and concrete block."

Joel laughed. "That's pretty standard college apartment furniture. Where did you go to school?"

"Pitt."

"Really? I'm on the Board of Trustees."

"You are?" She leaned toward him, her eyes earnest, "Then maybe you can explain to me why the chancellor . . ."

For Mitch it was like a switch just toggled off in his head. He was still sitting at the table, a participant by his mere presence, but the audio was off. Gina was having a good time and there was nothing he begrudged her about that. He wouldn't have predicted it when they left the house almost thirty minutes late because Emilie didn't want them to go at all. Had it been one of the twins, Mitch thought he would have handled it better, but Emilie's age and the fact that she was a girl made him impatient and softhearted at the same time. The need to be firm warred with his desire to give her anything she wanted—ever—in order to dry up those pathetic tears. It didn't help that the twins didn't hold out long in the face of their sister's distress, or that his mother and Gina were coaching him from the sidelines.

Then there was the argument with Gina over what they were driving. She'd arrived at his house before lunch, hung out with him and the kids through a Disney DVD and a trip to the library, and watched the twins while he and Emilie went grocery shopping. When it came time to leave he was prepared to follow her to her apartment in the North Hills, drop off her car, and continue into town in his truck. Gina balked before Emilie, insisting on taking the SUV. Pointing out that his cherry red truck matched the condom she was wearing hadn't exactly endeared him to her. He knew she was hoping that by controlling their wheels she could maneuver him to spend the night at her place. Mitch didn't like being manipulated, but he also knew Gina shouldn't have had to work so hard at it. She looked like a sex Popsicle in that dress and before the instant family, they would have been late because he'd have had to have her in *and* out of it.

Living with the kids had done something to his libido.

"Mitch?"

It was Thea's soft inquiry that brought him out of his reverie. He tilted his head politely and focused. "Hmm?"

"I asked if there's something wrong with your dish. The waiter's been surreptitiously eyeing you to see if you're ready for more."

He didn't need to look down at his plate to know he'd taken only a few bites from each one of the fresh pastas. "No. It's all fine. Better than fine." He speared a delicate spinach tortellini. "Fine is like damning it with faint praise."

Gina's smile was rather stiff. "I think we get the picture."

"Fine."

Thea hid her smile behind her linen napkin and gave him a sympathetic look over the folds. Gina turned her attention to Joel who had steered the conversation back to their mutual interest in real estate. Thea suspected that for Gina it was like sitting at the feet of the master. While Gina's own family had a significant percentage of the realty business in the tri-state area, Joel Strahern brokered deals that built stadiums and expansion teams all over the East Coast. Gina asked him questions Thea had never thought about. It had seemed to Thea that Joel had rarely wanted to talk much about his work, as if he suspected that Thea wouldn't be interested or understand, and she supposed she had reinforced his thinking by not pressing him. Now she found herself learning things in a single evening that he had never shared before. He was practically waxing poetic about the art of the deal, completely unself-conscious about the gap in their ages, telling stories of himself and his contemporaries that had happened years before Gina was born.

Conversation wound down over espresso. Mitch had

moved his chair around so he could lay his arm across the back of Gina's. Now she snuggled into the crook of his shoulder, replete and glowing from the meal and the attention. Joel made a few polite overtures regarding the children, and Thea was warmed by them because she knew he broached the subject for her sake. At that point Gina contributed more than Mitch did, and he made no attempt to elaborate on anything she said.

By the time they said their good-byes, Gina was out of patience. She turned on Mitch as she slipped the key in the ignition and gunned the motor. "What in God's name was wrong with you tonight?" It occurred to her that there had been too many conversations lately that started in a similar vein. "This evening was *your* idea. Let's all get together, you said. Joel Strahern made an effort tonight, Mitch, which is more than I can say for you. He asked about *your* kids. You might have said more than three words about anything, you know, but especially about the children."

"He asked about the kids because of Thea. He doesn't care about them. He did it for her."

Gina braked for a red light. Hard. Her head snapped around. "Now, there's a page in the playbook that you could study."

Mitch scowled.

"It wouldn't have hurt you to show an interest in what I was saying to Mr. Strahern."

Mr. Strahern? Where had that come from? Mitch wondered. All night long it had been Joel. What do you think about leveraged buyouts, Joel? What makes a successful portfolio, Joel? How about those Penguins, Joel? Mitch knew for a fact that Gina knew way more about hats than hat tricks, but she hung on Strahern's every word like she was making a powerplay. Perhaps she was.

"You could have supported me," she said. "Showed him I wasn't a complete child."

"Oh? And how should I have done that?" The light changed and Gina's acceleration pressed Mitch back in his seat. "You want to slow it down a little?"

Gina eased up on the gas but her fingers tightened on the steering wheel. "Little things," she said. "Like being more attentive. Treating me like your date and not your little sister."

"Joel Strahern would have been happier if you *had* been my little sister," Mitch said. "The man was interested in you."

"Oh, he was not. That's ridiculous. He's . . . he's a *legend*."

Mitch shook his head. "Trust me, he was hitting on you."

Gina sighed. "You definitely had too much to drink. Did you even see how he looked at Thea? And why wouldn't he? She's always so perfect. Perfect hair. Perfect nails. Perfect smile. Perfect. On top of that, she's a perfectly nice person. I hate her."

"Yeah, you were a regular troll in that—"

"Don't you dare call it a condom again."

Mitch's mouth snapped shut.

"Smart," she said dryly. "Anyway, I know now this dress was a bad choice for tonight. Too glam. I needed sophisticated-casual."

"As opposed to what? Liberty Avenue hooker?"

Without missing a beat, Gina's right arm swung out and clobbered Mitch across the chest. Satisfied with his *ooof,* she went on. "Cashmere," she said. "Like that fabulous sweater dress Thea was wearing. And the Jimmy Choo boots. Mr. Strahern looked as if he wanted to put her *on.*"

Mitch couldn't disagree. Like Gina, he had seen how Joel Strahern's gunmetal glance roamed over Thea. His perspective had been a bit rosier than Gina's, compliments of that second bottle of red, but it wasn't inaccurate.

Gina's voice was quiet, reserved, and even a little wistful. "That's how I want you to look at me, Mitch. Like you want to wear me." She pressed her lips together a moment and glanced at him sideways. "Don't make the obvious Trojan joke."

It had gone through his mind, but he had been smarter than to say it aloud. Gina deserved better than that anyway. Mitch took a breath and let it out carefully. "We probably need to put this in slo-mo." Out of the corner of his eye, he watched her. "That's what you're thinking, isn't it?"

Gina was long in responding, then there was a nod, cautious at first, more deliberate the second time. "I don't think I'm ready to be a mom, Mitch, even a weekend-girlfriend-stepmom type. I admire you so much for what you're taking on, but I'm not sure I can share it with you."

Mitch was surprised that he felt as lousy about her decision as he did. "I think you have more courage than I do," he said finally. "I don't know if I would have gotten around to ending it for a long time."

"Slo-mo," she said. "Remember? Not an end. I still want to see you. I really think we can be friends. I know people say that and don't mean it, but I mean it. Being friends could be good for both of us. And I like the kids. I do. But I'm going to like them a whole lot better when they're not standing in the way of what I want from you. They have no choice, Mitch. But I do. I'm making it before I end up resenting them for something that's not their fault."

It was a long time before Mitch spoke. "You know, Gina, I don't think I've ever been grown-up enough for you."

She reached across the console and touched his arm, patting it lightly. "It's all right. Girls mature faster."

Thea kicked the covers aside and sat up. She stretched, rolled her neck, and then flopped back on the bed rather than stumble out of it. The phone rang and she groaned, glancing at the clock. It was only seven-thirty. What if she had wanted to sleep in?

"Hello."

"It's Joel. What did I get you out of?"

"Bed."

"Don't tease me."

Thea yawned wide enough to crack her jaw. "I was just going to jump in the shower and get ready. We're on for nine, right?" There was a slight hesitation. "Oh, I guess we're not."

"I'm sorry, Thea. Something's come up. I wouldn't cancel with you if it weren't so—"

"You don't have to apologize," she said. "I know you wouldn't do it if it weren't important." It was the first time Joel had ever changed plans with her. During the almost two years they had been seeing each other he was the one who had gone out of his way to make certain he kept his dates with her. "It's not family, is it? Everyone's okay?"

"Oh, sure. They're fine. This is business."

"Anything you can talk about?"

"I can talk about it, but you'd fall asleep in the middle. It's that boring."

"Save it, then. You can tell me when it's over and you're the hero of the piece." His low laughter rumbled pleasantly in her ear. "I think I'm going to go riding anyway."

"I hope you do. There's no reason that you shouldn't go without me."

"Call me later?"

"Of course. It'll be after eight."

"That's fine." Thea added impulsively, "Thank you for last night, Joel. I know you did it for me and I appreciate it."

"I wish we had started out differently, but I had a good time in the end."

They spoke for another minute and then rang off together, slowly, even a little reluctantly, or so it seemed to Thea. She replaced the phone before she realized that Joel hadn't ended the conversation with "I love you." He was doing just as she asked him last night, giving her time, letting her think. In a perfect world, Thea thought, she would feel relieved that he had listened to her. Instead, what she felt was unaccountably sad.

Thea showered, dressed, and drove out to the stables. Because she had called ahead, Captain Henry Morgan was saddled and waiting for her, almost as impatient as she to be out. For several minutes, she talked loving nonsense to the gelding while she ran a hand over his glossy cinnamon coat. He preened under her attention, tossing his head when Thea ran her palm along his neck and shoulder. She led him out of the stable and mounted. She was offered a riding companion but she refused, preferring to be on her own on the trails with the Captain and her melancholy mood for company.

Thea rode for more than two hours. The trails were clear but a thin layer of snow clung to the overhead branches and limned the side of the tree trunks. Except for the sounds of their own passage, it was a silent ride. Thea could almost forget that she was not far from the highway or that if she veered off the trail and out of the woods, she would find herself in brick and concrete cul-de-sacs. When the trail opened up, Thea gave Captain Henry his head. Grateful for the chance to run, the gelding gave Thea exactly what she was looking for: moments in which she could think of nothing but the wind in her face, her seat in the saddle, and the powerful drive of the animal under her.

Afterward, Thea brushed him out, keeping up a stream of chatter that made the stable hand smile. "I don't get out here nearly often enough," Thea told him. "I always feel as if I'm making up for my neglect."

Thea thought about that as she was driving home. Neglect seemed to be a theme in her life. There was the physical neglect of her sperm and egg donors, the benign neglect of her adoptive parents, the self-neglect that had put her into rehab, the emotional neglect of her relationships, and the deliberate, perhaps selfish neglect of . . .

She paused, took a breath, and slowed herself down. She was forging ahead, wasn't she? In fits and starts, to be sure, but still moving in the right direction. Resilient, she reminded herself. God, but she wanted to be resilient.

The question of how that was accomplished echoed. It didn't come naturally to her, so maybe it wouldn't come at all. Her birth parents had no expectations except that she remain out of their sight, definitely out of their hearing. Her adoptive parents had no expectations except that she be a trophy child, on display as evidence of their generosity. It still remained for her to identify what she expected from herself.

Thea put the figurative brakes to her thoughts when she recognized they were not taking her anywhere she wanted to go.

Coming out of her reverie, she experienced several disorienting moments. She could not immediately identify her surroundings. Nothing about the landscape seemed familiar and she tried to think if she had missed her exit, projecting the image of the landmarks she should be seeing against the ones she was. When the Volvo completed a wide turn on the highway and Thea was confronted by the sign ahead of her, she finally realized she hadn't passed her exit but taken the one before it. Connaugh Creek was now only fifteen miles north of where she was. It was not particularly surprising, she thought, that her preoccupation on the subject of neglect should lead her to take this route. This, at least, was a place she was willing to go.

Activating her phone with the button on her steering wheel, Thea called Mitch. There was no answer and she couldn't think of any message she wanted to leave, so she hung up. Glancing at the clock, she realized Mitch and the children were probably all at church. By the time she reached their house, they would be getting out. It only took Thea a moment to decide to go on.

She parked in front of the house and kept the engine idling so she could have heat. Again and again her eyes strayed to the rearview mirror in anticipation of their arrival. She had no idea what she would say when she saw them; her mind remained a blank in that regard. She stopped trying to rehearse something in favor of letting things play out as they would. Maybe Mitch would think tongue-tied was charming.

Thea's concentration on the view behind her was such that she was blindsided. The tap on the passenger window made her jump in her seat.

"Sorry," Mitch said.

Thea was not given to dramatic gestures so the hand she placed over her heart was truly meant to keep it in her chest. She leaned back in her seat slowly; her head swiveled toward the window. Mitch did not look particularly apologetic. In fact, he looked as if he were trying to keep from laughing. Behind his glasses, his eyes were bright and there was the faint hint of amusement in the line of his mouth. Thea found the button for the passenger-side window and pressed it. "Where did you come from?" She winced as she realized how accusing she sounded. "I mean," she said more gently, "where did you come from?"

Grinning openly now, Mitch leaned into the open space. He used one thumb to point over his shoulder. "I live here, remember? Why didn't you get out and ring the bell?"

"I didn't think anyone was here. I was waiting for you and the kids to get home from church."

"I'm playing hooky again this week, trying to get some work done. Mum and Dad have the kids." His brow creased momentarily. "That was you on the phone? Four rings, no message?"

She nodded. "Do you mind?" she asked. "Is it all right that I'm here?"

"It's more than all right. It's perfect." He made a gesture that indicated the interior of the Volvo. "Unless you don't want to go car shopping with us. That's what we have on the agenda today. The kids are kind of looking forward to it."

"Then that's fine."

"Great. Turn off your car and come in. It'll be about ten more minutes before they get here. There's no sense in waiting out here."

Thea rolled up the window and depressed the ignition button. Mitch waited for her to get out and come around the car, and then he walked with her into the house. Thea joined him in removing her shoes in spite of his protest that she didn't have to. "I was riding this morning," she told him. "Trust me, you don't want what I might have on them tracked on your carpets."

Mitch took her jacket and regarded her jeans and cable-knit sweater with some skepticism. "Riding? I thought people like you wore those funny balloon pants when they rode."

"Jodhpurs."

"Yeah. Balloon pants."

"I do when I want to amuse people like you."

He grinned and closed the closet door. "Let's go in the kitchen. Can I get you something to drink? I have orange juice in a carton. You don't have to work for it."

"Sounds good."

Mitch went to the refrigerator and removed the carton. He hefted it once in his hand, making certain he *really* had something to offer, then poured her a glass. "Here you go."

Thea accepted the glass and sat down at the table. She thought she would feel uncomfortable in his kitchen, the site of that disturbing kiss, but the only thing that disturbed her was how uncommonly comfortable she felt. "You don't

have to entertain me," she said. "Go back to your work if
you like."

"I don't like." Mitch picked up his coffee mug and joined
her at the table. "I was taking a break when I saw you sitting
in your car. Now it will be a longer one. I'm working ahead
anyway."

"Isn't that a little risky for a political cartoonist? I thought
your work had to be timely to be effective."

"A day or two ahead doesn't usually catch me off guard.
A catastrophic event, something like a terrorist attack, for
instance, is immediately in the public's conscious and re-
quires a timely response, but satirizing or commenting on
broader issues, say, partisan politics or this administration's
domestic policy, doesn't necessarily require the same reaction time. In fact, sometimes the public needs a few days to
assimilate an issue so the cartoon's point of view makes
sense to them. They don't have to agree, but they do have
to understand the context."

"You like your work, don't you?"

Her question surprised him because of the hint of a pensive quality in her voice. Until just this moment Mitch
would have put money down on the fact that he and Thea
Wyndham enjoyed their careers equally. Now he suspected
it would have been a sucker's bet. "I'm very happy doing
what I do."

Expecting that answer, Thea nodded. "It shows—in your
work and in the way you talk about it." Before he could ask
her about advertising at Foster and Wyndham, she changed
the subject. "Will Gina be looking for cars with us?"

"On a Sunday? Never. Sundays are reserved for open
houses. I think she has three scheduled today. She'll be with
clients, pitching their homes to prospective buyers all afternoon and probably into the evening." Turning the discussion
to Gina and real estate reminded Mitch that he still hadn't
apologized for his boorish behavior the night before. He re-

garded Thea frankly. "One of these days I'm going to learn that if I didn't behave badly I wouldn't be saying I'm sorry so often."

She stared at him blankly.

"I'm talking about last night. I was not exactly the Good Humor Man. Gina would say I was a regular pain in the ass, but then she doesn't like to mince words." He lifted his coffee mug, shrugging slightly in the same motion. "Soooo," he said on a sigh, "I'm apologizing. Again."

Thea smiled. "I'm not keeping score."

"Good."

"Not on the number of apologies," she said. "I like to judge them in terms of form and degree of contrition."

"How'd I do?"

"Not bad. I give it a seven."

He laughed. "I hope that's on a ten scale. I lost points for my late delivery, didn't I?"

She nodded. "You appeared properly abashed but there was a certain lack of responsibility in your language. For instance, backhandedly describing yourself as 'not exactly the Good Humor Man,' instead of saying you were surly, and using terms that Gina would use, rather than acknowledging the ass thing yourself."

"Wow. There's a lot to this judging stuff."

Both of Thea's brows lifted. "Hmmm."

Mitch laughed again at her butter-wouldn't-melt expression and he realized quite suddenly how glad he was that she showed up. On the heels of that thought it occurred to him that she had never explained her presence. "So what brings you here?" he asked. "Not that I'm not grateful for the help today. Until you showed up I was going to have to take my mother's minivan out to the car lots. Frankly, it was killing me."

Thea gave him a quick, unaffected grin, the corners of her wide mouth lifting in appreciation. A single man who owned a restored Chevy truck and an Indian was understandably reluctant to get behind the wheel of a vehicle that symbolized family values, suburban settlement, and carpooling commitments. If it didn't kill him, he would at the very least be shaken. "Then I'm glad I was moved by impulse," she said. "I don't have a better explanation than that."

Mitch lifted his mug toward Thea. "To impulse."

She touched the mug with her glass and drank. "So why are you looking for a new car now?"

"I don't want to keep depending on Gina," he said. It was not a lie but it was limited as far as explanations went. "It isn't fair to her. The kids love her SUV, though. The banana car is all that and then some as far as they're concerned."

"Understandable. What are you looking for?"

"Something big enough to hold us comfortably that is not a minivan."

"Put a sidecar on your Indian."

"Don't think it hasn't occurred to me," he said dryly. "I'm open to most of the possibilities. The kids get a vote and I have the veto."

"How presidential." She hesitated a moment, uncertain how to pose her question without insulting him. Her lips pressed together as she mulled it over.

"What is it?" he asked, reading her expression.

Thea glanced at him. "Well, I was wondering . . . since you have to buy this car because the children are living with you . . . I'd like to help you finance it."

Mitch paused deliberately before he answered. He knew her offer was sincerely meant, but he couldn't help feeling that she didn't think he was able to provide for the kids on his own. "It's been a long time since I needed a cosigner for a loan," he said finally.

She reached across the table to touch him but let her hand fall short of the mark as she realized what she was about to do. "I wasn't thinking you needed help, Mitch. I was only thinking that I'd *like* to help. I'm not making this offer to salve a guilty conscience." Thea watched Mitch's brows rise another notch above the thin frames of his glasses as he greeted this statement with skepticism. "All right," she admitted, "not entirely because of that. My other reason is pretty straightforward: I want to provide for the children, too. I hope you're not going to deny me that at every turn."

Mitch's eyes narrowed faintly as he considered what she'd said. He studied her unshuttered expression and concluded that she was in earnest. Her hesitation in broaching the subject reminded him of how he had reacted to a similar offer at Wayne's office. It took some courage for her to bring it up to him again, especially since his instinct was to respond in exactly the same way. "Look, Thea," he said quietly, "if it's a choice between the kids seeing you or you helping to support them, then I'm going to pick the former. The kids will, too."

Her eyes widened. "No! No, it's not like that. Not one or the other. I understand why you don't believe me, but I'm not setting this up as a choice. I want to do both."

Mitch believed she meant it, but he was not as certain as Thea that she could follow through. "What does Joel think?"

There was a slight pause, then, "Joel supports what I want to do."

Which wasn't precisely an answer to his question, Mitch realized. He let it go because if Joel supported her, it didn't really matter what he thought about her decision. Outside, Mitch heard a car pull into the driveway. "Let's see what kind of cost I get into with the car," he said, getting to his feet. "There's insurance money from Gabe and Kathy's accident. Their vehicle was totaled. I think Wayne said I could expect a few thousand from that."

Thea wanted to protest that he was missing the point, but he was already moving away from the table to the side entrance. She had also heard the car and knew it signaled the kids' arrival. What remained of their discussion would have to wait until they were sequestered in a cubicle at the car dealer's.

Thea got as far as the hallway when Emilie rushed in. The little girl threw her arms around Thea and hugged her hard. "I knew you'd come back," she said, her face buried against Thea's thick sweater. "I told them you would." Emilie released her hold and looked up at Thea, her expression solemn. "You promised to do my nails."

It was the perfect reminder of how important it was to keep promises, even those hastily made. Thea felt something stir inside her, an anxiousness that came with the weight of the responsibility she was accepting, and conversely, a lightening in the region of her heart that felt very much like joy. She could not remember ever having such a keen awareness of opposing feelings, let alone being able to manage them both.

"Why are you smiling?" asked Emilie.

"Because you make me happy," said Thea. *And scare me to death.* "I have the polish with me. It's in my glove box. Come on. We'll get it out of my car." Thea got her purse and she and Emilie headed outside. The twins and Mitch were still in the driveway talking to Mitch's parents. Mitch was standing by the driver's side listening to what his father was saying while Case and Grant hovered by Mrs. Baker's window, holding out their hands for loose change from the bottom of her purse.

Mitch glanced at Thea as she walked out. "Here she is," he said to his dad. "Thea? You remember my father?"

"Of course." She handed her purse to Emilie and gestured toward her car. "It's a pleasure to see you again, Mr. Baker." Thea held her hand out to him. "It's been a long time."

Bill Baker reached through the open window and took Thea's hand. "So how's my favorite redhead?"

"After Lucy, you mean."

"Goes without saying."

Thea laughed. "I'm well, thank you. And you?"

"I'm not complaining." He released Thea's hand and cocked his head toward his wife. "I leave that to Jennie."

"I suppose a good marriage needs a division of labor."

"Exactly."

Thea was beginning to feel the cold seep in through her sweater but she bent lower to look in the window and greet Mitch's mother. "Hello, Mrs. Baker."

Jennie shooed the twins away, closed the window, and swiveled in Thea's direction, all with the fluid motion of a woman used to doing several things at once. "I thought that was your car," she said. "I told Bill it was as soon as we turned the corner. How are you, dear?"

"Fine, thank you."

Bill rolled his eyes. "She's shivering, Jennie. Let's let her get back in the house. You can grill Mitch later."

Jennie gave her husband a playful slug in the arm. "I don't grill my son," she told Thea.

Behind her, Thea thought she heard Mitch snort. "I'm going to the car dealers with them," she explained, trying to save Mitch the third degree later. "My Volvo's been commandeered. Apparently Mitch has some issues with your minivan."

Bill grunted in agreement. "Don't I know it. That's Jennie's car. Which is why, since we're going antiquing today, and I'm driving, we're in this one."

Thea suspected from the way Bill said it, that he and Jennie had been over that ground earlier in the day.

Jennie pulled a face. "Don't you listen to him," she said. "We're not in the van for one reason only, and that's because he thinks I can't buy anything bigger than a breadbox if we can't haul it home. What? He thinks I don't know about UPS?"

Thea gave a start as Mitch's hand lightly wrapped itself

around the nape of her neck and applied gentle pressure to get her to step back from the car.

"Trust me," he said. "You don't want to get involved in this." Releasing her, he took her place at the window. "Have a good time," he said. "Love you both. Don't spend my inheritance." He straightened, tapped the hood, and his father took his cue to put the car in reverse and back out of the driveway. Mitch waved at his mother who waved back gaily and blew kisses to the twins and Emilie. "That was close," he told Thea. "They almost had you."

Thea wasn't entirely sure what Mitch's parents had wanted her for but she knew he was right. "Then, thank you."

"If you really understood, your thanks would be a lot warmer than that." He placed his hand on the small of her back and gave her a nudge toward the house. "Inside. Before you freeze. C'mon, guys. Everyone in."

Emilie and the boys needed no further encouragement. Case and Grant raced inside, Sunday school papers flapping in their hands. Emilie followed a little more slowly, holding Thea's purse above her head like the Stanley Cup.

"What's she doing?" Mitch asked.

"I promised to paint her nails the last time I was here," Thea said. "And I never got around to it. I let her get the polish out of my car. I suppose she put it in my purse. We have time, don't we?"

"Sure. I'm going to make them lunch first. You can do it then."

Thea and Emilie retired to Emilie's room for girl talk and a manicure while Mitch made sandwiches and the twins played cars on the carpet road map in the living room. Emilie flashed her neon pink fingertips for everyone to admire during lunch. She had a hard time eating and watching her nails at the same time. Each time she raised her sandwich she went a little cross-eyed.

The children piled into Thea's Volvo as soon as the

dishwasher was loaded. Thea pointed Mitch in the direction of the driver's side door. "You know where you want to go," she said. "There's no sense in me driving."

Mitch accepted the duty gratefully and slid behind the wheel. "Thanks," he told her. "I appreciate this."

Thea just smiled and leaned back, enjoying having someone else in the driver's seat. They drove out of town to a strip of car dealers on the main throughway. At each location they spilled out of the car and began a search of the lot. Thea realized that Mitch had not been kidding when he said he was open to just about anything. They looked at American cars and foreign models, high-end and low-end in terms of cost and features. Thea showed the boys how to kick the tires while Mitch rolled his eyes; later she questioned salesmen as to why there were no cars in a color that matched Emilie's nail polish. Each time Mitch caught the gist of their conversation he buried his head under the hood of the nearest showroom vehicle and investigated engine mounting.

The dealers closed early on Sunday so after the doors shut behind them at the Ford showroom, Mitch decided they should retire to a local Mexican restaurant for dinner and discuss their favorites. The kids were willing to negotiate every aspect of the car purchase except one: they wanted a black car with smoked windows.

"We'll look like drug dealers," Mitch protested.

"Nuh-uh," Emilie said. "Movie stars."

"James Bond," Case said.

Grant got to the point. "We can make faces and no one can see us."

Thea bent her head, ignoring Mitch's plea for help, and began constructing her fajita. She smiled to herself while Mitch argued a little longer, but she could tell he was doing it for show. He wanted the kids to think they had won a big point when the truth was he was so happy they didn't want a yellow car that he could scarcely contain himself.

The kids did justice to their dinner, though Case drank too many Cokes and had to make an extra restroom run. They all passed on fried ice cream, sitting back in their chairs and examining their slightly distended bellies instead. Over their heads, Mitch and Thea exchanged amused glances, and without a word passing between them, mimicked their behavior.

We're just like a real family. The errant thought brought Thea upright and back to reality. She felt Mitch's eyes on her, watching her, almost as if he were privy to what she was thinking. Her stomach turned over and for a moment she thought she might be sick.

"Excuse me," she said, rising from the table. Without a word, she hurried to the restroom where she could look in the mirror and confront herself with the truth that she didn't belong.

Chapter 7

Mitch called Thea late in the week and asked to meet her for lunch on Friday when he would be in town. He could sense her hesitation, that almost infinitesimal pause as she searched for a plausible excuse. Before she came up with one, he dangled the hook: "I've decided on a vehicle," he said. Then he baited it. "I could use your help."

She bit and he felt guilty for about a nanosecond. He still didn't know what had gone wrong last Sunday, but he could almost pinpoint the moment when things tanked. He hadn't missed the look of panic in her eyes as she jumped up from the table at the restaurant and disappeared into the restroom. The kids hadn't thought there was anything odd about it, putting down the quick escape to a potty emergency. They were used to Grant waiting until the absolute last minute to announce he needed to go NOW, but Mitch doubted that Thea's hasty retreat was prompted by anything so simple as a call of nature.

When she returned to them, he sensed the change. She participated in their conversation, even seemed to enjoy herself, yet he couldn't shake the feeling that she was forcing herself in some way. She shied away from meeting his eyes, but when he caught her unexpectedly, the look he saw in hers was no longer panicked, but wounded and determined, the look of someone toughing it out. He did not have an opportunity to glimpse it again. Thea made sure of it.

He asked her to choose the restaurant and she picked a grill not far from her work. They purposely chose a late lunch in order to avoid the crowds and have a measure of privacy. Thea ordered a salad with oil and vinegar dressing; Mitch had a burger with everything. They merely shook their heads at what passed for each other's idea of a good lunch.

With the pleasantries and orders behind them, Thea pressed the purpose of their meeting. "So what kind of car are you getting?"

"Black with smoked windows."

She didn't smile. The line of her mouth even thinned a little. "That's a given."

Mitch realized he was in serious trouble. Thea wasn't simply tense; she had her shields up. "The Ford."

Thea nodded. "The SUV."

"Yeah. It fit us, the price is the going rate for one of those, it meets the kids' requirements, and it's not a minivan."

"How can I help?"

"They don't have the exact car that I want on the lot so it has to be driven in. I think they found one in Cleveland with a manual transmission. Apparently manual's a big deal. Not many people want one." He shook his head, mystified that people didn't want to really *drive* their car. "The first chance I'll have to pick it up is next Saturday, but I need a ride to the dealer. Mum and Dad are taking the kids that weekend—it's been planned for a while now—and Amy and her husband aren't available. I tried a couple of—"

"I get the idea that I was way down on the list."

"No," he said quickly. "Not exactly. I mean, you were, but that's because I didn't want to bother you."

"Right. You didn't want to bother me, but we're having

lunch together because you couldn't possibly have asked me this on the phone. I think you better tell me what's really going on, Mitchell."

Mitchell? Oh, boy. "Have you been talking to my mother?"

Thea gave him an arch look. "No. But it's tempting."

He surrendered, holding up both hands, palms out. "I wanted to see you again. That's all."

His honesty almost disarmed her. Thea said levelly, "You might have simply said that."

"Then you and I wouldn't be having lunch now." He lowered his hands. "You would have said no and I would be licking my wounds for a fifth time."

"This isn't a date."

He ignored that. "Anyway, I really do need a ride to the dealer."

"Mitch, you could have the dealer drive the car to your house. They'll do that for you."

"Really?"

"Yes, really."

Mitch leaned back in his chair and studied her, his head cocked to the side. "So," he said finally, "I can't get a ride from you?"

"I'll call the dealer for you and have them deliver the car."

He shook his head. "Don't bother."

"It's no bother. Driving out to your house and then backtracking to the dealer is a bother."

"You have something planned for that Saturday?"

"That's not the point. The fact is, I don't. Joel's off somewhere that week and I'm on my own."

"Then why won't you come out and spend it with me?"

Thea simply stared at him. He appeared perfectly serious. "I don't think that's a good idea," she said quietly. To punctuate her point, she raised her left hand.

Mitch's eyes did not stray once to her engagement ring but remained steady on hers. "You kissed me back."

Thea blinked first. "That's not fair."

"It doesn't matter if it's fair. It's a fact. Am I supposed to pretend it didn't happen?"

"Can't you?"

"Are you serious? Thea, why should I? There's always been something between us. I've never understood why you won't own up to it."

"But I have: every time you asked me out and I said no." Not wanting to be defensive, but hating that he thought she hadn't been honest in her own fashion, Thea let the words lie there.

Mitch's mouth pulled to one side as he mulled over her response. "*That's* why you won't go out with me? Because there *is* something there? What the hell kind of logic is that?"

"It's Thea-logical."

He couldn't help himself; he laughed. "God, I walked into that one." He shook his head in appreciation. "All right, so you've admitted to something in a backhanded kind of way. Where does that leave us?"

Before she could answer, the waiter approached with their orders. Thea thought her appetite had fled, but when the salad was placed in front of her, she realized the effect of Mitch's company was exactly the opposite. She was starving. It was difficult not to look longingly at his burger and fries.

"Live dangerously," he said, pushing his plate toward her. "Have a fry."

So much for not giving herself away. Thea chose the plumpest, greasiest fry in the pile and bit into it. Her mouth rejoiced. It was all she could do not to close her eyes.

Watching her, Mitch found himself grinning. The only thing that would have made the moment better was if he had fed her the French fry himself. "More?" he asked when she'd finished.

She shook her head. "That took the edge off. Thanks."

Thea splashed oil and vinegar on her salad. "Have you thought about letting me help you financially?"

Mitch had his sandwich halfway to his mouth. "You really want to ruin this burger for me, don't you?"

Thea waved at him to eat up and speared lettuce and a medallion of cucumber with her fork. "What if I pay the first half of your car loan?"

"What makes you so sure I got a loan?"

"Didn't you?"

"Yeah, five years, but you could at least pretend I paid cash."

She waggled her fork at him. "Now who's not facing reality?" Thea got away with her pointed question because Mitch's mouth was full of burger. "What if I pay the first two and a half years? Before you protest, consider that it's not even half of your real cost. You still have insurance and maintenance. Did you put anything down?"

Mitch removed one hand from his sandwich to make a circle with his thumb and forefinger. Big goose egg.

"Okay, so you're financing the whole thing. All the more reason I should help out."

Mitch swallowed, put his sandwich back on his plate, and took a drink. "Come out next weekend."

"Or what? You won't take my money?"

"Something like that."

Conscious of other diners, Thea leaned forward, her voice soft and insistent. "Where the hell is the logic in that?"

He considered the question. "Nope," he said, shrugging. "I don't have a snappy answer."

"Be serious."

"I am."

Exasperated, Thea watched Mitch pick up his burger, take another bite, and chew with evident enjoyment. "The children aren't even going to be there."

"So? Didn't you and I have a conversation about getting

to know each other? I happen to think it's important we do some of that away from the kids. Honestly, Thea, if I thought I could have just laid this out over the phone, I would have." Yeah, right. "But I figured you were going to take some convincing and it needed to be done in person. What can it hurt to spend some time together?"

Her eyes narrowed briefly, gauging his sincerity. "Then I won't have to fend off any smarmy seduction thing."

"I resent the characterization of my seduction as a thing."

"You're making me crazy," she whispered. "You know that?"

"You want to laugh. You know you do."

"Hah! I want to choke you."

"Who are you kidding? You're afraid to get that close to me."

Thea's mouth snapped shut.

Mitch's smile was smug.

They finished their lunch in silence.

She didn't call him at any time during the next week but Mitch didn't doubt that she would show up on Saturday. That's what he told himself. The reason he kept getting up from his drafting board and going to the front window was because he needed to stretch his legs and give the muse a little workout. It was a bald lie, of course, but he had no problem with that.

By the time she arrived, Mitch had finished inking, scanning, and sending his work to his editor. The cartoon skewered a congressional committee's prurient cross-examination of porn industry entrepreneurs. It had an ironic *ick* factor, and he thought it was probably good enough to get him some love-it/hate-it mail in the next few days. He considered blogging about it, but elected to keep a vigil by the window. When he saw Thea's car, he rolled off the couch and stepped back so she couldn't possibly suspect he had been looking for her. If someone was going to have the upper hand, he'd rather it was him.

He walked into the kitchen to get himself something to drink. It was all part of his plan to appear casual, not overconfident. He'd go to the door twenty or so seconds after she rang the bell, Pepsi in hand, and affect . . . what? Warmth? Mild surprise? Enthusiasm? He decided on mild surprise as the least threatening response. Pretty darn good plan.

There was a last-minute change of Pepsi to Dr. Pepper, but Mitch was flexible on these details. He popped the top, wiggled the tab free, and threw it into a plastic container on the countertop with the rest of the twins' collection. The elementary school was collecting them to help kids visualize the enormity of a million, and Mitch promised the boys he'd do his part, though he wished the school had decided to collect beer caps.

Okay, where was she? The doorbell should have rung by now. Switching soft drinks was one thing, but she was playing hell with his timing. Mild surprise could easily evolve into mild annoyance.

Mitch watched the clock on the microwave advance another minute before he sidled into the living room. He could see her car through the sheer curtains, but he couldn't make out whether or not she was still in it without parting them. He caved to curiosity and knelt on the sofa, inching the curtains open with his free hand.

She was talking on her cell.

Rolling his eyes, Mitch let the curtains fall in place. He turned around and dropped into a half-reclining position on the sofa, resting his head on the curved back and stretching his long legs out in front of him. He held the cold can between his palms at the level of his belt buckle and wondered how long he might have to wait her out. The question of the identity of the person on the other end of that call occupied Mitch's thoughts for a while.

The likelihood that it was Joel Strahern did not bode well for the smarmy seduction thing he'd been contemplating.

Thea pressed the phone closer to her ear. "What if this is a mistake, Rosie?"

"What if it is?" came the practical reply. "How you gonna know if you don't give it a shot? Anyway, isn't this a little late to be asking the question?"

"I've been asking it the whole way here," Thea said. "I just couldn't reach you until now."

"Robby was on the phone, and he never answers call waiting. That's another reason I'm going to divorce his ass one of these days. But back to you. Since this is the first I've heard about this trip and we've been on the phone about three times already this week, I'm thinking you don't really want to be talked out of it."

"Then why I am calling you?"

"You want my blessing."

"You think so?"

"Honey, I've been there. You're setting me up to take the fall if this doesn't work out."

"I wouldn't do that."

"Sure you would. But you'd be real nice about it. I'm giving you a gift here. You decide. You live with your decision. You live with the consequences. And no matter what happens, you don't beat yourself up or reach for the pills. It's just life happening to you, honey. Nothing more."

Thea took a deep breath and let it out slowly. Just life. She would rely on herself, not emotional painkillers. She *would*. "Mitch is going to be wondering what's keeping me," she said, glancing toward the house. At least he wasn't staring at her from the living room window.

"Let him wait. It won't kill him. And if it does, he'll die happy."

"Is that what Robby tells you?"

"No, that's what I tell him."

Thea laughed and the timbre of it was only a little shaky.

"See? You're sounding better already. What did Joel say when you told him about going up to Mitch's today?"

"What makes you think I told Joel?"

"Because as much as you don't mind foolin' yourself, it pains you to deliberately fool other people. So what did he say?"

"He said I should do what I need to do." There was a pause, and Thea could imagine Rosie was screwing up her face in disbelief. Her next words verified it.

"He really said that?"

"He really did."

"Then there's something's wrong with him, honey."

"He's trying to be supportive by giving me time."

"Time to step out on him? Supportive of you with the other guy? I don't think so. That man's whole life has been mergers and acquisitions."

"What are you saying?"

"Me? I'm not saying anything. You still wearin' that rock?"

Thea looked down at her left hand lying over the center of the steering wheel. "I took it off Tuesday after I talked to him."

"Then I guess you know what I'm not saying."

Perhaps she did, Thea thought. Joel hadn't put up much of a fight when she told him about Mitch's request. Thea hadn't really wanted to think about that. Rosie was right about her being willing to fool herself. "I didn't leave it at home. It's in my purse. I could still put it on."

Rosie snorted. "Sha-zaam!"

Silence followed. "I get your point," Thea said finally, quietly. "The ring doesn't have any magical properties to

protect me." Or at least it didn't anymore. If she put it back
on now she would know how self-serving it was, even if
Mitch didn't. She couldn't do that. It wasn't just that it was
dishonest to Mitch, but that it meant using Joel so dis-
honestly. "Maybe I should put it in the glove compartment."

"Leave it where it is. You can't find anything in that purse
of yours anyway."

Thea smiled. "I'm hanging up, Rosie."

"Have fun!"

Trust Rosie to get in the last word before she ended the
call. *Have fun.* Easy for her to say. Thea turned off her phone
and dropped it into her purse. She looked over at the house
and tried to remember if she had ever known how to have
fun. The fact that nothing specific came to her mind wasn't
at all encouraging.

Thea rang the bell, startled when the door opened immediately. Mitch was standing there with something like a
scowl on his face and a crushed Dr. Pepper can in his fist.
She actually took a step back. "Do I have the wrong day?"

"No." He held the door open for her but she didn't move
in his direction.

Thea's weight shifted from one foot to the other. "I'll wait
here until you get your coat. Or weren't you planning to go
to the dealer's right away?"

"That's fine." He disappeared into the house. Out of
Thea's sight he did a mock banging of his head against the
wall before he got his jacket. Feeling marginally better, he
pitched the pop can then found his shoes and slipped them
on. Thea was waiting by her car when he returned to the
front porch. He wouldn't have been surprised if she suggested he ride in the backseat.

She didn't. They got in simultaneously and buckled up.

Thea started the car but didn't take it out of park immediately. She looked over at Mitch. "Am I late?"

"You can't be. I didn't tell you a time."

"Then I interrupted you in the middle of something."

"No."

"So you're irritated because . . ."

"I'm not irritated." He flashed her a grin. "See?"

Thea regarded him skeptically, her mouth pursed to one side. "Never mind. I don't want to know." She put the Volvo into drive and started down the street. "You never did tell me where your parents took the kids this weekend. Emilie said something about skiing when I spoke to her but I wasn't sure I got it right."

"You did. They went to Seven Springs. Dad's going to spend the weekend in the hot tub, and mum will have the kids on the beginner slopes. It's still cold enough for making snow. If the forecast is right, they might get some fresh powder tonight."

"There's snow in the forecast?"

"A couple of inches the last time I checked."

Thea glanced at the sky. It was still clear and sunny, not a cloud on the horizon. Although she realized the temperature had been dropping since morning, she figured Mitch's sources were wrong about the snow. The first day of spring was only a week away, and there was that adage about March going out like a lamb to consider. Doppler radar was overrated.

"Why didn't you go with them?" asked Thea.

"I thought about it, but I realized I could get a lot done if they were gone. Besides, Mum and Dad really wanted to do it. They've taken the kids before, even when Gabe and Kathy were alive." He heard his words and fell silent.

More to herself than to Mitch, Thea said, "It's still hard to believe."

Mitch simply nodded.

"Last week I picked up the phone and called Gabe. I had his number on my speed dial. I didn't even realize what I'd done until I heard the voice telling me the number had been disconnected. I cried off and on for the rest of the day."

"Yeah, I know that feeling."

She believed him. "What do you do? I mean, with the kids around."

"They pick up on it pretty quick so there's no point in trying to pretend it's something else. I tell them I'm sad and why and we talk about it and go on. Emilie tends to cling a little more to me than the boys do. Maybe it's because they're identical and have some kind of twin weirdness happening."

Thea smiled. "Wonder twin powers! Activate!"

"How's that again?"

"It's from a cartoon show that Gabe and I used to watch. The twins would put their rings together and say that phrase and take on the bad guys. Maybe that's what Case and Grant do, in their own way."

"Makes sense to me. It's better than my alien theory." He glanced over at Thea and saw her smile had deepened. Better. "Anyway, getting Emilie out was a good thing, I figured. She was allowed to take a friend and that seemed to help. She only asked two or three times if I was going with them."

"I think she has a crush on you."

"Don't say that. It creeps me out."

"Why? She probably had a crush on Gabe. Didn't you ever read Freud? Then there's the whole transference piece that I don't really understand, but it's probably important."

"If you start talking about penis envy I'm throwing myself out of the car."

"Don't worry. No girl really wants one of those."

"I beg to differ."

Thea couldn't look over because of the traffic, but she bet he was smirking. "I don't think we're talking about quite the same thing any longer. Clean it up, Mitchell, or I'll throw you out of the car myself."

"Are you certain you haven't talked to my mother?"

"I'm certain, but I'm thinking more and more it's a good idea." The next sound Thea thought she heard was Mitch's mouth clamping shut. "It's perfectly natural for Emilie to develop an attachment to you. It will pass eventually. How does she act around Gina?"

That was hard for Mitch to answer since he and Gina hadn't done more than talk on the phone a few times since the we-can-be-friends speech. "For a while I thought there would be a catfight, but she's been better lately." That was true, at least.

The line of Thea's mouth flattened so she wouldn't laugh. A catfight? With Gina? Good for Emilie. When she was certain she was composed, she said, "One day you'll come to the realization that Emilie no longer thinks you hang the stars and—"

"And I'll hate it," he finished, resigned. "I know. I've thought about that. She has me wrapped."

Thea didn't say anything.

Mitch looked over and saw her pensive expression. "What is it? You think it's a problem she has me around her finger?"

Chewing on the inside of her cheek, Thea didn't answer immediately. How much did Mitch really want to know about her? How much did she want to tell? "I was thinking she was lucky," she said quietly. "It wasn't like that with my father. Either of them."

Either of them? Mitch frowned until he remembered the past that Gabe and Thea had really shared. "That's right. You were adopted."

She didn't glance in his direction. "I always wondered if you knew."

"Was it supposed to be a secret?"

"No, not really. I'm not ashamed of it or anything." There was a little catch in her breath as she heard herself say the words. In the back of her mind she could hear Rosie again. *Foolin' yourself, honey.* "Gabe and I were in the same foster home until we were five."

"The Reasoners."

Thea nodded. "They adopted him when he was four but they weren't allowed to take me. I had some medical problems. For a while the doctors thought I was going to lose a kidney. The surgery, the drugs, the aftercare . . . no one thought the Reasoners could financially handle it. There was no real help for adoptive parents in those days. They had to manage on their own. As long as I remained in foster care the county's children's services looked after me and paid my medical bills."

"But you were eventually adopted."

"Uh-huh. I stayed with the Reasoners another year as their foster child. They shuttled me to doctors, watched what I ate, made certain I had my medicine. I didn't understand there was any difference in Gabe's status in the home than there was mine. He was just my brother. I knew the Reasoners weren't my parents because I could remember my own, but it seemed to me that Gabe was really my brother." Thea paused and resolutely pushed down the lump in her throat. Her eyes remained dry. "Do you know what permanency planning is?"

Mitch shook his head. "I never heard of it."

"It's a policy that holds to the notion that foster kids shouldn't be shuttled from place to place."

"That seems reasonable."

Thea went on. "But stability isn't supposed to be achieved in a foster home if it can be helped. That's success of a lesser nature. Adoption is the holy grail."

Mitch understood the problem. "So, for permanency

planning to work for you, you had to be moved from the foster home. Is that what happened?"

"In a nutshell." She shrugged. "I suppose it depends on your point of view as to how well it worked. Children's services saw it as a coup. They got me off their rolls and into a family that could financially absorb my medical bills. The Wyndhams were like the poster parents for the adoption advocates, so it was good for them. I had to leave the Reasoners and Gabe but . . ." Thea simply allowed her words to trail off. It still caught her off guard sometimes, this pain.

"Thea?" Mitch said softly. "Are you all right?" Her face was pale and in profile her features appeared cast in marble.

She nodded, gave him a sideways glance, and smiled. "Oh, yeah. It's not Dickens, you know. No *Oliver Twist.* I was lucky." When she saw him frown slightly, she added more emphatically, "Really, Mitch. I was very lucky."

Mitch suspected she said that for his benefit. In spite of her quick grin and her words, there was something she wasn't saying. "Did you lose touch with Gabe and the Reasoners?"

"For a while. I didn't think Barb and John—the Reasoners—knew where I was. Later, I found out that they weren't allowed to contact me. Visits were prohibited by a court order. It was supposed to help me adjust to my new parents and my new home. No one explained that, though—or at least not in a way I could understand it. I thought they hated me." She shrugged. "Like most kids, I thought I had done something wrong."

Mitch just shook his head. Hearing it from her didn't make it any easier to imagine. It was that far outside his experience.

"Well," Thea said, punctuating a sigh. "Enough about me."

"Oh, no. Not so fast. How did you hook up with Gabe again?"

"You don't know?"

"I'm asking, aren't I? He was kind of tight-lipped about you. I never understood it. When Kathy first started dating Gabe I told all kinds of stories about her to him. When they got serious I actually told a few that were the truth. It was tough prying three words out of him about his friend Thea."

"You didn't even know me back then. We didn't meet until their wedding rehearsal."

"So? Kathy had a lot of anxious moments about you in the beginning."

"About me? That can't be right. Gabe was crazy in love with her."

"I don't try to understand it. I'm just reporting the facts. I figured if she saw you as the competition—and Kathy not being a slouch in the looks and brains department herself— you must be someone I'd like to know. My early plan was to make sure you didn't ruin things for my best friend by keeping you occupied myself."

Thea's head snapped around. "Oh, spare me! Are you serious?"

"Hey!" Mitch made a grab for the steering wheel. "Watch the road."

"I saw him," Thea said lamely. *Him* was the tractor trailer slowing to a stop to make a turn into a strip mall. "His brake lights are dirty."

Mitch merely grunted. He waited until Thea had clear road ahead of her before he continued. "I didn't tell Kath anything about my plan. I don't think she would have approved."

"She would have been insulted."

"Insulted? Why? I was looking out for her."

"Your actions suggest that you thought she couldn't keep Gabe on her own."

He sighed, running his fingers through his hair. "I don't get women."

"I know." She saw the car dealer up ahead and slowed to make the turn. "So what happened to your plan?"

"I couldn't get much out of Gabe about you. Tight-lipped, remember? He wouldn't hook me up with you." Not then, anyway.

"He was probably looking out for me," she said, grinning. "See how that sort of thinking worked against you?"

"I'm learning."

"Good." She pulled into the car lot and found a parking space on the side of the showroom. "Let's go see about your wheels, Mr. I-have-a-plan."

Mitch had to admit it seemed ludicrous in retrospect. At the time, he thought he'd had a stroke of genius. "Most likely, just a stroke," he muttered.

"What's that?" Thea asked, getting out of the car.

"Nothing." He pretended he didn't hear her laughing, but by the time they reached the doors, he was laughing himself.

Thea actually missed Mitch's company on the way back to Connaugh Creek. He followed her because she refused to have her view of the road blocked by his new SUV. Besides, she'd told him if he was stopped because he looked like a drug dealer, her plan was to drive on and leave him there.

The final paperwork on the car was finished without any arguing between them. Thea had her checkbook out before Mitch realized what she was doing. She paid the first thirty months off in one lump sum, essentially putting half down on the vehicle and reducing Mitch's monthly payments to a figure that was completely manageable. He could have stopped her, she knew, but he must have known she wasn't going to give in easily.

Mitch parked the SUV in the driveway while Thea stopped on the street. They walked in together through the garage. Thea noticed he'd made no attempt to make room for the new vehicle. It was doubtful there'd ever be enough space for it.

"I think you're going to need a larger house," she said. "Or at least a larger garage."

"I'm considering it." His voice held none of the humor hers did.

"You are?" Thea kicked off her shoes and padded into the house in her socks. "Seriously?" She took Mitch's jacket and her own to the closet while he went to the kitchen. "How long have you been thinking about that?" she called to him.

"Since about a week after the kids came to live with me."

Thea brought herself up short, sliding a little on the kitchen tile as she entered the room. "A week? But I thought you didn't even want the kids back then. You were still trying to get me to take them."

"I never thought that I wouldn't *ever* have them," he said. "Anyway, you weren't around and no one knew where you were, and I was thinking ahead to the what-ifs."

Thea leaned against the counter, her arms folded loosely in front of her, and regarded Mitch thoughtfully. He was looking for something in a cupboard, his back to her. "You really are one of the good guys, Mitchell Baker."

Mitch's hand froze over a bag of rice. He pulled it out of the cupboard, set it down, and turned around. "Yeah? You think so?"

She nodded. "I do."

His eyes narrowed faintly, consideringly. There was only about six feet separating them, and he closed the distance before Thea understood his intent. He heard her breath catch, saw her lips part, but he gave her no time to move or raise an objection. His mouth touched hers, lightly at first, and when she didn't push him away, he pressed his small advantage, tasting her lips carefully, finding the shape of them, first with his own mouth, then with the tip of his tongue. His hands rested on either side of her elbows on the counter, but they gradually moved closer together, cupping her arms, then gliding downward until he had her waist between them.

Her mouth was warm and soft. He touched the underside of her lip with the tip of his tongue. She was silky. Damp. His teeth clamped down gently on her lower lip. She made a tiny whimpering sound. Mitch shifted the position of his mouth, slanting over hers hard this time. His palms found her bottom and jerked her to him, pressing her thighs against his fly so there was no mistaking the response of his body. He surged against her, grinding his hips. Breath seemed to leave his lungs.

He tore his mouth away from hers. His nostrils flared slightly as he drew on the same air as Thea. There didn't seem to be enough. He took the next breath from her, feeling her moan softly against his mouth. His tongue slid over the ridge of her teeth. She opened for him. Her thighs settled heavily against him. He was supporting her now and she seemed almost weightless in his arms.

The kiss deepened. The pace changed to slow and drugging. Long seconds passed. Somewhere in the house a clock ticked. There was the sound of their kisses and the clock ticking. Then there was only the clock.

Mitch drew back slowly. He lifted Thea to the countertop and stood between her splayed thighs. His hands rested on her hips. Her head was slightly bowed and turned away. She wouldn't meet his eyes.

"You still think I'm one of the good guys?"

She didn't answer.

"That's what I thought." He backed up, leaving her on the counter, and tunneled through his hair with his fingertips. "You want to yell at me?"

She shook her head.

"You want to finish this?"

Now she raised her head and looked at him. The dark

centers of her eyes were so wide they nearly eclipsed the green irises. "I'm not ready."

He nodded. "I didn't think so." Mitch turned away, opened the refrigerator, and foraged for a beer. He held up the bottle of Corona. "You want one?"

"No."

Shrugging, he closed the door. He twisted off the top, tossed it on the counter, and took a long swallow of the beer. It was a relief to get something cold into his system though it was going to be a little while before his jeans fit comfortably. "I was thinking I'd make us some spiced couscous for dinner. Would you like that?"

She stared at him. "Who *are* you?"

"Hey, you saw me eat a burger, so you know I'm a regular guy." He shrugged. "I'm trying out new stuff with the kids. This way if I screw up, they don't have anything to compare it to. I apparently can't make Kathy's meat loaf right, even though I filched her recipe. After that debacle, I've been sticking to things that might satisfy uninformed taste buds. There was a lot of Vinnie's pizza in the beginning."

"Spiced couscous sounds great." She pointed to the package on the counter. "That's the rice you have out, though."

Mitch glanced at it. "I was distracted." He opened the cupboard, replaced the rice, and rummaged for the box of couscous. When he turned back with it, he saw Thea was still sitting on the counter watching him. There was still a little flush to her cheeks and her mouth looked ripe. She was wearing a loosely fitting purple turtleneck that looked great with her dark red hair and green eyes. Her socks matched her sweater. It made him wonder about her bra and panties and left him feeling a little sorrier he hadn't gotten under either the snug Levi's or the turtleneck. "You're kind of like a hood ornament sitting there: classy but not very functional. Why don't you set the table? We'll need bowls and forks. And find yourself something to drink. Napkins are—"

Thea slid off the countertop. "I remember." They traded places while she got out the dinnerware and he found the frying pan and set a kettle of water on to boil. They worked without conversation for several minutes. Mitch poured pine nuts onto a small tray and put them in the toaster oven. He gathered other ingredients as he remembered them.

"So how did you know?" Thea asked suddenly.

"Know what?" Mitch was frowning over the open cookbook. Before Thea could respond to his question, he asked her, "Can you get my glasses? They're in my office on the drafting board."

She disappeared, returning with them more quickly than she would have guessed. "Here. Don't strain yourself."

"Funny." Mitch put them on and bent over the book again. "Okay, that's a pinch of salt. I didn't think an inch of salt could be right."

"My taste buds aren't that uninformed," she told him. "I would have noticed."

He grinned, straightened, and checked the toasting pine nuts. "What was your question?"

Thea backed up to the other side of the table, setting the mats and bowls in place, before she answered. "How did you know I wasn't ready? I said I wasn't and you said you thought so. How did you know?"

Still stirring, Mitch turned halfway toward her. "You never once put your hands on me."

Thea's eyes dropped to the table. "Oh."

"It's okay, Thea. You're not ready . . . you're not ready." Mitch turned up the flame under the skillet and waited a few moments before he added a tablespoon of butter. It sizzled and began to melt. He hit the button on the mini food processor and it finished chopping the onion pieces he'd put inside. "I noticed you're not wearing your engagement ring. I probably made too much of it." He emptied the finely chopped onion into the pan and spread it out with the tip of his spoon. With his free hand he reached for his beer and took a swallow. "Plus, I was smarting from the good guy comment and the fact that I'd let you write that check at the car dealer's. Guess I thought I needed to show you I had a cock and balls." He saw her blink and a light flush steal over her fair features. "Sorry."

"It's all right." She knew her face was hot. "I know what they are and I know that you have them. I don't know why I'm blushing."

"Because you're a good girl."

"I don't mean to be."

He grinned. "You can't help it. Besides, I kind of like it." Mitch turned down the gas under the onion while he cubed an eggplant and sliced a carrot into thin medallions and a red pepper into strips. He swept the colorful contents of his cutting board into the skillet, added more butter, and stirred. When he was satisfied, he searched for and found a baguette. He put it in the oven to warm. "Tonight, ma'am, at Ye Olde Cock and Balls, our special is spiced couscous with fruit and—dare I say it?—nuts."

Thea laughed. "Do you have any lemon?"

"In the fridge."

She found it and cut a wedge for her water. "Do you want some?"

"I'm sticking with my beer."

"Beer and couscous?"

"It's my restaurant."

"Okay." She cleaned up around him, tossing a few of the things he was done with into the dishwasher, and the rinds and peels into the garbage disposal. "Look, it's snowing."

Mitch glanced out the kitchen window. "So it is. Open the patio blinds so we can watch."

Thea drew on the cord of the vertical blinds and pulled them across the track. The flagstone patio and walk, both of which had been cleared, were now covered. She turned on the porch light. It wasn't quite dark yet but the light still illuminated each individual snowflake. It was a mesmerizing dance from the moment they entered the arc of light until they fell to the ground. "Mitch?"

"Hmmm?"

"I need to tell you where I was when Gabe and Kathy were killed."

Mitch's stirring slowed. He looked over at her. She was standing at the window, her back to him. Her narrow shoulders were hunched as she hugged herself. It was a posture he didn't necessarily associate with cold. This was something else, more of a withdrawal, even as she offered to share. "That's up to you," he said carefully.

Thea turned slowly, her hands falling to her sides. "Are you familiar with Warwood Place?"

He considered her question. "That's not a Monopoly property, is it?"

She smiled faintly. "No. Not Monopoly. It's a clinic outside of Rapid City, South Dakota. At the foot of the Black Hills. Very exclusive. Very quiet."

"A clinic."

"Mmm. Rehab. Drug and alcohol." She saw his eyes shift to his beer as if he wanted to sweep it off the counter and hide it behind his back. "I've made a decision not to drink right now, but that isn't why I was there. I was abusing painkillers and tranquilizers. Pretty classic stuff. Something to keep me loose and something to keep me looser."

"Prescription?"

She nodded. "I didn't have to score illegally, if that's what you mean. It's like you said. I'm a hood ornament. Classy but not very functional."

"Jesus, Thea." Mitch dropped his spoon, started to take a step toward her, thought better of it. She was no longer hugging herself but neither was she exactly open to him. What did he have to offer her anyway? She was pretty clear earlier about not wanting someone to protect her. In any event, it was a little late for that. "I didn't mean any—"

"I know," she interrupted. "But it was a good description." She gave a short laugh that was not entirely self-mocking, but actually hinted at some humor. "I wish I had thought of it." She pointed to the skillet. "Don't burn our dinner."

Mitch automatically turned back to the meal preparation and went through the motions while his thoughts spun in a completely different direction.

Thea sat at the table and sipped her water. "Not many people know about my addiction," she said. "Gabe knew. He was the one who called me on it. Kathy sat with him while he told me I was a druggie. I think it might have been the hardest thing he'd ever done. He'd never looked at me that way before. I did the usual. Denied it. Told them they were crazy. Said I didn't really need the pills; that I could give them up. In a moment of complete insanity I tossed a full bottle of Xanax in their kitchen sink and ground them up, just to show them I could. Of course, on the way home from their house I was on the phone to my doctor to get a refill."

"He did that for you?"

"She. Not that gender matters. I had several doctors, Mitch. Dr. A didn't know about B and C, B didn't know about A and C, and so on. Some of them wouldn't have cared anyway. Besides, you can always find one who will do what you want if you're willing to walk. I was willing. If they wouldn't? Screw 'em. I found someone else who would."

"Shrinks?"

"Sometimes. It didn't have to be."

"How long?"

"How long have I been using?" Thea saw him nod. She watched him pour boiling water into the bowl of couscous before she answered. She didn't want to be responsible for him scalding his hands. When he put the kettle back on the stove, she said, "Off and on since I was eight."

Mitch's hand jerked as he pivoted to face her. "You're kidding, right?" He knew immediately it was a stupid question because he could see that she wasn't. *Holy Judy Garland, Batman.* He didn't even know he had spoken aloud until he saw her face go slack with surprise and then crinkle with laughter.

"Oh, Mitch, you really have no sense of the gravity of a moment, do you?" Thea dabbed at her eyes with one corner of a napkin. "Thank God. Rosie says I need to stop taking myself so seriously. I know she'd approve of you."

Mitch added ground coriander and a pinch of salt to the vegetables in the skillet, then tossed in raisins, chopped dried apricots, and the roasted pine nuts. "Who's Rosie?"

"My sponsor. I go to NA meetings. Narcotics Anonymous. And AA meetings when I can't find or make an NA. I went to one this morning before I drove here. It's part of the rehab aftercare. I see a counselor, too. Someone associated with the clinic, but local. It's a little bit like having a probation officer. I also agreed to random drug testing. Completely voluntary, since there were no charges in my case. It helps keep me honest."

"You're tempted?"

"Every day," she said. "Several times a day. Sometimes several times an hour."

Mitch sliced three tablespoons of butter, added them to the warm couscous and worked it through with a fork until it melted and the grains were fluffy. He turned off the gas and emptied the skillet mixture into the couscous and stirred. "Ready." He carried the bowl to the table, set it down, and then removed a baguette of French bread from the oven, tore it in half, and put one half on a small serving board. Almost as an afterthought he picked up his Corona. "Do you mind?"

"Not at all." Her eyes followed him as he sat down across from her. "You're not going to get all weird on me every time you have to take an aspirin, are you?"

"I'll try not to," he said dryly. Mitch realized he forgot the serving spoon for the bowl and got up to get it. "You first." He pushed the bowl a little in her direction.

"It smells delicious but I don't trust a cook who won't sample his own wares first." She grinned when Mitch started to pull the bowl back. "I'm kidding. Tear me off a hunk of that bread, buster. Feeeeed me." Her imitation of the man-eating plant in *Little Shop of Horrors* wasn't too bad, or at least Mitch was polite enough to laugh. He also drew back his hand quickly, proving he knew what Audrey II was after.

Thea filled her bowl and didn't wait for Mitch to serve himself before she tucked in. "Oh," she said around a mouthful of food. "Oh, yes. This is very good. Just the right amount of coriander and I'm tasting every one of those butter pats I saw you toss in."

"I tried it with oil before but it didn't have enough flavor."

"It's perfect now." She felt his eyes on her and froze, her hand and fork halfway to her mouth. "What?"

"You enjoy your food."

"Yes, I do." She put the forkful in her mouth and chewed with exaggerated relish. "More so since I left rehab. Seems as if I have time now."

The reference to rehab sobered Mitch. "How did it happen, Thea?"

She understood the question. "I was a neurotic child. Nervous. Worried. Afraid of most everything: snakes *and* sticks. It was as if I couldn't distinguish what could and couldn't hurt me. Everything seemed a threat to me. My parents politely referred to it as being high-strung." She saw his puzzled look. "I'm talking about the Wyndhams. I don't really remember the Reasoners ever mentioning it, but I was sick with the renal problems then, and I was very young, so perhaps that's why."

Or perhaps she'd just felt safe with the Reasoners, Mitch thought. He said nothing, figuring that's what she had a counselor for and just listened instead. He tore some bread for himself and ate it with the couscous.

"Mother decided it would be a good idea if I saw her psychiatrist. She was on antidepressants so the idea of medicating me didn't give her pause. I tried a cornucopia of meds from that time until I left for college. It wasn't a steady diet. More like supplements. After a while you get the idea they're like vitamins. I'd be on for a while, off again, and then Mother and Daddy would see signs I was regressing. Nightmares. Stomach and back pain. Crying spells. Things like that. Before I knew it I would be trotted back to the doctor for another round." Thea's voice deepened dramatically and took on the self-important resonance of a newscaster. "High-strung or strung out? *You* decide."

Mitch's mouth twisted to one side. He regarded her inquiringly. "So I guess the therapy wasn't working."

"Therapy? I was seeing my *mother's* psychiatrist. His practice wasn't children. He saw me for ten minutes and listened to a list of complaints from my mother before he scribbled something on his pad. When someone asked how I felt I rattled off a list of physical symptoms. It's what I understood and could talk about. That led to more tests and pain meds . . . eventually to other meds."

"How did you meet up with Gabe again? You never told me."

Thea took another bite of food. It was interesting to her that she could sustain her appetite and still talk about these things. It used to be that thinking about one shut down the other. "Gabe and I met at dance classes when we were eleven. We had the same instructor."

Mitch almost spewed couscous. "Gabe danced?"

"Mmm. He was good."

"He was built like a linebacker."

"Before puberty he was a ballet dancer. Even afterward."

"Now I understand why he never told me." Mitch shook his head, trying to take it in. "Gabe Reasoner, a ballerina. That's great."

"He was *not* a ballerina."

Mitch waved that aside. "So you met again at classes. Wasn't there a problem with court orders? I thought the Reasoners weren't supposed to be in contact with you."

"My parents didn't know Gabe was in my class. They didn't know that his mom, or sometimes his dad, sat with the other parents while we all practiced. They didn't know we found each other again because my parents never took me to lessons. I rode the bus into town alone or was dropped off. Seeing the Reasoners once a week was our secret for a lot of years."

And holding on to it had kept her stomach in knots and her nerves frayed.

Chapter 8

Mitch wanted to know more. A lot more. He was also aware that Thea had told him what she thought was important. She probably would have been satisfied telling him that she was an addict and leaving it there. That information alone put a lot of things in perspective.

Thinking of the secrets she had kept as a child, Mitch asked her, "Who knows about you?"

Thea was quiet a moment. "It's a pretty short list. Gabe and Kathy knew, of course. Joel knows. I've told Hank Foster, the partner at—"

"I've met him. I know who he is."

"Right. I forgot. I just got around to telling Mrs. Admundson. She's my administrative assistant. She and Hank have only heard about this since I came back. Mrs. Admundson wasn't shocked. She'd worked too closely with me not to suspect something. Hank, though, almost fell out of his chair." She made a small shrug. "Now there's you."

"Your parents?"

"They're in Greece right now. They've been in Europe since early December. I called them before I went to the clinic, tried to explain, but my mother mostly seemed interested in making certain I knew it wasn't their fault. I think it was a relief she could remind herself that we don't really share the same gene pool." Thea's chuckle was soft. "Growing up, we settled the nature/nurture argument by agreeing that if I achieved something of note it was nurture. If I failed, it must have been in my nature."

No pressure there, Mitch thought.

"The thing of it is," Thea went on, "I don't blame them, or at least I haven't for a very long time. There are lots of things I wish had been different, but I have some responsibility in that, too. I wasn't quite the daughter they wanted, and they knew from the beginning I didn't want to be anywhere but with the Reasoners. The wonder of it is that we made it work—after a fashion."

"Cheery," Mitch said wryly.

"Yes, well, we had our moments. My parents were doing the best they could, and I think more clearly about them when they're an ocean away."

Mitch laughed. He took a second helping of the couscous. "Maybe you could convince my folks to take a tour of the Continent," he said. "Or at least leave the commonwealth. It might improve my perspective."

She frowned, trying to gauge his seriousness. "You're kidding, right? Your parents are—" Thea stopped, searching for the right descriptors.

"Interfering?" Mitch supplied helpfully.

"Interested and involved."

"That's nice, Thea. Really. Even my mother thinks she's interfering."

Thea smiled because there was no mistaking the affection in Mitch's voice. "You love her, though."

"Oh, yeah. That's a given. Ask my sister. Mum doesn't give you any choice."

Thea thought there was probably a grain of truth in that. Jennie Baker could steamroll over you with affection, but what a way to go. "So how is it that she hasn't married you off?"

Mitch's head was bent slightly toward his meal. Now he raised only his eyes, looking at Thea over the rims of his glasses. He pointed his empty fork at her for emphasis. "Classic mother dilemma. She wants grandbabies but no woman is good enough for me."

"You are so full of it," Thea scoffed.

"God's truth. She's had a problem with every woman I've dated since I turned twenty-one." He regarded Thea with an expression of complete innocence. "Can you imagine? Even Gina. What could she possibly find objectionable about Gina?"

"You're right," Thea said dryly. "Gina is young enough to be your mother's grandchild. You'd think she'd be pleased by that. Then there's the fact that she's in her prime child-birthing years." The look of terror that passed over Mitch's face wasn't entirely forced and Thea enjoyed it immensely. "Obviously a factor you hadn't fully considered."

Mitch swallowed. "I appreciate the heads-up."

"No problem." Thea pushed aside her bowl and dabbed at her mouth with her napkin. "It seems to me that Emilie, Case, and Grant have solved your mother's dilemma. You have children without having to submit a woman to her for approval. The pressure's off."

"For the moment. Don't get me wrong. My parents love the kids. My mother would have been ecstatic if I had married Kathy. It was hard for her to understand that Kath and I could be so close and have no romantic interest in each other. Kathy got a similar push from her parents." The corners of Mitch's mouth lifted in a faint smile. "To satisfy them all we went to our senior prom together. Trust me, we were about the only couple there who didn't end up in the backseat of a car. We even tried groping a little, but it didn't work. Our hearts weren't in it." Mitch got up from the table and began to clear it. "I haven't thought about that in a long time. Thanks. It's a good memory. We had a lot of fun that night even though our parents were disappointed nothing momentous came of it. Mom's still got her eye out for another Kathy."

Thea pushed her chair back, stretching as she stood, and pitched in to make short work of the kitchen cleanup. He brewed a pot of tea while they worked and they went into the living room with their cups after they were done. Mitch saw her give the falling snow a glance as they sat down on the couch.

"You worried about it?" he asked. Little things, he thought, like whether she was wary of driving in the snow. Those were some of the inconsequential facts he wanted to know about her. He'd learned he was up to most of the big challenges he'd ever had to face, but the oddest details could do him and a relationship in. Just witness the way Gina's choice of an automatic transmission in the Xterra bugged the hell out of him. "Maybe you want to drive the SUV home? You paid for more of it than I did."

"Snow doesn't really bother me," Thea said, curling into one corner of the sofa.

Mitch lounged in the opposite corner. Bookends, he thought, and kind of liked the idea. "But if you had to drive it, could you?"

"Well, I'm not that crazy about driving someone else's vehicle . . ."

"But you *could*."

A small crease appeared between Thea's brows. "I don't know much about the all-wheel-drive feature. . . ."

"But you could *drive* the car. First. Second. Third. Shift the gears."

"Oh, that's right. It's a manual. Sure. My other car's a stick."

Yessssss! He almost punctuated his thought with a little pumping arm action. "You have another car?"

"An old Porsche. My father gave it to me when I landed my first big account for the firm."

"Sure. A Porsche. Old is code for antique, I bet. Mint condition. I mean, why not? If you want to show someone you appreciate their efforts, nothing says well-done like a Porsche."

"It was extravagant," she admitted. "Even for my father." She hesitated, watching him over the rim of her cup. "Does it bother you? I mean that my father could do things like that for me—and often did."

Mitch thought about it before he answered. She came from a different world than he did. Big money, if not necessarily old. An exclusive neighborhood. Private school. She probably finished college without a loan and paid cash for her first car, if she'd even bought it on her own. But all that was just trappings and from what she'd already told him, she'd been thoroughly trapped. Perhaps she still was. "My dad tells me when he likes my cartoons," Mitch said finally. "That's pretty good, too."

Thea smiled. "Yeah, it is." Still watching him, she sipped her tea. "Tell me something about yourself that will surprise me."

He liked the question. "All right," he said, thinking. "My second toe is longer than my big toe."

"Yikes!"

"I know. Freaky, right?"

"Carnival material."

Mitch laughed. "Okay, how about this? When I was kid I wanted to be a lawyer."

"A lawyer? Not a fireman? Astronaut? Race car driver?"

"Wayne's dad was a lawyer. He had this cool leather briefcase with a combination lock. Little gold tumblers that were set to a code Wayne and I could never break. I decided I wanted a job where I could have a locked briefcase like Mr. Anderson." Mitch sighed. "Wayne has lived the dream."

"But does he have the briefcase?"

"Of course. I bought one for him when he passed the bar."

Thea chuckled. "More, please."

Mitch obliged her, dredging up tidbits about himself that were silly, grave, amusing, and touching by turns. There were the inevitable warts to show, those qualities he was not particularly proud of. His intolerance for standing in line. The impatience he couldn't quite hold in check when people couldn't make change. The grief he could communicate to the waiter or waitress who tried to take his food away before he was done. "You might as well know now," he told her. "I'm a lousy shopper. My mother won't even go in stores with me. I embarrass her. Gina thought she could reform me."

"And?"

"And after three attempts she was happy to leave to me at home."

Thea thought she detected a real sense of satisfaction from him on this last count. A power struggle won.

"I won't hold a woman's purse, either."

One of Thea's brows lifted and her smile was wry. "I take it there was some early trauma."

That was Mitch's cue to regale her with the horror story of being left in the little girl's clothing section in a department store while his mother helped Amy in the dressing room. He was saddled with not one, but two purses, and the large blue-and-white shopping bag with all their previous purchases. Adding to the insult were the well-intentioned clerks, cooing over him for being so precious and mannerly. The final blow came when his occasional friend/nemesis Davey Druschell saw him. There were some things that took a boy a long time to live down.

Thea had set her empty mug aside a half dozen stories ago. She was turned sideways on the sofa, hugging her knees as she listened. What she felt right now, this settled sense of self, was something that did not often happen and she wanted to hold it as close to her as her knees were to her chest.

Mitch's last story wound down and they both fell silent. A faint smile lingered on Thea's lips and touched her eyes. Mitch cocked his head, studying her. "What are you thinking?"

"That this was a good idea. Coming out here. Picking up the car. Dinner. Talking."

"I noticed you left out the smarmy seduction thing."

She surprised them both by saying, "That was good, too." Their eyes met, held, then they both looked away simultaneously. The spark, the connection, the *something* that stirred when their glances caught was still there, still stirring. Thea swiveled on the sofa, unfolded her slender frame, and dropped her feet to the floor. She glanced over her shoulder to the window. "I need to be going before I have to follow the snowplows to get home."

Ask me to stay.

The errant thought made her shoot to her feet. What in God's name was she thinking? She wobbled a bit, getting her balance.

"Are you all right?" Mitch asked. "Don't fall over the coffee table."

Embarrassed by her gracelessness, Thea simply nodded. It was no good trying to laugh it off. It would come across as tremulous and uncertain and she would feel even more foolish. She could hear her mother's voice: "Stand straight. Don't slouch. You walk like a cow." The dance classes that had brought Gabe back into her life hadn't been suggested because Thea showed any aptitude, but because she had shown none. "I'll get my jacket."

Mitch stood. "Get mine, too. I'll help you clean off your car."

Thea didn't argue. She told herself she was happy for the help and grateful he wasn't pressing her even the slightest bit to stay the night. There was a truth in there somewhere. She honestly didn't know what her answer would be if he asked. Was it that she simply wanted the opportunity to say no, or that she really wanted the chance to say yes?

The wind swirled small eddies of snow around them as they cleared the car of four inches of powder. It was a white world everywhere they looked. Streetlights illuminated the falling snow and reflected off the surface of what was already covering the ground. For a night with no stars or visible moon, it was astonishingly bright. Thea had the engine running to warm the interior and defrost the windshield while they worked. In the distance they could hear the grating sound peculiar to snowplows as they cleared the main road.

"I don't know, Thea," Mitch said, looking up the street. The plows hadn't been down it yet and neither had much local traffic. "You might want to rethink this. We usually have one pass from the plows by now. If they're this busy clearing the main thoroughfares, then it must be pretty bad. Maybe you should spend the night."

Great. He'd finally asked her to stay and it was because of the weather. That was easy enough to turn down. She wasn't looking for a mercy invitation. "I'll be fine. Once I get out to the highway it won't be a problem." She saw he still looked dubious. "Really," she added. "I've been through worse than this with the Volvo."

"You know, just because it's Swedish doesn't mean it was made for snow."

"You're thinking of those ABBA chicks. My car will do fine." Thea opened the door and lifted one foot to the runner, ready to slide inside. Something she saw in his face made her hesitate. It was there, the invitation that she really wanted from him, hovering on his lips, reaching out to her with his glance. And then Thea understood and she put it into words for both of them. "It scared you, didn't it?" she asked him softly, searching his face. "The things I told you tonight about my drug abuse."

Mitch didn't respond immediately. His lips pressed together and his smile was at once wry and regretful. "Yeah," he said finally. "It did."

"I'm glad. It should. I know it still scares the hell out of me." She recalled with clarity the moment she realized that her best friend was right: she *was* an addict. The epiphany came to her weeks after Gabe's confrontation when even a steady diet of benzos and narcotics couldn't keep the gut wrenching terror and pain at bay. She'd fallen asleep in her car in the garage and couldn't make herself get out of it in the morning. She thought about starting the engine and letting carbon monoxide put her to sleep again. Instead, she called Gabe. He came. Rescued her, really, and three days later he and Kathy put her on a plane. It was the last time she'd seen them. The memory was bittersweet.

Thea raised herself over the edge of the open door and kissed Mitch on the mouth. It was brief, just a gentle tugging of her mouth on his, and she could almost taste his bemusement. When she drew back her smile was a trifle watery. "Thank you." She ducked inside the car, pulling the door shut while Mitch stepped back. Raising her left hand in a farewell salute, Thea pulled away from the curb. When she reached the stop sign at the corner, she glanced in her rearview mirror. Mitch was still standing in the middle of the road, his figure hunched against the cold and illuminated in a pale wash of light by the street lamp. She kept him in her sights until the falling snow drew a curtain over him.

Oblivious to the cold, Mitch slowly walked back to the house. He passed on a beer from the fridge and chose a soft drink instead. Wandering back to the living room, he picked

up the TV remote, turned it on, flicked through a few channels, and flopped on the couch. He didn't want to watch anything, didn't even want to listen. He left the TV on, tuned to
a financial station with a ticker tape of news running at the
bottom of the screen, and hit the mute button, silencing the
talking heads.

Thea *had* scared him with her revelation. She had always
scared him a little with her poise and frankness and cool de-
meanor. He had the suspicion that on the occasions they'd
met over the years, she was sizing him up and had decided
a long time ago that he was a boy's size Large. Maybe that
had changed recently, Mitch thought. He certainly hoped
that was the case, but he also knew it was no longer so important what she thought of him. He needed to decide what
he really thought of her.

He knew he liked her. At the rehearsal dinner for Gabe
and Kathy he had acted four kinds of stupid around Thea
Wyndham. That was his first hint that his feelings were engaged. At the wedding reception the following day, he had
offered an absurd number of toasts to the new couple's happiness in order to knock back another flute of cheap champagne and get his courage up to ask her out. Everything had
come out wrong, of course. His invitation, the one that he
hoped to communicate in a tone that was both smooth and
casual, came out in fits and starts. He was pretty sure he actually stuttered. Mortified, he changed direction, and fell
back on humor to help him get out from under Thea's patient, but mildly derisive smile. Somehow he managed to
suggest they retire to the fire truck in the garage to do the
wangy-bangy. Suave. He remembered her refusal as being
flat and firm. There was really nowhere to go from there.

It was true, he knew, that his interest in her had begun
before the moment of their first meeting. He had hedged a
bit when he told Thea that he was trying to remove her as a
potential rival for Gabe's affection. It was more to the point

that Kathy had begun to speak so often of Gabe's friend Thea, that Mitch wanted to meet her himself. Okay, so maybe that photo of the striking redhead he'd seen in Gabe's wallet had roused his curiosity and jangled his hormones, but he'd also paid attention to the little things they dropped in conversation about her. Most of it he still remembered.

Not once had anyone hinted that she had a drug problem.

It seemed likely they hadn't known back then, or perhaps Gabe had suspicions that he never shared with Kathy. Thea had been his boon companion, after all, and Mitch understood the urge to protect someone close. It was not as if Thea wasn't a functional abuser, at least as far as Mitch could tell, and that would have made her substance use problem more difficult to detect and confront. She probably hid it from everyone, most especially herself.

Mitch had done some drug experimentation as a teenager and college student, and when he looked back on it, it was with a mixture of astonishment at his stupidity and wonderment at his good fortune for emerging from adolescence alive. Drinking had always been more popular with his friends and he had participated enthusiastically in a mind-boggling variety of mind-numbing drinking games, driving or being driven under the influence, and sneaking home to collapse in bed still smelling like a brewery. Alcohol was plentiful, but there were opportunities to smoke a little weed at a football game or drop some acid, and Mitch was interested, so he never said no. On the other hand, he never went out of his way to say yes. If it was there, he didn't turn it down; if it wasn't there, he didn't go looking for it.

Even before he graduated from CMU, he'd lost interest and moved on. Now he drank the occasional beer and got his drugs at the pharmacy. Mitch sighed, and let his head loll back against the sofa, as this last thought brought him around to Thea again. She also bought her drugs at the pharmacy and he suspected she probably always had. He doubted she had ever done an illegal drug in her life; prior to Gabe's intervention and her stint in rehab, she might have considered Mitch to be the more serious drug abuser.

Thea Wyndham was a good girl.

He smiled a little wryly as he recalled telling her that. It wasn't that he had changed his mind, but now he wondered what had gone through hers when he'd said it. She knew firsthand about the cost of trying to be a good girl. There was a connection there, a small piece of the puzzle that was Thea Wyndham that Mitch could fit into place on his own.

He thought about what he knew of her childhood, then of all that he didn't. Except for a single, offhanded allusion to her biological father not caring for her, she hadn't said anything about her birth parents. She remembered them; Mitch recalled her sharing that much, but nothing else. The Wyndhams. The Reasoners. And then there was some couple whose name Mitch had never learned. What memories did Thea have about them? What part was fact? What part fiction?

Three sets of parents, Mitch thought. Biological. Foster. Adoptive. How was a child supposed to make some sense of that?

Thinking of the three children staying with his parents right now made Mitch's chest tighten uncomfortably. God, what if he screwed this up? What if they did all the stupid things he did as a kid and weren't as lucky to come out on the other side? He wasn't their parent. What the hell did he know about it anyway? Gabe and Kathy trusted him with their kids but it wasn't like they'd left an instruction manual behind. The closest thing he had was Kathy's recipes and he'd already proven he couldn't make her meat loaf to please the troops.

What kind of dad fed his kids spiced couscous with fruit and nuts?

Awww, jeez, he was losing it. Next he'd be asking Thea for a list of doctors that would prescribe him the choice drugs.

That thought made Mitch flash back to something Emilie had said about Thea weeks ago. *We make her nervous.* Thea had denied it, Mitch had covered for her, but Emilie, repeating something she'd overheard from her mother, had been telling the truth. Being around the kids *did* make her nervous, and it always had. Mitch realized that he was just ready to join her.

"Great," he whispered. "That'll really help the kids. Kathy? Gabe? What the *hell* were you thinking putting us in charge?"

There was no answer, which Mitch, in his present frame of mind, took as a good thing. Thea Wyndham, high school honor student, fledgling ballerina, Bryn Mawr grad, ad exec at the family-founded firm, and award recipient, was making him a little crazy.

What was he supposed to *do* with what she'd told him? Had her confession been in the way of an excuse or simply the explanation he'd been asking for from the start? Was he supposed to keep the kids out of her hair or let them pull her in? If she relapsed, who would be to blame?

"Strike that," he said at the end of a long sigh. "It's got to be on you, Thea."

The phone rang and Mitch almost let the machine pick up. At the last moment he realized that it was probably the kids calling to say good night and he made a mad dash to the kitchen, catching it a second before his recorded voice did.

"Hello."

"Mitchell, it's your mother."

He smiled. Some things didn't change and he was probably the better for it. "I know, Mum. What's up? Everyone's okay? No broken bones?"

"Your father parboiled himself in the hot tub, but other than that, we're fine. The kids want to talk to you."

Mitch glanced at the clock. "They're up kind of late."

"I'm the grandmother, dear. Things are different. You're the one saddled with the hobgoblins of consistency or some such thing."

"'A foolish consistency is the hobgoblin of little minds,'" Mitch quoted. "That's Emerson, Mum. Are you saying that I have a little mind?"

"Don't twist my words. In a few years you'll have no mind, with no chance of recovery. Do you want to talk to the children or argue with a woman who knows of what she speaks?"

Mitch didn't hesitate. "Pass the phone, please. I love you." He thought he heard her chuckle before Case's voice came over the line.

"What's a hobgoblin?"

"Ask Pap," Mitch said. "He'll be happy to explain. Did you have fun today?"

"Yeah. I made it the whole way down the hill without falling."

"Good for you. How many times did Nonny take a spill?"

"She didn't fall at all. She's good."

There was a relief, Mitch thought. "Put Grant on," he said. "Good night and I love you."

"Love you, too." There was some fumbling with the phone before Mitch heard Grant's soft breathing on the other end of the line. "Hey, Sport. What's the word?"

"Dis-com-*bob*-u-la-tion."

"Pretty cool word. Where'd you hear that?" As if he didn't know.

"Pap. He said that a lot after he got out of the hot tub."

"I'll bet. He was discombobulated, uh?"

"Yeah, that's it. Dis-com-*bob*-u-la-ted."

Mitch grinned at Grant's singsong pronunciation. He got

the skiing report and signed off after he asked for Emilie. "Hi, Em. How's my ski bunny?"

"Uncle Mitch! Nonny says that's a sexy remark."

"Sexist," he corrected her. "Put Nonny on the phone." He waited. The transfer was quick because his mother was hovering and had probably overheard the exchange. "Mum, what are you teaching her?"

"That she is something more than ornamentation on the slopes no matter how pink her ski clothes are. Emilie is actually quite accomplished and tomorrow I'm taking her on a bigger run."

"Okay, just checking. Put her on." The phone was exchanged again. "Sorry about the sexist remark, Em. I think you can be anything you want to be."

"I know that," Emilie said frankly. "But right now I want to be pretty."

In the background he could hear Case and Grant start to chant. *Pretty ugly. Pretty ugly.* "We'll work on loftier goals later, Em. Right now tell your brothers that 'pretty ugly' is an oxymoron and send them to Pap for the full explanation. That will put them to sleep." He waited while Emilie did as she was told. When she got back on the line, he asked, "So how was the skiing?"

"Good. Nonny says I'm a natural. I might even have a street name. Peekaboo."

Mitch laughed. "Nonny's talking about a skier named Picabo Street who won an Olympic gold medal."

"Oh. That's good, too."

"Sure is."

"What are you doin'?" Emilie asked.

There was nothing disingenuous about the question, Mitch knew. Emilie was fishing for information. "Watching TV."

"All by yourself?"

He shook his head, smiling wryly as her eleven-year-old guided missile system locked on to its target. "All alone," he told her. "Your aunt Thea was here but she's gone now. We picked up the car this afternoon."

"Miss Sommers didn't go with you?"

"No. I asked Thea to help instead."

"You like her more?"

Oh, boy. Mitch's collar felt a little tight. Emilie was a tough interrogator, but then he considered who was standing next to her and realized she was learning from the Jedi master. "I like her fine," he said. Take *that,* Mama Yoda. "Now, tell me more about your ski lessons." Mitch listened for another five minutes while Emilie gave him the excruciating details of everything she'd managed to learn that day. He signed off with "don't murder your brothers" and "I love you." When his mother got back on the phone he was prepared for her questions about Thea, and he fielded them with what he liked to believe was a certain casual grace. It wasn't until he was off the phone that he swallowed hard.

He managed to get halfway across the kitchen when the phone rang again. This time he did let the machine pick up.

"Mitch? Are you still awake?"

It was Thea. Mitch leaped back toward the phone. "Hey!"

"Mitch, it's Thea. If you're—"

"Thea! I'm here." He fumbled with the answering machine to make it stop recording. "I'm here," he said more quietly. "Where are you? You can't be home already."

"I'm not. I'm just south of Cranberry on 79. I'm waiting for a tow truck. I put the Volvo in the median and I can't get it out. I was wondering if—"

"I'm on my way." In his eagerness to get to her quickly, he almost hung up the phone. He caught himself. "Are you all right? Do I need to bring anything?"

"Hot coffee would be nice. Decaf."

"You got it. Call me on my cell if the tow truck gets there before I do."

"I don't think that's going to happen. They said it'd be about an hour and a half. That was twenty-five minutes ago."

She'd been waiting that long already? "Thea! Why didn't you call right away?"

"I did. Your line was busy. I guess you don't have call waiting either."

He hated call waiting, but he said, "At the top of my list now. See you in twenty minutes."

"Be careful."

Mitch hung up but not before he heard her teeth chattering. Wasn't she in the Volvo with the heat running? He grabbed his coat and gloves and then ran upstairs for a couple of blankets. The snowfall hadn't diminished since the last time he was outside. Mitch brushed off the new SUV and hopped inside. He was out of town in a few minutes and on the interstate not long after that. The roads had been scraped and salted but the surface was still visible only in isolated spots in the driving lane. The passing lane was all packed snow. The snowplows and salt trucks couldn't keep up with the rate of accumulation, and Mitch had to keep his speed under thirty miles an hour because of the reduced visibility. Even with only his low beams on, it was like navigating through hyperspace.

He had driven a mile and a half after the Cranberry exit when he saw flashing red-and-blue lights up ahead. The state police had found Thea first. Mitch slowed down to a crawl and pulled up carefully behind the cruiser. He left his motor running and jumped out. The officer was out of the car before Mitch's feet reached the ground. The cab light showed Thea sitting in the front seat.

"Is she all right?" he asked.

"Your name?" the officer demanded.

"Mitchell Baker." The SUV's headlights illuminated the officer and Mitch could see him lower his guard a fraction. "Thea explained she called me, didn't she?"

"She did. Just wanted to make certain it was you." He pointed to the median strip. "Her car's over there."

Mitch turned. He hadn't even looked for the Volvo once he'd seen the police car. Now he paled. The car was on its side in the snow-covered grass strip between the north and south-bound lanes. "She rolled a *Volvo?*" he asked incredulously.

"Not without some help. According to Ms. Wyndham a pickup passed her and then cut back into her lane too soon. He clipped her front headlight and she skidded, spun, and couldn't correct."

Mitch looked around. "Where's the pickup?"

"Gone. Didn't stop. We have her information. She caught some of the license plate. It might be enough."

He nodded. "She's okay, though?"

"Seems to be, and she says she is, but I'm no doctor. I'd get her to the ER to check her out."

"I'll take her there for coffee," Mitch said.

"Good idea."

Mitch rounded the back of the cruiser and went to the passenger side. He opened the door. Thea was still warming her fingers in front of the heater. "You ready to go? I have blankets in the car. Coffee's waiting for us at the hospital."

Her head swiveled. "I don't need to go to the hospital."

"Sure. We'll talk about it when we get there." Mitch waited patiently for her to get her purse and the papers she'd taken from the glove compartment of her car, then he escorted her back to the SUV. The officer made certain they had enough gas to wait out the tow truck, waved aside their thanks, and told them he had to go. Calls were coming in from all over, he said, shaking his head. Why didn't people just stay home on nights like this?

Thea didn't offer an explanation. She watched the cruiser pull safely onto the highway before she sank back in her seat. "I don't think he really wanted to hear my reasons for being out in this, do you?"

"Probably not," Mitch agreed. He took the purse and papers she was still clutching and put them in the backseat. He tucked the blankets he'd brought around her. They waited almost forty minutes for the tow truck. Mitch made arrangements for the car to go to a garage and mechanic he knew, and then he paid the driver and got back in the SUV.

"I have a bag in the trunk," Thea said. She yawned widely. "Please. Before he goes."

Mitch jumped out, ran up to the driver's window, and tapped on it. "The lady says she has something in the trunk she needs."

"Don't they always," the driver said. He accepted the twenty-dollar tip Mitch gave him and lowered the hoist to retrieve Thea's bag.

Climbing into the SUV for what he hoped was the last time before the hospital trip, Mitch regarded Thea's slim smile and sleepy-eyed thank-you in the cab light and decided it was worth it. He put the bag between the seats and buckled up before he adjusted the vents to direct more heat in Thea's direction. "What do you have in there that you couldn't leave behind?"

Thea closed her eyes as the car rolled forward and moved off the shoulder and onto the highway. "It's my just-in-case."

"Justin Case?" He frowned, certain he couldn't have heard her correctly. "What are you saying again?"

"You know. Just in case I have to spend the night. Just in case I get asked."

"I see."

"Don't flatter yourself," she murmured. "I always keep it there. I've had to do a fair amount of last-minute traveling for the business. I've found it's a good idea to have a grab-and-go bag."

"Handy."

"Sometimes."

He glanced over when she didn't say anything and saw

she appeared to be sleeping. Concern that she could have a concussion prompted Mitch to press a little harder on the gas pedal. He took the next exit, turned around, and got back on the highway heading north to the hospital.

Thea made a few protestations once he parked the car, but she didn't dig her heels in. Mitch helped her register, poking through her purse for her wallet and insurance card while she answered questions. His fingers stilled only once, and that was when they closed over the object that was undeniably her engagement ring.

The urgent care waiting room wasn't crowded and Thea was taken back relatively quickly. After an initial evaluation, the physician ordered a few X-rays of her neck and upper back as a precaution. The results, when they finally came, showed nothing unusual. Concussion had been ruled out early and the discharge recommendations were rest and over-the-counter pain relievers as needed.

"Told you so," Thea said, curling into the front seat.

"Yeah, but you looked real cute in that hospital gown."

"So that was your angle."

"Guilty."

Thea's smile was sleepy. "Take me home, Mr. Baker."

Mitch did.

Thea woke as she always did: bleary-eyed and unable to bring the room into immediate focus. This morning her disorientation was more than usual and then she remembered she was not in her own room, not in her own bed, and most importantly, she was not alone.

She sat up slowly, careful not to dislodge the covers, and took stock of her situation. On the floor not far from the bed was her overnight bag. It looked oddly deflated lying there, flattened and misshapen against the carpet. Thea blinked, trying to make sense of what she was seeing, or seeing poorly. In small increments, the brain fog began to recede and she understood that Mitch had unpacked the bag for her. Turning slightly, she groped for the contact wetting solution, hoping he would have put it in the same place she did on the nightstand. He had, and her fingers closed around it. One drop in each eye, a couple of blinks, and the watercolor on the far wall was identifiable as a cityscape with the Smithfield Street Bridge as its center. She couldn't make out the signature, and the painting was certainly different from Mitch's cartooning, but there were similarities in the bold, black strokes, and splashes of color, that made her know it was his work.

Plus, this was his bedroom.

Yep, she was a regular Sherlock. She hadn't even noticed the watercolor the first time she'd been here.

Thea's glance shifted sideways. Mitch lay sprawled on his stomach, half in and out of the sheet and blankets. His head was turned away from her, supported by the plumped-up pillow and the arm he had slid beneath it. There was a lot of shoulder and upper back showing, all of it covered by a wrinkled and roomy gray T-shirt. The leg that was stretched out and perfectly visible on top of the comforter was a remarkably attractive specimen of lean and muscular masculine contours. Thea's eyes followed its line from toe to thigh and back again. He even had rather nice toes, and sure enough, his second toe was longer than the big one.

She stared at them and then blinked. And blinked again. She wasn't imagining it: Mitch's toenails were varnished in neon-bright pink polish.

The sound that escaped her throat was something that held the nuances of despair and laughter, that was both surrender and acceptance. She stifled it by grabbing a pillow and hugging it to her, burying her face against the 300-thread count Egyptian cotton that still smelled vaguely more like him than her. Beside her, she felt Mitch stir and she risked a peek at him. He didn't rise. In the next moment his breathing was easy again and Thea slipped out of bed.

She padded silently to the adjoining bathroom and closed the door. Whoever had undressed her last night had had the decency or good sense to leave her in her panties and purple turtleneck sweater. Her bra had been removed but Thea had a hazy recollection of that happening under cover of the turtleneck.

That memory sharpened suddenly and Thea actually felt the tracks of Mitch's fingertips inching their way up her back. She shivered, but in a good way. Catching her reflection in the large mirror above the bathroom sink, Thea's mouth split in a wide, sappy grin. "You're a mess, Thea Wyndham," she whispered. For once the admonition was more playful than pejorative.

Mitch woke to the sound of the shower running in his bathroom. He groaned softly, regretfully. Another opportunity missed. Thea had been so exhausted by the time he got her in the house that she was practically drugged with it. Maybe that was an inappropriate comparison, but Mitch didn't think so. He sent her upstairs while he dealt with their coats and locking up the house, and when he found her again it wasn't in Emilie's room, but his own. She was already more asleep than awake, lying on top of the down comforter, one sock off, the other dangling from her toes. She had managed to unbutton and unzip her jeans, and even push them partway to her hips, but getting them off seemed to have confounded her.

Mitch shimmied her out of the Levi's, the socks, and—because she requested it—the bra. That took a little maneuvering, but he'd managed the thing without removing her sweater, and had ended up touching her just about everywhere *except* her breasts to achieve that end.

Mitch glanced over at the chair where all of Thea's clothes were folded neatly, the lacy bra on top. He smiled to himself. It had matched her purple sweater. The panties, too. There had been a certain amount of satisfaction in discovering he had guessed correctly about that. Thea was a monochromatic girl. Very sexy.

Rolling out of bed, Mitch straightened and stretched. He used the kids' bathroom for his personal needs but he drew the line at sharing their bubble gum flavored toothpaste again. Besides that, he needed to shave.

The shower was still going when he opened the door to his own bathroom. "You all right in there?" he called.

The soap thudded to the floor of the tub.

"Sorry," he said. "Didn't mean to scare you. You want me to get that?"

"Funny." Thea picked it up, held it too tightly and it leaped out her hand, ricocheting off the tub wall and thumping to the floor again.

"You playing racquetball in there?" Through the frosted shower door, Mitch could just make out the fuzzy shape of Thea's body as she twisted and bent for the second time. "Want some competition?" Her reply was muffled by the water pelting her face but Mitch understood enough of it. "Better wash your mouth out while you've got the soap."

Thea pressed her forehead against the damp tiles and closed her eyes. Hot water sluiced her shoulders and ran down her back. "What are you doing in here?"

Mitch already had his toothbrush and toothpaste in hand. "Dental hygiene. Do you mind? I didn't want to kiss you with bubble gum breath."

That brought Thea's head up. The bubble gum comment almost distracted her but she managed to zero in on what was important. "There's going to be kissing?"

"Uh-huh."

She glanced at the toothpaste and brush she had carried into the shower with her. She was ahead of him in some regards, but what if he didn't like mint? "I don't think that's a good idea."

"Why not?"

"You'll get wet."

Mitch grinned at his reflection. He was foaming at the mouth. "Yeah? Why's that?"

"Because I'm not coming out."

He spit and rinsed. "Okay by me. I'm gonna shave first, though." He looked around for his razor and shaving cream. At an angle behind him, via the mirror's reflection, Mitch saw the shower door slide open a few inches and a slim arm extend itself. At the end of the arm was a hand holding a can of shaving cream and his newest razor with four blades. He turned around, took the offering, and got an eyeful of slick wet thigh before the door banged shut. "Tell me you didn't use this already."

"You want me to lie?"

Mitch sighed. "You know, if you kept some cream and disposable razors in that grab-and-go bag, you wouldn't start off the morning on the wrong side of the guy who's gonna make you weak-kneed."

Thea swallowed. Her knees were already a little weak. She leaned back against the tiles and now the water drummed against her breasts and cascaded over her flat belly and down her thighs. Her voice was more hesitant than she would have liked as she asked, "I'm on your wrong side?"

"No woman needs a patented titanium quadruple blade system to remove hair from her legs," he grumbled. "You get facial hair, then we'll talk."

"Gee."

"I know. Serious stuff." Mitch lathered his face. "You want to watch?"

"I'll pass."

"I'd watch you shave your legs."

"I bet you would."

Mitch had to stop smiling in order to shave. The extra creases played hell with every one of those blades. "What are you doing now?"

"Rinsing the conditioner out of my hair."

"Can you do that and think about me kissing you?"

There was a pause, then, "I can now."

Mitch forgot himself, grinned wickedly at his reflection, and almost nicked his jaw. He stopped teasing Thea before he inadvertently severed a facial nerve. She probably would have less objections about the kiss if his mouth was not drawn back in a perpetual Joker-like grimace.

Splashing water on his face, Mitch wiped off the remaining shaving cream, and rinsed his razor. He smoothed the wrinkles on his T-shirt and snapped the elastic waistband of his boxers. Looked like it was a go. Turning, he took a step toward the bathtub stall and knocked politely on the shower door.

"Who's there?"

"Doesn't matter. I'm comin' in." He gave the sliding door a little tug on the handle and felt resistance from the other side. "I'll huff and I'll puff," he threatened. "I can do it, too."

"Mitch!" Thea opened the door wide enough to frame her face. Water dripped on the rim of the tub, Mitch's hand, and the carpet. "I want a towel."

"The water's still running."

"I know. I *want* a towel."

Amused, he yanked one hanging on a hook at the back of the bathroom door and gave it to her. She swept it inside, shut the frosted partition, and then called to him, "You can come in now. I'm decent."

Mitch opened the door and regarded Thea standing under the pulsing spray with the oversized bath sheet wrapped around her twice for modesty. "You are deeply left of center, you know that?"

"I'm learning it might not be such a bad thing."

Still in his boxers and tee, Mitch stepped into the shower.
"I kinda like it." Water pelted the back of his head and neck
as Thea made room for him. He shut the door. "Cozy," he
said, looking around. There were bottles of her shampoo,
conditioner, and moisturizer on the shallow shelves built
into the tiled walls. Peppermint foot cleanser and a pumice
stone were sitting on the interior rim of the tub. "You re-
decorated. I like what you've done with the place." His eyes
came back to hers and his humor faded. The centers darkened as he studied her upturned face. "You okay?"

"A little stiff," she said.

Mitch nodded. "I know the feeling."

Thea's eyes dropped immediately to the dampening front
of his boxers. Her brows lifted. "Little" was not an appropri-
ate adjective to describe what was happening south of the
border.

Following her glance, Mitch looked down at himself.
"What can I say? It's hard to pitch a tent in the rain."

In spite of her misgivings, Thea discovered she had the
capacity to laugh. He did that to her. Again and again he
gave her this gift, this opportunity not to take things so seriously that she wrung all the joy from them. She looked up at
him. Her lashes were wet and spiky. Water trickled down her
temples. "I thought I scared you," she said.

"You did. You *do*. But scaring me is different from scaring me off."

Thea thought about that and the distinction was not lost
on her. "Then I suppose you better kiss me."

"Hmmm. That's what I was—"

He stopped because Thea caught him full on the mouth
midsentence. That was the last chance she had to take charge
for a while. Mitch gave her a full body press against the tiles
and threw himself into that kiss.

Her mouth was damp and she tasted of mint, cool at first
but warming up nicely. His lips caught hers, the edge of his

tongue running along the sweet, silky underside and then across the ridge of her teeth. He plied her with small, nibbling kisses at the corners of her mouth, pacing himself, teasing her with the occasional foray of his tongue, hinting at deeper carnal pleasures. His hands bracketed her head but his body held her up. The bath sheet was sopping wet, heavy and thick between them. He didn't try to drag it from her. She'd shed it like a chrysalis when she was ready for him.

Thea whimpered softly under the steady onslaught of his mouth. This was carnage, what he was doing to her. Take-no-prisoners kissing. Insistent. Sensual. Wicked hot. He delivered on his promise to make her knees weak. The pressure of his lips, the sweep of his tongue, the deep, slow, pulsing rhythm of his kisses also left her light-headed and short of breath. It was a complete rush on every one of her senses, including common. There was nothing but his body pressing against hers and the hard, openmouthed frontal assault.

He broke the kiss suddenly and Thea couldn't even raise her heavy eyelids. She felt the pitch of the water change from pulse to spray and then his mouth was on her again, heavy and drugging, suckling her lips as if he were drawing honey from the comb. Thea's towel began to slide. She reached for it but he grasped her wrists and lightly held her hands at her sides. She didn't struggle. "Someone has his eyes open," she said softly.

"You bet." His voice was thick and rough-edged. "You have slippage." He drew her hands slowly upward against the tiles until they were raised above her head.

Gravity did the rest.

Chapter 9

Mitch's breath snagged in his chest. She was looking at him now, her eyes wide and luminous . . . and wary. "God, Thea," he whispered raggedly. "You're . . ." He lowered his head again because he didn't have words. Mitch only knew that if he were struck blind, he had already had a vision of the promised land. He kissed her on the mouth, slowly, warmly. His hands cupped her face lightly as he worked his mouth over hers. His fingers teased tendrils of damp hair around the curve of her ears.

Thea's heart thudded heavily. Of all the places he could have touched her when she stood naked and vulnerable in front of him, he touched her face. He made her feel . . . adored. She raised her hands and curved them around his wrists, tugging gently. Guiding him, Thea made his palms slide along her water-slick skin to her throat, her shoulders, and then, arching into him, her breasts. She swallowed his muffled groan with her own deepening kiss.

His palms were filled, amply filled. Gloriously filled. Her breasts swelled under his hands. The dusky pink aureoles puckered and the nipples stood erect, poking at the heart of his palms, then scraping against the crease of his life line as he moved his hands to cup her. He lowered his head and suckled.

Thea gasped at the first hot contact of his mouth on her breast. Rising on tiptoe, extending the long line of her leg, she slid upward against the wet tiles at her back and braced her arms on Mitch's shoulders. The source of heat spiraling outward from her breast was his mouth. The rough edge of his tongue lapped at her nipple. Flicked it. His teeth closed over the tip and he tugged.

She was scored by the heat all the way to her womb. Mitch's name was trapped at the back of her throat. Her lips hummed softly together, then the tremulous sound died away and she didn't try to speak again. It was all she could do to breathe.

Mitch straightened. He wondered if he looked as dazed as he felt, and for a long moment he stared at the darkly reflective centers of Thea's eyes looking for the answer. She watched him, intent and still wary, and he found himself intrigued by that guardedness. It seemed an emotion turned inward, as if she were not so uncertain of him, but of herself, and Mitch wondered at it.

"Good morning," he said softly. He bowed his head and pressed his brow lightly to hers. "Did I wish you a good morning?" If he hadn't been touching her he wouldn't have seen the nearly imperceptible shake of her head. He felt it, though. That small, slight movement sent a shiver all the way down his spine. "You're some kisser, Thea Wyndham."

His lips nudged hers. His breath was warm, sweet. Thea felt her eyelids grow heavy as Mitch's hands slid from the underside of her tender and aching breasts to her waist, then curved lightly at her hips. His thumbs made a pass across her skin. Back and forth. Back. Forth. Again. On her next breath she sucked in her lower lip, bit it to keep from crying out.

"Easy," he said. He kissed the corner of her mouth. "Where are we going with this?"

"You don't have GPS?"

"Smart ass." He was smiling against her cheek. "I know what I want." His teeth caught her earlobe and worried it. His tongue flicked the diamond stud. "I'm not entirely sure about you."

The truth was that Thea wasn't entirely certain either. "Can we kiss some more?"

"Yep. Vertical or horizontal?"

Thea felt his lips hovering just above hers again. "Vertical is good," she whispered.

Mitch bypassed her gently puckered, succulent mouth, and cocked his head sideways, placing a firm vertical kiss on the damp skin of her neck. "Good choice," he said. He sucked, applying gentle pressure until he felt her fingers curl into his T-shirt and stretch it taut. "You want to help me out of it?"

She nodded and her fingers caught more of the material until she had a fistful. Mitch ducked as she pulled and then he was out of it and Thea was left holding it in front of her. It lay slanted across her breasts and belly like a wet plaster and left the copse of dark red hair on her mons uncovered.

Mitch's eyes narrowed thoughtfully as he made a study of all that dewy alabaster skin exposed and the turgid nipples and taut belly perfectly outlined by his shirt. "All right," he said at last. "You can wear that."

She threw it at him.

Laughing, Mitch grabbed two slippery handfuls of Thea's bottom and jerked her upward against his groin. Her thighs parted and clamped around his hips for purchase. His cock pressed hard against her cleft. He backed her up to the tiled wall again; her arms circled him. Thea's head fell forward and was buried against the curve of his neck. Mitch heard her catch her breath. She nuzzled him with an openmouthed kiss. The tip of her tongue flicked the pulsing cord in his neck.

He turned his head and caught her cheek. She raised herself slightly and he kissed her jaw. Her face lifted completely then; her slender throat arched. She made herself available to his deliciously greedy lips, closing her eyes under this second rush on her senses. Her fingertips marked him with tiny white crescents where she pressed the back of his shoulders. His skin was taut over the defined bunching of muscles. Thea ran her palms up his back. A thin sheet of water covered him and droplets wedged themselves between her palms and his skin. The water was warm. His skin was hot.

She weighed next to nothing in his arms. Her long legs were locked behind him at the ankles. She rode up on him slightly as he continued to kiss her throat. Her breasts rubbed his chest. He fit himself snugly into the cradle of her thighs.

"Someone wants out of the tent," he whispered against her skin.

Thea groaned softly. "Why do men talk about their penis as if it's a third person in the room?"

Mitch lifted his head. "Hey, you live with the hand puppet all your life and it takes on certain anthropomorphic characteristics."

Something between a laugh and a sputter caught in Thea's throat. She plowed her fingers deeply into Mitch's thatch of wet hair and held his head still, simply staring at him, at once amused and disbelieving. Then she struck. Her mouth slanted across his. Hot. Hungry. She pushed her tongue past his, working it over and around his, sucking it into her own mouth.

She pulsed against him, clasping him tightly. His lean muscles shifted so that she felt the tension in the contraction. There was no mistaking the strength of his upper body or the fact that she was securely held in his arms. If his breathing was short, if there was a vibration running lightly under his skin, it was in response to passion, not fatigue. But in the event she was wrong . . .

Thea drew back slightly, tugging on his lips as she lifted her head. Her sigh was inaudible against the steady rush of water from the shower. "They say the bathroom is the site of the majority of household accidents," she said.

He grinned. "Don't trust me, huh?"

She searched his face. "Ummm. Maybe . . ." Her eyes darted in the direction of the door.

"Bedroom?"

Thea nodded. His grip on her relaxed and she was unfolded flush to his hard frame. "Leave your shorts here." She slipped around him and slid open the shower door. Thea felt him make a grab for her butt but his fingers only caught the curve of her left cheek. She was on the other side of the tub, dripping onto the carpet, before he had a chance to realize he had a handful of air and water.

Smiling to herself, she grabbed a dry towel from the back of the door and rubbed it furiously through her hair. She heard the shower stop, and in the immediate silence that followed she was aware of her thudding heart and lightly tingling skin in a way she hadn't been moments earlier. These sensations weren't courtesy of the sharp, pulsing water spray, if indeed, they ever had been. What she felt had its sweet nascence in the hot suck of Mitch's mouth and his hands cupped hard over her bottom.

And she was bearing it. More than that, she was embracing it.

The shower door slid open and, half-hidden in the towel draped over her head, Thea caught sight of five neon pink toes and a lean, muscular calf just before Mitch put his foot down. She tossed the towel at him and made a dash for the bedroom.

He caught her on the run, snapping the twisted towel at her thigh and catching her squarely on her taut buttocks.

"Ouch!" She stopped short, turning to get a look at the offended portion of her anatomy, and found herself lifted off the carpet and borne toward the bed in a dazzling offensive move that was a little carry and a lot of tackle. Thea felt some of the breath leave her body as they rolled onto the bed together. Mitch protected her from taking the brunt of the fall or bearing his weight and still managed to emerge holding the high ground.

He looked down on her, his expression a mixture of ornery satisfaction and wickedness. "You want to turn the other cheek?"

Thea got her fists between their bodies and pushed upward. He didn't budge. Her knuckles made small dimples in his skin, but the taut abdomen remained just where it was. Thea's hands unfolded and her fingers splayed across his midsection. She lifted one eyebrow. "Pretty impressive abs for a cartoonist."

Mitch gave her an aw, shucks smile at the same time he settled his hips heavily against her thighs. "You haven't said anything about my pen."

"Your pen is . . ." Thea rolled her eyes at her own gullibility. "You set me up."

"You say pen-is. I say pe-nis." He bent his head and kissed her softly, nudging her lips apart. His nose bumped hers. The shape of their mouths changed as they shared a smile. He kissed her again, sweetly this time, and tasted her sigh. Raising himself up on his elbows, he studied her face. His expression was watchful now, solemn and intent. "Thea?"

She knew what he was asking. It was there in the inflection in his voice as he said her name. Did she want this? Was she ready? Regrets? A mistake? "How do you know to ask?" she whispered. A heaviness settled inside her as her stomach clenched. "What am I doing wrong?"

Mitch exhaled softly, shaking his head. "No. Oh, no, baby." His hand came up to touch her face. The backs of his fingers brushed her cheek. Her skin was still faintly damp, glowing. Her short dark hair was freshly mussed and spiky from the hard rubbing she'd given it. He smoothed it back at her temple, then ruffled it again. "Don't even think it. It's not about what you're doing wrong."

"Then what—"

"It's about what I'm not doing enough of," he told her. He kissed the corner of her mouth. "I can still feel you tense when I touch you. I don't—"

Thea almost laughed. He thought it was *him*. She stopped Mitch by letting her hands run up his naked flanks and across his back. His breath hitched and she smiled faintly. Thea raised her hips, pushing herself against him, grinding, lifting. He was so hard and hot on her belly. Her abdomen contracted as he moved.

"Open for me," he said. "Wider."

Thea put her hands on his shoulders. Her heels sought purchase in the mattress. She wanted to do anything he wanted. Everything he wanted. He'd called her "baby" and she hadn't even blinked an eye. Maybe later her feminist sensibilities would find that endearment outrageous, but when he'd said it just now, it seemed tender and sweet, and she wanted to love him so much right then and there that there was ache inside her that was different from anything she'd ever known. She felt his palm curve lightly over her thigh. He was stroking her skin from hip to knee, slowly, carefully, watching her face, gauging her reaction, and doing nothing except this exquisite caress.

He moved suddenly but didn't surge over her or into her. Mitch slipped out from between her legs and flipped on his side. His hand never left her thigh, but now it had the inside track. His fingertips brushed the dark red hair of her mons. Once. Twice. He felt her inner thigh muscles start to close.

He leaned his head close to her ear. "No. Don't. Stay open for me." His hand cupped her mons. The damp, springy curls collapsed under the weight of his palm. He pressed with the heel of his hand as his fingers slipped between the lightly moist folds of her labia. He drew the moisture upward to her clitoris, rubbing the sensitive hood with his fingertip.

Thea's hips jerked. An inarticulate sound was trapped at the back of her throat and a tide of pale pink color flushed her breasts and washed upward to her face. Beside her, her hands sought something to cover herself. Coming up empty, they curled into fists. The next time he touched her she sucked in her lower lip and clamped her teeth over it.

"Okay?" he asked her huskily.

She nodded. "It embarrasses me a little."

One of Mitch's dark brows lifted. Watching her darkening eyes, he continued to caress her. "This? This embarrasses you?"

What he was doing flooded her with sensation. Embarrassment was just one of the ones she endured. "A little," she repeated. "Ah!" Her eyes widened almost imperceptibly. "Ummmm." She pressed her lips together, holding back the sound, swallowing it. If he had any sense of what she was feeling, or perhaps because he had *every* sense of it, there was no pause in Mitch's intimate caress. He wrested another cry from her and was smart enough not to smile when he did it. He kissed her instead, claiming that sound of her pleasure as his own, then eased a finger inside her.

Thea squeezed her eyes closed. She felt him close, his breath warm on her face. He nudged her mouth and his lips hummed against hers.

"Thea?" She was tense and tight and not nearly ready for him. If he tried to take her now, he'd hurt her.

"I think you'd better kiss me some more," she whispered.

Mitch obligingly touched the corner of her mouth with

his own and didn't make the mistake of telling her to relax. "Kissing helps?"

"The way you do it."

"Remember that. I may want to use you as a reference."

Thea's lips quivered. The man had his middle finger buried inside her and she was responding to his humor. Where was the dignity in that?

"It's okay to laugh, Thea. Really." Before she could answer he kissed her again, warmly, deeply. The inside of her mouth was damp and silky and sweet and he kissed her for a long time, working her lips and tongue with his own, opening her, making her accommodate his entry, changing the shape of her mouth with subtle pressure and cautious insistence. "That's it," he murmured on a thread of sound. "Wet. Make it wet for me."

Mindless. Senseless. Weightless. Thea heard Mitch's voice come to her as if from very far away. He had two fingers inside her now, easing them back and forth and she only felt a delicate ache where he pressed his entry and stretched her for his pleasure. She was wet for him and he had made it happen with his drugging kisses and sublime assault on her mouth.

It was not coherent thought that had her lifting her hips and pushing against him, making him go deeply enough to touch the tip of her womb. Thea's inarticulate cry was somewhere between a sob and a laugh but it came from her heart.

"God, you're so beautiful." Mitch removed his fingers slowly, allowing them to brush the silky nether lips with the same delicacy his tongue had had for her mouth. He watched the uneven rise and fall of her breasts as the cadence of her breathing changed in anticipation of what he would do next. He slipped between her thighs and pushed back her knees. "Put your legs around me," he urged her. "Just like you did in the shower." Cupping her buttocks, he lifted her. "Yes. Yes,

Thea." Then he lowered himself, teasing her with the tip of his cock, torturing them both. "Hold on."

Hold on? Hold on to what? Her fingers curled so tightly her nails made tiny crescents in her palms. The muscles in her thighs contracted, her own hips surged upward, and then her arms were around his shoulders and he was full inside her, not moving now, just letting her feel the exquisite ache of finally being joined to him.

Thea's eyes fluttered open and she stared at him. The care he had shown her and the restraint he had demanded of himself had not been without cost. There was a tautness to his throat, a thin sheen of perspiration on his brow. Strands of dark blond hair had fallen forward. Thea's fist uncurled and without a thought she lifted her hand to his face and brushed them back. His skin was pulled taut and the line of his mouth had thinned. Disciplined, even ascetic features did not change the fact that he was an astonishingly beautiful man. Thea's fingers trailed lightly from his forehead, past his temple, then along the line of his jaw. Her thumb made a pass across his lips and she felt his entire body thrum with tension. His hips jerked and Thea heard her own small gasp as he seated himself even more deeply.

Mitch's voice had a rough edge but the timbre was soft. "You know what I want, Thea?"

"I have a pretty good idea," she whispered.

He shook his head, his mouth relaxing enough to curve in a deliciously wicked grin. "You don't have a clue." He lowered his head and kissed her just once, then he said against her mouth, "I want to hear you *scream*."

She had no chance to catch her breath. He rocked against and in her. Pushing. Lifting. The thrust was powerful. Her fingers tightened on his shoulders and she felt the rise and fall of his body against hers, urging her without words to match his need. Thea's throat arched as her head was pressed back against the mattress. She felt his lips on the curve of her neck. His breath was hot. Moist. His tongue flicked her skin and he said something she could not quite make out, but that sounded so erotic in his low, sweetly rumbling growl that Thea nearly came right there.

Her hands trailed restlessly to the small of his back and up the length of his spine again. She plunged her fingers into his thick hair when he raised his face and held his head just there, above hers, watching his darkening eyes and the flair of his nostrils while his body surged between her thighs.

She contracted around him each time he withdrew. Her arms. Her legs. Her vagina. Mitch groaned softly. For the first time ever, Thea understood her capacity to give and receive pleasure. It was not merely that she felt she was supposed to touch him, but that she wanted to.

His skin was warm under her fingertips and fairly vibrated with tension. He was smoothly muscled, long and lean, with two small dimples at the base of his spine and the perfect swell of tight butt and taut flanks just below. The sensitive, aching tips of her breasts abraded his chest. Her soft flesh gave with the pressure of their contact. His did not.

Thea liked that about him. That, and the way he made her forget about being quiet and reserved and discreet. He made her want him so much, and want everything that he was doing to her even more, that when she heard her own ragged little moan she didn't flush pink with embarrassment. The emotion that put color under her pale skin was something else, something that . . .

It came upon her quite suddenly. One moment she was moving with him, aware of her skin, her breathing, the immediate response of her body to everything he did and then she was shattering. There was no fall as if from a great height, no teetering on a precipice. It was just that for a moment she was whole and then she was not. If it was not quite a scream that accompanied Thea's climax, then it was a good approximation. Her slender frame lifted in an arc.

Her head was thrown back, her mouth open. She offered herself up in a single motion, a beautifully taut thrust that exposed every sculpted line and curve of her body.

The strength of her orgasm took her by surprise. She flung one hand above her head. Tension uncurled; her body shuddered. Mitch found the hand that was still at the small of his back and raised it to join the other. He stretched out, holding her slim, supple wrists in place. Her thighs no longer held him so tightly and he felt the sole of her foot slide along his calf as her leg began to unfold. He shifted slightly and changed the center of the pressure he was bringing to bear and the rhythm of his thrusts. His fingers tightened on her wrists. Her breasts rose and her abdomen retracted as she sucked in her breath.

Then she felt it again, the little catch of pleasure each time he moved, each time his weight bore down in a certain way, and her eyes widened and her heels pressed hard in the mattress and her hands sought purchase but were contained by his. She was a single nerve ending, stretched tautly from the tip of her opalescent toenails to her flushed brow. Pleasure skittered across the surface of her skin. It rolled in waves, pounding, roaring, then crashed and curled deeply inside her and finally dragged her under.

This time she screamed.

It was all Mitch needed. His own hoarse shout, part laughter, part exhilaration, pushed him over the edge. He came hard, his hips pumping quickly and shallowly, then not at all. His body vibrated in the aftermath and he lay heavily on top of Thea for a moment, insensible of everything except profound contentment.

His fingers opened on her wrists and he lightly brushed the slender pulse cord with the ball of his thumb. She didn't jerk away or try to lower her arms. They remained above her head and she remained still beneath him. Mitch drew himself up slowly, resting most of his weight on his forearms, and looked down at her. "Breathe," he told her gently, then he watched, fascinated, as her generous mouth puckered slightly and she sipped air as if through a straw. Delicate. Precise. Refined. It made him smile.

Thea stopped breathing. "What?"

He shook his head. "Nothing."

She didn't press. Coherent thought was still difficult and he'd only told her to breathe, not think. She continued sipping air.

Mitch lifted his hips and eased himself out of Thea and from between her thighs. He rolled on his side, sliding one leg over hers and propping himself up on an elbow. Her skin was almost incandescent with a fine sheen of perspiration. He realized the room felt cooler now and he found the sheet twisted beneath him and after a little tussle, yanked it over his hips and across Thea. She lowered her arms and took the finished edge of the sheet in her hands. She fingered the hem but didn't lift it. The dark material lay against her skin just under the curves of her breasts.

Thea's eyes darted once toward Mitch then refocused their attention on the ceiling. "Some scream, uh?"

Mitch didn't miss the quiet self-mockery in her tone. "It embarrassed you?"

"Not just at that moment . . . but now . . ." She nodded. "I've . . . ummm, I've never . . ."

One of Mitch's brows lifted. "Never had an orgasm?"

Thea's mouth curled to one side in wry amusement. "Of course I've had an orgasm," she said.

There was no "of course" about it, thought Mitch, though she would have him believe that were the case. A hint of defensiveness in her tone made him wonder what she wasn't quite wanting him to know. His gaze narrowed, studying the face that she wouldn't turn in his direction and the dark green eyes that were apparently still captivated by his ceiling fan. "But . . ." he prompted, fishing.

Just considering what she might say brought a rush of color to Thea's cheeks. "Oh, God," she moaned softly, squeezing her eyes shut. It wasn't enough. Not nearly enough. Her hand fell to one side and she groped blindly for one of the pillows. When she caught one downy corner with her fingertips she clutched it like a lifeline and yanked it hard over her face, holding it in place with her forearms. "Bup nop wif somwom."

Thea's rose-tipped breasts were still very much visible so Mitch looked at those. "Yeah?" he asked. His fingers walked lightly up her rib cage and climbed her left breast. The aureole was puckered and the nipple stood erect. Good little soldier. He made his index finger circle it. The little guy practically saluted.

"Stumpf dat."

Mitch gave the same attention to her right breast.

Thea's smothered voice rose again from under the pillow. "Stumpf dat." This time she swatted his hand with one of hers.

"Oh," he said pleasantly, undeterred. *"Stop that."* He let his hand fall still at the level of her waist. "Your pillow talk needs a little work."

She groaned softly.

Mitch grinned. He could imagine her rolling her eyes. "So what was that other thing you said? About all those orgasms you've had?"

"Ah fad—"

Mitch lifted one corner of the pillow.

"I said," she repeated a trifle impatiently, *"but not with someone."*

It still took Mitch a few moments to understand the gist of what she was telling him. She'd had orgasms before, but not with someone. The sudden vision he had of Thea stretched out alone on her own bed, one hand caressing her breast, the other in finger play between her thighs, rendered him speechless. His cock even stirred a little, and after the workout he'd just given it, it was a tribute to the powerful clarity of the image in his mind's eye.

"Whoa," he said softly, letting the pillow fall back in place.

Thea came out from under it slowly, dragging it forward so that it covered her neck and chest. Her face was warm and she knew it didn't have a lot to do with the fact that she had just tried to smother herself. She glanced at Mitch, her eyes wary. "More than you wanted to know, right?"

His smile was a trifle lopsided. "No way. Guys always want to know. Women won't usually tell us."

She bit her lower lip. "Yeah, well, I've never been very good at the postcoital wrap-up."

"Oh, I think this one is going pretty spectacularly." He pointed to the light fixture in the ceiling fan. "Smile for the camera."

That made Thea laugh. She poked him lightly with her elbow.

Mitch accepted the nudge, then took the security pillow away from her and tucked it under her head. "Better," he said. Cupping one side of her face, he bent his head and kissed her. "Anything else you want to tell me?"

"Like what? You want to know if I use toys?"

The elbow that was propping Mitch up actually collapsed. His head thudded to the mattress. The leg that was lying over hers fell away as he rolled onto his back. "Don't tease me," he groaned feelingly. "That's not right."

Thea turned on her side to look at him. She drew her knees up, bumping his thigh under the covers. He had a great profile: well-defined jaw; squared-off chin; angular cheek. From the side she could see a faint rise at the bridge of his nose. His hair had fallen away from his brow. There was an indentation at his temple. Thea could just make out the regular beat of his pulse. She stared at it.

Mitch's head swiveled to the side and caught her out. She didn't look away, which he liked. "So do you?"

Thea gave him an enigmatic smile and said nothing.

"You're killing me, you know that?"

She nodded. Their eyes locked. Thea's smile slowly faded and Mitch's half grin disappeared. "I'm on Depo-Provera shots," she said quietly, seriously. "Every three months. You don't have to worry about a pregnancy, but—"

"Yeah," he said, sighing, "I blew the condom. I'm usually more careful." He'd always been with Gina. She couldn't use birth control pills or take the shots, so she had been using a diaphragm for as long as she had been sexually active. Condoms were part of the ritual with her and Mitch had never failed to remember. He hadn't even thought about it with Thea. "If it helps, I've been tested," he said. "Gina, too. There hasn't been anyone else . . . until you. Until now."

"What about Gina?"

Mitch exhaled softly. "Gina and I haven't been together for weeks. We've talked on the phone a few times since the night we went out with you and Joel, but we haven't slept together since . . . well, that's not important. I don't have any reason to think that Gina was sleeping with anyone else. She was the one who insisted on the testing in the first place so she's cautious."

Thea slipped one arm under her pillow, raising her head slightly. "Joel was the one who was adamant about it. I wouldn't have had the nerve to ask him, so I suppose it was good that he raised the issue. He hated condoms. He'd been married for thirty some years when his wife died and he'd never worn one in all that time. When he started seeing women again, started sleeping with them, the world had changed. He realized he had no choice but to use one if he was going to be responsible—and Joel is all that." She made a small shrug. "Sometimes I think he wanted to be in a monogamous relationship because it just made the sex details easier. It was his idea that I get the shots. No fussing with pills or a diaphragm. Spermacides. Jellies. He didn't want to have to think about any of it, and he was clear at the outset that he didn't want more children."

"That was all right with you?"

Thea hesitated before she answered. "I thought it was. I told him I felt the same and I believed it when I said it." Her expression softened. "Then Gabe and Kathy died and the children he didn't want were ones I knew and cared about and then I wasn't sure about much of anything any longer."

"Including you and Joel."

"Especially me and Joel."

Mitch ran a hand through his hair, nodding faintly. "I found your engagement ring in your purse." He didn't miss Thea's eyes widening. Before she accused him of something, he pressed her memory. "At the urgent care, remember? I was helping you register?"

"Oh." Her smile was a trifle lopsided. "I remember. You were holding my purse. It was kind of sweet."

He pinned her back with a narrow glance and a scowl. "Don't push it, lady." His expression relaxed. "So when did you take it off?"

Thea thought back to her conversation with Rosie. "A few days ago," she said. "It wasn't a last-minute decision, but just before I got out of the car, I was trying to decide if I should put it back on."

Mitch wondered who had helped her work it out. "Who were you talking to then?"

"You saw me on the phone?"

That was an easy admission and he nodded once. What he wasn't prepared to tell her was that he had been waiting impatiently on the other side of the window, slowly crushing a can of Dr. Pepper in his fist. "Was it Joel?"

It surprised her that he would think that. "No. It was Rosie. My sponsor."

"Rosie."

"Mmm. I needed to talk to her. I was . . . well, I was nervous about coming here . . . about seeing you."

"Nervous." Although he said the word flatly, Mitch still managed to imbue it with meaning.

"Anxious," she clarified. "More than fluttery. Like I wanted to come out of my skin." Thea sighed and said bluntly, "The precursor to a panic attack, and the kind of feeling that usually had me reaching for the Ativan or Valium."

"That's what I do to you?"

Thea shook her head. "No," she said firmly. "That's what I do to myself. Rosie's like a coach. She reminds me to breathe. To think. She reminds me that I'll live through it, whatever it is that's uncomfortable or scary." She took a little breath and exhaled slowly as her eyes roamed Mitch's still features. "You probably guessed already, but I've never been with anyone without taking something first. Ever." Her short laugh held no real humor; rather, it mocked her. "Wanna fuck? Sure. Let me find the Xannies in my purse. That's how I approached it, like something I had to get through. The pills dialed down the intensity of everything I was feeling. Mostly it dialed down the fear. Fear that I'd do something wrong. That I wouldn't be good enough. I could never figure out how to handle being in the moment. There's always a next thing, isn't there? I'm pretty much scared to death of the next thing. It wasn't about the sex. Not really. It's about being so close to someone. Physically. Emotionally. I'm mostly still a mess, Mitch, and that's *with* therapy. You shouldn't forget it."

He gave her a frank look. "Trying to scare me off again?"

"I don't know."

He appreciated how truthful she was trying to be and how much it pained her. "What do I need to do?" he asked. "Tell me."

"I don't know that either. I'm not certain I'm supposed to be with you now. That's why I was calling Rosie."

"For permission?"

Thea chuckled. "That's what she said I was doing. Looking for someone to blame it on if it didn't work out."

"And if it *did* work out?" he asked. "Because I thought back there in the shower we were working it out pretty good."

"Mmm . . . yes. The shower was good."

"And bed? That was the real thing, wasn't it?"

"Real," she said in a small voice. "Yes. Real."

"And what about now? What did you call it? The post-coital wrap-up? I think we've touched on the critical aspects. Just for the record, though, that *was* a scream we all heard."

She swallowed. "We?"

"You. Me. Every other living thing in a two-block radius."

Thea pulled the pillow out from under her head and whacked him with it. Mitch wrestled it free, pitched it over the side of the bed, and pinned her back to the mattress. It was a short battle but they were both breathing a little harder than when it began. Their smiles faded simultaneously.

Mitch regarded her gravely, choosing his words carefully. She would be a lot easier to scare off than he was. "I like you, Thea. You know I do. And I'm not with you now because of the kids, or at least not strictly because of them. I want you to be certain about that. Obviously there's a lot I've never known about you, but that was the point of yesterday, to get to know you."

"And the point of this morning?" she asked mildly.

"To get to know you better."

He said it with such practicality that Thea found herself smiling again. "Did I always suspect this about you?" she wondered aloud.

"Suspect what?"

Reaching up, Thea touched the side of his face. Her

thumb brushed his lips. They parted marginally under the
pressure, revealing the slightly uneven ridge of his teeth.
"That you don't take things too seriously."

Mitch didn't believe that. "There are plenty of things I
take seriously. Global warming. Nuclear weapons in Pak-
istan and India. The Steelers winning another Super Bowl."
He paused. "My family."

"Yes," she said. All of that was true. "But not yourself. It
makes you freer somehow that you can laugh at things, that
you always see the humor or irony, sometimes both at once.
I suppose that's what makes you so good at what you do."

"You're talking about my political cartoons, aren't you?"

Her smile broadened in response to his disappointment.
She tapped his cheek lightly. "You do all right for yourself."

The fact that she refused to stroke his bedroom ego didn't
bother him in the least. He wasn't going to forget how she
came under him anytime soon. Or how she came again. "Up
you go," he said, bussing her on the lips. "Let's get some
breakfast."

Thea's mouth watered. "French toast?"

"I'll speak with the chef."

Before he saw her drool, Thea gave his shoulders a little
push. Mitch rolled himself out of bed, taking the sheet with
him. He hitched it around his waist while he shamefully
ogled Thea before she tumbled out of bed on the other side.
She paid him scant heed, pivoting on the balls of her feet
and heading for the bathroom. Mitch enjoyed the view the
entire way. On the point of stepping inside, Thea gave him a
cheeky grin over her shoulder. "Pretty good ass, isn't it?"

"Amen," he said softly as she closed the door. Amen
to that.

It was over breakfast that they took stock of their situation. The snow had stopped sometime during the night but

there were ten inches of it in the driveway. The street had had one visit from the snowplow and was still largely impassable.

"What does this mean for the kids and your parents?" asked Thea.

"Another day at Seven Springs and no school tomorrow, maybe not even the day after. They're really going to hate that." He cocked an eyebrow to let her know he was kidding. "I'll call them in a little while and make certain Mum and Dad know about the weather here so they can decide how soon they want to try to leave. What about you?"

"I suppose I need to call about my car. Find out what the garage is going to do."

"It's Sunday," he reminded her.

Thea squeezed an extra dollop of warm syrup on her plate. She hadn't been thinking about the fact the mechanic was entitled to a day off. Sighing, she pierced a triangle of bread with her fork and slid it through the syrup. "Then I suppose whether or not I get home today depends on you."

"You know, I'm already regretting buying that SUV. My truck would have had a tough time in snow this deep."

"I'm not in a hurry," she said, glancing up at him. "I mean, if you're not eager to get me out of your hair or anything."

"You mean . . . ?"

She nodded. "Uh-huh. We could have a snowball fight."

Mitch's eyes gleamed. "A good second choice."

Thea's skin glowed warmly. Ducking her head to avoid his knowing glance, she speared another piece of bread.

"How do you feel?"

She almost said "happy," but then she realized that he was most probably referring to her physical health. He'd turned her brain to mush, that's what he'd done. Who the hell said "happy" when someone asked them how they were feeling? For that matter, who admitted to having orgasms only when they masturbated? Maybe you'd tell a girlfriend that, or write it in your journal, but telling the man who'd just made you pop off two in a row? He already proved he had way too much power and wasn't afraid to use it.

"Okay," she said, shrugging. "I'm okay." There was this delicious sense of space between her thighs; something that was almost an ache defined the hollowness. It made her conscious of her own body in a way she hadn't been before, and conscious of Mitch in a way she always had.

"Nothing tender? Sore?"

Her gaze flew to his. "I'm *okay*. I've had sex before."

"Well, good," he said carefully. It was a near thing. He almost choked on a mouthful of food. "But I was referring to your accident. You did put the Volvo on its side."

"Oh." She pressed her lips together as she evaluated her situation. On the one hand, she'd just made an idiot of herself, and on the other . . . on the other it was pretty much the same thing. Not exactly the balance she had been looking for. "There's never a trapdoor or one of those little Acme rocket seats when you need one."

"No, but those'd be great, wouldn't they? Maybe I'll have them installed in the new house."

Just like that, Thea thought, he'd given her a hand up. "New house?"

Mitch picked up his coffee mug. "I told you, remember?" He drank. "I've been thinking about it since I got the kids."

Thea glanced around Mitch's spacious and bright kitchen, looking for a rationale. "I don't understand. This isn't like your Chevy or the Indian. You have plenty of room here for everyone."

"It's not about room. It's about territory. It's been a tough adjustment for all of us." Mitch regarded her over the rim of his mug. "I'm not satisfied that I'm doing the right thing by making them live here. Sometimes—I don't know—it bothers me when there are video games under the coffee table or I step on cars on the stairs. There's no room in the garage for anything else. Emilie's bedroom was where I kept most of my books. Now they're stacked in what was the guest room along with a lot of other junk, and I haven't been able to put my hands on anything in under twenty minutes. That's sounds pretty selfish, doesn't it?" Mitch put his mug down and held up one hand to stop Thea from answering. "Don't bother. I know it's selfish. I'm just not sure what to do about it. You've seen my office, so you know I'm not a neat freak. The problem is, it's always been *my* mess. My space and my mess. I don't know why it's so annoying when it belongs to someone else, but I'm not sure I'm ever going to get used to it. I keep thinking that it would be less of a problem for all of us if we took a place that wasn't mine or theirs, but ours."

"How has it been a problem for the kids?" Thea asked.

"It isn't their home," he said simply. "Early on, I tried doing some weekend nights at their place. That didn't work."

"Perhaps it was too soon."

"Maybe. Probably. There were nightmares and lots of fighting, but it was more than that, too. I didn't fit there. It was like putting on someone else's shoes. In this case, there were two pair, and neither was comfortable."

"I see," she said gently. "So you're thinking about a family transplant."

Mitch considered that. "I guess I am. I thought maybe I'd talk to Gina about looking for a place for us. House hunting is her expertise, not mine."

Thea kept her expression carefully neutral. What had she thought? That he'd ask her to help? "You might want to find out what the kids think about this, and in the event they like the idea, you might want to consider what they think is important."

"Yeah, but then I'd end up with a pool in the basement and a half pipe for trick bikes in the backyard. I'll take your suggestion under advisement, though."

"It's just about letting them voice an opinion. They'll have one."

"They'll have three."

"And you'll have the final decision."

"You don't think they'll want to move, do you?"

"I don't know what they'll want or what they're ready for. That's the point of discussing it with them."

Mitch's head tilted to one side. "All right," he said finally. "I will." His eyes narrowed thoughtfully. "How'd you get so smart about it?"

Thea didn't know that she was. She stood, picking up her plate and silverware. She gave him a small, careless shrug. "I was a kid, I had opinions, and no one ever asked me what I wanted. It's not exactly rocket science."

No, Mitch thought. It was much, much harder.

After cleanup, Thea collected her toiletries from Mitch's bedroom while he called his parents. She put some moisturizer on her face and added lip gloss to her mouth before she tossed everything into her bag. Thoroughly conscious now of Mitch's territory and how he wouldn't want to be finding her things three days from now, Thea spent some time looking around for the stray article she was inadvertently leaving behind.

Mitch was still on the phone when Thea returned downstairs. Not wanting to disturb him, she sat on one of the lower steps hugging her knees and waited for him to finish his call.

From his side of the conversation Thea gathered he was talking to one of his parents. He gave a report of the local snowfall and cautioned them that they wouldn't be able to get into their own driveway if they tried to leave today. "Give me today to shovel you a way in," he was saying. "It'll be okay. There probably won't be school tomorrow anyway.

Sure, I know the turnpike is going to be clear, but trust me, you're going to get hung up in town."

Smiling to herself, Thea rested one shoulder against the banister, watching Mitch through the rails. He could have seen her if he turned around, so Thea didn't think of herself as an eavesdropper. Neither did she do anything to make her presence known. She liked the view she had.

"Yeah, Mum," Mitch was saying. "Uh-uh . . . right . . . well, I don't know. My political stuff is more about the national conscience. I don't think local snow removal makes much of a statement in a big picture kind of way. Yeah . . . but that's different. When the snow's in D.C., Mum, it *is* on a national level. A bureaucrat in a federal building can't get to work that day and some poor jamoke in Fargo doesn't get his social security. Uh-uh . . . yeah . . . tell you what, I think you better listen to Dad and put Emilie on. Mmmm . . . that's a good idea, Mum. Write a letter to the editor. He loves to hear from you."

Thea's grin deepened. Mitch was leaning into the kitchen counter by the phone base, his elbows resting on the top. He had the receiver propped in the crook made by his head and shoulder and he was tapping a pen on a piece of paper. Occasionally he wrote or doodled, but mostly he just tapped. It wasn't an impatient or agitated gesture, more like an absent one, a lazy workout to keep his wrist supple and his arm flexed.

"Hi, Em. I told Nonny you and the boys will have an extra day of skiing. Don't worry. No school tomorrow. Yes, I'm sure."

Thea saw him cross two fingers on his free hand.

"Umm, yeah. Aunt Thea's here . . . well, she decided it was snowing too hard to drive home so she stayed. . . .Yes, like a sleepover."

Aunt Thea noticed Mitch was not uncrossing his fingers.

"Uh, sure. She liked sleeping in your room. No, I don't

know if she slept with your animals. I'll let her know it's okay if she has to spend another night."

Thea's attention strayed from the conversation. Mitch was wearing a loose-fitting shaker knit sweater that matched his jeans in terms of faded color and comfort. He had the raglan sleeves casually pushed up to his elbows, and because he was leaning forward at the waist, the sweater had hitched up a few inches in the back and exposed his narrow hips and tight butt to an appreciative audience of one.

"Do you want to talk to her?" Mitch was asking. "Sure. She's around somewhere."

Before Thea could avert her glance, Mitch turned and caught her staring at his behind.

Surprise faded quickly and the left corner of his mouth lifted in a quirky grin. "Just a second, Em." He placed one hand over the mouthpiece and pointed to his butt with the crossed fingers of the other. "Pretty great posterior, eh?" Thea gave him a prim, butter-wouldn't-melt smile that in no way altered his good opinion of his own ass. Chuckling, he held out the phone to her, the mouthpiece still covered. "Em wants to talk. You heard what I said about where you slept?"

Straightening, Thea nodded. "Don't worry," she said. "I have a vested interest in this, too." Mitch met her halfway with the phone and Thea took it from his outstretched hand. "Hi, Emilie. How's skiing?" Thea felt Mitch step just behind her. His arms circled her waist and drew her back against him, fitting her snugly against his chest and thighs. "Oh, yes. I liked sleeping in your bed. No, I moved the animals to the floor. I didn't want to accidentally kick them while I slept."

Mitch was halfway to nuzzling her neck when he stopped. "I wish you had had the same consideration for me," he whispered.

"Just a moment, Em." She held the phone against her midriff and spoke softly to Mitch. "You want to sleep on the floor?"

"No. I meant that—"

"Then be quiet." She lifted the receiver. "Sorry, Em. Your uncle was being annoying. Mmm-hmm. Just like your brothers." Well, perhaps, not *just* like them. Mitch was nuzzling her neck now and the hands he had slipped under her pink cashmere sweater were inching their way up to her breasts. "Ummm. I guess I could punch his lights out. Is that what you do? No, I mean to your brothers, not your uncle." Mitch's low, rumbling laughter sent a little shiver through Thea. The consequence of that was Mitch electing to hold her closer. "Sometimes you hide their stuff? That's pretty sneaky, Em. It takes a little planning. What do you think I'd have to hide to annoy your uncle Mitch?"

Thea stiffened and in response, Mitch went still. "Say that again, Emilie? I'm not sure I heard you." Thea held out the phone so Mitch could hear her answer at the same time.

Emilie's voice was as perfectly clear this time as it had been the last. She said brightly, "His gun."

Chapter 10

Thea knelt on the sofa and drew the window curtain aside. Mitch was still shoveling snow off the driveway. He had two packed heaps of it on either side of the pavement and still had five feet to go to get out to the street. Like every other driveway on the block, Mitch's now resembled a luge run. Thea doubted anyone else was going at the job with the maniacal intensity that Mitch was displaying. He had already done the sidewalk from the house, as well as the sidewalk that paralleled the street, and he hadn't slowed yet. She watched him swing the shovel as if it were a weapon.

Shaking her head, Thea sank down against the plump cushions. She would have liked to have gone outside to help him, but he was clear he didn't want her. No, that wasn't quite true. He wanted to be alone and Thea understood there was a difference and she respected it. He was so terribly angry. There didn't seem to be anything she could say or do that would change that and he needed to get it out of his system. She could see that it was eating him up.

It was the gun. Mitch's face had gone ashen the moment he'd heard Emilie's voice saying those words. His hand actually shook as he took the phone from Thea and pressed it to his own ear. He asked Emilie a succession of questions in a no-nonsense tone that the little girl wasn't used to hearing from him. Where did you see it? Did you touch it? Do the twins know about it? Did you find the bullets? Even before he was done grilling Emilie, Thea could hear the child sobbing. It was at that point that his mother took the phone and let Mitchell know what she thought of his interrogation and the fact that he apparently had a gun in the house. Watching Mitch's pale stoic features, seeing the muscle twitch in his cheek as he listened to his mother was hard enough; knowing that Jennie wasn't telling him anything he wasn't already thinking, was harder still. Before Jennie had completely wound down, he simply handed Thea the phone and walked away.

She managed to diplomatically end the call a few minutes later and went in search of Mitch. She found him in the guest room on his haunches, an open lockbox near his heels and a Smith & Wesson revolver in his hands.

The sight of the gun had stopped Thea on the threshold. She wasn't afraid to hold one herself, but never was comfortable seeing one in someone else's hands. "Is it loaded?"

"No." He hadn't looked at her, but waved his arm to indicate the crowded expanse of the room. "The bullets are in here somewhere. I kept them in another box." He had lifted his head, then there was an expression of cold fear in his eyes at what might have been. "I stored the bullets in a goddamned crayon box, Thea. A goddamned *crayon* box."

That's when he had proceeded to tear the room apart, toppling stacks of books, opening packing crates. He went through an old album collection, cigar boxes with childhood treasures, and several large clear plastic containers that held infrequently used art supplies. Thea had not asked if she could help him; she pitched in without an invitation and although the contents of the room were turned on end, they couldn't find the bullets.

"Perhaps Emilie didn't know the twins had found them," Thea suggested. "Or she lied."

Mitch's head had snapped up. "Lied? Why would she do that?"

Because she was scared, Thea almost said. Instead, she told him with gentle practicality, "For the same reason most of us lie. Because we think we can get out of trouble. Trust me, Mitch. I know something about it."

"She wasn't going to be in trouble."

"Emilie didn't know that." Thea stood and offered her hand to Mitch. "Come on. I have an idea."

It had turned out to be a good one. They found several green-and-yellow boxes in the desk that the twins shared. Mitch immediately grabbed the one that advertised twenty-four colors on the outside of the box and flipped the top. The familiar crayon smell lingered but it was the bullets that were inside.

Mitch's relief was palpable although he didn't enjoy it long. Thea suspected he thought he had no right to feel it. He was up and down the stairs several times looking for a place to hide the lockbox and stash the bullets until he could get rid of both. He wandered out to the garage and down to the basement. Finally he disappeared into his office and when he came out he was empty-handed. It was after that that he had gone outside to shovel snow.

The sound of the SUV's engine pulled Thea's attention to the window again. She was in time to see Mitch backing out of the driveway. If he saw her looking out, he didn't acknowledge it. The SUV was headed up the street.

Mitch didn't return for more than an hour. Thea was sitting curled in a large chair in the living room, working the Sunday crossword when she heard the garage door open. Her first instinct was to go to meet him but she thought better of it. He made a noisy entrance, stomping snow off his boots in the breezeway. The snow shovel clattered in the garage. He had his jacket and scarf in hand when he reached the living room and stopped in his tracks. He wasn't quick enough to mask his surprise.

Thea knew that look. "You forgot I was here."

"I . . . um . . . yeah." Embarrassed, his cheeks puffed as he exhaled a short breath and his weight shifted from one foot to the other. "Pretty bad, uh? No question now that I've lost my mind."

Thea ignored that. Her eyes quickly took in his ruddy, weary features and asked softly, "You doin' okay?"

He shrugged. "I drove up to my parents' and cleared their driveway and the street entrance."

"I thought that's where you might have gone. Can I make you something hot to drink?"

Mitch shook his head. "There's still some coffee in the pot. I'll warm that up."

Thea watched him hang up his jacket and scarf and then disappear into the kitchen. His thick, gray woolen socks were soundless on the tile. She expected to hear him picking up the pot, getting a mug from the cupboard, or running the microwave. There was nothing. The silence lasted so long that it finally unnerved her. Putting aside the crossword and pen, Thea uncurled from the chair and went to see what he was doing.

Mitch was standing in front of the sink staring out the window, his arms braced against the stainless-steel rim, his shoulders slightly hunched. From Thea's vantage point she couldn't see what he was looking at. She suspected it was nothing outside the window that held his attention.

"Mitch?"

He didn't turn. A small shudder ran from his neck to the base of his spine. He quickly flipped the lever on the faucet and ran the hot water, cupping his hands under it, then splashing some on his face. He pulled open a nearby drawer, found a clean tea towel, and used it to dry himself. "Still thawing out," he said without looking at her. He tossed the towel on the counter and proceeded to get a mug. "Do you want some?" He lifted the cold carafe from the coffeemaker and held it up.

Thea stared at his back. "No, thank you."

Mitch poured coffee into his mug and set it in the microwave. He hit a few buttons. The noise the unit made effectively interfered with conversation for two long minutes. Thea, though, was waiting for him when the timer finished its countdown.

"Nothing happened, Mitch," she said. "No one was hurt. You don't even know if the twins ever knew about the gun or if Emilie knew about the bullets. This is a might-have-been, not a was."

Turning around, Mitch leaned back against the counter and held the mug between his hands, oblivious to the heat. His eyes were bleak. "I fucked up, Thea. That's pretty much it." His chin came up, almost daring her to say something in his defense. When she was silent, he jumped on it. "Good to know we agree on this."

"That isn't—"

He didn't let her finish. "I don't know if I can do this, Thea. Just when I think I can, something . . ." He shrugged again because his voice locked up. No words were going to move past the hard, aching lump at the back of his throat.

"What are you saying?" The look in Thea's eyes had gone from concern to wariness. Her body was already responding to the first inklings of panic. She could feel her insides curling, twisting, and the knots begin to form. "You're not thinking I could take them?"

His smile was derisive. "And send them from the frying pan into the fire? I don't think so. Stop worrying that you'll have to do something more than write a check or screw me from time to time. No judge is going to let a neurotic, pill-popping addict have the kids."

Thea simply stared at him. She would have given

anything to have been able to rein in her hurt, to not have let him see it, but her reaction was swift and clearly visible. Color flooded her neck and face and even her scalp felt hot. Her eyes were so dry that she had to blink to moisten them and her tongue was cleaved to the roof of her mouth.

A muscle jumped in Mitch's cheek. His entire body jerked in response to seeing the pain he had just inflicted. He felt hot coffee splash the back of his hand and wrist and knew that had he poured the entire mug of scalding liquid on himself, it was nothing compared to what he had just dumped on Thea. He put down the coffee mug and took a step toward her. He wasn't at all surprised when she took a step in the other direction.

Mitch stayed where he was, running one hand through his hair in an impatient, at-a-loss-for-most-words gesture. He swore softly because those words always came to mind. "Thea, I'm—"

She held up one hand. It was trembling slightly. "Don't you dare apologize to me for saying what you think. Most of it was true anyway. Let's just leave it."

"No, that's not what you and I need—"

"And don't ever presume to think you know what I need to do," she said flatly. "I'm going upstairs to get my bag. If you'll drive me someplace where I can get a rental, I'll get out of here. Obviously you need some time to feel sorry for yourself. You don't need me here for that."

"Thea, I don't think—"

She turned her back on him and started for the stairs.

"If it's the truth," he called after her, "then why can't we talk about it? Why are you running away?"

Thea paused briefly, her hand tightening on the banister. She stared back at him for a moment, on the verge of speaking, then shook her head slightly, thinking better of it. She continued up the steps.

Mitch had the keys in hand when she came back down.

Without a word he took her bag from her and gave Thea her jacket. "Give me a minute to warm up the car."

Nodding shortly, Thea sat herself down on the stairs. As soon as Mitch was gone, she dug in her purse for her cell and brought up Rosie's number. She almost wept when her call went straight to voice mail. "It's Thea, Rosie . . . I guess I'll call you when I get home. It's . . . umm . . . it's gone to hell in a handcart. I think I told Mitch too much, though he gave me some great sympathy sex, so maybe it was worth baring all." She groaned softly. "Sorry. Robby, if you get this message first, ignore that. Got to go." As an afterthought she added, "Oh. I'm doing okay. Mitch didn't have anything in his medicine cabinet except aspirin and antibiotics that expired in the last century." She tapped End Call. Rosie wouldn't have any trouble understanding what she was really saying.

Thea turned off the phone so Rosie couldn't call or text her while she was in the car with Mitch and then dropped it back in her purse. The SUV was warm but not toasty when Thea climbed inside. Mitch closed the garage door and backed out of the driveway after she was buckled in. Snow crunched under the tires as soon as they were out in the street but the all-wheel drive made short work of the deep ruts.

Thea swiveled sideways so she could drop her purse on the bench seat behind her. She caught Mitch's furtive glance in her direction. He was obviously looking for an opening to talk to her. "I'm not mad at you, Mitch," she said, turning to face front again. Thea pushed her hands inside her pockets. "If I'm mad at anyone, it's me. Joel warned me I should think carefully before I decided to tell people about my addiction, that there might be consequences I hadn't considered. I suppose this is one of those times I didn't think it completely through."

Mitch's strongest reaction was to Thea's reference to Joel as the clear-headed, cautious prophet. He had to make himself pause a beat to absorb the rest of what she was saying. "What consequences are you talking about?"

She looked over at him, disbelief making her mute for a moment. Hadn't he heard himself? "Look, Mitch, I know a judge still has to approve us being named legal guardians for the kids," she said. "Wayne explained that to me a couple of weeks ago. At the same time he told me a new judge would hear the case."

"Wayne told you that? Not that cold fish Childers?"

"I fired Avery the morning after we all met at Wayne's office."

Mitch wondered about that but he had the good sense not to pursue it. "Go on," he prompted.

"Isn't it obvious? I'm going to get cut out of the kids' lives because I'm a neurotic pill-popper. As soon as the judge finds out I've been to rehab and have less than six weeks of abstinence out of it, she's going to have cause to keep me away from the kids."

"What? You think I was making some kind of threat back there? I'm not going to tell her."

"No," she said softly. "I am. And don't pretend you don't think she should know. She has to be informed to make the best decision she can about the children's welfare." Thea turned slightly toward Mitch, drawing one leg up under her. He was staring straight ahead, his eyes fixed on the road, though Thea doubted that he was giving it his full attention. If he had glanced in her direction he would have seen the naked plea for understanding in her eyes. "Mitch, if you decide that you don't want the children—for whatever reason—I won't be the one to get them. They'll be placed in foster care. Perhaps they'll be able to stay together, but there are no guarantees. They could be separated."

He glanced at her, his expression skeptical. "Separated? They don't do that anymore."

Thea actually laughed, albeit without humor. Borrowing

Rosie's phrase, she asked, "Are you new to the planet? Mitch, it happens all the time. I sit on the board of a family services agency that operates foster care homes. No one likes to split children up but sometimes there's no single home available that can take all of them. Sometimes one child has more problems with the move than the others and the foster parents can't handle the misbehavior. That child can be removed and placed with another family and never be reunited with siblings again. Don't misunderstand me. There are wonderful foster parents out there. The Reasoners were like that and Emilie, Case, and Grant are great kids, so someone will come forward to adopt them, even as old as they are, and—"

"Like hell."

"And you'll be fortunate," Thea went on inexorably, "if you get to know where they've gone or how they're doing or even if they've been able to stay together. Then there's the whole problem of what the kids will think. You can tell them ten different ways to Sunday that it was *you* that fucked up and they'll live with the certainty that it was them."

"I've heard enough, Th—"

Thea talked right over him. "Tell them you let them go because you felt inadequate to the task of parenting them, that you forgot about a gun you had when you were a single guy, responsible to no one but yourself. Convince them it isn't their fault they're being taken from you because they stumbled on a lockbox in a room full of treasures and got curious. I swear to God, Mitch, that if they tell you they understand that they're not to blame, they're lying through their teeth. We all think it's our fault. We think if we had just been a little smarter, a little better, stood straighter, complained less, didn't cry, did our home—"

She fell silent abruptly. When had she stopped talking about Emilie and the twins and included herself in the circle of all children who believed they were to blame for the things that were done to them? "I'm sorry," she said softly, turning and facing the windshield again. Leaning her head back, Thea closed her eyes. She felt the press of tears against her lids and the dampening of her lashes when they could not be contained.

"It was never your fault, Thea," Mitch said after a moment.

Without opening her eyes, Thea offered up a faint, watery smile. "I know that," she said quietly. "I have for a very long time. The tough part is believing it." She turned her head toward the side window and impatiently wiped the tears away. She was glad when Mitch didn't say anything. There was some part of her that wished she had shown the same discretion when he had stood so forlornly at the kitchen sink and stared out at nothing. But no, she was so uncomfortable with all those unpleasant feelings, even when they weren't her own, that she had to try to fix them, ease them, make it better . . . not for Mitch, but for herself.

Thea's vision gradually cleared. She became aware of the bare-limbed trees lining the highway that were now perfectly outlined by the heavy snow. Branches drooped under the weight, making canopies that were like frosting and lace. Evergreen boughs were lowered toward their trunks, making the trees slimmer and more stately. They stood poised on the edge of the wood, still and serene, brides in waiting.

"Where are we going?" she asked suddenly.

"I'm taking you home."

Thea pushed herself upright. "I said I'd get a rental and drive myself."

"I heard what you said." He didn't add that he hadn't agreed. By now that was obvious to Thea. "There's not a whole lot you can do about it, so I don't know that haranguing me serves much purpose. Unless you need to do it on general principle."

Thea wasn't certain what that general principle was, but she didn't subscribe to it. She let him off without a fight.

It took them a little more than an hour to reach her home. They didn't speak again until Mitch turned the SUV into her drifted-over driveway. "You want me to shovel this for you? You won't be able to get your Porsche out."

She shook her head. "I have a snowblower. One of the kids in the neighborhood will come over if I call. I probably won't use the Porsche anyway. I'll get a cab or share a ride into town tomorrow." Thea opened the door. A blast of cold wind immediately filled the interior. "Thanks, though," she added belatedly. "It was a nice offer."

Mitch put the SUV in neutral and set the brake. "Listen, Thea, I hope we can talk about what happened today. If not now, then sometime soon. I don't want to leave it like this."

Except for the small vertical crease between her brow hinting that she understood, Thea's expression was perfectly blank. "I don't know what—"

"That's beneath you," he cut in. "You know very well what I'm saying. For God's sake, Thea, let me at least apologize."

In the act of pulling her bag and purse from the backseat, Thea paused. "I meant it when I said I don't want an apology, Mitch. I told you what I was and I made a point of asking you not to forget." She shrugged lightly, putting effort into careless-ness. "I just didn't anticipate it being thrown back in my face, is all. It's a good thing to know it can happen." Thea slung her purse over her shoulder and clutched the bag under one arm. "Thanks for the lift." She hopped down, sank halfway to her knees in snow, and still managed to smile brightly. "Bye."

Mitch almost recoiled as the door was slammed, if not in his face, then close enough to feel like it. He sat where he was and watched Thea make her way to the front door. It wasn't the graceful exit she might have wished for. The snow was too deep for her to do anything but make an awk-ward march up the sidewalk. She fumbled in her purse for the key, finding it only after a prolonged search that frus-trated her enough to drop-kick the overnight bag. Mitch was careful not to smile, certain that if she turned back and saw him she'd only be provoked by it. Even after she disappeared inside the house, Mitch remained in the driveway considering his options.

He could go after her, of course, but it was doubtful that she'd let him in at this point. More likely, if he hung around in her driveway too long, she or a neighbor would call the police. He had his cell phone in his jacket pocket. It was tempting to call her but too easy for her to hang up or simply not pick up. Just as important, Mitch wasn't at all clear about what he wanted to say to her; it was more that he wasn't ready to say good-bye.

It bothered him most that she wouldn't let him apologize. He had been so out of line saying those things to her. Just thinking about the words he'd hurled at her made him squirm uncomfortably. She'd taken it on the chin, not even flinching from the flailing he'd given her, but he knew he'd hurt her. It was more than the words he'd flung at her head; it was the fact that *he* had flung them. Thea had trusted him with something important and personal about herself and at the first opportunity, he had used that knowledge to shame and disrespect her.

So what was it that he wanted by making the apology? It seemed pretty clear to him that he was seeking absolution for himself, not for the words he'd used. Thea had known it, too— long before he had—and that was why she wasn't willing to hear him out. She wasn't going to play priest to his sinner.

He considered what she'd said that triggered his outburst. *"You're not thinking I could take them?"* He'd thought she was trying to avoid accepting any responsibility for the children in a tit for tat manner: if he couldn't take the children, then neither could she. But it wasn't that at all. She'd been trying to tell him that if he didn't assume responsibility, she wouldn't be allowed to. Thea was trying to warn him in that single alarming sentence what was in store for Emilie and the twins. Her mind had been racing ahead to all the possibilities while his own thoughts were mired in cataloging his inadequacies. Every time he made noises about not being able to handle his new role as a parent, Thea panicked. Not because she didn't want the children, Mitch was finally realizing, but because she was convinced she couldn't have them.

Swearing under his breath, Mitch jammed the SUV into reverse, released the brake, and backed out of Thea's driveway with enough speed that he fishtailed once he hit the icy street.

He wanted his life back, the one where he didn't have to think about school bus schedules and lunch money and the tooth fairy. The one where he could ask a woman to spend the night sans guilt. The one that didn't have a cussing jar, refrigerator magnets, and naked Barbies underfoot. He wanted the life that he had when he could put a gun away and not think about it again, when he could put bullets in a crayon box because no one would think to look for them there.

He wanted . . .

Mitch stopped. His chest felt tight, his eyes gritty. He glanced in the rearview mirror and saw a car sitting behind him, waiting for him to move. Before he could press the gas, the driver tooted his horn. With mock cheerfulness, Mitch flipped him off.

Yep, that was the life he wanted, all right, the one where mild annoyances could be answered by posting the bird and damning the consequences. Stepping lightly on the gas, he glanced in the mirror again and this time he saw that in addition to the driver there were two boys in the backseat.

He had just flipped off someone's father.

The epiphany for Mitch was that along with the tips of his ears reddening and the ruddy flush that colored his complexion, there was an undeniable sense of shame. He imagined trying to explain his behavior to Emilie and the boys,

and just as difficult, explaining away the behavior of someone else doing the same to him.

It didn't matter about the life he wanted; this was the one
he had. The one where he thought about his actions from a
child's perspective. The one where bicycles blocked door-
ways, where a sleepover with the opposite sex meant seven
of Emilie's friends were crashing in the living room. The one
where he owned an SUV, made sure there was something
green to eat at dinner, and checked the rating of every CD,
movie, and TV program for violence, language, and sexual
content. This was the life where he kissed warm foreheads
and drew the covers up small, snuggling bodies and listened
to prayers that asked God to make sure their parents' spirits
were having a wonderful time in heaven.

It was a good life. A great life, really.

Mitch felt the pressure in his chest ease. He could do this.
He could. Whatever the reason, it no longer felt as if he was
trying to convince himself of the truth of it.

Rosie sat at Thea's kitchen table with her feet propped on
the chair beside her. She had a cup of black decaf coffee and
a short stack of Oreos in front of her. Thea watched, fascinated, as Rosie dunked an Oreo into her coffee and pulled it
through the hot liquid in a figure-eight pattern. She seemed
to know exactly the right moment to pull it out to get maxi-
mum saturation without cookie collapse. It was remarkable.

Rosie plopped the entire Oreo in her mouth and sucked
the coffee out as the cookie melted on her tongue. Her smile
was beatific. "Manna," she said. She waved a hand, dismiss-
ing the attention to herself and asked Thea, "So what are
you going to do?"

Thea shrugged. "Not a thing. At least not right away. I
don't know when I'll be ready to talk to him again."

"You think he's really changing his mind about taking the kids?"

"I don't know," she said honestly. "I hope not." Her features softened. "You should see him with them, Rosie. He makes it look easy. Kathy and Gabe knew something when they asked him to look out for their kids."

"Oh," Rosie scoffed, "and they asked you because the children needed exposure to the dark side? I don't think so. If you feel strongly that the kids should be with Mitch, then you're going to have to talk to him again, Thea. And soon. The hearing's when? A few weeks from now?"

"April 17."

"Then you have time to convince him."

Thea's expression was patently skeptical. "I gave it my best shot before I left him. And then there was his crack about me not worrying that I'll have to do more than write him a check or screw him. That still stings. He thinks that I'm trying to avoid responsibility when I'm actually trying to take some."

One of Rosie's brows lifted and her eyes gleamed. "Yeah. About the screwing part . . . that would be taking responsibility, how?"

Thea's forearm was resting on the table. With a dramatic little moan she dropped her head against it and left it there.

"That's what I thought," Rosie said, grinning. "Robby got a kick out of your message. Sympathy sex. He liked that. Wishes he could get himself some. Of course I'd have to feel sorry for him first and that's not gonna happen."

Thea lifted her head enough to look at Rosie with one eye. "You torture that man."

"Uh-huh." She paused a beat. "So . . . was it good?"

Sitting up again, Thea nodded. "Better than good." Her voice softened. "It felt special." She held up her hand before Rosie launched into waterboarding mode. "That's all I'm saying. I'm not even certain what I think. I didn't plan it when I took off my engagement ring, but you and I know I opened myself up to the possibility."

"I still think you need to talk to him."

"Later," Thea said softly. "Much later."

Rosie abruptly cut to the chase. "And in the meantime, what are you going to do about the need for speed?" She stopped Thea's immediate denial and went on bluntly. "I know you weren't looking through Mitch's medicine cabinet for speeders, but if he'd had something in there to take the edge off—something in the Valium family, for instance—that was pretty damn close, Thea."

"I called you."

"After you had gone searching. Next time, get me before you do that. And if I'm not in, call a backup."

"I don't have a backup."

"What you have are excuses. Get a backup. Get two. And start thinking about how you're going to handle yourself the next time Mitch blindsides you. It'll happen and if your knee-jerk response is to go rummaging through medicine cabinets, you're gonna be in trouble faster than you can say benzodiazepine. You got that?"

Thea stared at her. Rosie hadn't waggled her finger once but that gesture would have been overkill for the lecture she'd just delivered. "I've got it," she said quietly.

"Good. Want an Oreo?"

The conference room at Foster and Wyndham was rectangular-shaped with a dark walnut table large enough to fit twelve people comfortably around it and still have space for a row of chairs against the wall on two sides. A bank of windows filled the outer wall and a screen for presentations had been permanently fixed to the wall adjacent to it.

At the moment the screen was filled with a blank blue field, the same image that was currently on Thea's laptop.

Six of the twelve seats around the table were occupied. Hank Foster slouched in one of the chairs against the wall. He wasn't wearing sunglasses this afternoon. Today he had on his antennae, a headband with two springs that coiled at sixty-degree angles from his thinning hairline and sported a miniature basketball at the end of each. Every time he moved his head, the springs wobbled and wavered so the basketballs arced like foul shots toward an invisible net.

March Mayhem. Glancing over at Hank, Thea shook her head, amusement tempering her mildly disbelieving smile. Last year she had been wearing the crown when three out of her four picks had made it through the Sweet Sixteen all the way to the Final Four. This year Hank was on top with only two of his picks in the last round while all of her college teams had tanked early in the NCAA regionals. No one in the agency seemed in a position to steal victory from him.

"It's not nice to gloat. That looks better on me anyway." She took the time to elicit a positive response from her creative Blue Team by making eye contact with each member in turn. "There you have it, Hank."

"Yeah, but what do they know?" He waved toward the big blue screen. "What you have up there now is about as effective as what came before it. I don't think you've licked this Shine and Shield thing yet." He looked around the room. "Anyone here think we're really ready to approach Carver Chemical with this yet?" No one said a word. "That's what I thought." He stood and headed for the door, the twin basketballs bobbling as he walked. "Don't forget. Final Four this weekend. Roundball party's at my house. Kids, spouses, and insignificant others welcome as long as they know the game's played in halves, not quarters." Hank shut the door behind him.

Five uncertain faces turned immediately to Thea at the head of the table. They were like grade school students, she thought, looking to her for permission to go to recess. Thea swiveled back and forth slowly in her chair, her head tilted to one side as she considered them. "I'm not going to say you can't go," she said. "But don't think Hank won't be looking for something brilliant from you during time-outs." A collective groan greeted this announcement. "Sorry. Sure, he looks like our resident alien in that getup, but you know he wants a real shot at this account."

Thea gave them a slight, sympathetic smile as they filed out of the room. "Shut the door," she called to the last one out. When they were gone, she kicked off her shoes and put her feet up on a nearby chair. She slumped in her seat, swiveling a few degrees so that she could see the screen easily when she turned her head. With her right hand, she tapped a few keys on the laptop and reviewed the presentation the Blues had put together. It wasn't any more impressive on a second go-through. Worse, it was uninspiring.

It wasn't that they hadn't made some decent attempts at showing the product in attention-grabbing fashion. Shine and Shield did not exactly lend itself to a sexy approach, but that had been tried. Humor. Straight. Standard. Functional. New product design. Celebrity. Cartoon. Music. One of Thea's favorites so far had been of a young mother using her Shine and Shield bottle like a microphone, rocking her way through a catchy pop number while she wiped down her kitchen counter, unperturbed by the mashed fruit her high-chair-bound audience was catapulting in her direction. It had humor, youth, product function, and the possibility of some rousing backbeats.

But Hank was right; it wouldn't get them Carver Chemical.

Thea lifted her feet and let her chair swivel toward the window. The blinds had been pulled to cut out most of the sunlight so their presentation was sharp and clear on the screen. There was still a hint of the bright, cloudless afternoon through small linear breaks in the slats. What would she be doing if she weren't here? she wondered. Where would she be?

She glanced at her watch. Three-twenty. The vision of herself standing on a street corner in Connaugh Creek, waiting for the approach of the No. 83 bus was so powerful that Thea could actually feel the pavement under her feet and the afternoon sunshine on her face. She'd never met the twins' bus before, didn't know any of the mothers who would also be there, but she knew about No. 83 from Case's account last night during their phone call. A push and shove match between a few of the older children had made quite an impression on the twins, especially the part where someone named Ben Henderson got a nose bleed and dripped real blood on Grant's book bag. Pretty exciting stuff, she'd told him—and meant it. Wished she had been there—and she'd meant that, too.

Thea massaged the bridge of her nose with her thumb and forefinger, closing her eyes briefly. This other vision of herself was startling. She'd never imagined herself doing anything but a professional career, yet in the two weeks since she'd last seen Mitch, the children figured largely in her recurring daydreams. Her recurring night dreams, on the other hand, were better left in the bedroom. It only required a fleeting vision of herself and Mitch together for Thea to have a physical response. Thinking about it now was enough to make her damp between her thighs.

Moaning softly, Thea jumped to her feet and padded over to the window. She twisted a wand on one set of blinds and let more sunshine into the conference room. She didn't move away from the light but stood there instead, lifting her head and feeling some of the warmth graze her face and throat. Behind her, she heard the door open. She didn't move.

"There's a call for you, Ms. Wyndham," Tamika said. Her hair beads clicked musically as she poked her head farther into the room. "It's Mr. Baker. Should I put it through?"

"Yes, that's fine," Thea said without turning. There was a

pause and the door didn't close and Tamika's hair beads didn't clack.

"Are you all right, Ms. Wyndham?"

Thea's arms were folded under her breasts. She let them drop to her sides. "Fine, Tamika. Put the call through." This time she heard the receptionist take her leave. A few moments later the phone on the conference table beeped softly. Thea impatiently dashed the wetness from her eyes and left her sentinel position at the window to take the call.

"Hello, Mitch. Is everything okay?" It was how she'd been responding to every one of his calls for the last two weeks. Focus on the children. Keep the discussion steady and about what they were doing, what they needed. Nothing personal. No chitchat. If he tried to do it differently—and he always did—she cut him off, politely but firmly.

"We're fine, Thea."

She hadn't been asking about him and he knew it, but he found little ways to insert himself into the conversation. For her own part, Thea shied away from any personal references. She had managed to get her car from the garage in Connaugh Creek without any help from Mitch, though she suspected the fact the mechanic had not asked for her insurance deductible payment had everything to do with Mitch making that payment himself. The Volvo was running smoothly again, even more quietly than before her accident, and all the new bodywork had removed the smaller dings and scratches she had never bothered to have repaired before.

Two days after she had returned home, still uncertain that she was ready to put her position about the children's welfare in front of Mitch again, she'd heard from his lawyer. Wayne wanted to know the name of her new attorney since he'd learned she'd fired Avery Childers. At first it felt like a slap in the face that Mitch was starting something through legal means that he hadn't discussed with her, then her cooler head prevailed and she knew that whatever he was doing was because of Wayne's advice. She'd given Wayne her lawyer's name and a phone number, exchanged some pleasantries, and hung up without knowing anything about Mitch's decision regarding the kids. That came the following day when her attorney informed her that Mitch was petitioning for permanent physical custody of the children and shared legal custody of them with Thea.

It was exactly what she had hoped for. She couldn't understand what it was about his decision that made her feel so achingly sad.

"You still there, Thea?" asked Mitch.

She nodded, then realized he couldn't see that. "I'm here. What is it?"

Mitch hated her cool, passionless voice. It was only like that with him. When the kids got on the phone she was bright and funny and curious. Sometimes he could hear her over the line, but even if he hadn't been able to catch the nuances of her tone, he only had to see the animated faces of Emilie and the boys to know how easily she had engaged them. "Case and Grant are standing by," he said. "They want me to hear from you *exactly* what time I have to have them at your house on Saturday."

Thea smiled. She could imagine the boys were practically standing on Mitch's feet as he spoke on the phone. "High noon," she said. "Hank's house is only a ten-minute drive from mine. Tell them we'll be there in plenty of time for kickoff." Her smile deepened as Mitch repeated the message verbatim and she heard the twins groan.

"Did you hear that?" Mitch asked. In the background Case and Grant were chanting, "Tip off! Tip off!"

"I promise not to embarrass them."

Mitch repeated that to the boys also. "They don't look reassured," he said. "Grant's asked me to write down a list of game rules for you."

Thea thought of the basketball crown she'd worn three

years running for her success in the office pool. Then there was her high school jacket, now in a vacuum-sealed plastic bag somewhere in the back of her walk-in closet, but still a reminder of four seasons of lettering in the sport. "You do that." She hesitated. "Is there anything else?"

"As a matter of fact," he said, "I've been talking to Gina about house hunting. I took your advice and said something to the kids. As near as I can figure out, they approve of the idea. We're still negotiating things like that indoor pool and a go-cart track."

Thea couldn't find it in herself to share his good humor. A weight just settled on her, not in her chest, but in her middle, the way it always did. It displaced the contents of her stomach and made acid rise as far as her throat. She fumbled in her suit jacket for an antacid. "Are you sure it's not premature?" she asked. "I mean, we haven't been to family court for the final decision."

"Wayne says it's a formality at this point. Your attorney tells him you're in agreement with this. That's right, isn't it?"

The first time she said the word, her lips merely moved around it.

All Mitch heard at his end was a long pause. "Thea?"

"Yes," she said. "Yes, that's right." After a moment she added, "It was good of you to include me in the legal custody, Mitch. I know you could have petitioned to take full legal guardianship and the judge would have probably gone along with it, even if it wasn't what Gabe and Kathy stated in their will. The judge is going to have some questions about my recovery. It might be a sticking point."

"Then we're stuck. I won't do this without you, Thea. Wayne knows that. Anyway, no one except you seems to be worried about what decision she'll ultimately make."

Thea took a deep breath and exhaled slowly. She leaned her hip against the conference table. Her fingers actually hurt from holding the receiver so tightly; she tried to ease her white-knuckled grip and couldn't make it happen. "What you said, Mitch . . . about not doing this without me . . . I want you to know that I understand that someday you'll decide you want to get married, and that it will be awkward for your wife if you and I are sharing legal responsibilities for the kids. She'll have a difficult enough time finding her place in this without me still being part—"

"Whoa! Thea. Slow down. You just went into warp drive. You're thinking light-years ahead of me now. That kind of thing gives me a brain cramp."

"Sorry. It's just important to me that you know I'm aware that things can change down the road. Sharing legal custody for the kids gives me a voice in some of the big decisions."

It meant more than that to Mitch. His current plan was to consult her about all the little things as well. Making certain they had joint legal custody assured him of a direct line to Thea for as long as he wanted it. Right now, in spite of what he'd said to Thea about her being light-years ahead of him, that line he wanted to maintain extended far into the future. "Yes?" he asked.

"Well, it's just that you may decide . . . or that your wife may decide . . . that it's . . . I don't know . . . awkward, I suppose."

"Thea?"

"Hmmm?"

"One day at a time."

Thea stilled. She knew that mantra. So did most people, whether or not they were part of a twelve-step program. It meant something more to her now than just a throwaway line or parting shot. Embracing it, when she was able to, had profound consequences. "Yes," she said softly. "You're right. One day at a time." Her bloodless hold on the phone suddenly eased with no real effort on her part. "Good-bye, Mitch."

"Good-bye."

* * *

Taking one day at a time carried Thea through March Mayhem and into April. Family court in the middle of the month was every bit as anticlimactic as Mitch had warned her it would be. The judge's decision came swiftly and without any admonitions or advisories. The judge was satisfied with the report from the children's court-appointed guardian ad litem, which included a home study and a summary of individual interviews conducted with Mitch and Thea, the people they provided as character references, and all three of the children. Mitch and Thea were granted joint legal custody while the children would remain in Mitch's home. The matter would only come before the court again if someone petitioned for a change in the arrangement. Thea's attorney explained to her privately that Mitch understood it would fall on him to take legal steps if he believed at any time Thea's judgment as it related to the children was impaired by substance abuse.

Thea accepted this, relieved only that it was over and that she had been allowed to have a substantially large toehold in the lives of her best friend's children. It was an obligation she accepted as a gift from Gabe, a responsibility she had come to cherish.

She returned Joel's ring to him the day after the court hearing. He accepted it reluctantly, not because he held out hope that he could change her mind, but because he had always meant for her to keep it. She had other things, she'd told him, that he had given her that she had no intention of returning: the signed program from the James Taylor concert at Heinz Hall; the little elephant pendant on the gold chain from their Saturday at the zoo; the platinum-and-diamond circle pin from Tiffany's. He'd chuckled about the Tiffany piece, but she could tell he was genuinely touched that she had remembered the others.

He invited her to join him for dinner that evening, and they returned to the same place they had had their first real date more than two years earlier. They just laughed about it; it was still a favorite spot for both of them. Thea could not remember that she had ever been quite so relaxed with Joel as she was that night. He, too, seemed different. At some point that evening it occurred to them that they really could be friends and they talked and joked and reminisced and it was two in the morning when Joel finally dropped Thea off at her home.

They chatted about twice a week after that. He never seemed to mind that her conversation often involved something Emilie, Case, or Grant had done. Thea realized he was no longer jealous of her attention to the children because they did not figure in his own life. He shared more anecdotes about his grandchildren, and she was reminded anew of what a warm and loving man he was.

"So, are you going to ever tell me about her?" she teased him. Thea was standing in her kitchen, stirring vegetable soup in a stockpot, while she spoke to Joel on the phone. "Don't pretend you didn't hear me. I know you're seeing someone. Who is she?" Her question was met with silence and both of Thea's brows lifted. "Oh, it's that serious, is it?"

"She's pretty special," Joel admitted. "We're having a bit of . . ." His voice trailed off as he began to have second thoughts. "Do you mind if we don't talk about it?" He sighed. "You know, Thea, when I fell in love with Nancy, I swear it wasn't so complicated. I knew. She knew. I never doubted for a moment when I asked her to marry me that she would say anything other than yes."

Thea paused in her stirring, hitching her hip as she considered this. "Were you so certain of me?"

Joel laughed. "I was *never* certain of you. Not once. What about you?"

"I've never been certain about anything," she said. But

she knew what he was asking and he deserved something better than a flippant answer. "No, Joel, I wasn't certain either. I suppose I thought it was time."

"Yeah," he said softly. "For me, too."

She smiled and began stirring again. "So you didn't love me quite as much as—"

He cut her off. "I loved you, Thea. I still do. But I know you were right to end it. It wouldn't have worked for us. This woman, the one I'm seeing now, it feels a lot like it did with Nancy, only . . ."

Thea waited. "Only what, Joel?"

"Only even better."

"Oh, Joel," Thea said. Her widening smile touched her voice. "That's wonderful." When he didn't answer immediately, she asked, "Isn't it?"

"We'll see," he said enigmatically. "Tell me about the kids. When are you getting the kids again?"

Thea allowed him to change the subject. "I'm taking Emilie horseback riding on Saturday afternoon. Sunday is Mother's Day. I'm not sure how we're going to get through that."

"You've been talking to Mitch about it?"

"A little."

"Did you offer to go up there? It might help if you were around."

"I wasn't invited, Joel." She had not been in Mitch's house since the day after her car accident. They communicated by phone, sometimes email and texts, and occasionally through his mother or the children. She saw him when he dropped the kids off or when she came to pick them up. He was invariably cordial and always a little amused, while she was wary and skittish around him. "I suspect that Mitch's mother will be the grande dame of the day. That should provide some diversion."

"Thea," Joel said gently. "Whose pain are you trying to divert?"

Chapter 11

Thea got out of her car when she saw Mitch's SUV appear in her sideview mirror. She followed its slow progress along the cemetery's circular drive until it finally reached her. The children jumped out first, all of them hurrying toward her. The twins had pictures they had drawn in Sunday school with them. Emilie was carrying a spray of pink, yellow, and white carnations, Kathy's favorite flower. Thea managed to kiss each one of them, fuss over the pictures they only waved in front of her, and compliment Emilie on her new straw hat before Mitch came up to them.

She lifted her eyes to meet his, uncertain of her welcome. This was not something she had planned with him, or even in her own mind. Joel's pithy observation was what had prompted her to come to the cemetery this Sunday.

Mother's Day.

Thea had only made the decision this morning, but her instincts were good. She suspected that Mitch or his parents would be bringing the children here after church and she timed her arrival accordingly. If she had been wrong, it would have been okay, too. She wasn't here just for the children, but for herself.

"You don't mind?" she asked Mitch.

"No. Not at all." He did something surprising, then. He leaned forward, cupped Thea's elbow, and brushed her cheek with his lips. Mitch felt her startled response in the slight stiffening of her body, but she didn't pull back. "You don't mind?" he asked.

"Ah . . . no." Thea's smile was tremulous at first, then more certain. "No," she repeated. "I don't mind." She heard the twins giggle, Emilie telling them to shut up, and the thudding of her own heart. "I need to change my shoes," she said because she needed to fill Mitch's silence. "I'll sink in the grass in these."

Mitch looked down. Following the line of Thea's slender, shapely legs, it seemed a long way to the ground. She was wearing a pair of canary yellow strappy sandals on her feet with at least three inches of heel. "Nice Manolos," he said.

Thea's eyes widened. "How on earth could you possibly know my shoes are Manolos?"

Mitch shrugged. "I've been studying." He tapped Emilie on the crown of her pink straw hat. "Who do you think picked this out?"

Emilie rolled her eyes. "I did, Aunt Thea. Nonny helped me. Uncle Mitch took Case and Grant to the arcade so they wouldn't have to hold purses."

"Traitor," Mitch whispered out of the side of his mouth. To Thea he said, "I suppose you have a pair of more practical shoes in your car?"

She nodded. "In the backseat."

Mitch opened the door and took the sneakers out. He eyed the Volvo critically, making certain it was clean enough for Thea to lean against. Her canary yellow suit wouldn't tolerate much dirt or dust. She'd look like Tweetie Pie after a fight with the putty-tat. "Here," he said, dropping to his haunches. "Give me your foot, Cinderella."

"You don't have to—" She had to catch her balance and

her breath as Mitch's fingers wrapped around her ankle and lifted her foot to his thigh. "I could do this, Mitch." Thea made an apologetic smile in the direction of the kids but Case and Grant were more interested in a bug they'd found scurrying along the curb and Emilie was admiring her reflection in the Volvo's window, cradling the bouquet of carnations in her arms like a beauty queen. No help there.

Mitch slid the thin leather strap down Thea's silky calf, shimmied the sandal off her foot, and replaced it with a white canvas tennis shoe. It made him smile. The sandals had easily cost her more than five hundred dollars and the sneakers ran about fifteen. They weren't just throwaway shoes, either. They were scuffed, comfortably worn, and in spite of having been washed a dozen times, smudges of garden humus and mulch still marked the creases. The canvas threads were stretched thin exactly where her big toe pressed against the fabric.

Mitch replaced the second sandal. His fingers lingered on Thea's ankle a moment before he released her. "There you go." He stood, brushing off his charcoal gray slacks at the knee.

"You missed a spot." Without thinking, Thea reached over and dusted off his thigh with her fingertips. When she realized what she was doing, she stopped cold and glanced up at him. "Yes . . . umm . . . well, you can get that yourself, can't you?"

Mitch was grinning. "As soon as you remove your hand from my person."

Thea's fingers flew back with the quick reflexes of some-one burned. Her cheeks went rosy. She was further discon-certed to notice the twins were no longer engaged in their nature study and Emilie had lost interest in her own image. Three pairs of eyes were watching her; four, if she counted Mitch. All of them curious and just a little slyly amused. It lasted only a moment, then the spell—if that's what it was—was broken. The skittering bug reappeared, sunshine glinting on the car window cast Emilie's reflection in a new light, and Mitch attended to the heel print on his trousers.

Mitch reached around Thea to tap Emilie on the shoulder. "Let's go," he said. "Case. Grant. Leave that poor insect in peace."

At first the boys ran ahead, but Thea saw as they approached the twin graves of their parents, they slowed and finally stopped, waiting for the rest of them to catch up and cross the last thirty feet together. They were silent as they walked. When they reached the bronze marker set in the ground, Emilie read the raised gold lettering aloud: "GABRIEL L. REASONER. KATHRYN A. REASONER. PEACE ETERNAL."

Case's paper fluttered in his hand. He caught it close, smoothing it across his stomach so the wind wouldn't tear it. "It's a picture of us, Mom." He pointed out the figures he had drawn. "Here's me and Grant. And Emilie. I colored her hat purple 'cause Jessica Swanson was hoggin' the pink crayon. And here's Uncle Mitch and Anthea."

Thea was surprised Case had included her in his picture. She tilted her head to get a better look at it, though why she thought she could see through the wash of tears was beyond her. It looked like she and Mitch were sharing a hand. She blinked, startled, but then Case's fingers covered up that portion of the drawing and he was explaining the three figures hovering at the level of the sun.

"This is you and Dad," Case said. "And Jesus. I gave you and Dad wings but not Jesus, because he can walk on water and stuff and I figured he don't need wings to fly." Case looked up at Mitch. "That's all I got." Then he remembered the reason they'd come. "Oh, 'cept Happy Mother's Day."

Mitch put his arm around Case's small shoulders and gave him a gentle squeeze. "That was great." Still protecting his picture, Case leaned into him. "Grant? You want to say something about your drawing?"

Grant unfolded his. "I drew a map. Mrs. Templeton helped. It's like the road rug we have for our cars 'cept this is our real town. This is our house now. And the church. Here's our house with you and Dad. This is the park and the swimming pool. This is the store. Nonny and Pap's house is here. I drew in some other houses 'cause Uncle Mitch says we might move, and I want you to know where we are. When he tells us which house Miss Sommers picks, I'll come back and show you."

"They'll *know*," Emilie said a trifle scornfully.

Mitch gave her a quelling look and said to Grant, "I think it's a great idea. We'll keep the map in the car so when we come back we'll be sure to have it. Em? You need help with the vase?"

Chastened, Emilie bent and gave the dial inserted into the grave marker a twist. She pulled hard and the vase lifted. She set the carnations in it and spent some time arranging them just so. "I forgot the water. I left it in the car."

"Case and Grant will get it," Mitch said. The boys thrust their drawings at Mitch and raced back to the SUV. "You okay, Em?"

She nodded, but didn't glance up.

Thea looked at Mitch, a question in her eyes. His encouragement and approval was in the faint lift of his chin in Emilie's direction. Thea hunkered down, disregarding the way her tight skirt rode up her thighs. "Did you pick these out?" she asked gently.

Emilie nodded again. "Mum liked carnations."

Thea smiled. Emilie had adopted calling Kathy Mum, just the way Mitch called his own mother Mum. "She sure did. And yellow and pink were her favorite colors. Look at us." She pointed to their clothing. "Yellow and pink." Thea touched the flowers again. "These white ones were a good idea. They accent the others. Did you think of that?"

Emilie glanced at Thea. Her smile was watery and tears glistened in her eyes. "Yeah, I thought it looked nice."

"Well, it does. You have a good eye." She said it because it was true, not because she wanted to lift Emilie's spirits. "Your mother let you pick out your own clothes as soon as she realized you had an opinion. I think you were not quite two. For a while, everything you wore had to sparkle. Do you remember?" She watched Emilie try to think back. "It's all right. There are pictures. Lots of them. Maybe Mitch will get them out and you could look at them later." There would be photos of Kathy, too. Gabe had loved taking pictures of his wife and daughter together. If Emilie was still too young to see how much of her mother still lived through her, Thea wasn't. Poring over Gabe's meticulously kept photo albums could be a good thing for both of them.

Emilie looked over her shoulder and up at Mitch. He was standing with his arms folded across his chest, his head cocked, watching them. "Can I do that when we get home?" Then, before he could answer, she asked, "Can Aunt Thea come home with us?"

"Sure."

"Oh, but—" Thea stopped because Mitch was shaking his head, the tiniest smirk shaping his lips and the glint of challenge in his eyes. *Just try and get out of this,* he was telling her. That was when Thea realized she didn't want to get out of anything. Perhaps she had even angled a little bit for the invitation. "I'd like that," she said softly, gratefully.

"We're eating at my mother's," he told her. "Amy and Dave will be there. We wanted to take Mum and Dad out for dinner but she didn't want to be bothered with the crowds and the service. Plus, in her own home, she's the queen mum."

Thea chuckled appreciatively. That sounded like Jennie Baker. "She won't mind an extra mouth to feed?"

"You're kidding, right? She lives for this."

The twins arrived at that moment carrying a plastic pitcher of water between them. Emilie popped the cap and poured water into the vase. The solemn moments had already passed and when she was done, she and the boys started back to the cars. Mitch and Thea were the ones that lingered at the graveside.

"I hate it that they're gone," Mitch said quietly. "But sometimes . . ."

Impulsively, Thea found Mitch's hand, slipped her fingers through his, and squeezed gently. "I know. The kids . . . they're so . . ."

"Yeah."

Neither of them said it. It was still too painful to admit that they had been blessed by the misfortune of two people they had loved. Still hand in hand, neither of them particularly conscious or self-conscious about that contact, Thea and Mitch walked back to where Emilie, Case, and Grant were waiting for them. Under the keen interest of the children, they parted a bit awkwardly, aware of their clasp as they had not been before. Emilie rode back to Connaugh Creek in Thea's car. The boys stayed with Mitch. They waved back and forth as they took turns passing each other on the highway.

Jennie Baker greeted Thea as though she were the distaff version of the prodigal son. When Jennie disappeared into the kitchen to throw another potato in the pot, Mitch whispered to his sister, "Great. Now she's gone back to kill the fatted calf."

"I heard that!" Jennie called from sink side.

Amy's pixielike features grew slack with wonder. "How does she *do* that?"

"I'm the mother," Jennie called again. "It's Mother's Day. I've got a synergy thing going."

Groaning, Mitch collapsed on the sofa and pulled Thea down beside him. She had to give her skirt a tug to keep her thighs decently covered. Mr. Baker rattled his paper as he lowered it. "Nice gams," he said. Then he glanced furtively in the direction of the kitchen, waiting to hear his wife announce she'd heard that, too. Everyone's laughter was what brought Jennie back to the living room to see what she'd missed.

Dinner was a relaxed, sometimes raucous affair. Food passed in both directions no matter how many times Jennie suggested a clockwise rotation. Whatever someone asked for always seemed to be at the other end of the long table. Savory pot roast, mashed potatoes, carrots, and fresh string beans kept circling. There was a basket of rolls that never bottomed out and a gravy boat big enough to need its own tug to find a berth among the platters.

Amy had been in charge of dessert and brought out two warm, deep-dish apple pies, the lightly browned crusts sprinkled with cinnamon and sugar. Thea, who didn't think she had room for another bite, found herself seduced by the aroma of hot apples and the sight of that flaky crust. When she was offered a scoop of vanilla ice cream to top it off, she didn't even hesitate.

Mitch, looking askance at her generous portion, said, "Tweetie Pie to Big Bird in one sitting."

"I heard that," she said, taking her cue from Jennie and otherwise ignoring him.

Jennie chuckled. "You tell him, Thea. I think yellow is your color, though I'm not certain about the tennis shoes."

Mitch spoke before Thea could. "She changed into them at the cemetery. You would have approved of her other pair. I certainly did."

Thea shot him a surprised glance. It required no effort on her part to draw on the sensation of his lean fingers circling her ankle while he removed her shoe. Her cheeks grew hot.

Jennie caught Amy's eye and rolled her own toward Mitch and Thea. Amy grinned and nudged her husband under the table when he looked as if he might comment. Smirking instead, he tucked into his apple pie.

Jennie excused the children to finish their dessert in the family room. They lined up single file to kiss her cheek and thank her for dinner. "At the little table," she called after them as they fled. "And bring your empty plates back here." Jennie smiled at Thea's amazement. "Isn't it sweet?" she asked. "Amy and Mitch used to do that after every meal. They got it from their father. When the kids were little, Bill never forgot to thank me for fixing dinner for him. He's gotten in the habit again with Emilie and the boys around. Isn't that right, Bill?"

Bill Baker was eyeing a carefully balanced piece of pie and ice cream on his fork. "Absolutely," he said, and everyone at the table laughed because they knew he had no idea what he'd just agreed to.

Jennie waved her hand at him and let him get back to his wobbling fork. "Where is your mother today, Thea? Still traveling?"

"My parents are in Scotland. Edinburgh, I think. I can't keep their itinerary straight. They're doing a walking tour."

"Oh, how wonderful for them. They're what? In their seventies?"

Thea nodded.

"They must be vigorous."

"My father would tell you they're stubborn."

"Sometimes that's just as good," said Jennie. "When are they coming home? It must be four months now that they've been gone."

"Five and a half, actually. They'll be back in June."

Only Mitch knew Thea well enough to suspect there was something like forced cheerfulness in her tone. He gently nudged the conversation in another direction.

After dinner, Amy and Thea tossed a coin to see who would rinse and who would load. Jennie kept them company sitting at the kitchen table but wasn't allowed to lift a finger

except to point where something was supposed to go. Mitch
and his dad turned on the Pirates doubleheader and cat-
napped. Emilie wandered into the kitchen and snuggled into
Nonny's lap while the twins went outside to play.

It was after five by the time Mitch herded them back home.
Emilie hadn't forgotten Thea's offer to look through photo
albums. She dragged her upstairs and into Mitch's former guest
room to find them. Mitch showed up a few minutes later with
Thea's grab-and-go bag in his hand. He winked at her. "Just in
case you want to change into something more comfortable."

Thea accepted the bag gratefully. Just in case. He'd remembered. Mitch ducked back out of the room humming
something under his breath that sounded suspiciously like
the Beatles' "Yellow Submarine." "You're not going to get
away with that, Mitchell!" she yelled after him. She heard
him pause on the stairs, chuckle, then call back, "I'll be in the
garage!"

Emilie pressed the photo album she was holding into
Thea's midriff, not hard, but enough to get her noticed.

"Easy there, girl," Thea said. "You'll make me pop a big
yellow rivet." She put her arm around Emilie's shoulders.
"Let's go in your room to look at these. Unless you think the
boys will want to do this with us?"

Emilie shook her head. "No way. This book's all about me."

Mitch heard the breezeway door open and someone step
into the garage. He was lying on an old quilted blanket on his
back under the Chevy truck. He scootched himself forward
as the footsteps neared. "Hey," he said, smiling as he finally
emerged. "Hand me one of those paper towels there, will you?"

He watched Thea as she reached for one of the heavy-
duty blue towels on his workbench. She'd changed out of
her mind-blowing canary yellow suit and into a pair of faded
jeans and an Oxford shirt the exact cool color of lime sherbet

with the Foster and Wyndham logo embroidered above the pocket. The tails were loosely tied at her waist and she had casually rolled the sleeves to her elbows. Her hair was ruffled as if she'd just run her hand through it and the left side of her face sported a pillow wrinkle from her temple to the corner of her mouth. Her green eyes looked vaguely heavy lidded and slumberous.

Uh-oh. Mitch accepted the towel she gave him and began wiping his hands. He sat up slowly, drawing his legs up tailor fashion. The grease-and-oil stained blanket bunched under him. "I'm afraid to ask," he said. "What time is it?"

"Ten-oh-five."

Both of his brows lifted. He used a relatively clean knuckle to push his wire rims up the bridge of his nose. "Case and Grant were just in here a few minutes ago," he said. "I promised to go up and tuck them in."

"That was at about eight-thirty," she told him. "Don't worry. All the nighttime rituals have been negotiated. I oversaw baths and prayers and read something called *Captain Underpants* to the boys. Emilie and I took turns with a chapter in one of the Harry Potters. Apparently I don't do the voices with the same gusto as you."

He shot her a brief, lopsided smile. "My stage training, don't you know," he told her in a credible Hugh Grant imitation, modest and self-effacing. "Mrs. Campbell's senior year production of *The Importance of Being Earnest.* I had the plum role and a star on my locker." Mitch got to his feet and tossed the paper towel in an empty bucket. "Listen. Don't go anywhere. Give me ten minutes." He had abandoned the accent but remained earnest. "I'll be right back."

A trifle bewildered, her smile fading slowly, Thea nodded. "All right."

He took a couple of steps toward the door, stopped, and looked back at her. "Promise. I need to know you're not going to drive away as soon as I leave."

That had not even occurred to her. "I promise." She made a crossing motion in front of her chest. "Really."

Still, Mitch hesitated. His eyes grazed Thea's face, making a quick study of her sincerity.

"Go," she told him, pointing to the door. "I swear. I'll be here." This time she held up two fingers. "Swear." Watching him finally go, Thea wasn't certain if he actually trusted her or simply realized he had no choice. For her own part, Thea had always intended to find a few private moments to speak with Mitch. After spending almost an entire day in his company, it had come down to waiting until the children were in bed, not so different, she supposed, than what married couples experienced on a daily basis.

It was a bit longer than the ten minutes Mitch promised before he returned to the garage. He'd looked in on each of the children, not because he thought anything had been left undone but because he needed to do it for himself. They didn't stir as he stood beside their beds and made good on his promise to tuck them in. The rest of his time Mitch used to spit and polish. He took the quickest shower he'd ever had, not counting his entire year as a nine-year-old when he'd tried to convince his mother he was allergic to water. He shaved, swished mouthwash, and ran a comb through his wet hair. Deciding the neat little furrows made him look completely geeky, Mitch mussed his hair again and raked it with his fingers. Better.

He was still tucking his shirt into the waistband of his jeans when he stepped into the garage. His first thought was that he shouldn't have wasted a moment cleaning up because Thea had fled. The overhead fluorescent lights had been switched off, but there was still a glow under the truck from the work lamp he had been using. He blinked, his eyes adjusting to the semidarkness, and saw Thea sitting inside the Chevy's cab. Her head was resting back against the upholstery and her bare feet were raised to the dashboard. He could hear the faint backbeat of an eighties tune coming through the closed window. Her toes were tapping out a rhythm, her lips parting softly around the words as she sang along.

Mitch walked around the truck to the driver's side and opened the door. Predictably, Thea jumped. "Sorry," Mitch said, climbing in. "Didn't know how to warn you I was here."

Thea let herself settle back again. Outwardly calm, her heart was hammering. He'd cleaned up, changed his clothes, and combed his damp hair with his fingers. Thea touched the side of her face and thought she still felt a pillow wrinkle on her cheek. Falling asleep in Emilie's bed had been a mistake. "What happened to the grease monkey?"

"Left him upstairs."

Thea almost flinched when Mitch closed the door. It was as though the Chevy cab had just been shrink-wrapped, squeezing the air out as space was collapsed. Physics had never been Thea's strong suit but she was fairly certain there was a law of the universe to explain it. "You didn't have to do it on my account."

Mitch turned slightly in her direction, drawing his knee up on the bench seat. "Yes," he said, his eyes grazing her profile. "I did. Fingerprints." He watched her swallow hard. Good. She got the message that he meant to touch her. Mitch was perfectly willing to let her wonder about when. He rested his forearm along the back of the seat, against the glass. If he stretched his fingertips he could have brushed her shoulder. He didn't. Thea was almost squirming now; he could sense it in her very stillness. "You want to tell me why you're here?" he asked quietly.

"You made me promise to stay."

"Thea."

She reached for the radio knob and turned it off, then let her hands cup her bent knees. Her bare feet still rested on the dashboard and she allowed her neck to relax against the curved back of the seat. "It was something Joel said, actually."

"Joel? You're seeing him again?" It wasn't what he wanted to hear. Not at all. Mitch's glance dropped to Thea's left hand. No ring. It didn't necessarily mean anything, he remembered. For the first time he wondered if she was still carrying it around in her purse.

Thea looked over at him, a slight frown changing the line of her mouth. "I'm seeing him because he's my friend. I suspect he always will be. It required breaking our engagement for me to realize how much I appreciate him in that way." She spoke in a matter-of-fact tone, without apology. *Deal with it.*

Mitch dealt. "What did he say?" he asked.

Shrugging lightly, Thea went on. "Just that I was avoiding some things to divert my own discomfort. I'm paraphrasing, but that was the gist of it. It's easier for me to get caught up in what someone else is feeling than pay attention to my own. It's not much of a test of my abstinence if I never allow myself to experience life."

Mitch was silent for a long moment. His brows lifted slightly; his features settled into contemplation. "Joel Strahern may be my new best friend."

Thea smiled faintly, her eyes forward again. "I thought he might be." She took a shallow breath and continued. "I decided I needed to be here today. First at the cemetery and then later with all of you. It was presumptuous, I know. But to do this right, I needed to risk rejection."

"Rejection was never a possibility," Mitch said. "You saw how the kids practically ran over each other to get to you. And me?" He offered a short, self-deprecating laugh. "Hell, Thea, as I recall, you had me kneeling at your feet inside of a minute." He stopped her before she took exception to what he'd just said. She wasn't prepared to hear what he'd admitted about himself under the guise of humor. "But I appreciate that you didn't know how it would turn out, and if I'd told you, you wouldn't have believed me."

"You're right," she said softly. "I wouldn't have. Seems I've always been a student of the long and hard way." Oh, God, she thought, hearing herself say those words. Please don't let him make a sex joke. Inside she was cringing, waiting for it.

"So what is it you want, Thea?"

She relaxed, rubbing her knees lightly with the palms of her hands. "How do people answer that?" she wondered aloud. "Do some of them really know? I don't. I think I'll always be working it out."

"Let me make it easier for you." He watched her carefully. "What do you want right now?"

Her hands stilled. "This," she said. "Talking to you." Thea's head swiveled to look at him. "You."

Mitch studied her. He swore he felt a current of electricity arc from the curve of her shoulder to his fingertips. It made him glance involuntarily at his hand, wondering if he'd touched her. No, his arm was still braced against the back of the seat, his fingers just inches from her shoulder. He hadn't moved. "What about tomorrow?" he asked.

Her smile was almost sad, regretful. "One day at a time."

Mitch released a long exhale. Could he do this? he wondered. Have her in his life with this impermanency so well defined? He knew better than most that no future was certain. The fact that Emilie and the twins were sleeping upstairs in *his* home was all the reminder he needed of that. But to go through each day with the purposefulness of not looking too far beyond it was not something he was sure he could live with. And what about the children? Was it fair to submit them to Thea's daily struggle?

He knew the answer to that almost as soon as the question formed in his mind. It wasn't fair not to. Keeping Thea at arm's length would certainly have consequences for the twins, but it seemed especially true for Emilie. Thea not only knew what to say to Em, she knew how to say it, and Mitch couldn't imagine denying Emilie that influence.

One day at a time. The phrase echoed hollowly in Mitch's mind, bearing no voice that he recognized.

Watching Mitch struggle with what she was offering was almost too much for Thea. She wanted to promise more of herself; she wanted to promise it for a lifetime. It would have been rash and inappropriate. She would have to remind him not to believe her. Not yet. "It was wrong of me not to let you apologize," she said on a thread of sound. "Those things you said . . . they did hurt. Even the true ones. I knew you felt bad after you heard yourself say them, not because you didn't think you were right, but because you understood you'd hurt me. I suppose that not letting you make amends was my way of punishing you." Thea ran her hands along the length of her legs from knee to ankle and back again, smoothing the fabric of her faded jeans and wiping her damp palms. "Pretty bad, huh?"

"Fiendish."

The shadow of a smile crossed Thea's patrician features. "Neurotic," she said.

"Quirky."

"You think so?"

"I'm sure of it." He hesitated. "About the other stuff I said . . . I was way out of line."

Thea nodded. "Yeah. You were."

"Did I ever thank you for helping me finance the SUV?"

"I don't want to be thanked, Mitch. I did it—"

Mitch flexed his fingers and this time he caught her shoulder. He laid his hand lightly there, drawing her full attention. "You did a nice thing, Thea. Let me thank you."

"All right," she said slowly, as if it were painful.

"Thank you." He watched her carefully. "Good girl. You took that right on the chin. Didn't even flinch."

She gave him an arch look. "You're not going to thank me for the sex, are you?"

"I'm thinking that would guarantee me never getting any again."

"Good thinking."

"So that leaves the pill-popping crack I made," he said.

"Which was accurate," she told him.

"I'm feeling my way here," Mitch said. "Am I forgiven?"

"You haven't actually said you were sorry."

"I'm sorry, Thea. You can't possibly know how—" He stopped because Thea had reached across the space separating them and placed one fingertip on his mouth.

"You're forgiven," she said softly. "Take it on the chin."

Mitch caught her hand just as she would have removed it and slipped his fingers through hers. She didn't resist. He made a point of looking around him so that she followed the direction of his glance. From the undercarriage of the truck, Mitch's work lamp glowed, illuminating their surroundings in a way that made the bikes and tools and trash cans all look a little less harsh, if not quite romantic. When his eyes settled on hers again, she was regarding him with a mixture of curiosity and humor. "You know where we are, don't you?"

"Your garage?"

"*A* garage," he corrected.

"Hmmm," she murmured.

"In a big red truck."

Her eyes widened a bit. "So we are."

"Exactly. There's even a hose and ladder lying back there in the bed."

Thea glanced through the rear window of the cab again. There was indeed a garden hose and reel lying on the cargo mat. The ladder was a stepladder. Her eyes narrowed suspiciously. "Did you put—"

"Practically a fire truck," Mitch said.

"I get it," she said dryly. "You really know how to wax nostalgic."

Mitch shrugged. "I'm not sure about that. I was going to

wax the truck, though. I started tinkering under the hood and ran out of time."

Thea couldn't help but smile. She looked out over the high-gloss finish of the hood. Light shimmered across the surface. "I don't know, Mitch. This Chevy might not be able to stand another buffing. It practically glows now."

"Shine and Shield," he said. "I just spray it on and—"

That was when Thea launched herself at him. Never one to look a gift horse in the mouth, Mitch accepted it, wrapping his arms around her back and pulling her close. She had kisses for his mouth, his cheeks—quick, smacking kisses that made him just grin as she placed them on his jaw, neck, and when he ducked a little, his forehead.

"You're a genius," she whispered against his mouth. "Do you know that?"

"Tough question. Is there a prize if I get it right?" Before she could answer, Mitch kissed her lightly, brushing her mouth with his. He felt the tug of her lips as he drew back. His fingers tightened on her waist as he sensed her starting to move away from him. "No way," he said. "You're not going anywhere."

Thea studied him, amused. She was also aware of her breath quickening. "I'm not?"

Mitch risked taking one hand off her long enough to turn on the radio. He kept the volume low. The La's "There She Goes" was just moving into the first refrain. Perfect. "I had a seduction thing going here. You're messing with my timing."

"I don't think I want to do that."

"Good." He bent his head and kissed her again, just as lightly as before. "You wanna neck?"

"Hmmm."

Mitch took that as a yes. There was no resistance as he pulled her closer. Thea slid across the wide bench seat easily and her lips parted as she raised her face. His hands left her waist and repositioned themselves gently on either side of her throat. The pads of his thumbs made an angled pass along her jawline. He felt the sweet rush of her warm breath a moment before his mouth closed over hers.

He nibbled. Tasted. Nipped. Teased. Frustrated, Thea arched into him, pressing herself against his chest, feeling the flattening of her breasts as a pleasant ache. Her arms circled him. She ran her hands along his back. Her fingers wound in the damp hair at the nape of his neck and ruffled it. She felt him shiver. When he kissed her again it was open-mouthed, hard and hungry and deep. Thea pulled at the tail of his shirt until it was out of his jeans. Her palms slipped under the material. His skin was warm and smooth, taut across his shoulders and along his rib cage. It retracted as her nails skittered up his abdomen.

Mitch felt the change in the line of her mouth. Her smile was still evident when he drew back and studied her darkening eyes and flushed face. "Like knowing you can do that, do you?"

Thea's answer was a small nod.

Mitch held up his hands in mock surrender. "I like it, too." He plucked the front of his shirt away from his chest and offered it to her. "Buttons," he fairly growled. "Make sure you get them all."

She made short work of them, surprising herself with the steadiness of her fingers, even if Mitch seemed to take it all in stride. This time when Mitch pulled her flush to him, her breasts felt the heat and hardness of his chest through only the material of her own shirt. It was a maddening barrier, deliciously abrasive and tantalizing. He played with her as they kissed again, running his hands up and down her thighs, slipping his fingers under the waistband of her jeans.

The heels of Thea's hands pressed against Mitch's shoulders. Her fingers uncurled. She tugged on his open collar, searching for the pulse beating in his neck. They shifted, breaking the embrace so Mitch could remove his shirt completely. It was pushed unnoticed to the floor of the cab while Thea found herself being levered back into the corner. Her thighs were splayed. Mitch fit himself between them, filling his palms with her butt, then lifting her so that when she came down again her seat was solidly against him.

He buried his face in the curve of her neck. Thea's fingers clasped behind his skull, cradling his head as he sipped her skin. His tongue darted out. Damp. Rough. Slippery. Sensation rippled through her and her hips jerked. She ground against him, lifting her pelvis, rocking so that she felt the outline of his erection against her crotch. "Touch me," she whispered raggedly. "My breasts." Her hands groped for his and brought them around to her chest. His palms lightly cupped her swelling flesh. She surged into Mitch, rubbing herself against him. "My shirt . . . please . . ."

Mitch's fingers showed far less consideration for Thea's Oxford than she had shown for his. One button ricocheted off the windshield and dashboard before it fell to the floor. Mitch helped Thea shrug out of the shirt and whipped it aside. He stared at her bra. It was only a shade paler than the cool lime color of her shirt. "Nice," he said huskily.

Then he got her out of it.

A shadow between her breasts defined the curve of them. Mitch touched her there first, making a pass with two fingers. He could feel the strength of her heartbeat. He made a long sweep with his fingertips, from sternum to navel and back again. Thea bit her lip, stemming a small cry of frustration. Her breasts ached. She arched, pushing herself toward him.

"Let me see," he said. "Do it." His palms continued to caress her sides, finding the swell of her rib cage and the indentation of her waist and taut belly. On one pass he unsnapped her jeans and worked the zipper open. What he did not do was touch her breasts. "I want to watch you."

On those few occasions that Thea wondered how she might respond to this very request, she'd never been able to sustain the image of herself complying. She found the idea of someone watching her embarrassing, even humiliating. But then the someone had always been faceless, an indistinct masculine presence unrecognizable as any of the men she had known. She thought it would have been easier to touch herself in front of a stranger formed only in her mind's eye. It wasn't. But for Mitch . . . for this man watching her now with the darkening eyes and unashamed interest . . . she could do this. She *wanted* to.

Thea watched him watching her. His fingers were splayed across her midriff. She laid her palms over the back of his hands first. Taking a shallow breath, she lightly dragged her nails across his skin, then across her own. Her hands lifted, skimming her ribs. She could feel the swelling of her breasts as she cupped them in her palms. Mitch's gaze seared her with heat as she gently kneaded her flesh. Her thumbnails scraped her nipples and sensation shuddered through her. Mitch was the one who gave it sound.

Thea's pelvis rocked again. She caressed her breasts, lifting them as though in offering, then covering them with her palms. The rose-colored nipples were sometimes visible between her fingers. She tweaked them with a scissoring motion that engorged them with blood, making them darker and exquisitely sensitive. For a moment she thought Mitch stopped breathing.

What he did was grab her wrists, remove her hands, and lift her so his lips could settle where her fingers had been. She cried out at the first hard suck of his mouth. His tongue laved her nipple. The wet contact ignited a fire rather than put one out. It was as if a flame were licking her skin. Sparks cartwheeled along her spine and when her lashes fluttered closed, they danced against the dark screen of her eyelids.

Thea found purchase in the waistband of Mitch's jeans. She felt him suck in his breath as her fingers dipped inside and skimmed his skin. She yanked on the snap and opened the fly. Her fingertips made immediate contact with the crisp arrow of dark hair. Her hand stilled and a startled, husky chuckle escaped her throat. Mitchell Baker wasn't wearing any underwear. He released her breast long enough to give her a grin that might have been sheepish if it weren't so thoroughly filled with the devil.

"I was in a hurry," he explained in a low growl.

"Yeah?" she asked softly, slipping her hand deeper inside his jeans, cupping him.

"Oh, yeah." He lowered his head again and applied himself to her other breast. His teeth worried the nipple. He pushed himself against her hand. It was at once too much and not enough. "Out of these clothes." His voice was muffled against her skin but the urgency was communicated even if the command wasn't. Mitch began working Thea out of her jeans.

There was a shifting of positions, an unwinding of tangled arms and legs as they tugged at the material, first on each other, then abandoning that as too complicated, on themselves. Mitch banged his elbow on the steering wheel hard enough to make his fingers go numb. He swore softly and clumsily tried to manage with one hand what Thea was speedily managing with two.

The light from under the truck brightened the interior of the cab as Thea opened the door long enough to pitch her jeans out. Mitch had a glimpse of little panties in the same lime sherbet shade as her bra. She was out of those in a heartbeat and then she was helping him, sparing a kiss for his elbow that he couldn't properly feel but imagined he did anyway.

Finding a position that suited them had all the elements of a wrestling match except for the referee.

"Here," he said, pinning her into the corner.

"I'll fall out."

"Lock the door."

She shifted, sliding under him. He had no choice but to follow her down. "You lock it," she said.

Mitch's tingling fingers caught the lock as his hips settled against her. She squirmed, trying to raise her thigh to give him a cradle for his body. He heard her head bump the armrest. "You okay?"

She nodded, bumping the armrest again. "This isn't going to work," she whispered. "You'll knock me unconscious."

They moved again, groping, straining, lifting. Mitch pushed them away from the steering wheel. Thea straddled his lap. "Better take the gearshift," he said.

Thea rolled her eyes but she circled his erection with her fingers. "This thing have reverse?"

He shook his head, groaning deeply, his head thrown back as she began stroking him. His hands found her hips. She came up on her knees. A choked cry of encouragement came from the back of his throat. There was the heady sound of the damp parting of her lips and the release of a musky scent that made his nostrils flare as he breathed deeply. She moved, rubbing herself against the tip of his cock. "Yes?" she asked, her voice at once a question and its own answer. "Yes," he said. "Oh yes." His fingers pressed dimples into her taut flesh as she lowered herself onto him. Her head fell forward. Her arms circled his shoulders. She kissed his neck, the hollow just behind his ear. Her teeth caught his lobe, pulling slowly as her own body was stretched and filled. "Mmmm," she murmured. She let him go and found his mouth, kissing him deeply, wrapping her tongue around his in an echo of the movement of her hips.

Mitch felt every contraction of the muscles in her arms and thighs and rocking pelvis. His shoulder bumped the rear window. His lean arms bunched. He leaned back, trying to give her more room and protect her head from hitting the roof of the cab. Their mutual laughter was short on breath. Thea lifted her hands and placed her palms flat on the roof. Mitch palmed her breasts. The interior of the truck was steamy with their heat and moist breath. He could feel himself starting to lose control. One shudder chased another and his own hips were trying to lift against hers.

He wedged one hand between them. His fingers brushed her clitoris and it brought her to almost immediate and complete stillness. Her mouth opened but her cry was silent. She moved again, this time more slowly, rubbing herself against him rather than the other way around. The pace was hers. She controlled the tempo and timing up until the very end.

She came moments before he did, the fluttering of contractions taking him with her. He gave a hoarse shout, levering her backward onto the seat and pumping himself into her with a rawness of passion that left them both weak and a little stunned.

Mitch lifted himself off Thea with far more care than he had used taking her down. He could feel the fine tremor of her body as he helped her up. His own muscles still thrummed with the barely visible vibration of a plucked string. Thea was massaging the back of her neck, her head tilted to one side. Mitch's expression took on a guilty cast. "Did I hurt you?"

She shook her head. The movement made her wince. "It's just a crick," she said quickly. "Maybe I shouldn't have locked the door. There would have been more room if it had popped open."

"There would have been more room if I had taken you to bed."

Thea smiled. She leaned toward Mitch and kissed him on the mouth. "There's that," she whispered. "But we seem to do all right in tight, cramped spaces." Thea patted his cheek lightly. "Stop looking at me like that. I'm fine, Mitch. Better than fine. If I have any regrets they have to do with turning you down all those years ago. I missed out by not climbing into that fire truck with you." Thea reached for her panties on the dashboard. The effort to untangle them proved too much and she threw them back. She accepted Mitch's help with her shirt instead.

"You going to button that?" he asked when she pulled it over her shoulders.

"No." She sat up a little, smoothing the tail of the shirt under her butt so she could sit down on it. "Do you have a problem with that?"

"Are you kidding?" He found his jeans and wrestled them on, only partially zipping the fly and leaving the snap open. "What?" he asked when he glimpsed her staring at him.

"Someone's going to get caught by his short hairs," she warned him. "But I like the look. Very sexy."

Mitch's mouth quirked as Thea wiggled her dark brows. "Come here," he said, reaching for her wrist and pulling her closer. One of her legs was drawn up on the seat. Her knee bumped his. His hand moved to her bare thigh, caressing her just above the knee. His own expression turned grave as he searched her face, looking for some hint of what she was thinking. "You okay with what happened?"

She nodded. "You?"

He murmured his assent. "You want to spend the night?"

"I—I'm not sure that's—"

"Forget it," he said quickly. "No pressure."

"No . . . umm, I was thinking about the kids. I don't know—"

He cut her off again. "It's all right, Thea."

She stared at him, a little exasperated by his unwillingness to permit her to pursue a complete thought or finish a full sentence. It was something that Gina had told her on the occasion of their first meeting, about her and Mitch not having much time alone. Thea had had the impression that Mitch's girlfriend did not spend the night. Now she wondered if she had been wrong. "I guess I'm not comfortable being here when the kids wake up," she said. "It just doesn't feel right somehow."

Mitch hadn't been thinking about the kids when he'd asked her. He blamed the blood loss to his brain for the oversight. "I know what you mean." He lifted his hand, cradling the side of her neck in his palm. Silky strands of dark red hair tickled his skin. His eyes shifted from Thea's face as her shirt parted and slipped over her right shoulder. Light glanced oddly off her upper arm, drawing Mitch's attention to a mark he had not noticed before. Her skin had a sheen here, the gloss of flesh pulled taut by an old injury. A faint but unmistakable band of scar tissue circled her arm halfway between her elbow and shoulder. Without thinking of any possible consequence, he touched it. Before he could ask her what happened, Thea was jerking her arm away.

"Sorry," he said.

Thea pulled her shirt up quickly. "It's nothing." She shrugged, her eyes darting away. "I'm a little self-conscious about it, is all."

A little? That hardly described her reaction to something that was barely there. Mitch decided he might as well be hanged for a sheep as a lamb. "Was it a burn?" he asked.

"No. Nothing like that." Her head came up, and she regarded him frankly for a long moment before she made her decision. "Can you picture one of those old-fashioned wringer washers?"

"Yeah, I know what you mean, but I don't think even my grandmother had one."

"My parents did," she said. "It was ancient when I was a kid. I remember it was rusted and battered and it sat on the back porch. I don't think my mother actually used it. It was the kind without the safety guard to stop someone from getting their hand caught between the rollers."

"Is that what happened?" asked Mitch. "You were playing around and put your hand in?"

"There was no playing. My father did the honors."

Chapter 12

Mitch lay awake in bed, his legs sprawled on top of the covers, his head cradled in his clasped palms. The light from a street lamp slanted into the room through the open curtains. An occasional breeze shifted the curtains and cast shadow play on the wall and the ceiling. He saw the movement out of the corner of his eye but he wasn't distracted by it.

He was thinking of Thea.

It wasn't exactly a new pastime. Mitch figured that if someone probed his brain they would find entire regions of it had been surrendered to the consideration of Thea Wyndham. Thank God for the autonomic nervous system; otherwise most days he wouldn't be able to breathe.

He slipped one hand out from behind his head and absently ran it up and down his chest. Her hand had made this same trail only a few hours earlier. He wished she was the one making it now.

Shine and Shield. He smiled now, thinking about it. It was the thing that had tipped the scales and catapulted her into his arms. He hadn't understood it then, but she had eventually explained. She always did that, he realized. If he had the patience to wait her out, she would find a way to tell

him what he wanted to know. Sometimes she found her way
to telling him things he didn't.

He conjured up an image of a wringer washer. The one
he saw had a large white enamel barrel and four spindly
legs. Two cream-colored rubber rollers, each about eighteen
inches long, were set in the wringer apparatus that extended
above the tub and could also be positioned out to the side.
Clothes could be fed from the wash water through the rollers
and into a laundry tub. The advantage of a moveable wringer
was that it could be repositioned over the divider of a double
laundry sink and the clothes could be wrung out a second
time. The one he remembered seeing rusting in some neighbor's backyard had had an automatic wringer.

That wasn't the kind Thea described. The one her father
had used to teach her a lesson was manually driven, which
meant he had not only fed her small fingers between those
hard rollers, but that he had flipped the lever to close them
over her hand, then turned the handle to make the rollers
begin their slow rotation.

Thea didn't have a clear recollection of it happening. She
imagined that she had screamed because a neighbor had
come to their apartment. She could hear the pounding on the
door with more clarity than the raw pitch of her own voice.
Later there were police and doctors. X-rays. Cries for her
mother that went unanswered. Strangers. Pictures. Angry
people talking in hushed voices, almost but never quite out
of her hearing. A Gund bear that was nearly as big as she
was to sleep with her in a consciously cheerful hospital
room. The certain knowledge that all of it was her fault.

The pain of that night was buried deep, but Mitch understood now that it leaked into every aspect of her life like
toxic waste in a landfill.

Some of what she knew, she'd been told, and so she told
him. She had her scars, some said, to remind her how fortunate she was to have been taken away from her parents. She

might have died in the care of her psychotic father and her terrified and terrifying mother. Failure to protect, they called it when they spoke of the woman who had done nothing except stand by as her husband tortured their child.

Doing nothing was tantamount to participating, the social workers argued, and the judge agreed. What Thea remembered was her mother clinging to her father as he was taken away and then turning accusing eyes on her.

"That's what I come from," she'd said when she had finished. "When I look at Emilie and Case and Grant, and I think of trying to be a parent to them, I can't forget what's in *my* blood. No laughter. No warmth. I remember hurt. Deep, abiding pain. I never wanted to know more about my parents. Never searched for them when I could have. I was afraid, I suppose, that what I would discover would be even worse than my memories. Emilie was right about me. She told you I was nervous around her and the boys. She just didn't know why. I'm not sure even Gabe understood. He never asked me about my arm. If the Reasoners ever talked about me in front of him, he never let on."

"You let me believe it was the drugs," Mitch said quietly. "Why would you want me to think that?"

"Because it's something I did to myself, I suppose. Talking about it doesn't make me feel entirely helpless. And people can relate to it in some way. There's hardly anyone who doesn't have at least one experience with drinking, eating, gambling, smoking, or spending too much." She had touched his face, then, cupping his cheek so gently in her palm that it was not pressure he felt, but warmth. "But this other thing . . . a father who puts his daughter's arm in a wringer because she annoyed him with her clumsiness and her crying . . . and a mother who did nothing because she was too afraid or too needy or as sick as her husband . . . well, it was done to me and it lives inside me and sometimes

I think I'm only containing all that ugliness, that it will come spilling out and I'll hurt someone, too."

Thea took a shallow, steadying breath. "Those medical problems I had as a child . . . the ones that kept me from being able to stay with the Reasoners . . . that was because of the abuse, Mitch. Getting kicked, tossed, shaken, a couple of times too often, I guess. My father had a short fuse. And in the event I took after him, I found drugs that kept my fuse long. Really long."

Mitch allowed her to talk. Even when she finished, he remained silent, watching her grave features settle until they became merely solemn. She actually believed what she was saying about herself, Mitch realized. It stunned him.

It still stunned him.

Somewhere in the distance thunder rumbled. A spattering of rain hit the open window, then stopped. He should get up and close it, he thought, but he made no move to do so. The curtains continued to beat a light tattoo against the wall and sill. Rain came and went and then came and stayed.

"Uncle Mitch?"

Mitch turned his head. The night-light in the hallway cast a penumbra around the figure at his open door. "Hey, Mutt. Where's Jeff?"

"It's Grant, Uncle Mitch."

Mitch smiled. "I know, Sport." He extended his arm over the side of the bed and beckoned Grant with a quick, curling gesture of his fingers. "You want to hop in?"

Grant's response was to hightail it over to the bed and jump on board. "You're not under the covers."

"You think I should be?"

"There's gonna be a storm. Can't you hear the thunder?"

"I hear it." Mitch also heard someone moving with exaggerated stealth in the hall. "Your brother's coming. Move over." Grant rolled himself across Mitch's chest and flopped on the other side. "Come on, Case. There's room."

Case peeked around the door frame. "How'd you know it was me?"

"I have X-ray vision."

That stopped Case in his tracks. His eyes narrowed in the semidarkness of the room. "You're just joking me, right?"

Mitch smiled at Case's word choice. "Teasing," he said. "Right."

Giggling, Case climbed in. "Hey, you're not under the covers."

"Seems to be the consensus."

"Huh?" Both boys questioned him at the same time.

"It means everyone agrees." His definition was met by silence. "Never mind," he said, sitting up. "Help me out here." They all tussled with the sheet and blanket together. It only took another boomer for the twins to find an opening and burrow deep. They wedged themselves on either side of Mitch. Their small bodies smelled of soap and sleep. The comfort was mutual. Mitch didn't bother asking them to leave him some room.

The rain began to fall steadily. Mitch could tell by the direction the droplets were hitting the house that the carpet in front of the open window was going to be damp. It didn't make him any more motivated to get up and shut it.

"You guys okay?" he asked. He felt heads nodding on either side of his shoulders. "Good. So what do you think's going on up there to make all that noise? Angels bowling? God talking? Thor's hammer?"

Grant raised himself up on one elbow and peered closely at Mitch. "Actually," he said with careful precision, "it's two air masses butting heads."

One of Mitch's brows kicked up. "Really? Who teaches you stuff like that? You sure it's not angels bowling?"

Case said importantly, "They teach kids a lot of different stuff now. Not like in the olden days."

Mitch groaned softly. "You guys are killin' me." As soon

as the words were out Mitch regretted them. Beside him he
felt the twins jerk to attention. "It doesn't mean anything,"
he said quickly. "It's just a way of saying that I can't keep up
with you two. You're too smart and fast for me. It's a compliment." He looked from side to side trying to figure out if
he'd explained it adequately. They seemed to be mulling it
over. "You understand?"

"Got it," Grant said.

"Got it," Case said.

"Good," Mitch said, relieved. "Go to sleep." There was
some snuggling, a few moments of peace, then the two air
masses butted heads again. The rumble actually shook the
house. Mitch thought the boys were going to crawl under his
skin. Apparently semiscientific explanations didn't signifi-
cantly reduce the fear factor. Still more surprising was
Emilie's continued absence from his room, then, as if on cue,
she materialized in the doorway. "What took you so long?"

"I just woke up," she explained with some dignity. Lightning flashed, illuminating her pale face on the threshold,
and dignity was no longer a consideration. Her feet barely
touched the carpet as she made a run for the bed. Case and
Mitch held up the covers for her and she threw herself under
them. The bed shook.

"Everyone accounted for?" asked Mitch.

"Where's Anthea?" Case wanted to know.

"Aun*t* Thea," Emilie said. "When are you going to get
some teeth, anyway? You sound like a baby."

Mitch cut it off before Case could retaliate. "No kicking,"
he said, grabbing one of the boy's legs. "Em, you used to
sound exactly the same."

Case voiced approval of Mitch's defense. "Yeah! You
were a baby, too. A *girl* baby." He managed to inject the
g-word with all the righteous scorn a five-year-old chauvin-
ist could muster.

"Enough," Mitch told him, thankful no one could see he

was smiling. He brought the subject around to the question that had started the ribbing. "Thea went home. She has to go to work tomorrow."

"You think she's afraid of the storm?" asked Grant. "Girls are sometimes."

Here we go, thought Mitch. But Emilie remained uncharacteristically quiet. "Sometimes," Mitch said. "But so are boys. And no one is always afraid of the same things. Thea might like watching a lightning storm."

"Really?" Case asked. "Mum didn't."

"I'm not crazy about them either," Mitch admitted. "But I bet you anything that Thea's watching this one."

"Can we call her?" Emilie asked suddenly. "Please, Uncle Mitch? Aunt Thea's all by herself. What if you're wrong?"

Mitch glanced at the clock. It was almost three. "I don't know, Em. It's not a good idea to be on the phone in an electrical storm." More importantly, Thea was probably asleep. He had worried about sending her home so late and as tired as she was, but she had her mind made up and in the end she had convinced him. "I'm sure she's fine," Mitch said lamely. On the other hand, he was wide-awake and so were the kids. Perhaps this was a moment she should share with them.

"Call her," Case said.

"Please," Emilie said.

"Seems to be the consensus," Grant said. The pitch of his delivery was higher than Mitch's, but in every other way—inflection, rhythm, and tone—it was a dead-on imitation.

Hearing not only his own words come back to him, but in a manner that mimicked him perfectly, just about took Mitch's breath away. Pride, amusement, a touch of fear at this reminder of his influence, he felt all of that. It was worth risking electrocution to share the moment. "All right," he said. "But I'm calling her and holding the phone. You can listen. Em, hand me the phone."

She did, reciting Thea's number for him before he could

find it on speed dial. The children were silent as Mitch held the phone a little away from his ear so they could hear the ringing. Thea picked up on four.

"Hello?"

"It's Mitch, Thea." He added quickly, "We're all fine."

There was a pause. "Mitch, it's three o'clock."

"I have two-fifty-seven." He smiled as she made a sound somewhere between exasperation and a sigh. "I've got company in my bed."

"Are you talking about the hand puppet?"

Mitch immediately pressed the receiver back to his ear and covered his mouth and the mouthpiece with his hand. "Jeez, Thea, I've got the kids here," he whispered.

"Oh. Well, you should have said that right away."

He could tell she was laughing. Mitch held out the phone again. "Are you having a storm there?" he asked.

"A spectacular one. Lots of thunder and lightning. You?"

"The same."

"Aaah," she said after a moment. "I understand. Are they listening?"

"Uh-huh. They wanted me to call. They were concerned that you might be afraid."

"Afraid? No. I love storms. I was sitting on the sunporch watching this one." There was a hesitation before her voice came over the line a little huskier and more intimate than it had in the moment before. "I couldn't sleep."

Mitch's own voice deepened. "Same here." Beside him, Case puckered his lips and began making kissing noises. Grant joined in almost immediately. Emilie started giggling.

"What's going on?" Thea asked.

"A little comedy routine," Mitch said dryly. He poked Grant lightly with his elbow. It had absolutely no effect. "Three kids who think they're pretty funny."

"Well, if they're laughing they can't be afraid any longer."

"I think you're right. Thanks, Thea. Good night."

She answered automatically. "Sleep tight."

The chorus finished. "Don't let the bed bugs bite!"

Chuckling softly, Mitch ended the call and passed the phone back to Emilie. He heard her fit it back in the base. "Satisfied?" he asked. "Told you she wouldn't be afraid."

"How did you know?" Emilie asked, settling back down.

Because a little girl who had her fingers forced through a wringer wouldn't be afraid of something so natural as thunder and lightning. That little girl knew about things that were infinitely more frightening. "I just knew," Mitch said quietly, tucking them all in. "I just knew."

Thea walked into work on Monday charged with energy. She gathered the Blue Team together in the conference room and told them her idea about Shine and Shield. "We'll do a product tie-in. Work up ideas for the Nissan Xterra, especially the yellow one they have. GMC. Ford. Toyota. BMW. You know the drill. Find a hot color and model." She saw some skeptical expressions. "Test it on your own cars if you don't believe me. I did. This morning. My Volvo"—she pronounced the make of her car very carefully and looked around to make sure no one was snickering—"shined like it was just off the assembly room floor. What I want to know is why didn't any of you know this?"

There was silence, then one brave soul ventured, "Because we use the laser car wash?"

"Exactly. So find out what those automatic washes are using and I'm betting we can pitch Shine and Shield to them as well. You know what this is, don't you? A new product use. Carver Chemical has never tapped this before."

"Is it safe?" someone asked.

"It was a 1953 Chevy truck, meticulously restored over a period of five years. Does the person who restored that sound like someone who would risk ruining a paint job by using something that *wasn't* safe? This truck looked brand spanking new. Mitch said he's been using Shine and Shield for years. Apparently his father told him about it."

There were a few more questions and comments. Everyone knew Carver Chemical already had a line of car products. In effect, Shine and Shield would be competing against them for a market share. On the other hand, if this product worked as well as Thea thought it did, it meant Carver had something to sell that had already been developed. The big costs were behind the company. They would have to run some tests, but they weren't going to be spending the kind of money they usually did on R&D. Thea didn't have any trouble convincing the Blue Team that meant extra money in Carver's advertising budget. The Foster & Wyndham creative team practically stampeded out of the corral.

Mrs. Admundson took a step backward to avoid being crushed. "Those people would kill their young for the next best idea," she said, entering the conference room. "What did you say to them?"

Thea made a three-sixty in her chair. Her smile was beatific. "I just gave them the next best idea, Mrs. A. And I might take the rest of the day off."

"But it's only nine-thirty. And it's Monday."

"I know. What could be a better way to start the week?"

Mrs. Admundson looked confused. That expression settled uncomfortably on her strong Nordic features. She held up a sheaf of pink message slips. "I have these for you," she said, waving them in her fingertips. "Plus, Mr. Baker is on line two. He's been holding for a while."

Thea immediately reached for the phone. "Leave those with me," she said, punching the line. "I'll take the call here." Thea lifted the receiver while Mrs. Admundson put the messages on the table in front of her. She mouthed a thank-you and fanned them idly in front of her, hardly sparing them a glance. "Mitch?"

"Oh, thank God, Thea."

His tone had her immediately sitting up straight. She didn't even hear her assistant closing the door. "I didn't know you were holding for me. What's happened? What's wrong?"

"It's Emilie," he said. "I had to pick her up at school this morning."

"Is she sick?"

"No, not what you'd call sick. Aww, hell, Thea, I don't know what to do. My mother and Amy are out shopping together and they must not be able to hear their phones. I hate to call you while you're working."

"It's all right. What's wrong with her?" Before he could answer that, Thea asked a second question. "Where are you, Mitch? What's that noise in the background?"

"I'm in Target. You hear the TVs in electronics. You need anything? I'm going through domestics."

Thea relaxed a little. He'd found his sense of humor so whatever it was that had him shaken was not a matter of life and death. "Where's Emilie?"

"She's waiting for me in the car. She didn't want to come in. Well, actually she *couldn't* come in. She . . . umm . . . she had an accident . . . sort of."

Her calm was short-lived. "Mitchell Baker, so help me God, you better tell me what's going on or I swear—"

"Emilie started her period." This announcement was met by silence. "You still there?"

"I'm listening. Go on."

"Well, it happened right after she got to school. One of her friends noticed the blood on the back of her dress and told her about it. Em, of course, was mortified."

"Oh, poor Em. What did she do? Is she all right?"

"Her friend has a cell phone—and don't think I won't hear about that later. Anyway, Emilie called me at home and I went and picked her up. She was too embarrassed to go to the office or tell her teacher. She was waiting for me outside."

"You forgot to take her clean clothes," Thea said.

"I didn't even think of it," Mitch admitted miserably. "I'm telling you, Thea. It kinda shook me up. This is way out of my league. I thought . . . you know . . . since you play for the away team, you might—"

Thea made a strangled sound.

"Are you okay?"

She reached for her bottled water and took a swallow. "Fine." She managed not to choke on the word, but only barely. He was deeply nuts. "I'm fine. Mitch? Why are you in Target?"

"To get . . . you know . . . stuff."

It was only the thought of Emilie sitting out in the car alone that kept Thea from spewing another mouthful of water. "You mean feminine napkins."

"Yeah. And tampons."

Thea set down her bottle and said slowly, "Listen to me carefully, Mitch. Do not, I repeat, do *not* purchase tampons for Emilie. Not now. I don't know what she understands about using them and—this is just a guess here—but I'm thinking you don't want to be the one explaining it all to her, you being on the home team and everything."

Mitch's sigh of relief practically vibrated the phone. "So what do I do?"

"What do you mean?"

"I mean," he whispered into the receiver, "what do I buy?"

"I thought I was clear. You buy her pads."

"Yeah, but *which ones?!*"

Thea realized he sounded a little panicked. She could almost enjoy this. "Tell me your choices."

"There are too damned many of them," he fairly growled. "Light days, medium days, heavy days, and superabsorbent overnights. Wait, I found a color code." He paused, studying the legend. "Pink is for light. Blue is medium days. Yellow . . . orange . . . green is blue and yellow. Who thought *this* was a good idea?"

"Go on," she said, tamping down her smile. "Emilie's counting on you."

He took a deep breath and let it out slowly. "Some have wings. Some are wingless. Deodorant. No deodorant. Scented. No scent. Thin. Wafer thin. Oh, God, there's something here that looks like a mattress."

Thea jammed her hand over the receiver to keep him from hearing her choke again. When she was composed, she said, "Go on. You're doing fine."

He grunted. It was as good a way as any of proving to himself that he wasn't lost to the feminine side. "Long. Longer. Wide. Double-wide. Tapered. Quilted. Thong. Contoured. Channels. No channels. Awww, jeez, Thea, this isn't right. This one has French drains."

Tears actually came to Thea's eyes. Her chest heaved with laughter too long suppressed, and for a moment she couldn't catch her breath.

"Emilie's waiting," Mitch reminded her.

That sobered Thea. She dabbed at the corners of her eyes with her fingertips. "Get her a package of the thin, regular absorbency quilted pads with wings. No deodorant or scents."

"Got it."

"Do I have to talk you through the checkout or do you think you can manage that on your own?"

"Amusing," he said dryly. "But I was already in hardware. I threw a power sander into my cart just in case I get any funny looks about this stuff."

"Good thinking." She hesitated a beat. "Mitch?"

"Hmmm?"

"When you get back in the car, will you let Emilie call

me? I could maybe . . . I don't know . . . maybe say some-thing to her that might help."

"Sure, I'll do that. She called you first, you know."

Thea sat up straight. "What?"

"Before me," he said. "She told me they wouldn't let her speak to you because you were in a meeting. I'm assuming she talked to Mrs. Admundson because I think Emilie could have wormed her way past Tamika in reception."

Thea looked more carefully at the messages in front of her. The third one was Emilie's. "I just found it," Thea said. Her shoulders sagged. "I didn't know, Mitch. I would have—"

She sounded so forlorn that Mitch stopped pushing his cart right in front of the nail polish. A glittery shade called In the Pink jumped out at him and he tossed it into the buggy. "It's okay, Thea. She's over it." Wrong thing to say. Mitch moved out of nails and leaned against the jewelry counter.

"She's *over* it? That means she was upset. I'm leaving work and coming up there. Don't try to talk me out of it."

Out of it? he thought. He'd been wracking his brain trying to figure out how to talk her *into* it. "You'll stay for dinner?"

Since it wasn't even lunch, Thea considered he was plan-ning far ahead. "I'd like that," she said.

"Good. How soon are you leaving?"

"Give me ten minutes and have Emilie call my cell."

"Got it. I'm out of here. Thanks, Thea."

Thea replaced the receiver slowly, her smile bemused and little off-kilter as she stared off into space. Monday morn-ings had never been her favorite part of the week. She was thinking she might have to revise her opinion.

In the next few weeks Thea spent more time in Connaugh Creek. Sometimes she drove up after work and stayed until the news was over at eleven-thirty. On alternate weekends they came to her home. Thea took Mitch and the children horseback riding. They went to the museum and the science center and a Pirates game. At the beginning of June school let out and there were swimming lessons and machine-pitch baseball. Emilie was lobbying heavily for dance camp. The twins wanted to live at the park.

At Foster and Wyndham the effort to pull together a campaign for Shine and Shield had moved Thea and every member of her Blue Team from drive into overdrive. She arrived at work as early as six some mornings so she could leave at four-thirty and miss some of the outbound traffic on her way to Mitch's. She attended NA or AA meetings on her lunch hour and kept tabs with Rosie several times a week. Joel caught her every few days at the office and they exchanged updates, his about a relationship on the skids, hers about the kids. For the first time her demanding schedule was not a distraction from life, but a purpose for it. She felt as if she were breathing, really breathing, and while she still took one day at a time it no longer required the sustained effort she had initially applied to the task.

Until Father's Day.

On that day she was a single nerve ending. Her parents had returned.

Mitch extended his hand to George Wyndham. "Glad to meet you, sir," he said. Wyndham's grip was firm, in spite of the knuckles being swollen and slightly misshapen with the effects of arthritis.

"And you," Wyndham said politely. "Thea's told us about you. She sent us some of your cartoons." He released Mitch's hand and sized him up with a glance, that in spite of its obvious interest, was still remote. "Not your best work, I suspect. You're a Democrat, aren't you?"

"Daddy," Thea interjected quickly. "No politics, please."

"Thea's right, George," Patricia Wyndham said. She gave him a tumbler of Scotch, neat. "You'll give yourself a stroke."

Mitch felt Thea's mother's cool, brittle smile turned on him. She was an attractive woman. Tall. Thin. Her hair was salt and pepper, expertly cut. She had a strong, linear jaw, and the choker of pearls she wore around her neck emphasized it. Her skin was too taut for a woman her age, which meant there had been a face-lift, probably several. Her nails were her own, buffed and polished with clear enamel. One of them tapped lightly against her cut-crystal tumbler. The ice cubes in her Scotch clinked together and against the sides as she regarded him for a long moment before she spoke.

"I liked your cartoons, Mr. Baker. You mustn't mind my husband. He left his sense of humor at Heathrow. It was a long and particularly trying flight."

Did they run out of Scotch in first-class? Mitch held his tongue and kept his expression carefully neutral. "I'm sorry to hear that, Mrs. Wyndham. It makes your invitation to have us here all the more gracious."

She lifted one eyebrow. "Do you think so? That is very kind of you." Patricia turned her attention to Thea. "Will you introduce the children to us? They appear to be at sixes and sevens."

"Yes," Thea said. "Yes, of course." She touched Emilie lightly on the shoulder. "Mother, this is Emilie Reasoner. Emilie, my mother."

"How do you do?" Emilie asked. Her concession to her own discomfort was the way she shifted ever so slightly toward Thea's side.

"Very well, thank you," Patricia said.

Thea completed the introductions all around. The twins marched right up to George Wyndham and shook his hand, just as they'd practiced with Mitch. Thea thought her father looked impressed, but it was always a bit difficult to tell. His smile was present but the eyes remained unreadable.

"Well," George said, "perhaps we should go to the living room. Berte will call us for dinner. Thea? Why don't you fix a drink for Mr. Baker? There are soft drinks for the children in the bar."

"Belly up to the bar, boys," Thea said, earning a disapproving look from Patricia as if she'd just said something vulgar. "It's from *The Unsinkable Molly Brown,* Mother. You took me to see it, remember?"

Patricia Wyndham was not sure that she did but her features softened marginally. She slipped her arm through her husband's and allowed him to escort her from the spacious den to the living room.

When they were out of earshot, Mitch said, "Make mine a double."

A glimmer of a smile appeared on Thea's lips as she walked to the bar. "They do seem to have that effect on people."

Case crawled up onto a leather upholstered barstool and pressed his stomach to the bar, taking Thea's invitation literally. "Double."

Chuckling, Thea looked in the refrigerator. "How about a Shirley Temple?" She saw Case exchange a look of confusion with his brother. "Never mind," she said. "Trust me. You'll like this. Emilie? Grant? You, too?"

While Thea made the drinks, Mitch looked around. "You grew up here?"

Thea had recently determined that she had lived here, but that she had only grown up after she left. She might tell Mitch that at another time; for now she only said, "That's right. There are eighteen rooms, not counting the baths. You saw the carriage house?"

"As we drove up."

"That's were Berte and John live. They take care of the

place for Mother and Daddy when they're traveling. Berte also cooks and John sees to the grounds."

Mitch whistled softly, accepting the drink Thea handed him. "Live-in help. Impressive." He had known her family had money, but this was something else again. "I had no idea the ad business was so lucrative."

"My grandfather and my father did all right for themselves," she said. "This house comes from my mother's family. She's a Carver."

It almost went over Mitch's head. When he got it he felt like he caught it on the rebound. "Carver?" he repeated, turning slowly. "As in Carver Chemical?"

"The same." She flashed him a guilty smile. "I really thought you knew. Grant, you can't have any more maraschino cherries in your drink. I'm not even sure they're good for you." She put the jar back in the refrigerator and took a tonic water for herself, adding a lime wedge to the rim of her glass. "Come on. Mother and Daddy will be wondering what happened to us."

"I think your mother and father are scary," Emilie announced, perfectly at ease in doing so.

"Me, too," Case said, sliding off his stool. "Like Cruella."

"Yeah," Grant chimed in. "And her boyfriend."

"Cruella didn't have a boyfriend," Emilie said. "Not really. Anyway, Mr. Wyndham looks just like Cruella, too."

Behind the bar, Thea felt a little weak in the knees.

"That's enough," Mitch said. "There better not be any Cruella comments at dinner. We're Mr. and Mrs. Wyndham's guests. Here, let me hold your drinks until we get to the living room. And don't touch anything on the way there. I won't make enough in a lifetime to replace what's broken."

Emilie handed her drink to Thea and clapped her hands close to her sides. Her brothers followed suit and the three of them began marching out of the den single file.

"Very funny," Mitch called after them. He looked at Thea.

"Your parents are scary," he told her. "And don't think you're done explaining the Carver Chemical connection. I didn't realize I was standing in the home Shine and Shield built."

Thea sighed, picking up Emilie's drink and her own. She came around the bar. "Actually, it was Avalon that built this house."

"The soap," Mitch said.

"That's right. 'As a flake, in a cake, all the suds you can make.' Soap *flakes*. *Cake* of soap. None of that rings a bell?"

"Afraid not, but you sing it real nice."

She continued with the ditty in her clear alto voice. "'As you glean, there's a sheen in all the clothes you can clean.'" Thea eyed Mitch. "Nothing?"

He shook his head.

"Well, it wasn't exactly a Barry Manilow jingle, but it was popular in its day. It sold a lot of Avalon even before it was set to music and heard on radio." Thea was the first into the hallway. She waited for Mitch.

"Let me guess," he said. "Your grandfather."

"Good guess. He wrote the words and later, the music."

There was more Mitch wanted to know but he was concentrating on not spilling the contents of the glasses he was carrying. The rug underneath his feet most definitely did not come from IKEA and he doubted it was something that was easily cleaned. Avalon or no.

"Are you going to be okay?" Thea asked as they reached the pocket doors to the living room.

"I was going to ask you the same thing."

"The strain shows?"

"A little."

Thea knew he was being kind. "Thanks for coming down with the kids. Your dad was great about sharing you and the kids today." Then, because his hands were full, Thea took a step toward him and kissed him on the cheek.

"You missed," he said.

She smiled. "I think I—"

Mitch kissed her full on the mouth. Her parted lips were damp and tasted faintly of the tartness of lime. "Let's go. It's too quiet in there."

Nodding, Thea parted the pocket doors and deliberately left them open once she and Mitch had stepped into the formal living room. The children were subdued. They were all sitting rather stiff-backed on the Queen Anne bench with the cabriolet legs. Emilie had placed herself between Case and Grant and had her hands neatly folded in her lap and legs crossed properly at the ankles. The boys' feet did not touch the floor. Their legs swung independently of each other, missing the synchronized beat every time.

No one was talking and everyone looked in need of rescuing.

"Oh, you're here," Patricia said, her tone more relieved than welcoming.

"I would hardly abandon you and Daddy," Thea said, "to the tender mercies of these three." With her back to her parents she smiled encouragingly to the trio on the bench. She handed Emilie her Shirley Temple while Mitch relieved himself of his extra glasses.

George Wyndham had risen slightly at their entrance. Now he indicated that Thea and Mitch should be seated. They each took an overstuffed chair on either side of the green-veined marble fireplace and George settled back beside his wife on the love seat. "Emilie has been explaining that she would like to attend dance camp," said George. "What is that exactly?"

"A summer camp," Thea said, glad to discover there had been some conversation in her absence. "Just the sort that I attended when I was her age, but with activities that focus on dance."

"What sort of dance?" Patricia asked, looking over Emilie. "She hasn't the figure for ballet." In a manner that was faux confidential, Patricia leaned slightly in Emilie's direction and said, "You like sweets, don't you, dear? It's all right. So do I."

Thea could not remember the last time she had seen her mother eat chocolate. Flushing, embarrassed by her mother's tactlessness and feeling Emilie's humiliation keenly, Thea threw herself into the breach. "Emilie is a talented dancer," she said. "She likes tap and jazz, but ballet is her first love. I shouldn't be surprised if Emilie wins the Clara role in a few years."

"Really?" Patricia sipped her drink. "*The Nutcracker?* At Heinz Hall? How extraordinary."

Thea felt Emilie's hard stare. It will be all right, Thea wanted to say, but she wasn't entirely certain it would be. In response to her mother's impolitic remarks, Thea heard herself speaking rashly, not really coming to Emilie's defense but putting pressure on her. Emilie had never once said that she might like to dance Clara's role. Right now Emilie aspired to be a sugar plum. Not a sugar plum fairy. Just the marzipan. "Yes," Thea said a little weakly. "Extraordinary. Emilie is extraordinary."

Mitch winked at Emilie. He took it as a bad sign that the corners of her mouth did not so much as flicker. "We're still in the discussion phase of dance camp," he told the Wyndhams. "Did the twins tell you they're taking swimming lessons?"

George shook his head. "We haven't heard from them."

It wasn't because they were afraid of saying the wrong thing, Mitch thought. It was because they were just afraid. "They're both going to take their final test this coming Saturday. One length of the pool. Deep to shallow. No stopping. Right, guys?"

Case and Grant stopped swinging their legs long enough to nod in unison.

George was thoughtful. "Didn't Gabriel swim competitively, Thea? I seem to remember that he did."

"Yes. In high school and college."

"I thought so. He was rather good at it."

"Yes, he was. And the twins are—"

"Enjoying themselves." Mitch broke in before Thea could promise her father the boys were headed for the Olympics. "They're regular water babies."

"I'm not a baby," Grant announced.

"Me neither," Case said.

Patricia blinked. It was as animated as her features became. "They're very forward, aren't they, dear?"

At first Mitch thought she was talking to her husband, but then he realized it was Thea who was meant to respond. Directed at George, Mitch might have been able to excuse the comment as a mere observation; directed at Thea, it took on the character of a mild rebuke. "Fast forward," Mitch said lightly.

"All day, every day," Thea said, darting a quick glance at Mitch to let him know she appreciated his timing and humor.

"Really?" Patricia imbued the question with a sort of regalness that was almost a parody. "And your nerves? You don't find it wearing?"

"On the contrary, I find it suits me."

"Really?" she said again in exactly the same tone. "How astonishing."

Mitch couldn't tell Patricia Wyndham's astonished expression from her disapproving one. He suspected it was because astonishment was simply a classy way of showing disapproval. His mother and sister had their own version of it at yard sales and craft fairs. When either one of them commented that some article was interesting, it was code for *Can you believe how tacky this is?*

Berte appeared in the doorway and announced dinner. Thea could have kissed her for the timely interruption. Instead, she encouraged the children to stand and accompany her into the dining room. "Leave your drinks here," she told them. "It's okay this time. Berte will get them."

Mitch could see from Emilie's expression that the advantage of having a housekeeper was not lost on her. She looked as if she could get used to the idea very quickly. He put a period to that idea with a single, quelling glance.

The dining room was finished in dark walnut. Each inlaid panel was polished to a reflective gloss. Stained-glass windows on the west wall filtered the late-afternoon sunlight into the room and splashed the white linen tablecloth with transparent color. The table was set with china rimmed in gold leaf and the silverware was silver, not stainless steel. The centerpiece bowl that held a fresh arrangement of pink hydrangeas was Waterford. So were the goblets and wineglasses.

Mitch looked over the table setting, especially the crystal, then at the twins. They had passed through the sippy-cup phase years ago, but they liked their drinks in boxes and pouches and plastic. He'd never seen them handle stemware. It was tempting to write a blank check at the beginning of the meal just so he could enjoy it.

The children settled into their chairs with aplomb, their hands folded neatly in their laps, their glances darting toward Thea for approval. That was Mitch's first clue that there had been a recent crash course in deportment. Emilie, Case, and Grant were acting as if they'd never fought over a Happy Meal toy in their lives. They didn't blink when sherbet in cold silver cups was presented to them as the first course. They didn't hesitate to choose the proper fork for the salad. They ate slowly, listened to the conversation around them without interrupting, and never failed to say please and thank you. No one made a face when they learned the meat dish was lamb and the green wiggling stuff wasn't Jell-O, but mint jelly. It was a stunning transformation and their exemplary behavior

did not go unremarked by Patricia Wyndham as the inter-
minable meal reached the dessert phase.

"They have lovely manners," she said, directing her comment to Mitch.

"Stepford training," he said without blinking an eye or
catching Thea's. He patted her back as she choked anyway.

"Stepford?" Patricia looked confused. "I don't think I—"

George Wyndham smiled thinly. "The Ira Levin book,"
he explained to his wife. "We both read it years ago. Perfect
wives and mothers. I believe Mr. Baker is implying the children have been brainwashed."

Case's brow puckered with real consternation. "I don't
think so, Mr. Wyndham. Because all I washed was behind
my ears and Uncle Mitch told me that was okay."

"That was fine," Mitch said. He noticed Case looked relieved. Clearly some sort of bribery had occurred. Thea was
being careful not to look in his direction and also to avoid
the children.

"You prepared the children, Thea?" George asked.

She looked up. "Yes." A little defiantly, almost as afterthought, she added, "I wanted them to be comfortable."

George Wyndham's expression did not change as he regarded his daughter. "That was good of you," he said after a
moment.

It struck Mitch that these stiffly spoken words were very
difficult for the man, that presenting Thea with a token, perhaps diamonds, or slipping her a C-note would have been his
preference. Patricia Wyndham, he noticed, had nothing to
say. She was too sloshed, though in a perfectly civil way.

Mitch dropped heavily onto a wide, overstuffed armchair
in Thea's living room and remained in a classic sprawl for a
full minute before he moved again. Finally, he undid the
already loose knot in his tie and pulled it off. It remained

lying limply over his knee and thigh until Thea passed within a foot of the chair, then he tried flicking her with it.

Amused, she shook her head as though disappointed in his poor effort. She took the tie from him and looped it around her neck. "You are one sorry individual," she said, pushing the ottoman in front of him. "Here, put your feet up." When he didn't, she sat down on it and invited him again, this time to put his feet on her lap. She ended up having to help him by pulling on his trouser legs.

"You never would have been able to drive home," she said, critically observing his heavy-lidded, slumberous eyes. His smile was faintly lopsided, endearingly so. She had not had any difficulty convincing Mitch that he should allow her to drive them all to her house for the night since it was so much closer to her parents' home. "How much did you have to drink after dinner?"

He held up one finger. "Never could seem to find the bottom of that glass, though."

"Ah, yes. I know that glass." She began massaging one of his stockinged feet, using the balls of her thumbs on his arch. He groaned appreciatively and let his head fall back again. "Like that, do you?" Mitch's reply was inarticulate but conveyed great pleasure. "It was my mother that kept topping off your drink, wasn't it? She can be insistent. She doesn't like to drink alone."

"Your mother's a lush, Thea."

"Don't laugh, Mitch, but I'm just realizing it."

He didn't laugh. "I read somewhere that lots of people don't figure it out about their own parents until they get into recovery themselves."

"You read that?" she asked, equal parts skeptical and curious.

Mitch shrugged. "Read it. Heard it. I don't remember."

Thea worked on the sole of his foot. "Now where would you hear something like that? I never said it."

"No, you never did. You don't talk much about it, not since you laid it out for me, so I figured I'd just find out some things on my own."

"On your own? What do you mean?"

"Well, I thought I'd go to some meetings. Open ones. Al-Anon—you know, the one for family and friends of alcoholics and addicts. It was interesting."

Thea simply stared at him.

"You wanna know why?" he asked.

She nodded slowly, afraid to know, afraid not to. Her thumbs pressed into the ball of his foot and stilled.

He grinned at her, one brow kicking up. "Don't stop." He wiggled his toes. "I like you, Thea. Like you a lot. Thought I should try to be a better friend."

Thea began massaging again. The fist squeezing her heart eased, but not as much as she would have thought. It made her wonder what she had been hoping he'd say. "You've been a very good friend," she said because she meant it and because it was true.

"But not like Joel."

"No, not at all like Joel. But that's not a bad thing. I need different kinds of friends."

"And lovers?"

She frowned. "What are you talking about?"

Mitch sighed as Thea transferred her attentions to his other foot and closed his eyes. "Do you need different lovers? We haven't been together since we fooled around in the truck. That was—"

"Mother's Day," she said. "Yes, I know. I was there. Fooling around. I just thought that with the kids and . . . well, I didn't think you . . . we're never really alone, Mitch. The kids are upstairs now."

"Conked out."

"That's not the point. They'll be awake in the morning,

and I thought we were in agreement that they shouldn't find us sharing a bed."

"Funny how you came to an agreement about something we never discussed." He wiggled his toes again to get her to resume her ministrations. "The real point is—and I'm coming to it—is that your father tells me you're still screwing Joel Strahern."

Chapter 13

Thea knocked Mitch's feet from her lap and rocketed off the ottoman. "That was a perfectly lousy thing to say."

He regarded her with wounded eyes as his heels thumped hard on the carpet. "What?"

"Don't look at me as if you're the injured party." Thea turned and started to leave. She managed only a single step before she found her wrist caught in Mitch's firm grip. She stared pointedly at her hand, then at him. "I think you should let me go."

He didn't. Instead he gave her wrist a tug. With no more effort than that he had Thea in his lap, though her revenge was to collapse against him with rather more force than was necessary. Mitch's grunt did not make her sympathetic. He had to release Thea's hand in order to rearrange her dead-weight across his thighs. "Guess this means I'm not gonna get laid."

"Good guess."

Mitch took her response in stride, "You wanna help me out here?"

Grudgingly, Thea slid her butt off his thighs and settled sideways against the widely curved arm of the deep, over-stuffed chair. Her long, slender legs made a bridge over his lap. This conciliatory gesture was balanced by the arms Thea folded somewhat defiantly across her chest. She gave him a challenging, narrowed-eye glance. "You better make this good, Mitchell."

He didn't know if he was up to it. "Do I get any kind of handicap on account of I'm drunk?"

Thea considered that. "I'll give you some leeway with the wording, but I'm not budging on the degree of sincerity."

"Deal." Mitch took a deep breath and exhaled on a thread of sound. When he finally spoke it was more to himself than to Thea. "No problem. I can do grovel."

Careful not to smile, Thea waited him out.

"I am most deeply sorry," he said. "Humbly sorry. Really, truly sorry. If I had their number, I would call back those words. If I had a receipt, I'd return 'em to the service desk. If I had a—"

"Hammered," she said softly. "You're hammered."

"Yeah." He gave her a slightly loopy smile. "Yeah, I am. Sincerely so."

Thea unfolded her arms, turned slightly, and let herself relax more comfortably in the crook of his shoulder. She closed her eyes. Mitch's breathing was quiet and even and sometimes it ruffled her hair.

"Thea?"

"Hmm?"

"Your dad never said that."

She smiled a little. "I know."

"Not those exact words."

"I know, Mitch. He doesn't talk like that."

Mitch rested his cheek against Thea's silky hair. "I was paraphrasing."

"Paraphrasing."

He nodded. "Communicating the gist of it."

"I know what paraphrasing means," she said. "It's the why of it I don't understand. My father said I was still sleeping with Joel . . ." Thea lifted her head enough to look at Mitch. "Did you believe him?"

"Actually, he said you were still in love with Joel."

With no hesitation, Thea repeated the same question. "Did you believe him?"

He didn't say anything immediately. The pause was not dictated by a need to arrive at the right response, only the truthful one. As it happened, the truth surprised him. "I suppose I did," he said finally. "I sure as hell reacted like I did."

Thea rested her head in the curve of his neck and shoulder again. "Good answer," she said softly. "Do you need to hear some sort of denial from me or can you work it out on your own?"

Mitch's neurons weren't exactly firing in sync, but this wasn't differential calculus. The math was pretty simple. "Your daddy likes Joel Strahern and he doesn't like me."

"Close enough," Thea said. "You do okay for someone plied with drinks all evening."

He took another stab. "Your daddy dislikes Joel less than he dislikes me."

"In a nutshell." Thea rubbed Mitch's chest lightly. "It's not at all personal. He's always been of the opinion that I should marry one of the Fosters. Cement the partnership. It seems vaguely incestuous, if you ask me. Hank is like an older brother. Annoying. Protective. Helpful. Familiar. It was a relief for both of us when he finally married. Evidently there was some pressure from his father as well. He has two brothers, neither of whom has any real interest in the agency—or me." She sighed. "My father has convinced himself that he was warming up to Joel. It only required that I break the engagement and deep-six the wedding plans for him to have that epiphany. What did you say to him anyway? He wouldn't have blurted out that I was still in love with Joel if he wasn't provoked."

Mitch shrugged. "Don't remember exactly."

Thea didn't believe him but she let it pass. "He means well, Mitch. He really does. It's another one of those things I'm beginning to understand. It never occurred to me in all the years that I've tried to win his approval, that he might have been trying to win mine."

"That's why he came back now, isn't it?" Mitch asked. "In time for Father's Day."

She nodded. "I think so. I'm not sure I ever knew how much stock he put in the day."

Mitch found Thea's hand and slipped his fingers through hers. "Did you tell him you love him?"

Thea nodded again. "I wish he hadn't been so surprised." There was a small catch in her voice. "Both of us are late to the realization that there's nothing about love that has to be earned."

Mitch smiled. "Figured that out, did you?"

"Yeah, I did."

"Good." He gave her hand a little squeeze. "Think you can help me to bed?"

"Sure." She raised her head and kissed him on the corner of the mouth. "But you're not getting laid."

It was an involuntary shudder that brought Mitch to wakefulness. That he was deeply aroused came more slowly to his consciousness. He groaned softly, pressing his head back into the fullness of the pillow. His back arched. He drew one knee up and felt his inner thigh caress the soft skin of a bare shoulder. His heel dug into the mattress. There was no pause in the hot suck of her mouth.

His eyes opened to tiny slits. The blue-green glow of a night-light defined the perimeter of the bedroom, then the boundary of the bed. He looked down the length of his nose, then his chest. The pale sheet shifted over his thighs. A crown of dark and silky hair emerged. He brushed it with his fingertips.

"Thea."

Now there was a pause. His cock was slowly, exquisitely released. "How did you know it was me?"

Mitch's low growl was part laughter, part need. Thea bent her head again, taking him in her mouth, sucking, using her lips and teeth and tongue to caress and tease and pull another response from him. Her fingers massaged his swollen balls. Her hair brushed the inside of his thighs.

"God, Thea! I'm . . ." He felt her swallow, taking him more deeply than she had before. She was so hot. Surrounding him with heat. Damp heat. Silky and wet and on fire. She stroked his thighs, his buttocks. The tiny noises she made at the back of her throat vibrated against his skin. Her tongue swirled, gently abrading, always arousing. His long frame jerked, stretched, and still he managed to contain himself in the taut confines of skin that no longer quite fit.

He caught her shoulder, then the tips of her hair. His hand curved around the back of her neck. Her name came to his lips as a soft, husky groan.

Thea lifted her head. Her eyes were dark, vaguely unfocused. "Hmmm?"

"Come here."

Smiling, she slithered forward over his hard belly and harder cock. "You have something in mind?"

Mitch rolled Thea onto her back and buried himself deep inside her. She accepted him without a murmur. The press of her fingers in his shoulders was the only outward sign that she felt anything at all. He found her silence oddly erotic. He kissed her mouth. Her lips were swollen and damp. She tasted of him.

He began to move inside her—slowly at first, then, because he could not do it any differently, faster and harder and with single-minded, selfish urgency. She embraced him, embraced his need. Her legs curved around him. She lifted, rocked. Her body contracted inside and out and each caress was both bold and somehow intimate. When he came she did not want to let him go. His body surged against hers and every line of tension that was in him became part of her. She watched him above her, his features taut, the muscles bunching across his back and upper arms. His mouth thinned; the jaw tightened. His entire body shuddered, then went slack.

Thea cushioned his fall. "No," she whispered when she felt him stir. "Not yet. Don't move."

He rested his weight on his forearms but otherwise remained as he was. The muscles of her vagina clenched like a fist around him. His hips twitched and he let his head fall forward, grunting softly. "You're doing that on purpose."

Thea stopped. "Is it too much?"

"A little."

She smiled. "You like it though."

"Are you kidding? Being the personal trainer for a woman doing Kegel reps? It's been a dream of mine."

It was all Thea could do not to laugh. Concentrating, she repeated the contraction, only harder this time. The movement made her catch her breath and she drew in her lower lip.

"Aaah," Mitch said softly. "Teetering on the edge, are we?"

"*I* am," she said dryly. "You came."

"Want some help?"

"Please." The tiniest inflection gave it the lilt of a question.

Mitch grinned wickedly as he eased out of her. Thea's protest was ignored and she forgot about it when his mouth hovered above her breast. "This oughta do it," he said. Just as if she were going under for the third time, Thea gulped air and held it when Mitch's lips closed over her nipple. He sucked hard, making her lift for him. His hand slipped between her open thighs; his fingers found her. With only a touch he closed the circuit. For Thea it felt as if every nerve ending in her body was part of an electric arc.

It was a perfectly lovely orgasm that rippled through her.

She lay quietly beside him for a while, unconcerned that he was watching her. The fact that he seemed to be inordinately proud of himself amused her. She gave him an arch look. *"'This oughta do it?'"* she asked, repeating his words with a wry twist. *"'This oughta do it?'* Did you think you were adjusting something under my hood?"

"I was . . . kinda."

Her hand snaked out around his neck and brought his head down. Laughter softened her kiss. "I think you must be very good for me, Mitch Baker."

Which was exactly what he had said to her father.

It was a few minutes after three when Mitch woke and discovered he was alone in Thea's bed. He listened for her in the adjoining bathroom but there was only silence. He got up, found his boxers on the floor and put them on, and then checked on the children before he headed downstairs.

Thea was sitting on an Adirondack chair on the back deck. From his vantage point in the dark kitchen, Mitch could watch unobserved. Her nightgown was almost as pale as her skin in the moonlight. It formed a tent over the legs she had drawn up to her chest. She was staring out over her knees, over the deck rail, in the direction of the woods and the horizon. In all the time he watched her, she never moved. He wished he could see her face. He did not think she would look so different than when she was sleeping, when her features were swept clear of every care, of others' expectations, and she dreamed of things that were all her own.

Mitch slid the door aside. She didn't stir, but it wasn't because she hadn't heard him, but because she had. "Come or go?" he asked.

"Come."

He hitched a hip on the wide, flat arm of the chair and stretched one leg out to the side. "Couldn't sleep?"

"I did for a little while. Sometimes I get like this. Restless. Unsettled. It helps to come out here. I used to take a handful of stuff for sleeping." She shrugged. "Now I do this."

Mitch noticed the phone lying on the opposite arm. "Were you talking to Rosie?"

Thea shook her head. "I thought I might call her. I found I didn't need to."

"Is it getting easier, Thea?"

"I don't know how to answer that. I can go days without thinking about using, then something happens—something small, something big—and I'm reminded that what I'm holding on to is a very slender thread. It's humbling." She lifted her head and looked up at him. "Today, for instance. My parents . . ." Thea's voice trailed off and she turned away again. "I should have done a better job protecting Emilie. What my mother said to her was unconscionably hurtful. Then I made it worse. Everything she said to the children felt like a criticism of *me.*"

"That's pretty much the way I read it, too," said Mitch. "I don't think your perception's so far off the mark."

She glanced at him. "Really?"

He nodded. "Your dad's in your corner, though. He doesn't seem to know how to say it, but that was my impression."

"Funny. It was mine, too. I should invite you and the kids to more Sunday dinners with my parents. At least I didn't throw up after this one."

"That's what you usually did?"

"When I was Em's age, almost every Sunday. I wasn't bulimic, just nervous. I had to eat what was served and my stomach would be in knots and . . ." She shrugged. "You get the picture."

Mitch did. "But you got through today without any pills."

Thea didn't miss the small inflection that made it a question. She chose not to be resentful of Mitch for having doubts. It made him prudent, she supposed. Cautious. She had to balance the respect he showed for her addiction with his wary trust in her. It couldn't be easy for him either. "Yesterday," she said softly, raising her face to the moon in the southwestern sky. "It was yesterday, but yeah, I got through it without taking a thing."

Mitch let his arm fall from the back of the chair to Thea's shoulders. She leaned into him without any more encouragement than that. A warm breeze stirred her hair. Strands fluttered against his skin. "Then you did good," Mitch said. "No one who didn't use did it any better."

Thea smiled. He knew the exact right thing to say.

In the morning the children found Mitch sleeping on the living room couch. They didn't know he had only stretched out there a scant hour before and they would not have changed much about their behavior had they been aware. Their idea of respecting his sleep involved stealthy movements on tiptoes and communicating in breathy whispers. The effect was more noise than if they had walked and talked normally. When they saw Mitch pull a pillow over his face and heard him groan with gusto, they pounced and eventually wrestled him onto the floor.

Thea discovered them sprawled on the carpet in a tangle of bed linens. She stood over them, her head cocked to one side as she fastened a gold hoop in her ear. "Cereal's in the cupboard above the microwave. OJ, milk, and bread is in the fridge. Butter's out. No coffee, Mitch. Sorry. There are tea bags in a canister on the counter."

Four heads lifted simultaneously and four pairs of eyes stared at her with laserlike intensity.

Thea patted her ear, making certain the hoop was in securely. "What? It's Monday. I have to go to work." Her words seemed to have no impact. They continued to stare at her. "I'm running late." She realized she wasn't getting through. "All right. I'll eat breakfast with you."

Case jumped up. "Waffles! Waffles!"

Emilie and Grant joined the chant.

Mitch merely smiled.

Thea caved.

Twenty-six minutes later they were sitting around the kitchen table, helping themselves to a warm stack of home-made waffles and bacon strips, sliding the syrup bottle back and forth like a hockey puck.

Mitch saw Thea glance at her watch. "You have a meeting?"

She nodded. "The Carver Chemical account. We're putting the finishing touches on the campaign. If it's as good as I think it's going to be I'll be trying to get a meeting with Carver in a couple of weeks."

"You're excited about this, aren't you?"

"I am," she admitted.

He studied her animated face. "It's nice."

Thea smiled. "It is."

Mitch was distracted by Grant's wildly waving fork. "Careful. You're going to spill your juice." He caught the glass in the nick of time and pushed it toward the center of the table. "For later," he said. "When you're done conducting." As soon as Grant speared his waffle, Mitch turned back to Thea. "So tell me about this Carver connection. Your mother's a Carver and I'm guessing Foster and Wyndham used to have the advertising account. What happened?"

"Nothing nefarious. Carver moved its corporate head-quarters out of Pittsburgh in the seventies and took its ad-vertising dollars to Madison Avenue. Except for voting by proxy and collecting dividends on her stock, my mother's involvement and influence with the company is nil. She used to be active on the foundation's board, but she lost interest in it after my father retired. There are only one or two

Carvers left in key positions. Management's been from the outside for years."

"Then if you get the account it will be on its own merit."

"Hell, yes."

Case and Grant were immediately attentive.

Thea sighed. "You guys are like robber barons. My purse is on the sofa."

Case pushed out his chair first and dashed to the living room to get it. He held it open for Thea so she could root out a quarter.

"Here," she said. "Put it in the jar."

"*You* have a jar?" asked Mitch.

Thea reached back in her purse. "Hell, yes." She tossed a quarter to Grant. "Jar," she said succinctly. "It was Emilie's idea the first time she stayed with me."

Emilie nodded serenely. "Aunt Thea has cable mouth."

Mitch blinked. "Cable mouth?"

"You know. Like cable TV. The channels where you can say *anything*."

Mitch gave a shout of laughter as Thea's cheeks flushed with color. He ignored her glare and patted Emilie on her shoulder. "Good one, Em. Come on. Let's help Thea clean up. We still have to get her car."

Thea shook her head. "No. I really don't have time for that. Drive me into town and I'll get a ride to my parents' house after work."

"All right." He sidled up to her chair and bussed her on the cheek. "Thanks for breakfast."

Thea's smile was still with her forty minutes later when she walked into the conference room at Foster and Wyndham. It faltered a little when she saw her father.

He stood. "You don't mind, do you, Thea? I stopped in to see Hank and he told me about your presentation. He invited me to stay."

"Did he?" Thea looked at the expectant faces around the

Jo Goodman

table. "Well, good. Give me a minute, please. I need to get some things in my office." She backed out of the conference room, shut the door, and took measured, even strides to her own office, trying not to look panicked.

Thea tossed her briefcase and purse onto the sofa and leaned back against the door. She drew in a deep breath and exhaled slowly through her nose. She tried it again, shutting her eyes this time. The exercise was only of marginal value. All she had to do to jump her heart rate and cramp her stomach was imagine facing her father in the conference room. Everyone would be turning to him after the presentation, looking for his approval. His opinion still mattered a great deal at Foster and Wyndham. Even new employees, who didn't know him to see him, were thoroughly familiar with his reputation and exacting standards.

She could do this. Thea rested the crown of her head against the door. *She could do this.* The truth was, she had before. In her first eight years at the agency she had faced her father many times pitching ideas for new ads. It was also true that she'd never done it without some choice drugs. What she needed right now was something to dial down the intensity. Valium. Xanax. Maybe a handful of Ativan.

Thea's fists clenched. Hearing papers crumple, she looked down and saw she was holding messages in her left hand—with no idea of how they came to be there. She realized Mrs. Admundson must have pressed them on her before she stepped in her office. Yes. A tranquilizer was definitely in order.

Or a painkiller. Something to mellow the senses. Vicodin. Someone in the office must have Percocet or OxyContin in their desk. That would give her a goddamn sense of well-being.

Breathe.

Thea sucked in air and let the messages flutter to the floor.

She counted to ten slowly and then pushed off from the door in the direction of her desk. Before she could begin rifling her center drawer Mrs. A's voice came over the intercom.

"Ms. Wyndham?"

"What is it?" Thea's voice was uncharacteristically sharp. There was a slight pause before Mrs. Admundson continued.

"Mr. Foster is wondering where you are."

"I'm here. Does he need a map?"

There was another pause. "Are you all right, Ms. Wyndham?"

"I'm fine. I need a few minutes." Thea cut the intercom and picked up the receiver. She punched in ten numbers on the base.

Four rings, then: "Hey there. Unless you're new to the planet—"

Thea hung up and tried another number. Two rings this time, then: "The cellular customer you are calling is currently not available or is outside the—" She slammed the phone down. No Rosie. No Mitch. There was no point in calling Joel. As supportive as he tried to be, he had never understood. Not really. Thea opened the shallow center drawer and began pushing papers and pens around. The paper clip tray tipped and spilled its contents. Markers. Scissors. Staple remover.

Her fingers dug a mint green pill out of one corner of the drawer. It was impressed with a V in the center. Thea palmed the Valium and kept looking. Loose change. Rubber bands. Stray business cards.

Thea fanned out the cards and found her counselor's number. She picked up the phone again and called. Almost immediately she was connected with voice mail. She was given the option of talking to someone else in the event her call was an emergency, but Thea didn't want to talk to a stranger. What would she say? She unfolded her hand and looked at the small green pill sitting in the heart of her palm. It was as innocuous as an after-dinner mint. How could she explain that right now she was feeling very much like a little girl whose fingers were poised at the rolling lips of a wringer?

Who knew anything about that?

Thea hit the intercom button. "Mrs. Admundson? Would you please ask my father to come in here?"

The presentation came off without a hitch. For Thea it was the easier of the two she did that day. The one she made to her father, the one where she put the Valium in his hand and made him listen to exactly what frightened her, was infinitely more difficult and ultimately more rewarding. It was the first time she had ever been able to acknowledge that the monsters that scared her were the ones that lived inside. It didn't matter that he was more than a little bewildered by her stream-of-consciousness confession or the passion with which she delivered it. She cared more that he was sitting on her sofa beneath the Warhol print he had always disliked and never once mentioned it. She liked that he gave her his full attention and that even when his mouth thinned in disapproval or disagreement, he didn't interrupt her. She shocked him, she thought, when she told him how much his good opinion meant to her—but that she wouldn't wreck her life being afraid of his poor one.

She was an addict, she told him, and though her explanation was not so different from the one she had given him before she went into rehab, she believed he finally understood what it meant. At least he nodded at all the right times.

George Wyndham wasn't changed by what he heard. Thea hadn't expected that he would be. She had put it all before him, without blame or censure, and she was the one who came to view life through a different lens.

When she came to the end, he simply sat there. His features gave so little away that Thea couldn't have said if he was stunned or simply being stoic. His very stillness caused her to take a step toward him.

"Daddy?"

He had looked up at her then, regarding her with something that passed for a smile on his face. "You're very forthright, aren't you, dear?"

"I suppose I am." It surprised her a bit, this admission. It was not how she would have characterized herself. "Yes," she said with more assurance this time. It was like taking that first step in a new shoe and finding you liked the fit. "I am."

"Good. It will serve you well." He paused, halfway to his feet, brought up short by another thought. "But you're not a lesbian?"

Thea burst out laughing. "No, Daddy, I'm not a lesbian."

George Wyndham nodded once, straightening. "It wouldn't matter to me," he said rather gruffly. "But your mother would certainly drown in her Scotch."

Thea sank into the chair behind her desk, slipped off her black-and-white Ferragamo heels, and put her feet up. She pulled the phone toward her, fit the earbud in place, and then began returning calls. Between the ones relating to business, she tried Mitch. She finally got him on her third attempt.

"How'd it go?" he asked right off the bat.

"Great. Wonderful. Not a single glitch. Oh, and my father's relieved I'm not a lesbian, although he says it wouldn't matter if I was." She smiled to herself as silence filled the airway. "Kind of tough to know what to say to that, isn't it?"

"Yeah, well, I've got a picture going in my head now that's going to be hard to shake."

Thea rolled her eyes. "You're such a guy."

"Thank you."

"I just finished setting up a meeting with Carver Chemical. I'm flying to New York next week." She glanced at the calendar on her laptop. "Thursday afternoon. I'll be back Friday night."

"You're going alone?"

"I'm taking half the Blues with me. Hank might go. He's pumped for this."

"Are you going to drive up this evening? Case and Grant have a ball game."

Thea's disappointment was real. "I can't, Mitch. I still have to pick up the Volvo and I invited my mother and dad out to dinner. It's going to be late before I can leave the office anyway." She leaned forward and began scrolling through her calendar. "Tell me when the next game is."

"Thursday, a week from now, but you'll be in New York. There's nothing after that until the All Stars on the Fourth of July. That's the season finish."

Thea entered the information. "What time does the game start?"

"Five-thirty. But Thea, you don't—"

"I'll think of something," she interrupted. "Now, tell me about the cartoon you're working on." That was when Thea leaned back, closed her eyes, and let herself be lulled by the sound of Mitch's sexy, sandpaper voice.

Emilie tugged on the back of Mitch's T-shirt hard enough to choke off his *batter-batter-batter-swinnng* cry.

"Whoa! Em. What is it?" He pulled his shirt back in place and glanced at her. She was pointing to the entrance to the field, her mouth parted and her eyes wide. When he followed the direction of her finger, he saw what had rendered her speechless. His own jaw went a little slack.

It wasn't every day a woman in a Chanel suit and a ball

cap wriggled her way through the crowd at the concession stand and came away carrying three footlongs with everything and a cardboard holder of drinks.

Mitch watched Thea's parents each relieve her of a hot dog and then follow her past the dugout and toward him and Emilie in the bleachers. "Jesus, Mary, and Joseph." Although he said it under his breath, and with a certain amount of reverence, he caught Emilie's look and knew she wasn't fooled. "I'll pay later," he said, hopping down. Dust puffed around his Nikes as he hit the ground.

"Surprise," Thea said, handing him the drink holder but keeping a good grip on her footlong. "What's the score?"

Mitch found his voice. "Two - zip. Bottom of the first. We've already been to bat. The twins are in the outfield. You made good time."

"Nice sports update. You do the weather?"

He ignored that and held out his free hand to Thea's father. "I didn't expect to see you so soon." Translation: Not in this lifetime. Mitch nodded to Patricia Wyndham who was holding her hot dog in two hands and looking as if she had no idea what to do with it. "May I help you to your seats? It's pretty crowded today. The Squirts and Little Rotary always draw a lot of spectators. We're up on top."

Thea had more difficulty than her parents. After all, they had just come back from walking the craggy moors of Scotland, while she was wearing a narrow Chanel skirt that did okay on the gentle incline of her office treadmill, but couldn't be wrestled into modest coverage while climbing the bleachers. From where Mitch stood behind her, it was a great view.

Patricia Wyndham waited for her husband to spread a handkerchief on the rough wooden seat before she sat down. It was a tight squeeze between Emilie and George. "I don't

know why we couldn't have gone to a real ball game," she
said. "Doesn't the agency still have a box?"

"This is a real ball game," Emilie told her matter-of-
factly. "You have a hot dog, don't you?"

Patricia blinked. "I was speaking to my husband."

Emilie shrugged. "I know."

Mitch tried to catch Emilie's eye but she deliberately ignored him. Thea tapped Mitch's knee and shook her head. "I
don't want her to be rude," he whispered.

Thea cocked an eyebrow at him. "My mother's the one
being rude. Let them work it out." Out of the corner of her
eye she saw her father was actually smiling.

There was no time to appreciate the moment. The batter
hit a ground ball, which took a bad bounce past the short-
stop and the second baseman, both of whom were watching
the sky for UFOs anyway. Case, sharing center field with his
brother, remembered to run for the ball but overshot his
mark and went flying chin first into the grass. Grant managed to dig his uniform out of his behind just in time to get
his glove back on. The ball was now just lying there. He
picked it up but didn't appear to be entirely certain what to
do with it.

Thea jumped to her feet and began yelling directions to
him along with every other parent in the crowd. "Second
base! Throw it to second!"

Emilie shot up and hopped onto her seat. Unencumbered
by a hot dog, she waved her arms madly. "Second, Grant!
Second base! Hurry!" She reached down and pulled on Patricia Wyndham's arm. "Come on! You're missing it! This is
the good part!"

The footlong wobbled in Patricia's hands but she gamely
got to her feet. She was witness to Grant overthrowing
second base and being a hero anyway because the runner
was already on his way to third. The third baseman snagged
the ball and there was some dashing back and forth before

a tag was made. "It does seem like the good part," she said dryly, sitting down again. "I believe you missed it, dear."

"No, I didn't," George said.

Patricia followed the direction of his glance. Thea was still on her feet, arms raised, dancing in place and cheering at the top of her lungs. The ball cap had been refitted backward and the Chanel suit had dust on the jacket and skirt and a splinter in the hem. A dollop of ketchup and relish spotted the left sleeve. Her face was flushed. Strands of hair fluttered at odd angles on either side of the cap. Her eyes were almost feverishly bright.

She looked radiant.

Patricia Wyndham felt a pang of jealousy, not merely for Thea's vitality, but the expression of it. This is what she fought to control in herself and later, tried to contain in her daughter. What had made her think she could curb that wildness in Thea when it had always been so difficult for her?

Blood would tell. It invariably did, didn't it?

Patricia passed her footlong to a surprised Emilie and reached past her husband to tug on Thea's skirt. "You're making a spectacle of yourself," she whispered with some urgency.

Thea looked down at her mother. "I know. Isn't it wonderful?" She grinned fulsomely. "Here, have my hot dog."

Mitch leaned backward on the bleacher so he could look around Thea's taut backside and long legs. "You look like you could use a drink, Mrs. Wyndham."

With a devilish little smile, he handed her a Coke.

"Gina found a house she wants me to look at," Mitch told Thea as soon as Emilie handed him the phone. He was the last one to talk to her. The twins had already apprised her of their win on the field and what flavor of ice cream they'd had at the subsequent celebration. Emilie's conversation went the distance, covering her current favorite pop star, her hair, her best friend Nicole, and what she should do about Joseph Allen, the boy who was torturing her with bugs in homeroom. "I'm going to check out the house tomorrow," Mitch said. "Gina says I'll like it."

Thea was silent.

"Thea? Are you still there?"

"I'm here." The slight squeezing around her heart eased enough for her to push out those words. "That's great." What had she thought? That he would invite her to look at it with him? Yeah. That's exactly what she'd thought. "Where is it?"

"Can't tell you. Gina wouldn't say. She's been secretive about it."

"Gina? Secretive? That doesn't sound right."

"That's what I thought. She's been . . . oh, I don't know . . . kind of weird lately."

"Weird."

"Don't ask me to explain it better than that. She's just been different."

"You've seen a lot of her?" Thea winced. Only one day out of town and she was sounding possessive. "I mean, I guess you've seen a lot of her. About the house and everything."

Mitch did not try to keep the smile out of his voice. "Sure. About the house . . . and everything." He thought he heard Thea's muffled groan. "Are you okay?"

She uncovered the receiver. "Fine." She cleared her throat. "Fine."

"Did you get the flowers?"

Thea looked over at the extravagant bouquet on her hotel room bureau. "They were waiting for me. Thank you."

"They're from the kids, too."

"I know. I thanked them."

Mitch hesitated when she didn't say anything else. "Was there a box?"

Thea's eyes fell on the open box at the foot of her bed. Tissue paper blossomed from it. The lid was lying on the carpet next to the pair of Stella McCartney black mesh pumps she'd bought especially for this trip and presentation. "What kind of box?" she asked, leaning back against the headboard. She looked down the length of her bare legs to the canvas sneakers her feet were favoring at the moment.

"I don't know. A box. Twelve by six by four. About like that."

"Hmmm. Let me look around."

Something about her perfectly executed nonchalance made Mitch suspicious. "Thea?"

"Yes?"

"You're wearing them, aren't you?"

"Uh-huh." There was a catch in her voice. She whispered, "They're perfect." Every inch of canvas was covered with artwork. Her left shoe sported caricatures of Mitch, Emilie, and the twins, rendered in Mitch's bold style, while her right shoe was a neon bright kaleidescope of color compliments of the kids and Crayola. "Just perfect."

Mitch figured he was going to have trouble sleeping no matter what, so he asked, "You wearing anything else?"

She fingered the thick terry sleeve of the standard-issue hotel robe. "Nope. Not a stitch."

"Awww, that's not right."

Thea smiled. "You know what else?"

"What?"

"I'm not alone." She heard him suck in his breath. Before he could speak, she said, "I'm with Danielle, my dark-haired *bonne amie* from boarding school."

"You didn't go to boarding school."

Thea's mouth puckered to one side. "Work with me here."

"I'd rather work with you *here*."

She chuckled. "The kids aren't still standing around, are they?"

"They're getting ready for bed."

"Good." Thea plumped the pillow at the small of her back. "Thank you for the shoes, Mitch. They're . . . unexpected."

"They're lucky shoes."

"Yeah? How do you know?"

"Tap your heels together three times and repeat, 'Shine and Shield is the power I wield.'"

"You just made that up."

"Not bad, huh?"

"It's awful."

He laughed. "Knock 'em dead tomorrow."

Thea closed her eyes and massaged the bridge of her nose. "God, Mitch, I need to think about something else."

"Like what?"

"I don't know. Something besides 'Shine and Shield is the power I wield.'"

"It sounds catchier the more I hear it." This time there was no mistaking her groan. He grinned. "Good night, Thea. Get some rest. Oh, and there's one more thing . . ."

"Hmmm?"

"I love you." Fairly certain he'd given her something else to think about, Mitch hung up.

Thea arrived home late Friday night, more tired than triumphant. She had tried to call Mitch a half dozen times and kept getting the answering machine at home and voice mail on his cell. There was no message that she wanted to leave so she didn't try texting. At first she was disappointed that she couldn't talk to him, but she reasoned that it would be better to tell him in person. And there was still the matter of his sign-off the night before. If he was going to say something like that again, she wanted to see his face when he said it.

The cab slowed as it neared her driveway. "Looks like someone's waiting for you," the driver said.

Thea leaned forward in her seat and peered through the windshield. The light was on in the interior of the SUV. Thea couldn't see the driver but she recognized the vehicle.

The cab pulled into the driveway. "You know who it is?"

"Yes, it's all right. I'll be fine." Thea paid the driver and got out, pulling her overnight case and boxed flowers with her. She shut the door with her hip and waved the cab off. The door of the SUV opened before she reached it.

Gina Sommers stepped down. She pushed the door closed.

"Regina," Thea said. "What are you doing here?"

"Waiting for you."

"That's the obvious answer." She looked Gina over. The landscape lighting created small glowing pools near their feet. Gina was casually dressed: sneakers, socks, khaki shorts, and a sleeveless shirt of indeterminable color. Her dark hair had been hurriedly scraped back from her face with two metallic clips. The severity of the style highlighted her drawn features. Thea almost dropped her flowers. "What's happened?" she demanded. "Is it Mitch? The children?"

Gina shook her head quickly. "No. Oh, no. I'm sorry. I should have realized you'd think . . . no, it's nothing like that. They're . . . they're fine. I'm the . . . I'm the one that . . ." Gina glanced over her shoulder toward Thea's front door. "Can we go inside? I know I'm imposing . . . I just . . ."

Thea had heard enough. She thrust her flowers into Gina's arms. "This way. Just let me unload my case at the door and then we'll talk." Thea started up the walk. "Have you been waiting long?"

"About an hour."

"How did you know how to find me?"

"Mitch." Gina paused while Thea searched for her keys. "He told me you were out of town but that you expected to get back tonight. I did some sleuthing and found you'd already checked out of your hotel. There were only a couple of flights you could have come in on so I came by."

Thea pushed open the door and gestured Gina to step inside first. "Light's on the right."

Gina flipped the switch and flooded the foyer with light from the chandelier. "I'm sorry about it being so late," she said. "But I . . ."

"Kitchen's straight ahead," Thea told her, heading for the stairs. "Put the kettle on for tea. Here, give me the flowers back."

Gina pressed the box into Thea's arms. "I really appreciate this, Thea. I didn't know who else I could . . ."

Thea turned away from the newel post as Gina's voice trailed off again. It wasn't entirely the lighting that made the younger woman's complexion sallow. "Go on," she said gently. "Give me a minute. I want to put these in a vase." What she really wanted was a moment to collect herself and an opportunity to try Mitch again. It occurred to Thea that perhaps he knew something more about Gina's strange behavior than he had let on. Mounting the stairs, she tried not to leap to conclusions of exactly what that might be.

The teakettle was whistling shrilly by the time Thea entered the kitchen. Gina was sitting at the table, her back to the stove, apparently oblivious to the sound. She didn't stir until Thea was pulling mugs out of the cupboard.

"Oh," Gina said softly, surprised. She twisted in her chair. "I didn't hear you come in."

"I noticed. You were thinking hard."

"No. Hardly thinking."

Thea nodded. "I do that sometimes, too." She poured hot water into a blue-and-white china teapot and allowed it to steep. "Are you hungry? I have crackers. I think there are some cookies somewhere." She tried to remember if Rosie had finished them off.

"No, nothing for me," Gina said. "You go ahead, though."

Thea didn't want to admit that her desire for a late-night nosh had faded the moment she saw the banana car in her driveway. She carried the teapot and mugs to the table. "Sugar? Milk?"

Gina shook her head. She accepted the tea Thea poured for her and held the warm mug between her palms, making no attempt to drink it.

"It's cool in here," Thea said. "Would you like a sweater?"

"No. I'm okay."

That was the last word Thea would have used to describe Regina Sommers right now. Thea sat down and picked up her own mug. She sipped her tea, watching her uninvited guest over the rim. Gina studiously avoided making eye contact. "So," Thea said finally, "perhaps you want to tell me why you're here."

"You didn't talk to Mitch?"

Thea flushed guiltily. "He wasn't home. I haven't been able to reach him all day."

"His parents swung by while I was showing him a house. They wanted to take the kids to Storybook Forest. I guess it was a last-minute thing. Some kind of ticket deal. Mitch decided to go along." Gina flicked her wrist and looked at her watch. "Maybe they ended up getting a room somewhere."

"You're probably right." It didn't explain why she couldn't reach him on his cell phone. Thea realized she must have telegraphed her thought in some way because Gina said, "He was complaining about his cell phone this morning. I don't think the battery's completely charging anymore."

That sounded right, Thea thought. Mitch had never gotten around to getting a backup battery. She looked over at her phone. No blinking light, no messages. Thea could have let herself get sidetracked by that. She refocused instead. "You're going to have to tell me what's going on yourself, Regina, now that you know Mitch didn't."

Gina's small half smile was more gently derisive than amused. "I suppose I should have trusted him not to say anything. That's what I asked him to do."

Thea said nothing, waiting.

"Did you ever want children, Thea?"

The question surprised Thea. She considered the possible responses and then answered honestly, "I didn't think so."

"Because you're an addict?"

In the back of her mind Thea could hear her father's carefully modulated voice: *You're very forthright, aren't you, dear?* Tamping down her smile, she swallowed that reply and asked a question of her own. "You know about that?"

Gina nodded.

Well, Thea thought, she'd never asked Mitch to keep it a secret. It didn't bother her that Gina knew, only that Mitch had never mentioned telling her. It made her wonder what else he had shared with Gina.

"I don't think less of you," Gina added quickly. "I mean, I think it takes a lot of—"

Thea made a dismissive gesture with her hand. "I'm not insulted, Regina. In fact, I'm not even sure I care what you think." She saw Gina's sloe eyes widen. "Sounds bitchy, doesn't it? It's taken a long time to realize I don't need to worry about how other people judge me. What I haven't figured out is whether I should tell them so."

Gina tentatively raised a couple of fingers above the rim of her mug. "I vote no."

Thea smiled. "I'll remember that." She sipped her tea and then slowly set the mug down. "Actually, Gina, my thinking about wanting children doesn't have a whole lot to do with my drug use. It's more basic than that."

"What do you mean?"

Her manner matter-of-fact, Thea said, "I was an abused kid before I was adopted and I didn't trust myself not to do the same thing. It seemed the wiser course was not only not to have children of my own, but not to want any."

"But you've changed your mind," Gina said, watching her carefully. "Because of Mitch?"

Thea hesitated. "That's more personal," she said after a moment. "Why do you ask?"

The tips of Gina's fingers whitened as she pressed them tightly on her mug. "Because I'm pregnant."

Chapter 14

Pregnant. Thea actually flinched. A droplet of hot tea splashed the back of her hand. She barely felt it. "Why are telling me, Regina? Shouldn't you be talking to—"

Agitated, Gina broke in. "I need *you* to talk to him. Please, Thea. I don't seem to be getting through."

"I don't know," she said softly, shaking her head. It astonished Thea that her voice wasn't shaking. "This is something that should be between the two of you."

"I think he'll understand how serious I am about keeping this baby if he hears it from you."

"Keeping the baby?" Thea thought she couldn't be startled by anything else Gina said. She was wrong. "You mean he actually suggested an abortion?"

Gina nodded. "And adoption. He thinks I don't know what I'm doing, wanting his baby."

No longer *this* baby, Thea thought. *His* baby. Regina Sommers was in love. "How far along are you?"

"About seven weeks."

Thea pressed the rim of her mug to her lips, stifling a tiny moan. Seven weeks back was just before Mother's Day. Mitch had been all over her in his Chevy truck that Sunday. She'd never once considered that he might have been with

Gina the day before, or the day before that. Remembering how much she had wanted him, Thea wasn't convinced that the knowledge would have changed anything. *He* had known. It hadn't made any difference to him.

Gina dashed a tear from her eye and looked around for a tissue.

"In the bathroom," Thea said. "I'll get them for you."

Gina stopped her. "No, I'll get them."

Thea pointed her in the right direction, and Gina slid her chair out and hurried off. It was several minutes before she returned. Her eyelids were puffier than when she left. "Hold still," Thea said. "Close your eyes." She plucked a small piece of tissue from Gina's dark lashes. "That's better."

Gina gave her a watery smile.

"Have you told your parents?" asked Thea.

"No. I wanted to wait. I . . . I didn't think he would be happy about it, but I . . ."

"What is it you want from him, Gina?"

There was no hesitation. "Marriage." The word was split by a little hiccup. "I want to marry him." She mocked herself with a derisive chuckle. "Can you believe it?"

"Actually," Thea said quietly, "I can."

That closed Gina's mouth. She nodded slowly. "I suppose you can." She crumpled the tissue in her hand. "Will you talk to him, Thea? He thinks there's too much of an age difference. You know better than anyone how little that matters. You were engaged to Joel."

"It matters, Gina," Thea said. "But maybe it shouldn't."

"That's what *I've* been saying. He won't hear me, though. He thinks I don't know my own mind."

"And you're certain you do? This is what you want?"

She nodded to both things and pressed the crumpled tissue to each eye.

"I can't make him marry you," Thea told her.

"I know that," she said wretchedly. "But I thought that if

you told him . . . that is, he feels so protective toward you . . . like there's some obligation . . ."

"Obligation," Thea repeated. Her voice sounded dull and wounded to her own ears, but when she darted a look toward her guest, Thea realized Gina was too caught up in her own misery to notice. And rightly so. "So you want me to make sure he knows he doesn't owe me anything, that he doesn't have to look out for me. Is that it?"

"Yes." Tears squeezed out from under her lashes even as she tried to blink them back. "I think he loves you, Thea. That's why . . ." Gina couldn't finish. She sucked in her breath as a shudder vibrated her small frame.

"What if I love him?" Thea asked frankly. "Had you considered that when you came here and asked me to be a go-between? Did you even once think about what my feelings for him might be?"

Gina's head snapped up. She was so clearly startled by the idea that Thea proposed that there was no way she could say differently now. "But I thought . . . I mean, I was so certain that you . . ." Her shoulders slumped and she stared at her hands folded on the tabletop. "Oh, God. I'm an idiot. I'm such a fucking idiot." She pushed her chair away from the table and started to get up.

Thea heard her mother's voice come out of her mouth, cool and deliberate, and brooking no argument. "Sit down."

Gina sat.

"Good. You will stay here." Single syllables, each word carefully enunciated. "And we will talk. And you will choose a course, if not now, then in the morning."

Gina nodded jerkily.

Thea added some tea to her mug. She relished the warmth as she sipped it. "Do you love him?" It was her own voice this time, gentle but candid.

"Yes."

"Do you know how he feels about you?"

Gina hesitated. "I thought I did." She spared an uncertain glance for Thea. "He told me he loved me."

Thea did not so much as blink. "Is he saying something different now?"

"No. But he hasn't said it since I told him I was pregnant."

"Shock."

"That's what Mitch said."

"It's understandable."

Gina drew one foot up to the corner of her chair and hugged her knee. "Maybe," she said, "but I didn't set out to get pregnant. I would have sworn under oath that I didn't want children. Not now. I've been accepted for an MBA program in the fall. I like working in real estate. I'm learning a lot about properties and investing. I want to do more of everything, not less." Gina's tears had dried up but her dark eyes remained brilliant. "I can't take the pill," she said. "Or the shots. I didn't want an IUD. I told him that. I used a diaphragm. Always. He promised me he would use a condom. He *promised.*"

"But sometimes he forgot," Thea said. She understood all too well how that happened.

Nodding, Gina asked plaintively, "Is that supposed to be my fault?"

"Is he saying it is?"

"No," she said after a moment. "No, not really."

"Then there's no point in assigning blame."

"He could have had a vasectomy," Gina said, determined to have another word on the matter.

Thea felt the corners of her mouth lifting, not in amusement at Gina's situation but in appreciation of her youth.

Gina caught the look. "You think that's a stupid idea."

"I think it doesn't matter now."

"You're right," Gina conceded. "It doesn't."

Thea's eyes slid to the clock in the microwave. "Listen, it's late. I want you to stay here tonight. There's a bedroom you can use; the bed's made up. I think we both need to sleep."

"I don't know if I—"

"I promise you I'll talk to him," Thea assured her. "I need to think about what I'm going to say and right now I can't think at all. You're not exactly clear-headed yourself and you need to be." She waited for Gina's assent before she continued. When it was offered with a mixture of reluctance and relief Thea knew she had been right to suggest it. "Now, is there someone I should call to let them know where you are?"

"No. I have my own place. I talked to my mom earlier tonight. She probably hasn't called again. No one else will worry if I'm not there."

"You're sure?" When Gina nodded, Thea went on. "All right. Let me show you where you can sleep. A hot bath might not be a bad idea either." To further tempt her, she added, "I have a whirlpool tub."

"Oh yes," Gina said softly. "Yes."

Mitch's insides gave a peculiar lurch when he saw Gina's SUV. What was she doing at Thea's at—he glanced at the dashboard—at seven twenty-five in the morning? For that matter, what was she doing at Thea's at all?

"Oh, God," he said under his breath. There was no other explanation that fit. "She must have told Thea about the baby."

Mitch parked behind Gina, switched off the ignition, and sat there for a full minute before he got out of the car. When Thea finally reached him an hour ago, he was so full of apologies and excuses for not being available yesterday that he jumped at the chance to see her—even at this ungodly hour. She had listened patiently while he told her about his spur-of-the-moment decision to go with his parents and the kids, how Case had gotten sick at the park, the back and

forth about should they stay or go, the freaking cell phone
battery being low, his mother complaining about the heat,
the traffic, the crowd, Grant wandering off, Emilie flirting
with boys, and—the coup de grâce—the oil light in the
minivan coming on between service plazas on the turnpike.
They were so beat by the time that was taken care of, they
got off the next exit and found a motel after being turned
away only three times by NO VACANCY signs. It was late then,
he'd told her, he didn't want to disturb her.

Lame. That was Mitch's evaluation of his delivery and the
content as he reviewed it now. Really lame. The worst part
came at the end when he'd taken a breath and flippantly
asked, "And how was your day, dear?"

He tried to remember if Thea's quiet chuckle had been
genuine or merely pitying because he had been so pathetic.
At least he'd remembered to ask about her presentation at
Carver. She wouldn't tell him how it went, though. That was
when she had asked him to meet her at her house. Thea must
have known there was about a zero chance that he'd turn the
invitation down. She'd reeled him in dangling just a hint of
good news and let him make up the part in his own mind
about maybe getting laid.

Jeez, he was such a guy. On the other hand, Mitch reasoned, he was sensitive enough to know that the presence of
Gina's SUV didn't mean that Thea had arranged a threesome.

"Keep that to yourself, Mitch," he whispered. "You'll live
longer."

He opened the door and hopped out. Thea stepped out
onto her small front porch at the same time. Not only was he
expected, but she had been watching for him. Mitch wondered if she had seen him talking to himself.

"Hey!" he said, jogging up the walk. "What's Gina doing
here?" Take the offense, Mitchell. He saw Thea's welcoming smile falter a little but she held out a hand to him.

"Come inside," she said. "We need to talk."

Mitch took a step up but he left his stomach on the sidewalk. Her hand was cold. She was pissed he hadn't told her about the baby. Mitch had an image of himself dangling on this particular hook for a long time. The metallic taste in his mouth was very real.

Inside the foyer, Thea released Mitch's hand. "Did you have any trouble finding someone to watch the kids?"

Mitch followed her down the hall to the kitchen. "You kidding? Saturday morning? Amy was thrilled to have her butt dragged out of bed. I owe her big time."

"Sorry." Thea's terse apology didn't exactly resonate with guilt. She went straight to the coffeemaker. "Have a seat. You want a cup?"

"Yeah." He noticed the bag of coffee on the counter was the same brand he used at home. She'd picked it up for him. That eased his mind a little. He pulled out a chair and sat down at the table. "So where's Gina? That *is* her SUV, isn't it?"

"It's hers. She's still sleeping."

"Sleeping?"

"She spent the night." Thea handed him his coffee. "You want toast? Eggs? Cereal?"

"No. Coffee's fine. I had all that junk food yesterday; I'm still full."

Thea nodded absently. She turned away and retrieved her cereal bowl from the breakfast bar. She didn't join Mitch at the table but leaned against the counter instead, palming her bowl in one hand. "You must have only gotten home when I called."

"About ten minutes earlier. Long enough to put the kids to bed. They were wiped." He was aware he was frowning. "Is this really what you want to talk about?" he asked. "I can tell you the motel left a lot to be desired. My mother assigned herself to roach patrol and apparently didn't sleep a wink. She waited until first light, and then she herded us out of there. We got home. You called. End of story."

Thea blinked. "Are you angry at me?"

"No," he said, his voice clipped. "Not yet. I'm working up to it."

She took a bite of cereal, calmly chewed and swallowed. She said, "Let me know when you're up to a full head of steam. At that point I want you to imagine a pressure ten times greater and then you'll have some idea how ticked I am at you right now."

Mitch's eyes narrowed as they skimmed her set features, then the rest of her. There were pale shadows under her eyes and a fine crease between her brows. The mouth that he had always thought of as generous was markedly thinner. There was very little color in her face. She was wearing an old chenille robe, the frayed belt cinched tightly around her waist and double knotted. She wasn't coming out of it anytime soon. His gaze dropped to her bare feet. One slender ankle was turned so that she could rub the instep of one foot with the sole of the other. It was an absent, uneasy gesture, and it gave Mitch some hope that she wasn't quite as angry with him as she would have him believe.

"Look, Thea," Mitch said with credible calm, "I know how this works and I'm not going to say anything to incriminate myself. You better tell me what you know or what you think you know, and we can go on from there."

Thea set her bowl down but she didn't approach the table. The one small advantage she thought she commanded was the high ground. "Gina told me about the baby," she said after a long moment. "She came here, I suppose, because she didn't think anyone else was listening to her. She feels as if she's being blamed for the pregnancy."

"I didn't blame her," Mitch said.

"She didn't say anyone did. She just feels that way. If you can accept her feeling as fact, then you can understand how real it is for her. She's confused about a lot of things, but she's definite about wanting to have this baby inside a marriage."

Mitch's cheeks puffed slightly as he exhaled. "Yeah." He finger raked his hair. "She said that to me, too."

"And did you tell her she was too young?"

Had he? "I don't know. I might have said something about the age difference."

"I think she's heard a lot of that."

"It's a fact," Mitch said. "More fact than your feeling stuff."

"Feeling stuff?" Thea bristled. "You weren't sitting with her last night while she sobbed into her hands. You didn't watch her go through the motions of getting ready for bed on autopilot. Her heart's breaking, Mitch. That feeling stuff is as real as it gets."

Mitch set down his coffee cup and held up his hands, palms out. "All right. It's real. But so is the age difference. For cryin' out loud, Thea, when I was seeing her, she didn't know Don McLean's "American Pie" from *American Pie* the movie."

"Well, don't just sit there!" She pointed upstairs. "She's in the guest room. Take her out and shoot her."

Sighing, Mitch slid forward in his chair, stretching his long legs under the table and jamming his hands in his pockets. He shook his bowed head slightly. "Okay, I don't believe I said that either." He darted her a sideways glance, his sheepishness not feigned. "You're not packin' heat, are you?"

Thea held up her index finger, cautioning him. "No, but the steak knives are within easy reach. Don't tempt me."

He nodded. Mitch pushed his heels against the ceramic tile floor and tipped his chair back on two legs. "What do you think I should have done when Gina told me, Thea? I take it that's where we are right now. You have some opinion of what I was supposed to do."

"Yes," she said, "I think you should have told me."

"Even though she asked me not to say anything to anyone. Did she tell you that?"

"I got that impression."

"It was not an impression that was given to me," he said, dropping the chair back to all fours. "It was a clear request to keep a secret and I gave my word."

Thea was silent for a moment. "I know," she said quietly. "But can you appreciate what it was like hearing it from her?"

Mitch's brow creased. "It's Gina's news," he said, watching Thea closely. She had the oddest expression on her face. The anger she professed to have didn't appear to be in danger of exploding at all. She had it perfectly contained, ready to implode on her. What in God's name had she been telling herself? "Why shouldn't it have come from Gina?"

Thea's smile was slight. "Because I wasn't prepared to hear it." She walked over to the table and finally sat down in the chair closest to him. "And because she wasn't prepared to tell it in a way that made any sense. I didn't sleep much last night, thinking about our conversation, trying to give what I'd heard some sort of logic or rationale. Maybe if I had been able to talk to you before I sat down with her"—Thea shrugged—"that might have helped. You might have said what I needed to hear to put the pieces in place sooner."

"I tried to explain about that, Thea. I'm sorry you couldn't reach me or that I didn't—"

She waved his apology aside. "I know. You don't have to be connected to me, Mitch. That's not what I'm asking from you. We've gotten so used to the Net and cell phones and immediate accessibility that self-reliance is an afterthought, not the first choice. At least I have. I realized some of that when I had to make the presentation at work in front of my father. I tried Rosie. You. I called my counselor. None of you were available. I had a Valium in my hand that I found in my desk drawer and I was thinking I was a smart woman who knew her limits and why not take it with a whiskey chaser."

"Oh, Thea . . . you never said—"

She couldn't quite meet his eyes. "Yeah. Well, I was ashamed by how close I'd come and I was afraid it would scare you off."

Mitch leaned forward in his chair and took Thea's hands in his. "I told you before, there's a difference between scaring me and scaring me off."

She nodded, swallowing hard. "I'm starting to get that part." She lifted her eyes to him again. His hands made a pocket around hers. They were warm and strong and Thea didn't make an attempt to slip free. "I didn't take the pill, Mitch, though it was a narrow thing. I ended up asking Mrs. A. to call my dad in and I gave it to him, along with a piece of my mind."

"And?"

"And he listened to me. He probably only understood a third of what I said or was attempting to say, but he listened, and later I realized I wouldn't have tried talking to him if anyone else had been available. It wasn't that I would have just missed an opportunity, Mitch. It was that I wouldn't have seen one."

"Okay," he said slowly. "And that's like last night, how?"

She sighed and gave him a small, half smile. "Boy, I'm really going to have to connect the dots for you, aren't I?"

"Only if you want me to have the same picture as you."

"All right. Last night, after Gina finished telling me everything she could, in her own jumbled sort of way—and I couldn't reach you—I had to work it out for myself. I kept thinking about what she'd said. The suggestion of abortion. Adoption. The problem with the age difference. No offer of

marriage. Not using a condom. Saying I love you. The time-
line of all of it." Thea pressed her lips together momentarily as she considered whether she'd said it all. Deciding she
had, she went on. "Some of it fit; some of it didn't."

"Fit what?"

Thea connected the last two dots. "You."

Mitch pushed backward so hard he almost tipped the
chair. It wobbled as he leaped to his feet. "Me?!"

"That's why you should have told me," Thea said, unapologetic. "Then I wouldn't have thought for even a moment that
you were the baby's father."

"Me?!" He pointed at his chest in the event she thought there
was some other *me* in the room. "You thought it was me?!"

"I don't think it was you now. I told you, I worked it out.
That was my point about not being able to reach you. It
forced me to think for myself."

"But you *thought* it was me."

"At first." Some of her exasperation was revealed in her
voice. "I'm not proud of it, Mitch. I've been thinking that I
should have trusted you more."

"You should have trusted me. Period."

"Maybe."

"Maybe?" Agitated, he plowed his fingers through his
hair. "Jesus, Thea, I just told you I loved you."

"I know. And then I didn't hear anything from you for
more than twenty-four hours—and that was because *I* called
you. It started to feel more like a hit-and-run than a declar-
ative sentence."

"A declarawhat? Who talks like that?"

Her chin came up. "I do."

"Well, stop it. I can't argue if you're going to get all poly-
syllabic on me."

Thea stared at him.

He stared back.

She broke first. A smile lifted the corners of her mouth a mere fraction.

His grin flashed like quicksilver.

"You want to sit down?" she asked.

"Yeah." Mitch spun the chair around and sat on it backward, resting his forearms across the curved rail.

Thea inched closer to Mitch and propped her feet on one of the rungs of his chair. Her robe split down the center of her thighs and revealed a lot of bare leg. She was aware of Mitch's glance and the fact that she was self-conscious of it only in a good way. "Did you ever have a conversation with someone and you think you're talking about exactly the same thing and you're not at all?"

He dragged his eyes back to her face. "I think I just did." She was wearing little yellow panties and a cropped top under that frumpy robe. That wasn't right.

"No, you didn't." Her hair swung lightly against her temples as she shook her head. "What you and I just did was nothing compared to what happened between Gina and me. She talked about the baby and the baby's father and—"

"She said *I* was her baby's father?"

"No. That's just it. She never said who it was. I mean, I think she *thought* she was telling, but she never did. Not really. And I never exactly explained that I thought she was talking about you. So we just kept on talking about the baby and about the baby's father and never using any names except a couple of times that confused things more than it helped." Thea stopped to take a short breath. "It was like this big misunderstanding was unfolding and we had no way of knowing it."

"But you know it now," Mitch said cautiously, feeling his way.

"Yes! That's what I'm saying here. What I've been saying. I wish it hadn't taken me so long to figure it out." She leaned forward and this time when she touched his forearm, she let her hand lie there. "But I don't have any regrets about the process. It forced me to consider the one thing that I've been ducking these last few months."

"And that is . . . ?"

"That I'm in love with you."

Mitch's heart slammed so hard against his chest that he thought he actually jerked in his chair. He looked down at himself, realized he was in exactly the same position he had been a moment before, and then returned his eyes to Thea. He heard himself say, "All because you thought I was the father of Gina's baby?"

"All because I figured out why you weren't."

"Oh."

She smiled gently. "You don't really understand, do you?"

He shook his head. "No, but as long as one of us does."

"Yeah," she whispered. "That works for me, too." Thea closed the small distance that was separating them and kissed Mitch on the mouth. His lips were firm and dry. She moved over them warmly. They parted. She caught the upper one and tugged, came back and caught the lower one.

Mitch's hand curved around the back of her neck, under feathery strands of dark red hair. He held her to him. Returning the kiss. Hard. Sweet. Heat and tenderness. The corner of her mouth. The parenthetical dimple. He touched those with the tip of his tongue.

They stood as one. Still holding her, Mitch shoved his chair aside. It toppled to the floor. He cupped her bottom, lifted, and set Thea on the table's edge. She groped for the coffee cup and pushed it away. Her thighs parted and Mitch stepped between them, still kissing her. Changing the slant of his mouth, first one way, then another. She fumbled with her double-knotted belt. "It's okay," he whispered against her mouth. "You don't have to take it off. Get mine."

Thea pulled at the cedar brown, leather weave belt at Mitch's waist. The buckle opened. She undid the button on his khakis, then the fly. She plunged her hands into his briefs and cupped his cock and scrotum. He sucked in his breath and took hers with it. She drew back shakily, sipping air. He didn't give her a chance to get much, bringing her right back to him, hard and needy. "Think we can get you out of these panties?" he asked.

Think? She was counting on it. Thea lifted her bottom while he tugged on the skimpy material. They slid down her thighs. She squirmed, wriggled, and they dropped to her knees. One careful kick later and they were on the floor and Mitch was standing between her parted legs again. "Drop trou, buster," she told him.

He did. Thea scooted to the edge of the table. He pressed forward into the cradle she made for him. Her thighs tightened on his hips and her hand slipped between their bodies. She curled her fingers around him. He bent his knees, thrust, and then he was inside her. Thea gasped, caught her breath, then pressed her lips together. Her throat arched. She closed her eyes and her head fell back. Mitch's mouth was against her neck, sliding toward her shoulder. The sleeve of her robe slipped over the curve of her arm. His hands came up from her waist and slipped under the thin, loose cotton crop top. He kneaded her breasts, made the nipples bud, made her flesh swell, made her bite her lower lip to keep from doing more than whimpering his name.

The table shook. Neither of them noticed that the shudder was anywhere but in them. The vibrations carried Mitch's coffee cup to the edge of the table where it finally fell. The crash barely registered.

"Lie back," he whispered hoarsely.

"What?" She couldn't focus.

"Lie back."

She did. His hands grazed her ribs and abdomen. His thumb brushed her navel. Her skin retracted. He held her hips, plunging into her. Deep. Deeper. The crown of Thea's head pressed against the unyielding oak. Her back lifted, arched. She found the edge of the table and gripped it with her fingertips. The sense of him inside her made her feel deliciously full. The pressure on her clitoris came and went and came again. There was a dizzying spiral of heat that spread out in all directions from the point of their joining. It widened as it turned, raising a flush that seeped under her skin, ratcheting pleasure up another notch.

Mitch finally had to brace his arms on the table. He ground into her, pressing his hips hard. He spoke to her in short, rapid bursts, his words rising inarticulately from the back of his throat. "Go on," he said. "Do it. I want to see you do it."

With a frustrated moan, Thea released the table with one hand and let it fall against her thigh. She barely had to move her fingers. He was pushing into her, making her body slide so that she caressed herself with no effort. Her fingertips walked down her inner thigh, then between the moist folds. She could feel the heat of his belly. When she looked up at him it was to find him looking down at them, their joining, her hand cupping herself intimately, her fingers moving, stroking, making herself come.

"Aaaah." She flung back her head again. "Aaah." She panted, drawing a sweet breath. "Mmm . . . Mitch." Thea hummed his name and her pleasure at the same time and she thought she might faint.

"Come with me," he coaxed. "Let me feel you come."

Thea's hips jerked. Her legs extended, stretched. She reached for him. Her fingers flowered open and she felt tension in his corded muscles. It was there, then it was gone. His shoulders heaved once. His hips moved shallowly. He groaned softly, his body trembling, then he was still.

It was a couple of moments before Mitch's breathing calmed. "Holy shit," he said quietly.

"Jar."

"Hmm?" He leaned over her, bracing his palms flat on either side of Thea's waist.

"Pay the jar."

"Later." He bent, kissed her on the mouth, and straightened slowly. "What else are you serving for breakfast?"

Thea's laughter came in a staccato burst as she sat up. "Look at us, Mitchell. You just had me on my kitchen table. I'm going to have to buy a new one."

He was unrepentant. Stepping back, he pulled up his briefs and khakis, and tossed Thea her panties. "Nothing a little Shine and Shield won't take care of."

"Hah! A lot you know." She slid off the table. "It's not for wood products."

"No one thought it was for cars either." He tucked the tails of his shirt and fastened his belt. "So how did it go at Carver? Or can't you tell me yet?"

"I can tell you," she said with a certain amount of sass. Thea smoothed her robe and adjusted the belt. Now that her fingers weren't trembling she undid the knot and retied it easily. "But maybe I don't want to."

"Hey." He gave her a swat on the butt as she turned away. "I'm the guy that gave you the lucky shoes. I should get to know if they worked or not."

Thea gave him a big, over-the-shoulder grin. "They worked."

"No kidding."

"That's right." She went to the door that led to the garage to get a mop and dustpan. When she returned with both items she handed the mop to Mitch. "I'll get the broken glass; you wipe up the coffee."

Mitch leaned on the mop handle. "So they really liked your ideas."

"Yep. I wasn't expecting to hear one way or the other after we pitched them the ads." She dropped some of the big shards in the dustpan, careful to keep her robe hem out of the coffee. "I thought I'd get some sense of their interest, maybe hear something in a week or two if we were lucky. They got us at JFK before we boarded and said they'd made their decision. Hank and I were working out the details all the way back. The rest of the Blue Team got stupid in business class." Thea stood, emptied the dustpan in the trash under the sink and waved Mitch into action. "It was showing Carver what we could do with Shine and Shield that clinched it for us. They loved the product overlap. The car manufacturers get to show off their hot models and Carver shines them up. Shared advertising costs. A little back scratching. Everyone wins. Everyone's happy."

Mitch spun the mop around, gave it a little Fred Astaire flourish, and sang, "Shine and Shield is the power I wield. I will never yield my Shine and Shield."

"Give it up, Baker. We're not using it. Even the new stuff."

He shrugged. "Your loss." He carried the mop over to the sink, wrung it out, then took the dustpan from Thea and returned both to the garage. When he got back to the table Thea had a fresh cup of coffee waiting for him.

Thea opened her mouth to say something but snapped it shut when she heard footsteps pounding on the stairs. The sound was so loud, so deliberate, that there was no mistaking Gina meant to be noticed. Thea's eyes flew to Mitch's. "She heard us!" she whispered, tugging on his sleeve.

It was easy for Mitch to remain unfazed when Thea was flushed from her neckline all the way to the roots of her hair. "She heard you," he said. "I didn't knock over the coffee cup or go off like a siren."

"I didn't kn—" she began indignantly, and stopped because she saw he was trying to get a rise out of her. "Ooooh!"

"Careful. She'll think we're at it again." Chuckling, he swept his coffee cup off the table and pulled it close to his chest before she decided to upend it on his crotch. "Come on down, Gina!" He called back toward the hallway. "Coast's clear."

Thea gave him a look of mock disgust, but the kick in the shin was real enough. She danced out of his reach before Gina entered the kitchen. "Coffee?" she asked. "Or I can make tea."

"Coffee's fine." Gina was wearing a silky emerald green robe. On Thea it would have been fingertip length. On Gina the hem brushed her knees and the sleeves had to be rolled up three turns. "I found this on a hook in the guest bathroom. I hope you don't mind."

"No. I put it there for you. I don't think I've ever worn it."

Mitch gave Gina an appreciative once-over, then looked pointedly at Thea's ratty chenille robe. He just shook his head.

"What?" Thea said. "That was a Christmas present from Mother three years ago and it's not at all my thing."

"Did I say a word?" asked Mitch. He looked at Gina for support. "Did you hear me say a word?"

Gina held up her hands. The silky sleeves pooled around her elbows. "I *know* I'm not getting in this." She nudged a chair out with her bare foot and sat down. "Mornin', Mitch."

He smiled. "Good morning. How are you feeling?"

"Not too bad." She no sooner said it than she blanched as her stomach did a twist and heave. "Thea? Do you have some soda crackers?"

"They might be stale."

Mitch looked at Gina's pale face. "I don't think her stomach cares about stale."

Thea found the crackers in the pantry and put them on the table, along with Gina's coffee. "You should think about decaf," she said.

"I do think about it," Gina said. "I just won't drink it. I am a one-cup-in-the-morning girl now. Do you have cream?"

"Sure do." Thea pulled the carton out of the refrigerator while Gina opened a stack of crackers. "Here. Use lots of it."

Gina nibbled on a cracker with one hand and poured with the other. She set the carton down and looked at Mitch. "I suppose Thea's told you why I'm here."

It was Thea who answered. "You know, I'm not certain I ever did get that far."

Mitch lifted his coffee cup. "She didn't," he told Gina dryly. "Apparently Thea had a little confusion about paternity."

Gina looked from Mitch to Thea, her eyes widening. "What?"

Thea shrugged. "You never really said who the father was. I thought it was Mitch."

"Mitch!" Gina's jaw actually went slack. "You're kidding."

"Oh, no, she's not," Mitch said.

"Well," Thea began defensively, "how was I supposed to know?"

Gina shook her head, her mouth pulling in a wry twist. "Because Mitch *never* forgets to wear a condom."

Mitch nearly blew a mouthful of coffee across the table. Thea stepped behind him and pounded his back—hard.

"You okay, Mitch?" asked Gina. "Your face is red."

He made a strangled noise, part cough, part wheeze. Thea gave him another hearty slap between his shoulder blades. "He'll be fine," she assured Gina. "I think the coffee just went down the wrong pipe. Isn't that right, Mitch?"

He didn't try to talk this time. He simply nodded.

"See? He's fine." Thea turned away, retrieved her half-eaten cereal from the counter, and sat down at the table. "Can I get you anything?"

Gina nibbled on her cracker. "This is fine. I might be able to eat in an hour or so." She regarded Thea consideringly. "You do know who the father is, don't you?"

She nodded. "I figured that out as soon as I realized it

wasn't Mitch. There wouldn't have been a mistake at all if someone had told me you were seeing Joel."

That gave Gina pause. "Joel never told you?"

Thea shook her head. "He was pretty secretive about the woman he was seeing." She saw Gina's shoulders slump and her eyes well with tears before she ducked her head. "Oh no, don't misunderstand," she said quickly. "The relationship was very special to him. I think it made him uncomfortable to talk about it casually."

"Yeah," Gina said mockingly, "right. He's ashamed by what he feels and embarrassed to be seen with me."

Mitch cocked an eyebrow, patently skeptical. "The Joel Strahern I met was *not* embarrassed by your attentions, Gina. Quite the opposite. He was flattered. In a big way."

"Oh, come off it, Mitch." She swiped her eyes with the sleeve of her robe. "I was dressed hot that night. The Pope would have given me a second look."

"She's right about that," Thea said. "She was pretty hot."

"Thank you," said Gina.

"I don't get it," Mitch said. "He was engaged to you, Thea. And Gina's only ten years younger."

Gina bit off another corner of her cracker. "Nine. I'm twenty-three now. Anyway, Thea's a lot older than her birth certificate. No offense, Thea."

"None taken."

"You know what I mean, Mitch?"

"Oh no," he said, shaking his head. "You're not going to get me to say anything like that."

Thea smiled to herself and took another bite of soggy cereal. "You know, Gina, you were wrong about some things you said last night. I didn't really question them because I thought you were talking about Mitch, but since you weren't, you need to know you're dead wrong. Joel is my friend and I think he genuinely cares about my happiness, but there's no

special sense of obligation on his part. No need to protect me.
I know he knows that. He doesn't have feelings for me
beyond friendship."

"How can you know that?"

"Because I know what it feels like to be loved. And it's
nothing like what Joel felt for me."

Gina's eyes darted between Thea and Mitch. A smiled
edged the corners of her mouth upward. "Okay. Well, that's
good."

"Yes," Thea said, sliding Mitch a glance, "it is." She
watched the tips of his ears start to redden, and he looked as
if he wanted to be magically transported to a duck blind with
five camouflaged buddies, sucking back beers and loading
a really big gun. Thea patted his forearm lightly and turned
back to Gina. "I know what Joel said about the woman he
was seeing, and I know what it meant. He told me it was like
it had been with Nancy—only better. He loves you, Gina. I
have no doubt about that. The issue here isn't entirely about
your age. It's about the baby. Joel was clear with me that he
didn't want children and that suited me back then. It's probably true that if Gabe and Kathy hadn't been killed, Joel and
I would be married—" Thea looked over her shoulder at the
calendar on the refrigerator. "Today, actually. How about
that? We would be going through the ceremony, not entirely
happy, but probably not realizing it. Each of us settling for
what we had. We would have been comfortable. Stable. Easy
with each other. And bored."

Thea's eyes narrowed as she studied Gina's still features.
"You better be damn sure you love him, Regina, because I'm
thinking Joel is a whole lot less certain of you than he is of
himself."

Gina nodded slowly. "I do know it, Thea. I do."

Thea said nothing for moment. Gina wasn't wearing her
heart on her sleeve. It was in her eyes. "All right," she said
finally. "I'll talk to Joel."

Mitch, who had been tipped back on the chair again, dropped it hard to the floor. "Whoa. That's what you wanted, Gina? For Thea to talk to him?"

"Yes. Why? Is there a problem?"

"Problem? Not yet. Right now you have a situation, not a problem. Once she talks to him, then you'll have a problem. You don't want Thea in there."

Both of Thea's brows shot up. "Oh? You have another idea?"

"Yeah. This should be between Gina and Joel."

The cracker in Gina's hand snapped. "He won't listen to me, Mitch. I need to get his attention."

"Fine. Then let me beat the shit out of him."

Gina and Thea exchanged glances. "I don't know," Gina said. "What do you think?"

"Could work," said Thea. "Sure, why not?" She turned to Mitch. "Okay. You can beat the shit out of him."

"Ha-ha." He took a swallow of coffee. "I should—just to show you how it works—but I'll give diplomacy a shot first."

"Oh, goodie," Thea said dryly.

Gina was more enthusiastic. "Really? You'd do that for me? But what will you tell him? Do you know what to say?"

"I know what not to say," Mitch said. "I'm *not,* for instance, going to tell him that Thea thought I might be the father of your baby." He regarded his companions pointedly. "Unless you ladies don't mind if he beats the shit out of me."

Chapter 15

Mitch had no difficulty spotting Joel Strahern in the booth at the back of the downtown tavern. He would have preferred sitting at the bar himself. A good bar fight never started in a booth. The tables were secured to the floor and the wall, for one thing. No one could tip them over. Mitch allowed the place was a little too upscale for a fight anyway, which was probably why Thea had suggested it. He didn't know if she didn't trust him or Joel. She made noises on the phone earlier that morning about being in touch with a bail bondsman. Ha-ha, he had said.

Mitch arranged the meeting himself. He refused offers from Gina and Thea to set it up. It didn't have to be so complicated, he told them. This was just two guys getting together for a beer. They had rolled their eyes. Apparently neither one of them thought of Joel as a guy. A lot they knew. Every man was just a guy at heart. Joel Strahern dressed better, was all.

Mitch slipped into the booth and extended his hand on his way down. "Strahern."

Joel accepted it and shook it briefly and firmly. "Baker."

Mitch grinned. "That's about the extent of my macho posturing. Call me Mitch."

"Joel."

"Good. You order yet?"

"No, I just arrived. I didn't know this place existed."

"You're on the other side of town. They have some good deli sandwiches. The Reubens are terrific." Mitch waved to the waitress and asked Joel, "What'll you have to drink?"

"Heineken."

"Okay." He held up two fingers to the waitress. "Heinekens." She nodded, gave them both menus, and left. Mitch flipped his open but he didn't look at it. "Look, Joel, you might as well know that I had this idea of just beating the shit out of you. Thea and Gina talked me out of it."

Joel Strahern hadn't gotten where he was by being moved by threats. He didn't so much as blink. "Lucky for you," he said without inflection.

One of Mitch's brows lifted ever so slightly. "Good one."

"I wasn't kidding."

"Yeah? Well, neither was I." They stared each other down across a table that Superman would have had a hard time tossing. Luckily the waitress brought their beers and distracted them. Mitch took a swallow. "How much time do you have?"

"As much as I need. You?"

"I turned my stuff in to my editor this morning. I'm free."

"I've seen today's cartoon. I take it you're not happy with the Supreme Court's latest ruling on gun control."

"Automatic weapons specifically," Mitch clarified. "Those were assault rifles the justices were packing."

Joel nodded thoughtfully and took a drink of his beer. The waitress reappeared asking for their orders. He got the turkey club. Mitch had the Reuben. "So," he said after the waitress left, "you weren't clear on the phone about why we should have lunch together."

"But you came anyway."

"Don't flatter yourself. I was curious."

"Whatever works," Mitch said, shrugging. He lifted his bottle, took another swallow. "It's about Gina."

Joel nodded, expecting it. "Regina told you that we've been seeing each other."

Mitch cocked an eyebrow. "She told me a little more than that. She says you have not practiced responsible birth control and that just won't do. I know you grew up thinking women would handle that, but the times, Joel, they have a-changed."

"I'd rather you beat the shit out of me," he said dryly, "than murder Dylan again."

"Deal." Mitch gave Joel a small salute with his beer bottle, then he became serious again, getting to the heart of the matter. "Look, I don't know you at all, and I don't know what you're thinking or feeling about what's happened. Personally, I think it's between you and Gina to work out, but she says she can't get your attention. She thinks that maybe you're still feeling something for Thea."

"Oh, for God's sake," Joel said. "Where did she get that idea?"

"Who knows? My guess would be it has something to with you not wanting to marry her." Mitch watched Joel's knuckles whiten as he gripped his Heineken. "But that's just a guess."

Joel grunted softly.

"I also hear you suggested that she not have the baby."

He didn't try to deny it. "It seemed like a reasonable solution until I heard it come out of my mouth."

"Yeah, I know what you mean. It's hard for girls to get over that, though. That kind of thing sticks. Especially since you followed up with the adoption suggestion."

Joel's gunmetal gray eyes narrowed and his chin jutted forward. "Goddammit, is there anything she *didn't* tell you?"

"Probably not. She was pretty upset when she first talked to me. Things just kept falling out of her mouth. Then she showed me a house last Friday morning. She was doing okay for most of the tour but when we got to the room that had been used as a nursery . . ." Mitch simply shook his head. "Well, you can use your imagination. What I didn't know before, I learned on that round."

"And she talked to Thea, too?"

"Yep. She had some insane idea that Thea should talk to you. If it turns out that I have to kick your butt, remember I saved it in the first place."

Joel Strahern swore softly. He finished his beer and got the waitress's attention to order two more. "You want one?" he asked Mitch.

Mitch chuckled. "Sure."

"Three," Joel called to the waitress. Out of the corner of his eye he caught Mitch's look of surprise. "I'm kidding," he said. Then he changed his order back to two. "I can get a cab back to the office, but I really need to drive home."

The cold beers arrived quickly and the sandwiches came a few minutes later. Mitch pulled the toothpick out of one half of his Reuben and dropped it on his plate. He picked up the sandwich in two hands. "Thea thinks that maybe this isn't about whether you love Gina. She says you do. She thinks it could be that you're not sure what Gina feels for you." Over the top of his dark rye bread, Mitch saw Joel Strahern flinch. On the money, he thought. Thea was on the money. "But that's just her opinion."

Joel pushed his plate a few inches away and picked up his beer. He tipped it back and drank, then he regarded Mitch frankly. "What would you do?"

Mitch shook his head. "No way I'm answering that."

"All right. Then what do you think I should do?"

Mitch didn't say anything immediately. He put his sandwich down, wiped his fingers on his napkin, and took a swallow of beer. "Is it your plan to ignore your child?"

"Hell, no."

"I'm not talking about sending a monthly check, Joel. Gina doesn't need your money anyway. I'm talking about spending time with your kid. Ball games. Dance lessons. Diapers. Whatever it takes."

Joel's jaw tightened and a muscle jumped in his cheek. "I don't need lessons from you about raising children. You've been in charge of runny noses and bedtime stories for six months. I have grown kids. I have grandkids. I know something about what it takes."

"Then maybe the question is: Do you have what it takes to do it again?"

"You mean do I want to?"

"No, that isn't what I mean. Frankly, I don't give a shit if you want to. Gina doesn't want to be a single mother, but she'll do it because the alternatives don't work for her. You do it because it's the right thing to do. Period." He paused and when he spoke his voice was low and a little rough with emotion. "Then, if you're damned lucky, you'll find you want to."

Joel stared at him. After a while he asked, "Is that what happened to you?"

"Pretty much. You have an advantage, Joel. Emilie, Case, and Grant weren't mine."

"But they are now?"

"Oh yeah. In every way that counts. I had a family transplant that took."

"Thea?"

"I can't speak for her, but yes, I'm guessing she feels the same way about them that I do."

Joel set his beer down and turned the bottle slowly. "Are you going to marry her?"

"Not because of the kids."

"No?"

"No. There's only one reason I'm going to ask her to marry me—and only one reason I'm hoping she'll say yes."

"Let me guess," Joel said, his mouth lifting in a wry twist. "It's the same reason I should propose to Regina."

"You said it."

Joel's cynical smile faded slowly. "I don't know if it's enough," he said quietly. "I'm older than her parents. There will be talk. She doesn't deserve to be subjected to that."

"No, but you can't control what other people will say. And shouldn't she have some part of that decision? Anyway, do you really care what people think? You'll be happy. So will she." Mitch gave him a dead-on look, the kind that closed deals in Joel Strahern's world. "Isn't that the best revenge?"

Thea swiveled in her chair to face the door to her office. It swung open and she looked up expectantly. Mitch stood on the threshold. His features didn't give anything away. Her eyes narrowed, looking for bruises.

"Nobody beat up anybody," he said, stepping inside. He shut the door behind him and leaned against it. "Are you disappointed? I thought that's what you wanted."

"It was." She paused for effect. "Mostly."

"You know, I wish you had been clearer, because there was a moment that I really wanted to smash his face."

"What happened?"

"The moment passed." Mitch pushed away from the door and flopped on her sofa. "Are you working late?"

"Mi-itch." Exasperation pressed Thea to make two syllables out of his name. "What happened?"

He shrugged. "We had a couple of Heinekens—a vastly underrated diplomatic beverage, by the way—and talked. I had a Reuben. He ordered the turkey club but didn't eat much. We both had fries. Afterward, we shot darts."

"You shot darts?!"

"Yeah, he's pretty good, too. I won best two out three then I got the hell out of there before he made it three out of five. The man's competitive."

"You shot darts," she said softly.

"Uh-huh. So, are you working late tonight? Don't forget tomorrow's the Fourth. You get a day off and there's a parade and people throw candy at you from fire trucks. I mostly go after the Tootsie Rolls if there aren't a lot of kids around me."

"That's very mature of you. Now tell me what Joel said. What's he going to do?"

Mitch frowned. "How should I know? It wasn't that kind of talk. I planted seeds and we'll see what happens."

"You . . . planted . . . seeds."

"Yeah." He leaned forward and rested his forearms on his knees. "Thea, the man's sixty-one years old, and by the look of things, he's done okay for himself. I wasn't going to sit there and tell him what to do." He stopped, thought about what he'd said to Joel, then added, "Well, not tell him much. It's up to him and Gina."

Thea pressed her lips together briefly as she considered. "Are you hopeful?"

"Let's put it this way," he said. "They were good seeds and the ground was fertile."

Laughing, she got to her feet and dropped into his lap. "Farmer Baker," she whispered, putting her arms around his neck, "you wanna plow the lower forty?"

Thea stood on the curb of Connaugh Creek's Main Street and dodged candy missiles while Mitch made a surreptitious search of the street and sidewalk for midget Tootsie Rolls. There was a toddler giving him a lot of competition.

"She's cramping my style," he told Thea.

"You are a sick man. You really would take candy from a baby."

"Look at her. She must be at least four and already she has no heart."

Rolling her eyes, Thea moved so she was standing in front of him. She found his arms, brought them around her waist, and held them there. She leaned back against him. "Just keep you hands on this tootsie."

Mitch nudged her hair with his chin. "Firecracker."

"You better believe it."

"Mmm," Mitch murmured against her ear. Thea was wearing navy blue shorts and a white cotton top with silver-glitter stars. Her red hair was like a burst of fire in the sunlight, giving the impression the fuse had already been lit. Which it probably had. "Look. Here come the bicycles."

Thea glanced down the street and tried to pick out Emilie and the twins in the sea of children pedaling their way. She caught sight of Case almost immediately. He was flanking the large group, coming up on their curbside. Like every other kid's bike, his was decorated with crepe paper streamers woven in the spokes and around the handlebars. Red-and-blue streaks in his pale hair helped him stand out. In the event that wasn't enough to catch the judges' notice, Case had a horn he tooted whenever he was confident enough of his balance to take one hand off the plastic grip.

Emilie spotted Thea and Mitch before they saw her. She waved with both hands, showing off until she was certain she caught their eye, and for a little while after that. "Hands on the wheel!" Mitch yelled.

Emilie grabbed the handlebars so hard the bike wobbled and she almost took a spill.

"Okay, now you've embarrassed her," Thea said. "Look at your parents. Do you see them embarrassing the kids?" Jennie and Bill were sitting in lawn chairs a few feet away. Jennie had just pulled her camera out and was yoo-hooing to get the children's attention so she could take pictures. Bill was unwrapping a midget Tootsie Roll. "Never mind. It will scare you."

Mitch laughed. "I know. Do I have some great genes, or what?"

Grant pulled in front of them just then for an Uncle Sam hat adjustment. Thea refitted it on his head so it wouldn't fall over his eyes while Jennie took more pictures than a paparazzo. "Careful," she said, and gave him a push off. "Love you."

"Aunt Thea!" Grant ducked his head, the hat fell forward, and he had to adjust it again. His legs churned on the pedals so he could catch up with his brother.

"Now who's the embarrassing one?" Mitch whispered. He opened his arms again to allow Thea to step back in his embrace.

"Sssh," she hushed him, dashing away the tears that had suddenly filled her eyes. "I'm having a moment."

Mitch let her.

The parade ended thirty-five minutes later with fire trucks and emergency vehicles representative of the nearby municipalities bringing up the rear. It was an impressive display of community and volunteerism and wholly fitting of the spirit of the Fourth.

Thea and Mitch caught up with the children on their walk from Main Street to the park. They all wandered the grounds eating hot dogs and homemade pie and listening to a brass band play show tunes and Sousa marches in the gazebo. There was a double-header All Stars ball game in the afternoon. Case and Grant were up first with the younger players, then their Little League heroes took the field. Afterward Thea and Jennie went to the pool to watch the kids swim while Mitch played in a cornhole tournament with his father.

"Do you think there are perfect days?" Thea asked Mitch as they were walking back to his house. The children were riding ahead on their bicycles, weaving in and out of each other in a spontaneously choreographed pattern.

"I never thought about it," Mitch said. "You think today is one of those days?"

"Uh-huh."

Mitch found her hand and slipped his fingers through hers. "There's still burgers on the grill and fireworks to come."

She smiled, dropping her head to his shoulder for a moment. "It just keeps getting better."

They had a backyard cookout. Mitch's sister and brother-in-law joined them, along with Jennie and Bill. Emilie was allowed to invite a friend to keep the squabbling with the twins to a minimum. There was more food than they could possibly eat, sustained laughter throughout the preparation and cleanup, and some prickly exchanges when politics came up front and center. At dusk the children were finally allowed to have their sparklers. They paraded around the yard, air writing with wands of light and alternating between playing Star Wars and Harry Potter.

When it was time to return to the park to watch the fireworks, Mitch managed to get Thea to hang back with him while the others went on ahead.

"What's going on?" she asked. "We won't be able to find them if we don't catch up."

"They won't get lost."

"I'm not worried about—" Thea looked at Mitch suspiciously. "What *is* going on."

"Nothing. I swear." He took her hand and guided her toward the curb so they could cross the street. "Come on."

"The park's the other way, Mitch. Everyone else is—"

"The best fireworks view is this way."

"But—"

He started across the street, pulling her with him. "Trust me."

She did. They walked counter to the direction of the park for three blocks, dodging people and cars going the other way. It did seem odd to Thea that no one else appeared to know about what Mitch called the "best fireworks view." Apparently it was also the best-kept secret in town.

The cross street signs read Elm and Orchard when Mitch turned Thea off the sidewalk and onto the private walkway of a large Victorian style home on the corner. The wide lemonade porch wrapped around two sides of the house. White gingerbread accented the eaves and gables. The trim on the porch was also white and the house was painted pale yellow. The home was situated so charmingly on the wide corner lot that a white picket fence would have been overkill.

"Who lives here?" asked Thea.

"No one right now." Mitch easily overcame her slight resistance and pulled her up the steps to the porch. He released her at the front door and searched his pocket for a key. "I got the key from Gina. Sommers Realty has the listing."

"This is the house she showed you last week?"

"Uh-huh. After months of dragging me out of town to look at homes in places with names like Woodfield Glen Timber Crest Estates—which have no trees, by the way— she finally heard me when I told her that wasn't where I wanted to live."

"So she found this place? Amazing."

"I know. She says she did it by thinking of the last place she'd ever want to live."

Thea chuckled. "Well, there you go." She stepped inside when Mitch opened the door for her. He reached behind her and flipped a switch, flooding the foyer with light. The entrance hall was wide with hardwood floors, white wainscoting, and a staircase that curved gently to the second floor. She allowed Mitch to take her hand again and lead her through the downstairs, one room flowing into another:

living room, dining room, kitchen and family room, pantry and laundry.

"Grab that newspaper on the counter," Mitch told her before they circled back into the entrance hall. "Gina will blame me for putting it there."

Thea picked up the folded paper and slipped it under her arm. "What's in the basement?"

"A basement." He caught her arch look. "Okay, half of it's been remodeled into a playroom. The rest is storage. Come on. There's more." Mitch led her to the staircase and up the steps. He showed her to rooms he'd picked for the kids. There was even an additional bedroom that would work for when the twins no longer wanted to share sleeping quarters.

Thea listened as Mitch described his thinking about how he and the kids would fit into this house. There was finally space for all his books and treasures that were crammed into the small guest room in his home. The kids would still share a single bathroom, which wasn't a bad thing in his opinion, since it forced a little cooperation.

"You have it all worked out," Thea said, forcing a note of enthusiasm into her voice.

"You don't like it." It wasn't a question.

"No," she said quickly. "No, I like it. I like it a lot."

"Then what's wrong?"

Thea shook her head. They were standing in the doorway of the large master bedroom, similar in size and layout to Mitch's current bedroom. She was trying not to think of where she would put the king-sized bed, or what the dresser would look like with her favorite perfume atomizer sitting on top. "Nothing. Really. This is lovely. I'm happy you found it. It's perfect."

"I don't know about perfect, but it gives us more elbow room." He inched toward her. "Though cozy works." Mitch bent and kissed her lightly on the mouth. "I haven't made any decisions yet. Whether or not I make an offer depends on what happens with another offer I'm preparing to make."

"Another offer? There's another house?"

In the distance there was a loud BOOM. He drew back. "Come on. You don't want to miss the fireworks. This way to the attic."

Childhood memories of a dark, airless attic with dead sash flies scattered on the floor and windowsills did not make Thea particularly enthusiastic about following him. She was pleasantly surprised to find that after climbing the narrow staircase, this floor of the house had been completely gutted and remodeled to create an aerie. She immediately filled the space with Mitch's drafting table, his towers of magazines and newspapers, his computer sculpture, and a dead plant. It was exactly right for him.

BOOM!

South-facing French doors framed a shower of sparks against an inky sky. Thea let go of Mitch's hand and hurried over to the doors. "Do they open?" She rattled them.

"Sure." He dimmed the lights and crossed the room to her side. "The door sticks sometimes. There's a balcony out there. It's safe, but be careful. It's small." Mitch found the latches, jiggled them a little, then drew the doors inward. "Go on."

Thea stepped out. BOOM! Whirligigs of gold light made a high-pitch whine during their dizzying descent. A spray of blue and green and purple followed, one bouquet of color blossoming after another. "Oooh! Beautiful." She glanced over her shoulder. "I love fireworks. Come out here and ooh and aah with me."

It was a good offer, so Mitch followed her, shutting the doors behind him. A pool of light from the interior outlined the perimeter of the balcony. They stood leaning against the railing for a while, Mitch adding dry color commentary until Thea poked him in the ribs with her elbow. "Ooh and aah only," she told him.

Mitch complied for a few minutes. "You know we can sit down," he said. "Here, give me that paper. I'll spread it out under us."

"I can do it." She slipped it out from under her arm and unfolded it. Out of habit she glanced at the headline. Frowning, she looked at Mitch. "I think this is today's paper." She squinted at the date. "It is."

"Something wrong with that?"

"Well, you know what this means, don't you? Someone else has been in the house today. Other people are interested in this place, Mitch. Have you talked to Gina about a deposit?"

BOOM! A net of red, white, and blue light was cast across the sky. Strontium. Magnesium. Beryllium. The explosion of rockets sprayed sparkling color in all directions.

"Aaah," Mitch said on cue. "Or were you supposed to say ooh first?"

Thea ignored that. "Did you hear me? Someone else is interested in the house."

"I'm sure a lot of people are," he said casually. "It's a great house. I just don't know if it's for us. And there's still that other offer."

"What do you mean? What other offer? I thought you liked this place."

"Boy, I'm really going to have to draw you a picture, aren't I?"

Thea frowned. "What do you—" She stopped as Mitch took the paper from her hands and opened it up.

"Good thing I already have," he said, "because I don't have a pen with me now." He snapped the paper, folded it lengthwise, then in half. It was now open to the editorial page and Mitch's cartoon was front and center. "You told me once that you looked at my work every day. I took you at your word."

She was still looking at him, not the paper. Thea's expression was contrite. "I do look at your work every . . . well, almost every . . . well, this morning I was in a hurry to get up here."

"Thea, it's okay." He stepped closer to the French doors to make use of the attic light and held the paper so she could see it clearly.

Thea looked down. In a simple pen and ink line drawing, Mitch had connected all the dots.

It was a house. This house. Peaked roof and gingerbread. Lemonade porch. A sagging banner was strung from one upper-story window to another. It read: IN(TER)DEPENDENCE HALL. The figure in the forefront—perfectly recognizable as Mitch—was on one knee preparing to light a large Roman candle. Leaning over the attic balcony, watching the sky, was a slim figure with cropped hair and eyes too big for her face. The caption below the cartoon was printed in neat, block letters. OF THEA I SING.

Overhead, in the midst of an explosion of fireworks was a simple message.

She stared at the paper, then at him. "Yes. Yes! YES!" Dropping the paper, Thea launched herself into his open arms.

"Oooh," he said.

"Aaah," she said.

BOOM! BOOM! BOOM! BOOM! BOOM!

For some it was the grand finale. For the two people slipping behind the balcony rail at Elm and Orchard, it was a great beginning.

Epilogue

The bride was escorted down the aisle by her father. She was glowing; he was reserved. The mother of the bride stood in the pew of honor occasionally pressing a handkerchief to her eyes, waiting for her husband to join her. The groom's vision was darkening at the periphery—and he thought he might embarrass himself by being sick—but at the center of all that he saw was his radiant bride, and he knew he did not want to be anywhere else this afternoon. The groom's children, on the other hand, had a long list of places they'd rather be, but no one cared, least of all their father.

Thea slipped her arm around Mitch's as the congregation was directed to be seated. She whispered to him, "Do you think we looked like that?"

"Like what?"

"Well, scared for one thing."

He shrugged. "I was. But you looked like you knew what you were doing."

Thea chuckled under her breath. On the other side of her, Case and Grant had already grown bored by the proceedings and were drawing pictures of monster trucks on the service program. Emilie, though, was watching with a great deal of interest and occasionally making notes.

At the back of the church a baby whimpered softly. A few heads turned. When the same baby began crying in earnest, most of those gathered smiled in understanding. It was always an iffy proposition to have an infant at a wedding, but in this case the infant was the child of the bride and groom and the howling took on a deeper meaning to many in the congregation. There were those who thought it was a distinct sign of approval and an equal number who thought exactly the opposite.

Gina, who felt her breasts swell and begin to leak, knew the truth. It was only that her baby was hungry. She took Joel's hand without the priest's prompting and squeezed it reassuringly. For a moment it seemed as if that was all that was holding him up.

Once tiny Sara Strahern's greedy mouth clamped around a bottle of expressed milk, she was mostly quiet. During the exchange of vows, she was asleep, and in the receiving line, she was a star. Her smiles, even those prompted by a bit of gas, were remarked on by everyone. People commented that she certainly took after her mother—or her father—depending on which side of the church they were seated.

It was late in the afternoon when Mitch and Thea corralled the kids to leave the reception. Emilie and the twins had made friends with Joel's grandchildren and had disappeared several times to explore and adventure in other parts of the country club. When Case and Grant returned with grass stains on their knees and a convoluted story involving the eighteenth hole, ducks in a pond, and a lost titanium golf club, Mitch decided it was time to get out of Dodge.

On the way home, the twins fell asleep in the backseat while Emilie stared thoughtfully out the window. Mitch watched her in the rearview mirror. "What are you thinking, Em?"

She glanced at him. "Why do brides wear white?"

Mitch looked at Thea. "You field this one."

"Coward," she whispered. To Emilie, she said simply, "It's tradition."

"Oh. Thanks."

Thea reached across the console and patted Mitch lightly on the knee. "Sometimes the best explanations are the simplest ones."

Emilie fiddled with her shoulder harness, pulling it away from her chest and letting it slip back. "Do you think I could wear pink?"

"Sure," Mitch said, keeping it simple.

"Was I at my mom and dad's wedding?"

Mitch gave Thea a quick grin. "Back to you."

Thea turned slightly in her seat so she could see Emilie better. "No, Em, you know you weren't at the wedding. You were born about ten months later."

Emilie considered that. "I wish I could have been there. I think Sara was lucky."

Mitch chuckled. "That's one way of looking at it."

"Do you want to watch the video tonight?" asked Thea. In the course of the move to Elm and Orchard Mitch had come across a recording of Kathy and Gabe's wedding. They stopped everything they were doing, hooked up the DVD player and TV, and sat down on the floor to watch. The quality certainly wasn't hi-def and the camera work was jumpy, but those production values were immaterial in contrast to the power of the images. In retrospect the bride and groom looked absurdly young. There was no doubt, however, that they were deeply in love. Listening to them exchange vows again was poignant; watching them do the chicken dance at the reception was very nearly hysterical. In the end they all laughed more than they cried and the disk was carefully re-boxed and placed with other keepsakes and moved to their new home. "I know just where we put it," Thea went on. "It's no trouble to get it out."

"No," Emilie said. Then, in adultlike tones, she added, "I

think one wedding is enough today." She turned back to staring out the window, planning her gown, bridal party, and reception right down to the number of flowers on her cake.

Much later that night, after the kids were tucked in bed, Mitch found Thea sitting in the darkened family room watching the DVD she had offered to show Emilie. She hit the pause button and made space for him on the sofa.

"It's all right," he said, putting her legs over his lap and running his hands lightly over them from knee to ankle. "There. That's nice. You've got great gams, Thea Baker. Anyone ever tell you that?"

"Your father," she said dryly.

Mitch chuckled. "Yeah, well, he's always been a leg man."

"And you're not?"

"I have diverse interests. Legs *and* breasts."

"That doesn't exactly make you a Renaissance man." Before he could respond, she aimed the remote at him and hit the mute button. Mitch's mouth clamped shut. "I'll be darned. It works." She hit it again. "Are the kids all down?"

"Down, but not out. Case and Grant are nodding off. Emilie wanted to read in bed for a while so I said okay."

Thea nodded. She laid the remote on the arm of the sofa and settled more comfortably into the corner. "Mmm. That feels good," she said softly as Mitch continued to massage her bare calves and feet. "I thought it was interesting that Emilie passed on watching this."

"Don't put too much stock in it. She might decide to do a marathon of viewing tomorrow."

"I know. And that's okay. I just can't remember her passing on an opportunity to do anything related to Gabe and Kathy before. It's hard to know whether to feel relieved or concerned."

"She's working it out, Thea. So are the boys." They had marked the first anniversary of Gabe and Kathy's deaths quietly, honoring their memory by making a contribution to the

Mothers Against Drunk Driving chapter in their community. It was a bittersweet time for Thea because it fell on the heels of her first year being drug free. "We're all still trying to know how to think about it. Their misfortune. Our blessing. I mean, what do you do with that except thank God that you're able to move on?"

Thea sighed quietly. "You're right."

Mitch's brows lifted. "Can I hear that again?"

She tossed him the remote. "Press rewind, then play."

"Think you're pretty funny, don't you?" He pushed the remote between the sofa cushions to get it out of the way and went back to rubbing her legs. "So what did you think of the wedding?" They hadn't had an opportunity out of Emilie's hearing to discuss it before now. "Particularly Joel's children."

She pulled a face. "Do you think that's what people look like when they have to face a firing squad?"

Mitch laughed softly. "That was my take on it, too. They could have used blindfolds or hoods. Still, they toughed it out."

"They love Joel that much. It wasn't all that easy for them when they thought he was going to marry me, but they came around. They will for Gina, too. And Sara. She's a little beauty, isn't she?"

Mitch chose to reserve judgment. "She's got a set of lungs on her." He began massaging Thea's right foot. "Gina really put Joel through the paces these last months. I wasn't sure she was ever going to agree to marry him. Even today I thought she might back out. You know, I don't get women. She wanted to marry him, he says no, then he says yes, will you marry me, and she says no. Explain that to me again."

"It's your fault," Thea said simply.

"That's a given."

She laughed. "Gina thought you threatened Joel in order to make him propose and she didn't want his proposal under those circumstances. You did volunteer to beat the shit out of him, remember?"

"Yeah, but no one took me seriously. Especially not Strahern."

"Gina did."

Mitch was skeptical. "Personally, I think she wanted him to crawl."

"I think she wanted him to be sure."

"Of whom? Him or her?"

"Both of them. And you know what? I don't applaud her methods, but her intention was right on target. You saw for yourself what they'll have to cope with from friends and family. Family on both sides, I might add. The wedding had to be public and Gina didn't want to go down the aisle being led by her belly. Besides, Sara turned out to be a great ambassador. Who's not going to love her?"

"Maybe it will all work out," said Mitch. "I told Joel that being happy was the best revenge."

"You said that?"

"Yeah. A long time ago. When I was planting seeds. Who knew I was so smart?"

Thea smiled. "Or such a great farmer."

Mitch gave her knee a squeeze. "That's why you married me?"

"One of the reasons. That, and the fact you give a good foot massage." She drew her foot back as he tried to tickle it. Laughing, she asked him for the remote. "I want to finish watching the video. I was just up to the part where you make your third toast of the evening."

"That's right before I asked you to go fool around with me in the fire truck."

"Yep. That's how I remember it."

"Damn shame you didn't."

"Seems that way now." She shrugged. "Then, I was afraid of you."

Mitch had started to give her the remote, but now he pulled his hand back. "Afraid of me? Did you think I meant to hurt you?"

"No. Nothing like that. Not physically hurt me. I just wasn't ready for you. I can't explain it any better than that. I wasn't prepared to be different, and you wouldn't have liked the person I was then. Not once you got to know me better. I did both of us a favor by staying off your radar screen all those years."

"A lot you know. You were *never* off my radar screen."

"Yeah?"

"Absolutely." He handed her the remote. "Fess up. Didn't you have a little crush on me back then?"

Thea rolled her eyes. "Watch this and ask me again." The TV flickered from blue screen to an image of a much younger Mitch standing at the bridal party's table raising his champagne flute for a toast. "'There once was a girl from Nantucket,'" he began. Thea hit pause and gave Mitch a wry look. "I rest my case."

"So it wasn't my finest hour. But I looked good in a tux."

"You looked excellent in a tux," she told him. "It was no reason to fall in love with you, though. That came much later."

"How much later?"

"Years."

"Oh."

His slightly wounded ego made her smile. "It might have happened earlier," she said. "But I was practicing a lot of denial in those days." She watched his features soften as he accepted the truth of that. "So, do you want to know when I realized I loved you?"

For Mitch loving Thea had come about so gradually that he accepted it as if it had always been that way, as much a part of him as the memories of his childhood. He'd never thought about it being a different experience for her, yet he

somehow had always known that it was. "There was a defining moment?" he asked. "Really?"

"Really."

"Okay," he said. "I'll bite. What was it? Our first kiss?
The scream? That time in my Chevy truck?" He wiggled his
brows up and down. "It was the Chevy truck, right?"

"It was your neon pink toenails."

Mitch was silent.

"That's right, sissy man," Thea said. "Your toenails. I saw
them the morning of the first time I woke up in bed with
you. We hadn't even made love yet. Remember? The shower
came later."

"Pink toenails." Mitch said it as if he couldn't believe it,
which he couldn't.

"Neon."

"Awww," he said, putting a hand over his eyes. "That's
not right. Now I'm going to *have* to go beat up someone."

Dropping the remote on the floor, Thea squirmed out of
her corner and put herself on Mitch's lap. She pulled his
hand away from his face and raked her fingers through his
brown-and-gold streaked hair. "I liked your toes," she whispered. She kissed him lightly on the mouth. "It was the same
shade I bought Emilie. What did she do? Ask you if you
wanted a pedicure?"

Mitch shook his head. "I conked out on the couch one afternoon and she and the boys did that to me."

Thea believed at least part of it. "You might have been
napping when they started," she said. "But I'll bet you played
possum through most of it. You let them do that to you."

He shrugged, a little embarrassed. "They were having a
good time."

"See?" she said. "That just turns my heart over." She
paused a beat, her eyes darkening. "Although I like it when
you make me scream."

He tickled her first, made her breathless and helpless

with laughter, then he wrestled her easily from the sofa to the carpet. They made love there and it was uncomplicated for them, familiar in a way that made it good, then better.

The last six months had been crowded. From proposal to wedding only took a few weeks. They kept it small and intimate by choice. A few friends, family, and the children were witnesses to the event. Wayne Anderson was Mitch's best man. Thea asked Rosie to be her matron of honor. The reception dinner was held in the town's historic hotel and afterward the bride and groom caught a plane to the Virgin Islands. They stayed three days, called home, and had Bill and Jennie put the kids on a plane for Orlando. The rest of the honeymoon was a family affair at Walt Disney World.

In September the driver who crossed two lanes of traffic to collide headon with Kathy and Gabe came to trial. Mitch and Thea were in the courtroom when the sentencing was decided. It provided some closure, if not satisfaction. Thea was prepared for the sentence, but Mitch came late to the realization that no number of years would have satisfied him. He spent the better part of the week feeling nothing but numb.

The holidays pushed them all forward. Halloween. Birthdays. Thanksgiving. Christmas. Each one a nodal event in that it was the first one without Gabe and Kathy. There was no struggle involved in enjoying themselves, only in not feeling guilty for it. In the end they discovered ways to find joy in remembrance and appreciate each other and the family they had become.

Not that it wasn't without its trials. Emilie threatened to run away when Mitch put his foot down about a cell phone. She actually packed a suitcase and walked out the front door, hollering they'd never hear from her again since she didn't own a personal communication device. "Obviously she's forgetting about her mouth," Mitch said in a dry aside to Thea. But he went after Emilie anyway and got her to come back without promising her what she wanted. Mitch took her cell phone shopping a month later. Just because.

The twins squabbled often, sometimes in earnest, sometimes because they didn't know what else to do with themselves. The playroom afforded them a place to keep it contained but they found ways to bring it up from the underground. They called Thea Cruella under their breath when she sent them to opposite corners. She pretended not to hear and went to her room for a time-out. Mitch was the one who pointed out to Thea that even when she was at her wits' end, not once did it occur to her to put their hands through a wringer. The revelation stunned her. She had smiled then, realizing she was doing much better than okay. She felt like she was becoming the mother she wanted to be.

The Shine and Shield campaign went national in January at the Super Bowl and the ads were among the most talked about the following day. In February Thea decided to go part-time at the agency. Hank Foster had been anticipating her doing just that; he was only surprised she'd held out as long as she had. The successful acquisition and launching of the Carver Chemical account gave her the perfect opportunity to take a step back.

But Thea and Mitch weren't thinking about any of that now. His hand. Her breast. Their mouths. These were wonderfully selfish moments and they didn't allow themselves to be distracted.

Afterward they lay on the carpet half covered by an afghan Mitch had pulled off the sofa. "We can't sleep here," Thea said. "Emilie will be up first and she'll find us."

"No problem. You can explain. Just remember to keep it simple."

"Mitch. She knows about what men and women who love each other do. I've *had* that conversation with her."

"You have?"

"Yes. Way back when you had the FPE at Target."

"FPE?"

"Feminine Protection Emergency."

He groaned, remembering. "Don't talk about that now. You just can't imagine . . ."

"Traumatic, was it?"

"Not quite that, but . . ."

Thea turned on her side, raised herself on one elbow, and studied his face. He stared back, his features relaxed, a little amused by her regard.

"What is it?" he asked.

"It's just that you did it anyway. You didn't even hesitate. You really are one of the good guys." She smiled faintly, tracing the line of his chin with her fingertip. "You know, there are times I'm still frightened," she said quietly. "Even now. Maybe especially now. Because of how much I'm in love with you."

"That scares you?"

"A little. Sometimes."

"But you stay right here."

She nodded. "I learned that from you. Constancy of the heart. The difference between being scared and being scared off." Thea slipped into the crook of his shoulder again and lay there without speaking. He simply held her, occasionally brushing her with his fingertips. Her arm. Her hair. The curve of her hip. He had no need to fill the silence.

Sometimes the best way to love Thea was quietly.